Finding
Rose Rocks

by

Karen Ginther Graham

Finding Rose Rocks

Cover Art by *RJMorris*

The Wild Rose Press, Inc.
PO Box 708
Adams Basin, NY 14410-0708
Visit us at www.thewildrosepress.com

Publishing History
First Mainstream Women's Fiction Edition, 2016
Print ISBN 978-1-5092-0737-4
Digital ISBN 978-1-5092-0738-1

Published in the United States of America

The prairie met the edge of the deck

with no yard to serve as a buffer. Jennifer liked it that way. On the west side of the house, a thick row of junipers had been planted ages ago as a shelter belt to block strong spring winds and dust that churned up at planting time. Other than a grove of mature oaks off to the east, this side of the property remained the windswept expanse it had always been.

With the aid of a wheelbarrow and thick leather gloves, Jennifer retrieved her gnarled driftwood from its storage place in the barn. She set it on the edge of the wide deck steps. In an instant the weathered wood ceased to belong to the coast and transformed itself into a sun-bleached piece of the prairie. Her former beach combing expeditions became a search of the fields for interesting rocks to arrange on the steps, just so.

Troy joined her outside one day. He handed her half a geode the size of an abalone shell. "For your collection."

She cupped it in her hands. "It's lovely. The color reminds me of a ring I've had my eye on in Chester's shop."

He watched as she tucked the geode in among the other rocks. Its presence suggested their flinty outsides also beheld these lavender gems. It caught the sun's rays. Jennifer turned and looked up at Troy. Was that a trick of the light or a spark of love in his eyes?

Kudos for Karen Ginther Graham

In 2014 *FINDING ROSE ROCKS* won first place in Oklahoma City Writer's contest and second place with Chesapeake Romance Writers.

Dedication

To David

Chapter One

At eight o'clock sharp Monday morning, the phone's trill cut into Jennifer's dark thoughts about her business. She glimpsed the long-distance number, no doubt a misdial or telemarketer. Then again, it could be a potential tenant, someone coming to Oklahoma City for an extended stay. She told herself to face reality and stop hoping for prospects, but her heart remained defiant.

Her professional tone disguised her excitement. "Hello, Alcove Management. This is Jennifer."

"Good Morning, I'm Troy Stanhope." The voice was deep and slow, a rich chocolaty sound.

"How can I help you?"

"I saw your website. I've got a project startin' up in a few weeks' time, and I need to lodge my crew of about forty men. Can you tell me 'bout the apartments?"

Forty men! It would mean a full complex. She flitted around the room, all energy. Then she cringed at the image of dirt and grime covering her pristine carpets and furniture. She'd scoured the city and hand-picked every piece in all thirty units. Alcove Apartments had been an upscale haven for white-collar professionals. Time to ease up on her lofty standards or sink deeper into financial straits.

"I'd be glad to tell you what we offer. Each

apartment is furnished, including linens, kitchenware, and a laundry room. There's central heat and air, cable TV, and Internet service. All your employees would need to bring are their duffle bags." She usually said 'suitcases' but 'duffle bags' sounded more in line with construction workers. How quickly we adjust when our livelihoods are on the line.

"Says here you want first month's rent, plus three hundred cleanin' deposit, that right?"

"Yes, it is."

"Do you have enough rooms to accommodate them all for upwards of twelve months?"

His words, delivered in a precious Oklahoma drawl, fell on her ear like magical chimes. She moved through the house with the phone pressed to her ear.

Yesterday she'd stood on the lawn of her complex scowling up at it. Wooden blinds covered every window without a single slat out of place. The building's stark façade reflected its empty interior. She knew then she could wait no longer. The time had come to disband her furnished setup and suffer the massive loss. After that she'd high-tail it out of this god forsaken state, leave it in a cloud of red dust and go back to California. She'd turned away from the building and yanked at a stalk of Johnson grass, bent and bobbing from the weight of its seedy head. The tough fiber resisted and cut her palm. She'd winced and brought it to her mouth and then began the slow walk of defeat toward the parking lot.

Less than twenty-four hours had passed, and things looked much brighter.

Her response came out too chirpy. "We'd be happy to accommodate your crew, Mr. Stanhope. What's the name of your company?"

"Call me Troy. My son, Russell, and I run Stanhope Construction, based out of Albuquerque. We'll be general contractin' a commercial mall in Coahoma."

"I know the project well. Sunday's paper had an article about it. They've named it West County Fair."

"That's the one."

Coahoma was the center of a farming area northwest of Oklahoma City. Its residents were divided about the mall. It would bring commerce, but Jennifer sympathized with those who wanted to keep the small-town feel. Coahoma couldn't meet the housing needs of Stanhope Construction. Alcove Apartments stood on the western edge of the city, one of the nearest businesses of its kind to the job site. Troy must've considered that.

"My foreman and I plan on bein' in Oklahoma City through the weekend. Mind if we take a look at your place?"

Jennifer's hand shook as she picked up a red marker and held it over the calendar on her desk. "Not at all, will Saturday at ten work for you?"

"It'll work just fine."

"Great, I look forward to meeting you both."

She wrote 'show apartments' on the date and drew circles around it. Not that she'd forget with five short days to go and no other interested parties.

"Have you looked at many other complexes?" She pressed her fingernails into her palm. *Say no. Say no. Say no.*

"Nah, we've got some places lined up to see, but it'll be our first trip to scout out housin'. We'll drive in from New Mexico on Wednesday."

"That's a long journey."

"Yep, it's all we'll do that day."

"I'm glad you called Alcove Apartments."

A background voice drew close on his end. "'Scuse me a sec," he told someone he'd be with them in a minute, and returned to the line. "Where were we?"

"Sounds like you're busy. I won't keep you." Keeping him on the line, with his gentle voice and the hope it held like a lifeline, was the very thing she wanted to do.

"Saturday at ten, right?"

"Right."

"See you then, darlin'."

"Okay…Troy. Bye."

She sank into a chair and let the full weight of the potential windfall hit her. Then she popped back up, spring-loaded. The crucial showing needed preparation, but she wasn't able to sit still. Bent over her keyboard in a position of the worst form, she fired up her computer to study prices and amenities of her competition.

Her six permanent tenants wouldn't mind construction workers as neighbors, but they'd object to their peace being disturbed. Quiet construction workers? Yeah, right. Still, if this deal went through her cash flow problem would be over, at least for now. For that, she'd find a solution to noise and dirt.

Four years ago, Jennifer stared at the reflection of a forty-one-year-old woman with a brand new divorce decree. A brief but intense pity party followed. To take part in middle-aged dating made her shudder. Besides, who'd want an old cast off like herself?

Throughout Jennifer's married life, her husband invested in apartment buildings on the side. Jennifer discovered a passion for renovating them and a flair for management. Post-divorce, her experience might've qualified her for a job at a large apartment complex, but doing so held no appeal. She had another idea and shared it with her banker. He approved the funds, and she got busy.

The decree had awarded her sole ownership of a thirty-six-unit apartment complex. She threw every ounce of herself into transforming it from standard rentals to upscale living spaces for corporate travelers. A hyper-focused taskmaster, she drove herself and her team to the limit. With little more than a leap of faith, she'd completed the redo on a shoestring. She'd canvassed decorating outlets, bargain basements, and out-of-the-way thrift stores rumored to carry large inventories of furniture. In the end she created smart, gender-neutral apartments she could show with pride.

For over three years her business flourished. It catered to air traffic control personnel from all over the country. Then the federal government shut down its flight training operation in Oklahoma. In three months' time, Alcove went from a teeming complex with a waiting list to one of resounding emptiness.

Now eager to share her good news, Jennifer puttered in her yard until her next door neighbor, Evelyn, arrived home from work. There wasn't anyone else. Aaron, Jennifer's twenty-one-year-old son, was busy with his university studies. The rest of her family lived fourteen hundred miles away in San Diego. They'd never been close. Jennifer had accepted it long ago.

Evelyn had been a haven when Jennifer first moved in and wanted to hide from the world. Jennifer's old friends were moms first and foremost. Evelyn had been different. She'd been a stepping-off place into an interesting unknown, a luxurious indulgence.

Evelyn pulled into her driveway.

Jennifer shouted across the lawn, waving her over. "I almost declared an emergency and called you earlier."

"Why? What's up?"

"This is the break I've waited for. Of course, it comes at a cost."

Jennifer's rush of words continued while she and Evelyn went into the kitchen for iced tea. Jennifer wiped clean counter tops and paced.

"Any other apartment owner would jump at this opportunity. I don't know what to think. I picture mud and construction dirt everywhere. What if he chooses mine?"

"For the love of god, lighten up. First get online and check out the company."

"I did. It's legit. Dunn and Bradstreet gave it a decent rating, knocked down a bit because of a legal matter they'll have to explain, but not unusual for a company of its size."

Jennifer didn't mention she'd done a personal check on Troy Stanhope. New Mexico's judicial website for civil and criminal activity showed nothing. She'd tried Oklahoma's system. There, records on him were minimal, but she'd scrutinized every tidbit; fifty years old, a couple of speeding tickets, a marriage, and a divorce. Despite an intensive search, she found no photograph of him.

Evelyn turned up her palms. "Why hesitate? A golden opportunity just dropped into your lap. You've dealt with unruly tenants before. Hell, they end up afraid of you."

Jennifer snickered. True enough. When it came to her apartment complex, she was a formidable enforcer, small but feisty. To replace a carpet or couch now and then was pocket change compared to the income she'd receive. She forced her feet to stay on the ground and reserved her happy dance for when she had a signed contract in hand.

Chapter Two

Jennifer's oversized watch slid down her arm, a reminder of the forty-minute drive ahead. She readied herself, headed out, and arrived early despite construction on the interstate.

The Spicy Bison was a trendy cafe near the University of Oklahoma in Norman. Her son Aaron wanted to meet there for lunch and try the restaurant's famous buffalo burger. Jennifer perused the student art on the walls in the waiting area but took none of it in.

The move to Oklahoma had been a stopover in her husband's career—twenty years ago. The state remained a paradox to her. Unlike her native Southern California, there were seasons here. Winter graced the state with just the right amount of snow to cause wonderment at its falling. Turbulent spring skies made for dramatic theater. Yet the pervasive undercurrent of religious zealotry continued to be a source of discomfort to her.

Jennifer missed San Diego's beaches, hilly terrain, and inland mountains. She longed for the familiarity of the place she still called home. She'd tried to dismiss her discontentment as a business woe. After all, there'd been no pining for California when she'd built her little empire or while it thrived. Selling would've been foolhardy when the occupancy rate hit a miserable thirty percent. She didn't plan to leave until Aaron graduated in a year but finding herself stuck with an upside down property made her all the more desperate to get out.

She'd tried everything to attract tenants, but without a primary employment source to tap into, she couldn't make the business work. Other complexes suffered high vacancy rates, too. Their loud banners announced a month's free rent or a wide screen TV with a years' lease. Jennifer had resisted gimmicks and opted to market the quality of her property. Now she wasn't so sure. Worry often kept her awake at night. On the plus side, she had time to spend with Aaron if he hadn't been so busy with school and work.

He walked in, and they hugged. Small talk passed between them while they waited for a table. After they sat and placed their order, Jennifer plunged in.

"You said you weren't sticking around Oklahoma after graduation, so I've been thinking more and more about a move of my own, back to San Diego."

She'd spared him the details of her failing business. He had concerns of his own.

"Really? Cool!" His head of untamed blond curls bounced. If her announcement caused him alarm or sadness, he didn't let on.

****

Troy called again Wednesday evening with a muted radio and the hum of an engine in the background. "I was wonderin' 'bout something."

Brightened by his call, Jennifer's response escaped too soon. "What's that?"

"How long a lease is it?"

There was that voice again, smooth as Tennessee whiskey. Alcove Apartments' website contained this information. He's bored by the empty miles, but why call me? Wasn't there someone else to phone, a girlfriend or second wife? If he'd remarried outside of Oklahoma or New Mexico, it wouldn't have shown on state records.

She spoke up so Troy could hear her over the truck's engine. "Most of the time, the need is for short-term stays, so we offer a three-month lease. I'd be happy to send you a copy."

"Nah, checkin' is all. I'm not lookin' to get tied to a year's obligation, just in case."

"No, you wouldn't."

"Well, okay then."

The conversation stalled. A crackly version of Vince Gill's mournful ballad, 'Never Knew Lonely' filled the miles of air space between them.

"Sounds like you're on the road." Obvious, but she wanted to converse with him and couldn't think of anything to say.

"Yeah, we got hung up at the office and started out later than planned."

"At least there're two of you for company."

"That's true, and it's Dean's turn at the wheel. He isn't bad as far as driving companions go, but he's a long shot from being my first choice."

"Yeah, it's no picnic looking at your ugly mug for hours on end," Dean shouted.

Dean must be psychic. He'd voiced the very thing Jennifer wondered about.

Troy chuckled. "You probably didn't hear that clearly. Dean here says I'm the best lookin' son-of-a-gun he's ever had the pleasure of driving with."

Garbled words and clear expletives came from

Dean. Jennifer laughed. "You guys are miles apart in your opinions."

"You'll have to take my word for it."

"My picture's posted on Alcove's website, so you already know what I look like." Jennifer wished she hadn't said that. It sounded like she hoped for a compliment. Plus, it revealed her curiosity about him.

"And a fine-lookin' lady you are."

Good thing they weren't face to face. Bravery could be faked over the phone. "Thanks. Tell your traveling companion hello for me."

Troy conveyed the message, and Dean shouted a hello in return.

Jennifer started to relax. She drew her feet up onto her desk chair. "How do you like living in Albuquerque?"

"You'd have to put that question to Russell or Dean. I live in Cimarron, out in the Oklahoma panhandle. I'd be on my cattle ranch now if Russell didn't need a hand due to setbacks on another project. Scouting out lodging for the crew isn't in my job description. I'm supposed to be the silent partner, you know, a behind-the-scenes-guy."

"I don't picture you being silent." She clamped her hand to her mouth, hoping she hadn't blown her deal. At his chuckle, she relaxed. Even more, her mind drafted a physical image of the man. She shook off the buff, bare-chested romance-novel cover image. Nine times out of ten, the voice didn't match the body. Troy was probably a troll.

"I work on a ranch with cowhands not much given to long-windedness. Lotta gaps that need filling. I don't wanna talk to those guys anyway."

This brought laughter and more unintelligible commentary from Dean. Jennifer swiveled away from her computer screen and rocked herself with one foot. A full moon's white orb shone through the window.

"I'd love to hear about your ranch."

"We call it the Lazy J. My great-grandfather, Jasper, was anything but lazy. He acquired the acreage and built the place. Gus oversees things. He and his hands mark the condition of the cattle and look after springs and water holes to keep them clean and ice-free. That's a bit of what ranching's about."

"Are you involved in all of that?"

"Not too much. I'm more of an armchair cowboy now days. I oversee the business interests of the construction company and the ranch, including selling bulls and heifers, land management, leasing out hunting rights, and so on."

"Interesting, I've never been on a cattle ranch."

"Folks get fanciful notions about it. Lotta hard work to scratch out a living."

"So the construction business supplements your income?"

"Nah, I'm set up okay. Russ asked me to come on board a couple years ago. Guess he figured I didn't have enough to do. Hadn't planned on so much traveling, though. He needs t' get himself a partner or hire a general manager so I can step down."

"Sounds like a lot of work on your part. You must be a devoted father."

"He was in a bind. Still is. Business is going gangbusters. I don't mind helping him out. I never know who I'll meet."

Jennifer liked their conversation, but Troy's last

remark made her uncomfortable. "Well, I should get going. I enjoyed talking to you."

"Same here, I'll see you real soon."

"Okay, bye."

She disconnected and remained in her chair. The same moon, shining like a spotlight through her window, lit the way for a cowboy with a velvety voice who was closing the distance between them.

Chapter Three

Saturday morning Jennifer dressed a bit better than her usual apartment garb, choosing her favorite ivory tee. Business attire was so off her grid that dressing up in a power suit or even slacks and a blouse never crossed her mind. She ironed her good Levis, the ones without holes in the knees, and slipped into strappy, low-heeled sandals. A rummage through the cabinet under the bathroom sink produced a dusty makeup mirror she wiped with a towel. She added blush and mascara to her minimal makeup regimen, the importance of the meeting causing her hands to shake.

She pulled up to the apartments with plenty of time to spare. Alcove didn't have an office, so she kept a leather briefcase containing pertinent documents in her car. No laptop. She was a desktop kind of gal. Flipping down the visor, she looked into the mirror. Too much blush. She wiped her cheeks with a tissue.

She unlocked three apartments, turned up the air conditioning and staged them with lamplight, lazy ceiling fans, and blinds turned to the perfect angle.

Back in her Jeep, she tapped a finger on the steering wheel. Too restless to sit, she got out and stood on the sidewalk in front of the building. Her outward serenity and inner turmoil copied the short bursts of wind against the warm southern surface of the brick wall at her back. She set the briefcase between her feet, shoved her hands in her pockets and peered around, then pulled her hands out and inspected her nails. They were fine. She checked her watch. Ten minutes to go.

Joe Running Bear drove in, parked, and emerged from his car.

Jennifer smiled and nodded, then turned away, pretending to search for something in her purse. The last thing she wanted was to be trapped in conversation with Joe, or anyone, when Troy arrived.

She studied the property. The two-story building sat deep in the lot, thus the name Alcove. It had an attractive terracotta hue and black wrought iron railings. A low wall ran along the front, with an ornate gate at its center. Each apartment faced a central courtyard of ornamental pear trees above a carpet of fescue. She and her husband had co-owned the complex for fifteen years. Over time, every facet of the place had been repaired, replaced, painted, or addressed in some other way.

There were few cars parked in the lot and no traffic. A brown pickup with a splattering of bugs on the grill pulled in. It had to be them.

Her stomach fluttered. She walked to the edge of the sidewalk and gave a small wave. The truck eased into a parking space. Its windshield reflected billowy white clouds, blue sky, and roof line, but obstructed the view of the two figures inside.

Jennifer's initial glimpse of Troy was a worn cowboy boot when he opened the door on the driver's side and started to step out. She knew him by the way he looked straight at her while the other man, Dean, gave her a quick nod and then gazed at the building. Troy's and Jennifer's eyes met and held. A long, thirsty glance told of their mutual curiosity.

"Jennifer?"

"Yes, hello."

"I'm Troy. This is my foreman, Dean." He removed his ball cap, revealing short, white-blond hair.

Wow, what a gorgeous hunk Troy is. He stood five-foot-ten or eleven with a light complexion, broad shoulders, and a sturdy build. He tossed his ball cap through the truck's open window and then looped his thumbs into the front pockets of his jeans. Her eyes dropped to his slim hips and she felt his gaze sweep the length of her body.

She gripped her trusty briefcase with both hands like a life preserver before going under. Her broad smile and words were never more genuine. "Nice to meet you."

Troy extended a hand.

Her heart thumped. Sweat beaded at her temples and on the back of her neck.

His handshake held restraint, telling of an accustomed firm grip with other men and conscious gentleness in shaking hers.

"Did your drive seem longer than it was, I mean, was it a long drive?" She might as well have tripped and fallen for all her verbal fumbling.

Attractive smile lines appeared around his eyes. "I felt every mile. I'm gettin' too damn old for this traveling."

"We appreciate the opportunity to show you Alcove Apartments. Right this way." She led them up the walkway and felt eyes on her behind surely as a hand cupping her butt cheek. Her steps became a little bouncier.

Troy drew up beside her. "Do you own the apartments?"

She bristled. "They're owned by a corporation."

This standard reply, in a dismissive tone, was a slightly skewed version of the truth but served to end that line of questioning. She disliked it every time someone asked. Being the owner made her vulnerable to those who wanted to haggle over price or amenities. As the manager, she claimed a duty to follow the rules. She'd taught herself to say 'we' rather than 'I' as protection from opportunists and contentious tenants.

They drew up to the first unit, and she held the door. "Please come in and look around. The furniture in each apartment is microfiber or Naugahyde. We have the carpets cleaned after each resident vacates and replace them as needed. Notice the two closets in the bedroom."

She handed each of them a glossy flier showcasing several apartments and listing prices, amenities, and square footages. They went into a second unit. The beeping of her phone interrupted the showing. She glimpsed the number. It was her sister Allison. Jennifer let it go to Voicemail. A text followed: 'call me ASAP.' Allison was self-absorbed and easily alarmed. Chances were good there was nothing urgent.

Dean raised his eyebrows and whistled. "These are the best ones so far."

She smiled at his reaction. "I have additional apartments to show you." She liked to show off her decorating flair. Artwork, lamps, and furniture were all of clean, contemporary design. The results never failed to impress.

Troy walked from the bedroom back into the living

room, glancing around. "We don't need to see any more. How many did you say you have?"

"There are twenty-five ready for move-in. We expect five more to be available next month."

He and Dean looked at each other, and then Troy turned back to her. "That's not enough. We'd have to find other places for the rest of the crew."

Disappointment hit her hard. Once prospective tenants saw an apartment, she almost always secured deals on the spot. There had to be a way to win their business.

"Have you found other complexes that can accommodate your entire crew?"

"Unfortunately not. We may have to put them in more than one location. We'll have to think on it, and I don't like to do that on an empty stomach. Any place you'd recommend for lunch around here?" Troy asked.

"There's a new deli down the street that's good."

"Care to join us?"

Her cheeks warmed, and she started to sweat again. "Okay."

Troy and Dean walked ahead while she closed up the apartments and locked them with her massive ring of jingling keys. She wiped the moisture from her palms onto her jeans. *It's a simple business lunch.* Her day-to-day interactions were with tenants and maintenance people, necessitating a professional distance. Other than the Chamber of Commerce, there were no organizations to tap into, no conferences to attend. She ate lunch alone in restaurants while surrounded by coworkers enjoying comradery.

Jennifer caught up with the men. "Do you want to follow me there?"

Troy nodded. "We'll be right behind you."

She got into her Jeep, lowered the window and then added, "If I lose you it's a mile west, on the northeast corner of Council and Airport Roads."

"If you lose us? How fast you plannin' to go?"

Being inside the Jeep gave her bravado. "Oh, not fast at all. I like to take things slowly." She smiled and raised the window.

Chapter Four

Driving along, Jennifer gave herself an *atta girl* for maintaining professionalism in the face of a hodgepodge of emotions. Once parked, she took a look in the mirror, fluffed her hair, and stepped out.

Troy held the deli's door for her and smiled when she passed through. His eyes shone. No doubt hers did too because it's how she felt when she looked at him. They placed their order at the counter, Troy paid, and they weaved their way to one of the last available tables.

Troy's big, suntanned hands picked up the sandwich and brought it to his mouth. He appeared at ease.

In contrast, she remained hyper-aware of every nuance.

He paused between bites, sat back in his chair, and shook the ice in his drink. The movement appeared sexy somehow.

Despite her hunger, she found her thick Reuben daunting. She never ordered this kind of sandwich; chicken salad was more her style. Because of the knot in her stomach, she could only nibble on it.

Troy glanced at Dean, back to her, and asked the very question she wished she had the courage to ask him. "So, you married?"

She hesitated. To thwart a tenant or workers come

hither was nothing new, but blending business and personal attraction was uncharted territory.

"What's the relevance of that to your renting from me, ah, the corporation?"

"None. I'm wondering is all."

She grinned. *He wondered? Well, she wondered too. Game on.* "The answer is no, how about you?"

"Single."

Her smile joined his with this new tidbit of information dangling between them. *This is flirting. I am sitting here unabashedly flirting with this man.* The sexual tension between them made her squirmy. Dean was involved in the apartment decision process. He appeared content to plow through his sandwich, taking bites the size of his hand, but social grace dictated she include him in the conversation.

"So, Dean, I understand you'll oversee housing?"

It hadn't been necessary to worry about excluding him. He cared more about his lunch than conversation and answered with a mouthful. "That's what they tell me."

She rested her forearms on the table. "From what I've seen, there are a lot of dives out there."

"Yeah, we've seen a few of those."

"If you all need to house your crew in more than one facility, you could use Alcove for your supervisors."

Troy chuckled, "Nothing wrong with getting your pitch in."

She tilted her head and gave an exaggerated eyelash flutter. "Only doing my job. Did I mention our wireless Internet and expanded cable?"

"Twice." He held out his bag. "Chip?"

She reached over to take a few. Their fingers brushed, and their eyes met. The moment held exhilaration. Unspoken words were at deafening volume.

Dean continued, "Your place is nice, but like we were saying, it would be simpler to have the entire crew in one location."

A sudden thought occurred to Jennifer. "Some of our apartments are furnished with hide-a-beds. Can your crew double up?"

Troy looked from her to Dean. "That's a good idea. It would save us a hell of a lot of money."

"If you'd like, I'll inventory our sofa sleepers and get back to you."

Dean produced a crumpled card, tried to smooth it out on his shirt, and handed it to her with an apology.

There was the usual shuffle and scrape of chairs as they got up to leave. Once outside, she paused on the sidewalk. "Thank you for lunch and the opportunity to show you Alcove Apartments. It was nice to have met you both, and I hope we can do business together."

"Nice to have met you, too." Dean swung into the truck.

Troy walked her to the Jeep and opened the door. She slipped inside, and he leaned into the open doorway. "I'll get back to you either way."

"I'd appreciate that. Okay, until then."

"Until then." He nodded and closed her door.

As Jennifer left Oklahoma City, her mind reeled, and she pressed hard on the accelerator. Would she ever hear from them again? Fifteen minutes into her drive, her phone's jingle startled her, and she jerked her foot off the pedal. It must be Allison calling again. A quick look showed it was Troy.

"Hi, Troy."

"Hi there."

"That was fast. Good news?"

"I'd say so. I'm wondering if you'd like to go to dinner with me tonight."

Her heart strained to burst through her chest. No preamble. Directness was his style. She gripped the steering wheel, slowed down, and focused on the road.

"Um, you've caught me by surprise. I don't know what to say. There's not much call for business dinners in my job."

"My asking you out is personal. In fact, let's not discuss business."

If she weren't on the road, she'd be able to think. "Not even a little?"

"Nope."

He sounded so confident while she was a bowl of jelly. Her mind spun through its search for the right words, something clever and light with a touch of reservation. "Okay, you rent from me, and I'll go to dinner with you."

"Good try. You seem like a person of principle. Wouldn't you rather have your apartments chosen on merit?"

Her mind reeled. "You have a point. Now I'm ashamed. Should I go to dinner with you out of a sense of shame?"

"How 'bout we have a nice meal together and enjoy ourselves?"

"I have a lot to do this afternoon. Maybe I can get it all done. Sure, I'd like…" Nervousness caused her to finish the sentence by slurring the words 'to' and 'that.'

It came out 'tat', making Troy laugh.

If not for being on the interstate, she would've pulled over until she'd regained control of her senses.

"Seven o'clock? I'll pick you up."

"Seven's fine, but it's a long drive out to my house. I'll meet you at the restaurant." *Isn't that the way things were done nowadays, for safety?*

"I'm taking you to dinner, and I'd like to pick you up."

"I think it would be better if I met you."

"I invited you, and I'll drive."

"Why don't we meet in the middle? I'll wait for you in the lobby of the Best Western on I-40."

"Nope."

"I suspect you're used to getting what you want, right?" she asked.

"Pretty much."

"I always seem to give in."

"Then we make a good team."

No doubt Evelyn would notice his truck pull up. Come tomorrow, she'd be at Jennifer's door for the full scoop. That's fine; they'd giggle together. A good-looking man was taking her out on a date. The only thing to stop her from a joyful shriek was she had yet to secure his business, and she'd pursue that with everything she had.

Chapter Five

Jennifer's huge orange tabby, Fuego, watched from under a holly bush while she pulled into the garage, got out, and walked to the mailbox. She yelled a greeting to him, and he withdrew further beneath the hedge. He thought he was sly, and she'd called his bluff. Her laughter changed to self-reproach for humiliating her beloved pet.

Her phone's blinking light reminded her to return Allison's call, and she settled on one of the couches in the living room. The room's ambiance soothed her. Polychromatic rococo in shades of beige, tan, and taupe made the most of its limited square footage. A modern couch of fawn-colored leather faced an ivory cloth sofa, soft like chamois. An over-sized marble-topped coffee table stood between them.

Allison was two years younger than Jennifer, and a long-time resident of Del Mar, a posh coastal town north of San Diego. There was no real animosity between the sisters, but they were rarely in touch. Phone in hand, she pushed her sister's number.

Allison picked up before the end of the first full ring. "I've been waiting for your call."

"Hello to you too. I didn't know it was important."

"My text said ASAP. That was hours ago. Like three."

Allison's wail grated on Jennifer's nerves, and she

held the phone away from her ear. "With you everything's urgent. I don't know if you're crying wolf or not. Why didn't you call again?"

Other than a dramatic exhale, the remark passed. "You know about that girl Mom's letting live in her house, right?"

"Vaguely."

Jennifer had trouble keeping track of her mom's tenants. With so much distance between them, she had to rely on whatever sketchy facts her mother chose to share.

"What? She's been there six months, supposedly paying rent," Allison said.

"I do recall that, but Mom's made no mention of it during our conversations. I assumed all was well."

"No, it isn't. The girl's name is Sadie. It hasn't been that bad having her in Mom's house but I drove up yesterday and found two more people living, or should I say squatting, there. A stringy-haired skanky chick who's pregnant and her low-life boyfriend have moved in."

"That's Mom, queen of half-truths and intentional omissions."

Her mother, Blanche, had spent twenty years as a nurse at Los Colinas Women's Detention Center. She'd developed a rescue complex for these types of people, young ones in particular.

Allison continued. "Mom's eighty-one and vulnerable. I think she's being taken advantage of, but she defends them. They're scumbags. You should see it around there. I wouldn't be surprised if they were dealing. Plus, mangy dogs and cats are tearing the place up."

She had Jennifer's full attention. "What do you suggest we do? She likes those kinds of people, and she doesn't want to live alone."

"Will you call her? If we both show concern, maybe she'll listen."

"My conversations with Mom are always one-sided; it's all about her. You know how it is between us. She blabs on about herself and then gets her digs in before I have a chance to end the conversation."

"Will you please phone her?"

"Yeah, I guess. I'll call you back afterward."

Her mother's number hadn't changed in over forty years. She'd lived in the same house in the small town of Las Casitas, tucked into the hills of northeastern San Diego County. After she divorced Jennifer and Allison's father in 1977, the property's five acres were maintained, more or less, by an occasional hired hand. It sat at the end of a dirt road with few neighbors to offend with its untidiness.

After three rings, a male answered. "Hello?"

"May I speak to Blanche?"

"Uh, who's calling?" said the dull voice.

"I'm Jennifer, Blanche's daughter."

"Hang on."

She expected her mom to come on. Instead the voice said, "She wants to know if you're Allison."

"No, this is her other daughter. Put my mom on right now."

After background murmurs and shuffling her mom answered. "Who's this?"

"It's Jenny, Mom. This is your phone. I shouldn't be interrogated before I can speak to you."

"I don't want to be bothered by junk callers. These

kids live here, and I'm fine with them answering the phone."

Jennifer wasn't going to have the 'you need a cell phone' argument. There were more important issues to discuss.

"Alli called. She's concerned about a few things. I'd like to have a private discussion with you. I don't suppose you can take the phone to the patio?"

Blanche's phone had a cord long enough to reach other rooms, but so tangled it couldn't be moved one foot. Jennifer had untangled it more than once, and it stayed that way for maybe a day.

"Hold on." Blanche's tone carried imposition. She bellowed into the room without moving the phone from her mouth. "Hey, can you guys go outside?" Shuffling and a long pause followed. "Okay, what's up?"

"Did you run background checks on your tenants before they moved in?"

"Sort of, I asked their friends for references. You remember what a sweet little girl Sadie was, don't you? Every time I ran into her around town she'd say 'Hello, Mrs. Bradford, how are you?' I think drugs messed her head up, but she seems okay now."

"I don't know her or her family. Why doesn't she live with her parents?"

"She got kicked out."

"For what?"

"Oh, I don't know. I'm not her parole officer. She said something about fighting with her mother and was accused of starting fires in her neighborhood."

"Lovely. What about the other people living there?"

"They're all from the same crowd. Nice enough

kids, it seems; a bit down and out is all. They pay rent when they can."

"You said they're twenty or so, that's adult age. Do they have jobs?"

"Off and on."

Jennifer knew all her mother's phrases and their accompanying gestures. At that moment, Blanche waved a dismissive hand in the air.

"Sean works nights at 7-11. The other one, what's her name, Kayle, is a part-time home health aide and sometimes moonlights at the Red Dog. None of them seem to hold jobs for very long."

"The Red Dog? That place was the crummiest bar in town way back when, and I bet it hasn't changed. How do they pay rent?"

"Eh, they manage. I don't charge much." Blanche changed the subject without a pause. "What did you know about bars in town? You were too young."

"Everybody joked about the Red Dog."

This exchange sparked one of Jennifer's frequent and fierce headaches. Phone at her ear, she closed her eyes and pressed down on the top of her head. She walked to the bathroom for aspirin, finding one left in the bottle.

"Have you thought about whether your tenants are using drugs or selling them out of your house? This is serious. You don't need the money. If you're careful, you can get by on your Social Security and pension."

"I'll speak to them."

"That's not enough. If they're dealing in your home, it could bring you legal trouble."

"Oh, I doubt it."

"You should consider making them move out. Alli

says one of them is pregnant, and there are stray animals on the property. This isn't good, Mom."

Jennifer's headache throbbed. She went to the garage, grabbed the bottle of aspirin from the glove box of her Jeep, and headed to the kitchen for water.

"Kayle's not sure what she's going to do with the baby, but I told her I don't want my sleep disturbed. She'll have to make other arrangements."

"What about the animals?"

"They stay outside. Rex is a good boy, and the cats don't bother anyone."

"From what I hear there're several strays."

"They're not strays, and they're here temporarily. Sadie's keeping two dogs for a friend, and the tenants are trying to find homes for the cats."

"This is insane. You've got to get rid of those people and their animals."

"I don't need you, or your sister, telling me what to do, dammit. If I want to take in tenants, I will." Silence followed. Blanche had hung up. Most of their calls ended that way.

Jennifer called Allison back. "You're right to be concerned. I'll bet she's being manipulated. The situation could go from bad to worse. She needs an apartment in one of those senior living places."

"She'd fight it."

"Just the same, would you look into retirement places in Las Casitas? If she looked at one it might get her to consider it. She wouldn't want to move out of town."

"There's a new one that's nice. I forget the name. It advertises independent living. But I don't have time. We leave tomorrow for a week in Puerto Vallarta, and I haven't even packed."

"Didn't you just get back from somewhere like that?"

"That was with my girlfriends. This trip's for Matt and me."

Between Allison's social life and her demanding job as manager of a popular full-service salon, she had little time for anything else. Jennifer started to make a comment to that effect but held back. Tonight was too important to let a family argument ruin her mood. Instead, she leveled her voice.

"All right, look, if you talk to Mom today about moving, I'll check into housing tomorrow."

"Okay, I will."

"Good. By the way, I appreciate your checking on her."

"I'd do it more often, but with traffic it's an hour's drive. I've got to go. Love you."

"Love you too, Sis. Bye."

****

At the gym, Jennifer wriggled into her leggings and tee and stepped onto the treadmill for a thirty-minute power walk. These workout sessions could be a bore. Too bad Swarthy wasn't around. She liked watching the buff Hispanic guy lift weights and do pull-ups. Most days, she used the time to keep current on world news, but today she stared at the blank TV screen. An important date lay ahead. As a forty-five-year-old woman with high stakes in securing Troy's business, a dignified demeanor was best. Without breaking stride, Jennifer wiped her brow with a hand towel. Three sets of twenty crunches were next, followed by a machine to keep her triceps in check. Troy wanted this evening to be personal. She'd like nothing more than to have a fun time with this gorgeous man, but it would be unwise. She had to present herself as a competent manager and do so with grace.

The empty yoga room awaited her, silent and dim, with bamboo floors polished to a high gloss. Before the mirrored wall, she raised her arms above her head, reaching ever higher, inhaling and expanding her rib cage. She bent sideways, long and slowly, one way then the other like a petite ballerina. She folded her upper body forward and down, nose to knees, giving her legs a good stretch.

Using one towel per person was the polite thing to do during busy times, but it was too early for the after-work crowd, and the locker room was empty. Thoughts of tonight's dinner date made her feel luxurious, so she helped herself to three towels. She stripped off her sweaty gym clothes, left them sprawled on the bench, and stepped into the curtained shower stall.

Cool spray refreshed her after a hard work out. Turning the spigot to steamy hot, she closed her eyes and rubbed liquid cleanser on her breasts, thighs, and between her legs, imagining Troy touching her there. It had been a long time since she'd felt a man's hands on her body, well before the onset of her divorce. This awakened sexuality wouldn't be going back into hibernation anytime soon.

She dried off and peered at her image in the full-length mirror. How would she appear in Troy's eyes? She'd exercised faithfully for years, so she looked pretty good. Her backside was fuller and lower than it used to be, her breasts no longer plump, some cellulite and loosening of the upper arms, but nothing unexpected. She'd nursed a baby for eight months, and now she was middle-aged.

At home, she chose her makeup and assembled it on the bathroom counter. It reminded her of a surgeon's operating tray. She dabbed mousse into her short blonde curls and scrunched them, creating a mussed look.

Her careful choice of clothes waited on the bed. Raising her arms, she let the soft material pour itself over her skin. She buttoned and unbuttoned the blouse's V area, deciding on open. Did the burgundy hue say 'confident woman' or 'sexy siren'? Slipping her nylons over her calves, she discovered a large run, pulled them off and threw them in the trash. Her other pairs were too dark; she'd have to go bare-legged. It was a sexier look, nice but not the business image she was trying for.

She was ready and waiting when Troy's truck engine announced his arrival, a trumpeter's call in baritone. Her nerves were on edge, and she breathed purposefully to calm herself. The truck's door closed, his footsteps approached, and there was the sing-song of the doorbell.

Her temples throbbed. What the hell am I doing? It was too late to chicken out. Steps away, a man waited who stirred something in her like never before. She stood, smoothed her skirt, placed one high-heeled foot in front of the other, and walked to the door.

Chapter Six

Troy stood on Jennifer's porch, smiling warmly. She hadn't noticed his dimples earlier in the day. They added cute to his strong face. Slacks, a western belt with an ornate silver 'T' on the buckle, a jacket, and a shiny version of the day's scruffy cowboy boots replaced the morning's form-fitting Wranglers.

"Hi, Troy."

"Hello there, Jennifer."

Their eyes met, and then his dropped to caress the silky folds of her blouse. They continued down to her hips, clad in a camel-colored suede skirt, and further down to her legs and pumps before they rose back up again and met her smile.

"You look terrific."

"Thank you. So do you."

"Ready to go?"

She nodded and stepped outside.

"Wow, your perfume's a knockout."

She'd chosen the most pheromonal fragrance she had. "Oh, you like it? It's Jean-Paul Gaultier. I dabbed a little right here behind my ears." She touched the space behind her earlobes. *Why did I say that? It's not in my script. And why that perfume?*

She walked ahead of him to the driveway.

"Sorry, the truck's all I have."

The dust and bugs had been washed off, and the

truck shined. The high step into the cab made getting in tricky. She would normally have scrambled in without a problem, but not in a skirt and heels with him standing right behind her.

"Can I give you a lift up?"

"No, I, um, maybe if I turn backward like this." She struggled, getting nowhere.

"Let me help you." He gripped her waist with his strong hands and lifted her in. She laughed at the awkwardness of it and caught his woodsy scent. He walked around the front of the truck, smiling when he passed by, and got in. The engine gave a manly growl when he cranked the ignition. He grinned at her and slipped the truck into gear.

"I made a reservation for Arthur's downtown. It came highly recommended by the front desk employees at my hotel."

"It's supposed to be nice. I've never been."

Streetlights flickered on while they drove through town. The last thing Jennifer wanted was those long silences she knew were a part of Troy's personality.

"I made time for the gym this afternoon."

"Best thing you can do for yourself."

"Do you work out?"

He moved his right hand from the steering wheel to his thigh, as if posed for a better view of his brawny torso.

A ladies man used to the effect his physique has on women.

"Every day. I had a lap pool built and set myself up with a home gym."

"Oh, nice."

"It's an indoor pool, so I'm able to swim year

round."

"I like to swim, but the pool at my gym is the only one nearby and has limited lap hours. Swimmers are expected to share a lane with one or two others. I can't get a good cardio workout when I have to keep watching out for everyone. I want my own lane or nothing, so nothing it is. The treadmill and the machines are nice, though." She pressed her lips together. *Stop rambling.*

"I wouldn't put up with sharing a lane either." He swept her body with his eyes again, not hiding the pleasure at what he saw.

She surprised herself by enjoying it.

"Are you from Oklahoma?" he asked.

"No. I'm from Las Casitas, a small town in San Diego County."

"What brought you here?"

"In ninety-two my former husband and I came for his job. I mean, he wasn't my former husband then, but..."

"I know what you mean."

"I'm moving back when I figure out an exit strategy. There're mountains around Las Casitas, and I used to spend a lot of time at the beach."

"After twenty years I'd think this would be your home. Do you visit there?"

"Yes, but it's not the same. Oklahoma was a great place to raise my son, but I don't want to be an Okie all my life."

"That right? I'm Oklahoman born and bred, and I like it." His hand went back to the steering wheel.

Silence followed. Waylon Jennings spun out a tune on the radio, with the volume turned low. *Why did I make the Okie remark?* She tried to relax and let her favorite line in the song "Amanda"—the line about looking in the mirror at the age in his eyes—calm her nerves. She crossed and uncrossed her legs and tugged at the bottom of her skirt.

"Nervous?"

She shrugged. "No, it's…I don't know how good I am at this."

"Do you mean dating?"

"Yes. I'm rusty. I've been preoccupied with marriage recovery and making a living."

"It's easy. Relax. Ask this ol' Okie whatever you'd like."

"Well, are you divorced?"

"Ah, the preliminaries. Eight years now. Next you're gonna ask me why my marriage failed."

"Irreconcilable differences are the usual reason."

"True enough. We met in college, married and had three kids. She got restless living on the ranch and wanted to move to Denver, so that's what she did."

"Living on a generations-old ranch seems so romantic. Do the women you date think it's too isolating?"

"Women clamor to live with me there, but none of them are the one."

Jennifer raised her eyebrows. Was he kidding, bragging, or what?

He shrugged. "I'm stating a fact. I don't shy away from female companionship. Plus, I'm not at the ranch all the time. I visit Russell in Albuquerque, my daughter Stephanie and her kids in Denver, and another son Keith near Pueblo. He's the one most likely to take over the ranch when I retire."

"When will that be?"

"They'll have to chase me off with a stick. How about you? Marital status, I mean?"

"Divorced for four years now." The road became rough because of uneven brick streets. "Bricktown's revamped from an old industrial area."

Troy parked, and Jennifer waited for him to come around to help her out. Her blouse was staying tucked, her skirt wasn't creeping up, and her heels weren't cutting into her feet. If she could manage not to insult him any further, things might turn out well.

Couples came and went from under the emerald awning of Arthur's. On Troy's arm, Jennifer stepped into the dimly lit restaurant. The soft flicker of candlelight on each table and slow dance of flames in the fireplace across the bar suggested romance. Tables were set to accommodate small parties, and servers dressed in black glided among them. Thick green carpeting added to the hush of the room. Murmured conversation and the clink of dishes formed pleasant background sounds.

Jennifer took it all in. "I like the ambiance here. Not quite right for a power meal but…"

Troy wagged a finger at her. "Uh uh uh, that's not allowed tonight. This is a nice intimate setting."

A slight man with jaunty step came forward in greeting and led them toward the back. He held Jennifer's chair while the firelight of an amber candle shone on the white linen tablecloth. Nearby, a pianist played softly. The host presented them with a wine list.

Troy perused it. "How 'bout we order a bottle?"

"I'm good for two glasses."

"Red or white?"

"I prefer white."

The server arrived, and Troy asked, "How's the Gray Riesling?"

"Dry, with a slightly fruity top note, an excellent choice, sir."

Troy turned to her. "That sound okay to you?"

"Sounds fine." She liked his authority. How nice it was to let someone else take care of her after oh-so-long.

The server returned with the bottle, opened it with a flourish and poured some into Troy's glass. He took a sip, nodded and set the glass down. She liked his style. The ritual of sniffing, swirling, and holding the glass to the light seemed an affectation for all but genuine connoisseurs.

After touching glasses and taking few sips, he asked, "So am I what you imagined based on our phone conversations?"

The attraction was there, but she wondered about his conceit. "What makes you think I imagined anything?"

"You must've formed a mental image. I know I did."

"You're fishing."

"Yes, I am. Did I hook one?"

His words and flirty smile emboldened her. "I find you presentable and interesting. I'm intrigued. There, I played right into your hands."

She picked up her wine glass and sipped, holding his gaze over the rim.

He laughed.

She liked the way his eyes crinkled when he was amused. Very sexy.

"Presentable? That's a new one. When I looked at you standing on the sidewalk this morning, I thought you were the prettiest thing I'd ever seen."

"And now?"

"Now you're the one fishing." He leaned forward, creating shared intimacy. "You're stunning tonight, with curves in all the right places, and your scent is giving me palpitations."

"I bet you say that to all your dates."

"No, I don't."

They shared a smile, and the moment swirled like glitter in a breeze.

She broke the silence. "Note that I'm honoring your wishes and not bringing up leasing issues."

"Very clever. To say you're not mentioning something is mentioning it." He unsnapped a leather case on his hip, withdrew his phone and started typing.

"Is that your little black book?"

He handed it to her, open to a calendar. She read aloud the current date and the words *first time out with Jennifer*.

"You're sweet." She added a winking smiley face and handed it back.

Troy took a pair of reading glasses out of his coat pocket and put them on. "It's a little dark in here." He perused the menu. "What sounds good to you?"

"I'm leaning toward the petite filet special."

The waiter appeared, and Troy said, "The lady will have the filet with burgundy mushrooms, and I'll have clams linguine."

"How would you like your steak, Miss?"

"Pink in the middle." She took another sip of wine. It was helping her relax.

When the server left, Troy asked, "What are you grinning 'bout over there?"

"All this pampering, it's so pleasantly unexpected."

"Maybe we can do it again sometime."

"Maybe. Tell me about your children."

"Stephanie's oldest. She's a pediatrician, divorced with three kids, including twin girls. More wine?"

Jennifer nodded.

Troy refilled their glasses. "My son Keith and his wife run a feed store east of Pueblo. They have a son and daughter. Russell's in construction, as you know. His wife's expecting their second, a girl they plan on naming Wynter, spelled with a *y*." He studied Jennifer's face.

"Do you like the name?" she asked.

"It's a little strange."

"I think it's lovely."

The server appeared with a pitcher of water. "Everything all right?" Ice cubes plopped into glasses. Jennifer nodded to him and turned back to Troy.

"So almost seven grandchildren, you must be proud. What are their ages?"

"They're all young yet. The twins are still babes. Hell, I'm only fifty."

"And not chasing younger women?"

"I'm in hot pursuit of you, aren't I?"

She gave an indulgent half-smile. "You and I are close in age."

Troy shrugged. "Flattery will get you everywhere."

"I believe the expression is 'Flattery Will Get You Nowhere.'"

"I bet you won't tell me your age. Women rarely do."

She straightened and raised her chin in mock propriety. "'One should never trust a woman who tells her real age. If she tells that, she'll tell anything.' Oscar Wilde."

Troy raised his wine glass to her comment.

Their dinner arrived. After a few bites, he rolled some linguine onto his fork and held it up.

She hesitated. Eating off of it seemed too intimate. Then she leaned in and took it. "That's good, but mine's better." She offered him a bite of her steak in the same manner.

"Um, it is good, but I made the wiser choice. It hits the right spot for me. So, Jennifer, you have the one son?"

"Yes. His latest plan is to go to Korea and teach English, but I'm sure it'll change."

All too soon, the waiter was standing at their table reciting the dessert menu, French pastry cake, chocolate mousse, a raspberry torte, and apricot strudel. Jennifer didn't want the wonderful dinner to end. The desserts sounded tempting, and ordering one would prolong it.

"I'd like something sinfully rich. Will you share some chocolate mousse with me?"

"Nah, I'll have an espresso."

Jennifer savored the mousse, taking small bites and sliding the spoon in and out of her mouth in slow motion. "Delicious."

Troy stirred his coffee and watched.

She waved a bit toward him. "Taste?"

"Thought you'd never ask."

She reached across the table and fed him.

"Mmm."

They shared bites until the mousse was gone. Troy

signed the bill and said, "What do you think, Jennifer, should we go for a drive through Bricktown? I caught a glimpse of it once before, and I'd like to see more."

"I'll show you around."

Troy held her chair and placed his hand on the small of her back. She was aware of its warmth as they left. Once at the truck, he pushed the remote to unlock it and swept her off her feet. She let out a squeal and wrapped her arms around his neck. He fumbled with the door until it opened, and set her on the seat. He got into his side, started up the truck and pulled out of the lot.

"Which way?"

"Have you seen the canal?"

"Nope."

"Okay, let's go there. Turn left."

They parked, got out, and strolled along the sidewalk parallel to shore. A tour boat slipped through the light streaming from restaurants and reflecting in the dark water.

"Dinner cruises on the boats are supposed to be nice, but I don't know anyone who's taken one. Tourists, I guess," Jennifer said.

"Is it something you're interested in doing?"

"Not really. I like this, strolling with you watching them drift by."

He put his arm around her shoulder. "I find myself wondering how long I'll be in town. It might be selfish, but I wouldn't mind if Russell's other job delays him longer than the two weeks he's projecting."

"Two weeks isn't much time to get to know a person."

"Depends on how the time's spent."

On the drive back to her house, Jennifer said, "I

43

mentioned moving back to California, but it won't be for a long time, at least a year or more."

"Maybe you'll change your mind altogether."

Chapter Seven

Troy pulled into the driveway. The area around the door had just the right amount of light from the street lamp. If she'd left the porch light on, moths would flutter around. Once at the door, he held her waist with a light touch.

"My coming to Oklahoma City was fate."

She smiled up at him. "I believe in fate."

He lifted her chin and kissed her with a touch as soft and light as the velvety brush of a rose petal. "See you soon, cupcake."

This was the part where she should've slipped inside and gently closed the door behind her. She slid the key into the lock and felt it click, but the door wouldn't open.

"I installed weather stripping inside the frame. I rarely use this door."

"Let me help you with that." Troy stepped forward, grabbed the handle and gave it a hearty shove. It whooshed open like a vacuum-packed canister.

Jennifer laughed. "Talk about a clumsy moment."

He looked at her, and his expression softened.

To hell with propriety. She wrapped her arms around his neck and gave him an appreciative lingering kiss. He tasted like wine, and there was that woodsy scent again.

He cradled her head in his hands and returned her

kiss, intense, urgent and barely restrained.

She sighed. "See you soon."

"You'd be one sweet landlady."

Once inside, she kicked off her heels and, with a big grin, reveled in the sensation of his lips on hers.

****

At nine o'clock Sunday morning, Jennifer still lolled about in her pajamas, unwilling to trade the previous evening's warm glow for daytime's obligations. One more hour, she'd told herself twice.

A call from Troy boosted her mood even more.

"Hello, pretty lady. Have you been outside? It's a beautiful day."

She laughed. "You sound happy."

"I am. I wonder if you have some time to meet Dean and me at your apartments today?"

"I'd be glad to. Does this mean you've made a decision?"

"Not quite. Dean spent most of yesterday searching and wants to take a second look at yours."

"Great. I'm pleased to be in the running. Alcove will be considered on merit, right?"

"Mostly. Fact is, and I could be way off here, you and I hit it off last night. That'll affect things, like it or not. Can you be there by ten thirty?"

She glanced at the clock—lots of time. "Sure, I'll see you then."

Certain they'd choose Alcove, she started copying tenant information documents. Her new copier was worth its high price for this transaction alone. In dressing with care, she lost track of time and scrambled to get out of the house. On the drive, her speedometer's needle eased ever farther to the right. If she secured the apartment deal, she'd be back in the black. Add a heady romance to the scenario and she did well to stay on the road. She eased up on the accelerator. An armadillo waddled out from the underbrush. Its armored plates were no match for a speeding car. These critters were a common sight on the roads, lying dead like army tanks after a battle. She slowed down some more.

Troy and Dean stood beside their truck as she hurried up the sidewalk, rummaging in her briefcase for the keys. Troy was back to his snug jeans and cowboy boots, looking fine.

"Morning. Sorry I'm late."

She directed them along the sidewalk. Unable to resist a little showboating, she led them to a stylish apartment dominated by black leather-like furniture, a bold orange Georgia O'Keeffe flower poster framed in black, and a Salvador Dali desert print.

Troy caught her checking him out and gave her a wink. She smiled and turned away but remained keen to his every word and gesture. She played her part like an actor and looked forward to the time when she could drop the business pretense and engage him on a personal level. Unabashed flirting is what she had in mind, but her priority had to be his signature on the bottom line.

Dean took a cursory look around. "I have a few questions about your place."

"Sure. Shall we sit down?"

They assembled at the small kitchen table.

Jennifer jumped back up and moved the vase of silk flowers to the kitchen counter. "What can I answer for you?"

Dean had a small notepad in front of him. "Can a

maintenance man be reached nights and weekends?"

"Yes, for emergencies. Everything else is handled during normal business hours."

He appeared to weigh her every word. She smiled to put him at ease.

"About parking, are there enough spaces for everyone's car?"

"The size of the lot allows for one vehicle per apartment, plus four extra spaces for short-term guests and second cars. It does get crowded on occasion, and I send out notices to remind everyone of the rules. That's solved the problem so far. We haven't had to assign parking spaces, but we will if necessary."

Jennifer could see Dean ticking off questions in his mind. "This place is non-smoking, right?"

"That's right."

"A lot of our guys smoke."

Jennifer had anticipated that issue. "We haven't rented to smokers because of liability issues and damage to interiors. Considering the number of units Stanhope Construction is interested in leasing, we'll make an exception. If the residents smoke outside, we can rent to them. It'll be enforced by a once a month inspection when maintenance changes the filters. If smoking is detected a two hundred dollar cleaning fee will be charged. Your workers can put ash cans by the doors, but we don't want cigarette butts littering the grounds. She grinned at him and added, "especially on rainy days. It makes them wet and hard to light."

This coaxed a smile onto Dean's stony face. "The crew would go along with that."

Jennifer studied the dynamics at play. Troy was co-owner of the construction company and would sign the contract. In him, she had an ally. However, he appeared to be turning the housing decision over to Dean, who would oversee the workers and live among them. She needed to convince Dean. Would Troy make his preference known? His comments that morning implied it. How much power did Dean have? Would he cater to Troy's wishes? To win this deal meant recognition among the apartment community and a name for herself and her business in the construction industry. There was another factor, too. She liked Troy. No, more than that, every part of her ached for him. Romantic promise floated like perfumed mist between them. If he allowed another complex to win the contract she'd resent it, no matter the reason. Romance would wither and die. She had to secure this deal.

Dean looked at her with squinty eyes. "You mentioned sofa sleepers?"

Troy had sidelined her from inventorying them last night by whisking her off on the exhilarating dinner date.

"I haven't had a chance to do an inventory yet." She shifted her gaze to Troy but couldn't read his impassive expression.

Dean nodded and cleared his throat. "What we were thinking was that we'd still need all your available apartments, but each one would sleep two guys."

Jennifer agreed, ready to overcome any obstacle put to her.

Dean withdrew the flyer she'd given him yesterday from his shirt pocket. He unfolded it and pointed at the prices on the page. "And the rates would be the ones listed here?"

She was caught short. How had she overlooked

rates for double-occupancy? The dynamics in the room shifted. Dean was in a strong bargaining position and knew it. Heavy negotiations weren't her forte, particularly without preparation. To waive a late fee or bend a rule was easy, but this was bigger. She'd always managed the properties but relied on her husband for this sort of thing.

Dean's ordinary features and quiet demeanor belied a sharp mind. He and Troy watched her like birds of prey. This was too intense. She wished Troy would step away. In fact, she wanted them both to get the hell out so she could think. Her tension set off a coughing fit.

"Excuse me, I'll be right back."

She went to the kitchen for a sip of water, but it didn't help.

Bypassing the dining room where the men sat, she went straight to the bathroom for needed refuge. There, she patted her face with a damp washcloth and then stared at her reflection. What a somber expression. It wouldn't do. Let them wait. She sat on the closed toilet until her thoughts were in order, square and tight like the bed corners her father used to make.

In the kitchen, Troy leaned against the counter. Dean hadn't moved. She rejoined him and smiled. Smooth voice, confident manner.

"You asked about our rates? Those listed in the brochure are for single-occupancy. With a modest adjustment for doubling up we'll be happy to accommodate your crew. Of course, it means additional expense for management to purchase and transport bedding."

Dean shifted in his chair. "So, ah, what sort of

adjustment do you have in mind?"

"To figure an equitable up charge isn't simple. Fifty percent for the second occupant is our usual rate, but because of the number of units you're interested in, we'd cut it to forty percent."

Troy did a half laugh and stared at her wide-eyed.

Dean whistled and shook his head. "Forty percent? I'm thinkin' not. Listen, my men won't be tearing your place apart."

Jennifer remained poised. "Of course not. Naturally, double the occupancy means to double the water, plumbing, electric, and general usage."

Dean looked at Troy but received a blank stare. Troy had retreated into observer mode. Dean was on his own, like Jennifer.

"I'd understand the plumbing issue better if we were doubling up with wives and girlfriends. My background's plumbing, so I can say this with knowledge. Womenfolk have a tendency to put things into a system that shouldn't be there, but we're all men. Besides, Sycamore Gardens is only asking ten. Why shouldn't I take their offer?"

"Their ten percent doesn't cover utilities, including cable. There'd be no Wi-Fi."

"That so? Sycamore's closer to the job site."

"You don't want to be down on Tenth Street, believe me."

"Well, dang, we don't have the budget for this. I guess I could go fifteen percent, but not a dime more. That's my final offer." He sat back and folded his arms.

Jennifer remained quiet, considering.

Dean spoke again, this time to Troy. He didn't seem to know whom to address. "Lantana Apartments has no up-charge and sits right next to a convenience store. The men will like that."

It may have been poor form to speak ill of one's competition, but these were desperate times, and she had to make a point.

"Dean, I'm sure you've noticed. Lantana backs up to a liquor store and sits across the street from Chancy's Strip Club. With their cover girl sign flashing red all night, why tempt fate? As you've said, your men are here to work. Do you want them out drinking and such at night?"

"My men aren't angels, but they don't go whoring and drinking, at least not during the week. You must be thinking of Troy's old crew. Sorry, boss, I had to add that. Like I said, fifteen's my ceiling."

Jennifer needed an iron stomach for this. She plunged in again. "You drive a hard bargain, but thirty's more than fair. At that rate, it'll cost us big time. Tenants lie. They promise to only smoke outside and then turn right around and do so inside too. There'll be cigarette burns on our counters and furniture."

Dean shook his head. "Not my guys."

Jennifer held up her hand in a stop motion. "Don't tell me it won't happen. My years of experience prove otherwise."

Playing arbiter, Troy stepped up to the table. "Okay look, we've got enough to consider. Let's call it a day so y'all can think on it."

Jennifer forced a smile. "Okay. How about lunch? This time it's on me."

Dean shook his head. "Thanks, but I'll have to skip it. I've gotta pick my wife up at the airport."

Jennifer's pasted-on smile remained. "Another

time then."

Troy and Dean waited at the door while Jennifer closed up. Two showings and still no deal. She wanted to slam the chairs into place, slap at the light switches and give the blinds a swift sideways kick and a yell, as in karate. Maybe she'd punch a wall, too, so her maintenance man would have something to do.

Chapter Eight

Dean, Troy, and Jennifer walked along the apartment's sidewalk, and Troy asked, "Is the Greek place down the street any good?"

Jennifer brightened. At least one positive thing would come of the meeting. "Kostas? Yes, it is. I have an idea. There's a park nearby. Let's pick up gyros and eat there."

Troy glanced at the sky. "It's a nice day for the park."

Jennifer knew he and Dean shared a vehicle. "I can drive and drop you off at your hotel afterward if you'd like."

"That'll work."

She moved her few things out of the passenger seat. Troy got in, buckled up, and looked in back. The seats were folded down, a ladder and broom ran the length of the cargo area with blue storage tubs on each side.

"You can tell a lot about a person by the inside of her car."

"Oh great, I'm hauling toilet flanges and wall mud." She liked the sound of his hearty laughter.

"But it's all neat and organized. Do you clean the apartments yourself?"

"No, I have someone who does it. I might be spotted sweeping up cigarette butts while muttering curses. Poison pen notes to the tenants don't stop the problem."

"I thought the place was non-smoking."

"It is. Guests cause most of the problems. I tell the tenants they're responsible for the actions of their friends, but it doesn't always work. I used to think I could control everything that went on here and at other apartments I've managed. It isn't possible, so I've mellowed."

"Like a good wine."

"Right, spelled w-h-i-n-e."

Jennifer and Troy ordered their food to go, drove to the park, and carried it across an expanse of grass to a picnic table. They sat side by side and ate while watching a game of Frisbee golf from a safe distance. Troy finished and turned his back to the table with his elbows resting on each side. He tilted his face to the sun and closed his eyes.

Jennifer ate some lamb with her fingers and studied him. His close-cropped haircut gave him the appearance of a sergeant. She wondered what it would look like grown out some. He had a strong, squarish face. The lines around his eyes and mouth appeared to be from laughter though he'd been through a divorce, so he hadn't escaped sorrow. She wanted to follow each of those lines with her fingertips. He carried a bit of excess weight around the middle, but a small paunch was perfectly tolerable. Jennifer liked men with lean body types. Stockiness had never appealed to her, yet one glance at Troy and her tastes forever changed. If he were a dog, he'd be one of muscle and broad chest, like a Mastiff, in the most flattering sense. The image made her smile.

He turned to her. "I'm curious about something."

"What's that?"

"Why so many empty apartments?"

She shrugged. "It happens now and then. They're easier to manage that way."

He gave her a blank look.

"I'm kidding."

To be frank about her desperate situation meant a weakened bargaining position. Troy might not use the information to his advantage, but Dean would hone in on the most subtly dropped word.

Troy may have picked up anxiety in her voice, because he changed the subject. "What are you doing for the rest of the day?"

"I promised my sister I'd check into retirement places for my mom, after that not much. Why do you ask?"

"Would you like to go for a swim at my hotel this evening, and then grab a bite to eat? It's a nice-sized lap pool, and no one else seems to use it."

The earlier bargaining and failure to secure a deal left an ache in her belly. Yet she sat in the sunshine's warmth beside a wonderful man. Nothing sounded better for her jumbled emotions than vigorous exercise. Her heart sang at the thought of a second evening with Troy. It wouldn't hurt her chances of winning his business, either.

"I'd love to."

They returned to the Jeep and headed into the heart of the city toward his hotel.

Troy wasn't a compliant passenger. "You don't have to stop when making a right turn on a green light."

"I'm being careful. Traffic's heavier than usual,

and I don't want to make you nervous."

"No chance of that. Let's see if we can make every red light."

"You're trying to rattle me."

He rested an arm on the back of her seat and stretched his legs. "Now why would I do that?"

"To mess with me."

"Nonsense. You're doing a fine job, Granny, if we ever get there."

She dropped him off in front of his hotel with a promise to return later and then waited to pull back into traffic. Her apartments weighed on her mind. Of the thirty-six units, thirty had been converted to corporate dwellings, and six remained in their original unfurnished state, like a rainy day hedge fund. How well she remembered the fateful moment a tenant had approached her on site.

"Jennifer, you got a minute?"

"Yes?"

"You know there's a hiring freeze in effect at the FAA, don't you?"

She'd waved him off. "That rumor's been going around for years."

He shook his head. "It's for real now. With the election over, the sequestration's lowering the boom. Washington's shutting us down. I got a notice. When my current course ends, they're not starting up another one. This'll be my last month. Sorry, I assumed I'd be here longer." He'd held up a letter.

She took it, verified the truth of his words, and handed it back. "Thanks for letting me know."

Like the exodus of Okies during the Dust Bowl era, she had watched her residents move out one by one.

The apartments had sat empty except for an occasional newly estranged husband or nomadic roofer that blew into town. Taunting winds howled through the breezeways and brought gritty soil from distant fields.

A phone call interrupted Jennifer from her unhappy reverie while she navigated through traffic. A quick glimpse showed a number with a San Diego area code. After her conversation with Allison yesterday, she'd called the Las Casitas sheriff, explained her mom's situation and asked him to check on her. Would he have looked into the situation already?

"Hello?"

"Ms. Ellis?"

"This is she."

"Sheriff Whiting here, I sent a deputy to your mother's house."

"Wow, your department's fast."

"Yes, ma'am. There's nothing we can do about the tenants. They reside there with your mother's permission. She appears to be in no danger to herself or others and is not disabled. She even invited the deputy in for a cup of coffee."

"Sounds like my mom." Always a sucker for a man in uniform.

"We found no cause for intervention. However, the deputy noticed a pungent odor he believes was coming from the two dozen or so cats in the barn. We've notified Animal Welfare. They'll send someone out to look around."

Jennifer tried to recall whether California had a no-kill policy for strays because her mother's menagerie had to go.

"That's fine. Can you continue to keep an eye on

the place?"

"Unless you call with something significant, all we can do is drive by and stop in once a month."

"That'd help. Thank you."

****

Jennifer returned to Troy's hotel that evening and met him in the lobby. Poolside, he removed his robe to reveal a pair of minuscule racing briefs. His body looked fit, and she couldn't miss the large bulge down there, but those skimpy Speedos had to go. She'd nix them the minute she knew him well enough to do so.

Troy's swimming skills were in sync with her own, athletic and proficient, except Jennifer was out of practice and became winded. After four laps, she stopped to rest and watched him do several more. He drew up beside her and raised his goggles. Silver droplets of water beaded on his thick blond chest hair.

"You're a powerful swimmer," she said.

"I never stopped after competing back in college. You're graceful in the water."

"Thanks. I swim like my father. His strokes were long and slow. It was a problem for me years ago in lifeguard training. I had trouble with the timed segment. The instructor said, 'Don't worry about looking pretty. Just go for it.' I tried, but it was like thrashing around. This is how I swim."

Jennifer braced her feet on the wall of the pool and gave her legs a stretch. "My feet are like my dad's, too. Long and thin with high arches. They make good flippers."

Troy laughed. He began a set of push-ups on the pool's edge. What a show-off, except that his effort to impress her worked. The muscles on that man! Those arms could hold her like never before. She stared as his biceps flexed, relaxed, and flexed again.

He stopped to catch his breath. "Did you pass your test?"

Jennifer's mind whirled around heaving triceps and thrusting pecs. She focused her reluctant eyes up into Troy's face. "Pass what? What test?"

He smiled. "Did you make it through training and become a lifeguard?"

She shook off her confusion. "Oh, that. Yes, eventually. I'm sure the instructor gave me more tries than were allowed. It turned into a big deal. The whole class came out to cheer me on. It was awful."

"I like your moves, kinda slow and easy. Maybe you'll rescue me some time."

"From what?"

"I'll think of something."

"Maybe I will." She smiled and pushed off the side for her best rendition of a provocative backstroke.

After their swim, Jennifer declined Troy's offer to accompany him to his room to get ready for dinner. Too intimate. Instead, she made do in the small poolside bathroom. There was a sink but no counter space. She had to set her things on a towel laid out on the floor. She and Troy were going for a casual bite, so she spent little time in preparation.

His hotel sat on a strip of similar dwellings and restaurants geared toward easy access by car, but not convenient for foot traffic. Cars whizzed by as the two made their way single-file along a happenstance dirt path until Troy took Jennifer's hand and walked street-side in the weeds. The Italian place they entered was part of a chain found in every city, but offered a reprieve from the road noise and the fare wasn't half bad. They sat at the bar with mugs of beer, ordered too much food, and tried to foist it onto each other. Back across parking lots and weedy fields, he walked her to her car and left her with a sweet kiss and a promise to call.

Chapter Nine

Three days passed without word from Troy. With every replay of their time spent together, Jennifer found no crucial misstep in her business or personal interactions with him.

Alcove's rates were higher than the competition, but they came with a better amenities package and were nicer all around than the other complexes. She wondered if Dean wanted a different apartment, Troy conceded and was hesitant to break the bad news to her. Pride kept her from contacting either of them. She almost called Stanhope Construction's main office to ask if they'd made a decision but resisted. The inquiry might get back to Troy.

Hours passed, and Jennifer's despair deepened. The week had been a whirlwind fantasy, nothing more. She'd been flattered by Troy's attention and had read too much into it. She was a passing fancy, a distraction. Twenty-six years had gone by since she'd played the dating game. She no longer knew the moves and had misinterpreted them. Plenty of women were younger than she and eager for a man like him. He had lots of them; he'd said as much on their date, but she'd dismissed his words as bravado.

Jennifer ate poorly and slept worse. Exertion at the gym would have helped relieve her stress, but she had little energy and couldn't face it. She didn't feel like telling Evelyn the whole messy story. Rather than seek her out as an understanding friend, Jennifer avoided her.

Despite the negativity, Jennifer set her computer to ping with every new e-mail and pounced on each one. Phone calls and texts caused her to give a start in that they might be Troy.

On the afternoon of day four with still no word, she picked up the phone to call her doctor for advice, maybe a temporary medication to help her sleep. It wasn't something she'd ever done before. At the same moment, Troy's number flashed on the screen. An instant later it vibrated and rang. She ventured a cautious hello.

"Hi Jen, sorry I haven't called. I've been busy."

"Oh? I wondered if I'd hear from anyone in your company."

"Listen, how would you like to go for a ride with me out to Coahoma?"

"When?"

"Ah, I'm thinkin' now."

After all the anguish, to head off on some errand of his with no explanation? "No, I can't."

"I'd like to see you."

Her eyes welled up as she recalled the last three days of anxious misery. To lose both Troy and the apartment deal would've been too much. She lowered herself onto the couch.

"Oh? What's on your mind?"

"An issue came up with the outfit hiring us. I had to fly to Albuquerque. We almost lost the contract. The whole f..., the whole thing had to be renegotiated. My plane's touching down in Oklahoma City. I've gotta drive out to the site to see Dean. It shouldn't take long. I thought you might like to come along."

His voice carried weariness. Her negative thoughts over the past few days vaporized, and her heart went out to him. How dare that son of his run his father ragged like this?

"I'll be ready and waiting when you get here."

She stood in the driveway and watched him pull up. He leaned across the cab and pushed her door open. She climbed in, gave him a shy peck on the cheek, and studied his face.

"You look tired."

"I'm beat."

They neared the construction zone where pickups lined the sides of the makeshift road and sat helter-skelter in the fields. Troy parked beside a white trailer with its window air conditioner churning in the heat. Dean broke away from a group of men and strode toward them, looking more comfortable in mud-splattered jeans and rubber boots than at a negotiating table. Jennifer waited in the truck while he and Troy stood outside and talked.

The sky's pale blue wash was a backdrop for scripted chaos. Earthmovers, cranes, and backhoes toiled like domesticated dinosaurs. Men in safety vests and hard hats were dwarfed by beasts clawing away at the red clay soil.

Troy ducked his head into the truck. "Can you come out here a minute?"

She picked her way toward them in her nude pink ballet flats, pitifully inadequate on this terrain. The smell of engine exhaust wasn't concentrated enough to be unpleasant. It blended with the rich scent of churned earth so prevalent she could feel it on her tongue. Motors accelerated, gears ground, and high decibel beeps wailed. The racket meant they had to yell.

"Hello, Dean."

"Ma'am."

He was a hard study. Jennifer didn't yet have a read on him. "Please, call me Jennifer."

Troy began, "Let's see if we can get this apartment business squared away." He said something else, but the scream of hydraulics drowned out his words. He climbed the trailer's steps and tried the door, looked in the window, and turned to Dean with an unlocking gesture.

Dean shrugged and looked around.

Troy returned. "Never mind, we'll make do."

A man approached with three hard hats and thrust one toward Jennifer in a way that said wearing it wasn't optional. The too-large white shell teetered atop her head. To hold a discussion here meant drawing close together. It brought into focus the vast difference between her height and the men's. She shrugged off her self-consciousness with a quick internal pep talk. *I might be little, but I'm a spitfire. Bring on the negotiations.*

"Have y'all talked any more about housing?" Troy yelled.

Dean looked at the ground and shuffled his feet. "I haven't had a free minute apart from what's been going on here."

So Dean should've been in touch all this time. He'd caused her anguish. She used her hand like a visor to block the sun and glare at him before speaking.

"After our last meeting I called my insurance

agent. My fire and liability premiums will double with smokers on the premises."

Troy rested his eyes on her face. "Let me check with my carrier real quick."

He walked to the driver's side and got in. She and Dean stood outside with their hands in the front pockets of their jeans. Nearby, a backhoe swung around and dumped a load of gravel. The thundering rattle ceased, and wispy white dust settled in its wake. She understood why this kind of work attracted men and a few women, too.

"Have you ever thought of providing ear protection for the workers?"

"We'd have to mandate it before they'd wear 'em. Maybe we should."

"This place is like a monster-sized ant pile that's been disturbed. I'm sure there's a master plan to it all."

Dean chuckled. "Supposed to be. You'd be surprised all the hassles come up on a job this size."

"I can imagine. Are you still chief negotiator for housing?"

"Nah, I'm covered up here. 'Fraid Troy's efforts to get me into a shirt and tie haven't worked out too well."

Jennifer shrugged. "It's hard to do two jobs at once."

"Try three or four, but there are worse ways to earn a buck."

"That's true. If you all decide on Alcove, there'd be enough apartments for you to have one of your own. No doubling up for the supervisor."

"I appreciate that."

Troy rejoined them. "There's a supplemental rider I can buy to cover any property damage the men might cause, including all hazards and liability with a three hundred fifty deductible per unit. I'm willing to do it, but it'll have to be at twenty percent."

Jennifer smiled. "You've sweetened the deal, and I appreciate that. It's very kind and does help, but there's still a gap. Where we left off, I had thirty on the table."

He shook his head. "Can't go thirty, it'll have to be twenty."

Someone bellowed Dean's name, and he excused himself. After a minute he yelled, "Hey Troy, over here?"

Troy nodded to Dean and touched Jennifer's arm. "Be right back."

She watched him stride away. He offered a fair deal, and she wasn't in a position to ask for too much. On the flip side, there'd be more wear and tear on the units than ever before. All the bills would fall to her. She had to try for the best possible agreement.

Troy broke from the others and headed back. His walk held power and grace. Behind him, Dean started toward them in an ambling gait.

"Dean has an idea. How 'bout we leave it at twenty percent and include any plumbing or HVAC issues that arise?"

She tipped her head to the side. "That's an interesting idea. I'd need first and last month's rent, our standard cleaning deposit, and a supplemental smoke damage deposit of three hundred fifty per unit, refundable of course."

Troy looked at her with unfocused eyes. She almost heard calculator keys click in his mind. His expression turned outward. "Agreed."

A smile stretched across her face, and her

shoulders unclenched. The negotiations were over. She'd won the contract. Inwardly, she shrieked with joy and danced the jig of a leprechaun beside his pot o' gold. No more 'empties' while the bills tumbled in and no having to sell the contents of each apartment—a huge collection of furniture and household items. She'd have a full complex and steady rent for six months, guaranteed, with another six or more based on Troy's projection.

She grinned at him. "I'd like a disclaimer stating I didn't influence you with feminine persuasion."

"Hey, I'm no pushover. Like Dean said, your place is the nicest we've seen. You're one hard-nosed businesswoman and worked yourself a hell of a deal."

"Hard-nosed? You think I've been unfair?"

He drew back. "No, you made sense, fought, and you'll get your terms. A deal's a deal."

She shook hands with Dean and turned to Troy to do the same, awkward after their passionate kiss a few nights ago. Still, he'd just consented to pay her a monthly rent topping twenty-eight thousand dollars.

Troy and Jennifer left the site and put the jarring gravel road behind them. Late afternoon sun filled the cab.

Troy raised his visor. "What are you doing this evening?"

"Counting all my money."

He smiled through his weariness.

"I have to put a lease together for you to sign," she added.

"There's time for that later."

She looked at the heavy shadows under his eyes and his slumped shoulders. "I want to make a nice dinner for you but not tonight. You should go back to your hotel and rest."

"Good idea."

After being dropped off at home, Jennifer went inside, threw her purse on the couch, and darted over to Evelyn's.

"I got the contract. Alcove will be full!"

"All right Jenny! I've gotta say it. I told you so."

They shared a big two-handed high five. She returned home and e-mailed Troy the application. He completed and returned it within the hour. Her next e-mail thanked him for his quick response and scolded him for working rather than resting. With the new information, she analyzed Stanhope Construction's creditworthiness. Except for the legal settlement Troy had mentioned, it was an impressive six figure monthly balance.

Jennifer poured a glass of wine and stepped onto her patio. She settled into a chair while the late sky turned deep violet. Running Alcove would be busy but low-stress: bookkeeping, overseeing maintenance and keeping the tenants happy. Stanhope Construction's project would end, and she'd have tucked away a nice nest egg. Who knew, a similar contract might come along, or the stalled air traffic program would resume. Beyond those possibilities, she'd convert to standard leasing and sell.

Her newfound peace of mind would enable exploration into other aspects of her life. Would a relationship with Troy come to be? Did he prefer a variety of women to one? He happened along and turned her life on end, but the last few days were a wake-up call. She'd look out for number one. His roots were in Oklahoma while a return to San Diego was her long-term goal. She closed her eyes and lifted her face to the kite-like zephyr wending over distant counties and state lines.

Chapter Ten

Jennifer remained low in the patio chair with her feet propped on the table. The crystal goblet caught glints of moonlight and the merlot's deep hue blended with the night. Fuego leapt up and made himself comfy on her lap. Jennifer sipped her wine and stroked his soft fur.

She'd won the contract. What a relief. Negotiations had been a lone battle, no husband at her side or lawyer's keen advice. She wished her ex, Mark, could see her now. They'd shared a desire to invest in multi-unit properties but had opposing management styles. Jennifer had called him a slumlord and he'd accused her of playing fast and loose with discretionary income. The thought transported her back to more stinging memories.

Five years ago, she and Mark sat in his truck in the parking lot of an apartment complex. A lone streetlight struggled to illuminate the entire building and grounds.

Jennifer frowned at the boarded windows. "This area's creepy. I don't want to invest here."

"A buddy and I worked it out. He'll manage and maintain them. You won't be involved."

She shoved her hair behind her ears and then crossed her arms. She'd heard it all before. Nothing she said reached him. Necessity drove her to discover her talent for renovation and management though each

71

project took its toll. Battle fatigue and the weariness of rescuing Mark from his messes had settled in. That moment began the end of their marriage.

Round one in divorce court ended in Jennifer getting temporary possession of the home. Afterward, she and her attorney, Linda, walked to their cars.

Jennifer turned back toward Mark and his attorney, Ms. Welch, walking a distance behind them. "New clothes and a stylish haircut have replaced Mark's laissez-faire appearance, but it won't last. He'll tire of the charade. Instinct tells me he and his lawyer have a relationship beyond the normal client-attorney one. It's like I'm the opponent in a territorial cat fight with the house as the prize."

Linda shifted her eyes. "Speaking of which."

The new, improved Mark walked swifter than his usual meandering gait to keep pace with Ms. Welch's brisk stride.

"The Cobra in red pumps with D cups," Jennifer said.

"Shh."

Mark and Ms. Welch passed by, and everyone smiled politely. Jennifer's heart ached to reach out to Mark, but the Cobra was always at his side.

Time went by while offers and counter offers shuffled between the attorneys. Legal fees mounted. Jennifer vowed to maintain the property's three acres. Aaron should've helped, but at seventeen he was always elsewhere. With the sorry state of his home life, she didn't have the heart to push him. The house's upkeep and yard work grew oppressive. There was no money for hired help. She'd have to give it up.

Armed with new resolve, she once again sat in

Linda's cold leather chair; a Victorian miscreation in oxblood with oversized nail heads running up and around like a device used for torture.

Linda sat dwarfed behind her monstrous desk. "I think you've made a wise decision. What time frame do you have in mind for the final ruling?"

"I need a few months to find another house."

Linda scratched out some notes. "Okay, I'll request an extension. Mark will want a deadline."

Divorce and deadline were such ugly words.

Jennifer wanted to stay in Mustang and found a cute house there. It didn't stop her from fearing a lifetime of regret for giving up her home.

The square gray courthouse blocked the morning sun. Its shadow chilled Jennifer as she approached. She hoped never to return after that day, knowing it would forever evoke the despondency of the moment.

After the final judgment had been pronounced, Jennifer gazed across the aisle in search of comfort from Mark's gentle face. Only the steely eyes of the Cobra stared back. With head high, Jennifer walked out of the courtroom and then nearly ran through the corridors. She threw the outer doors wide and rushed to her car. She had no memory of the drive home. Inside her tiny house, she turned off her phone, climbed into sweats, and curled up in bed, where she remained for the next three days.

****

In the weeks that followed a signed contract with Stanhope Construction, the bond that formed between Jennifer and Troy lacked its earlier sizzle. She rebuked herself for her tomboy ways. Why run around in jeans and sneakers, clamoring to be shown the latest developments of the sawdust-choked construction site? What need did she have to burn her lungs in the pool trying to out-distance Troy? Rather than intimate dinners and lovemaking, they grabbed take-out and watched movies at her house or exercised and then devoured deli sandwiches. Those activities weren't devoid of romantic potential, but none existed.

Occasional weekends passed with no word from Troy, and Jennifer went crazy picturing another woman in his arms, an elegant beauty, tall and sophisticated, unlike her own rough and tumble self. Still, she liked to think she and Troy had a magic of their own, a cagy allure. Her assertiveness as an apartment manager didn't carry over to Troy. It wouldn't work to question him about their relationship or how he spent his time. Meanwhile, his stay in Oklahoma City stretched from two weeks to nine.

An art culture had grown up in the city's Paseo District. It was a commercial area of Spanish revival architecture in lively pastels along cobblestone pedestrian streets. Jennifer and Troy stepped into a studio there and were both drawn to a large oil painting. In it, a woman held a red umbrella over her head as she meandered along a country road. Beneath her feet was the deeper, reddish-brown Oklahoma soil. Sun shone through the rain, highlighting golden wheat fields on both sides of the road.

Jennifer stood back and studied the painting. "I love its pensive mood."

"The vibrant colors draw me in." Troy checked the price.

She gazed at it until he took her by the elbow and led her out.

The painting stayed on Jennifer's mind for days. She asked herself why not, reasoned that she'd earned it, and returned to the gallery intent on its purchase. The rickety screen door creaked as she opened it. The painting hung in its same place but with a red tag tucked into its corner. SOLD it read in bold black letters. Jennifer turned and fled.

That evening she recounted her tale of woe to Troy.

"Hang on a minute."

He went outside and returned, struggling through the front door with something large. Jennifer went to help him and recognized the size and shape of the parcel wrapped in brown paper.

"Is it...?" It couldn't be the painting, could it? Gift giving wasn't their way.

The parcel's width encompassed Troy's full wingspan. He turned sideways, maneuvered through the entry, and propped it on the couch.

"Is that for me?"

"Of course."

She tore at the wrapping.

He laughed. "Careful Jen, it's delicate."

"It's the painting! Troy, it's more stunning here than in the gallery. Oh, thank you." She threw her arms around his neck and kissed him.

They hung it above the fireplace where russet bricks made a perfect backdrop. She poured each of them a glass of wine and snuggled up beside him.

"I'm still in awe. Look at how rich the colors are."

"Yep, it was a good choice."

"The woman hasn't made much progress on her walk since the last time we saw her." Jennifer intended the remark to be funny.

Troy didn't laugh. "She's walking a country mile. It won't do her any good to be in a hurry."

Her words weren't meant to be metaphorical; did Troy take them that way? If so, it presented the perfect lead-in to a discussion about their lack of intimacy. Better not to. She cherished the painting, and the occasion was special. She didn't want to taint either one.

Before Troy left at the end of the evening, he kissed her. Not with the longed-for passion, but rather like a honeysuckle's droplet of nectar on her lips.

****

It took twenty minutes to reach Coahoma from Oklahoma City. The quiet farm town seemed to have been in hibernation until its discovery. Its rise in popularity changed pastures and wheat fields into housing tracts and gated mini-mansion communities. The change saddened Jennifer, yet the town's growth spurt represented her business's saving grace and the reason for Troy in her life. At least the county fair still had its rural appeal. Jennifer and Troy meandered toward the pungent barnyard smells of the livestock exhibits.

She petted a sheep, white with a velvety-black face and ears. "Her wool is so thick and fluffy."

Calm was interrupted by the piercing squeal of a pink pig charging full speed toward them on its dainty hooves. Jennifer screamed and leaped aside. Troy tried to halt the runaway animal by stepping in front of it, but it swerved around him without breaking stride. A pack of 4H students chased it, and the crowd cheered for both pig and kids.

Troy put his arm around her. "You okay?"

"Yeah, just shaken up. Geez, I thought the beast would ram me."

"It's a young thing, more terrified than you were."

At the beef cow pens, Troy demonstrated his area of expertise. He bent and pointed between the corral's metal slats at a blue ribbon winner.

"See how the carriage is broad and sits evenly on the shoulders, the base in line with the spine?" With animated body language, he gestured toward the animal while he spoke.

Jennifer smiled at his boyish enthusiasm.

A crowd gathered as he continued, "Judges look for a long frame because it holds more meat and one with the most muscle possible while staying in proportion to the size of the body. It's important to have strong, sturdy legs."

The scent of fresh popcorn wafted from the exhibit hall, and Jennifer bought a bag. She and Troy meandered through homemade quilts, woodworking, and scroll art with their arms around each other's waists. She didn't want to let go of Troy, but couldn't eat the delicious-smelling kernels, so she dipped into the bag by mouth.

He laughed and fed her some. "You're like a horse with a feedbag."

"Gee, what a flattering comparison. Can you at least make it a pony?"

They paused to watch a cake decorating demonstration and then moved on to a mineral and gem exhibit. It featured a collection of rose rocks, Oklahoma's state rock.

Jennifer read aloud, "250 million years ago barite

crystals and sand formed a circular array of flat plates in the shape of roses in full bloom. Iron content gave them a burnt sienna hue. Far and away, Oklahoma has the world's largest concentration of these interesting minerals."

She swiveled to face Troy, "I know some rose rock lore."

"Yeah?"

"Cherokee legend says the rocks represent the blood of braves and the tears of maidens who made the Trail of Tears journey in the late 1800's to the southern central Plains Indian Territory, eventually Red Man, or Oklahoma."

****

Jennifer's huge armoire lacked the modern look she wanted. It had to go, along with the ancient television inside. Goodwill Industries agreed to pick the items up if they were in the garage. Aaron pulled in, and Troy arrived soon after with a handcart.

Jennifer smiled. "Hi Troy, this is Aaron. Aaron, this is Troy."

They shook hands. Troy carried more bulk than Aaron, but they were close in height.

"It's a pleasure to meet you, Aaron."

"Pleasure to meet you, as well."

"Your mom's talked about you so much it's like I already know you."

"She does that."

Jennifer relaxed. "I'll leave you guys to it."

A simple lunch of sandwiches involved a lot of stuff—bread, packaged turkey, condiments, pickles, chips, iced tea, and dishes. Aaron had somewhere else to go and wanted to make it quick. She sliced tomato and washed lettuce with an ear to the other room. Aaron liked the idea of his mom not being alone and had asked to meet Troy. The two entered the kitchen in a tumble of activity.

"Mom, is there any cheese?"

"I knew I forgot something. There's Pepper Jack and Swiss in the refrigerator."

Jennifer made sandwiches, and Troy filled glasses with ice. The grind of metal against ice and the sharp clink of cubes hitting glass dominated the room.

"I can't believe you're getting a wide screen," Aaron said. He addressed Troy. "My mom used to consider TV evil. She wouldn't let me watch it."

Jennifer laughed. "You watched all the time."

"Right, Mr. Roger's Neighborhood, and I had to ride my bike around the block three times before I could turn it on."

Jennifer set a stack of napkins on the table, and they all sat. "You loved Mr. Rogers."

Aaron glanced at his watch.

"Your mom says you're going rock climbing today," Troy said.

"Yep, rappelling at Rocktown. Have you heard of it?"

"No, I haven't."

"It's converted from a grain elevator. There are sixteen silos. Some climbs go up ninety feet. I'm meeting my friends Brian and Carly there. Do you guys wanna see it?"

Jennifer and Troy looked at each other.

"We don't have any other plans today," she said

He shrugged. "Sure, let's take a look."

"Cool. You know where it is, right Mom?"

"I've driven you there."

Aaron paused between bites. "So Troy, how long will you be in town?"

How long indeed. Troy and Jennifer's eyes darted around like prisms, lighting on Aaron and then anywhere but each other's faces. Aaron had inherited her intuition. The marked shift in the room's emotional climate must've confused to him. Jennifer would explain the situation to him later.

Troy's eyes were sad and a little shifty. "I've already been here longer than expected. There's some unfinished business in Albuquerque. I've gotta put in some time there."

His unexplained business hung in the room like frozen fog, but now wasn't the time to ask. After Aaron's innocent stumble, she knew he wouldn't either. She rose and lifted the pitcher from the counter.

"More tea, anyone?"

"No thanks, Mom. I gotta go."

Aaron set his dishes in the sink. "So you guys are coming, right?"

Jennifer nodded and looked at Troy.

"I'd like to see it," he said.

Aaron and Troy walked outside and wrestled the dolly back into Troy's car. Jennifer liked how they smiled and nodded at each other. Troy and Dean no longer shared a truck. Troy hated his small rental but saw no point in paying for a bigger one. When he and Jennifer did things around town, they took her Jeep.

Heading east on I40, she glanced over at him. "What kind of unfinished business do you have in Albuquerque?"

"It's unpleasant. I don't want to talk about it."

"I hope it's not too serious. Is it work related?"

"Did you not hear me clearly? I'm not going to discuss it. Don't bring it up again."

What vehemence. He'd never snapped at her before. Was the company in trouble? She couldn't ask Dean. As Troy's faithful second-hand man, he wouldn't tell her. Like everything else concerning Troy, she'd have to wait and see.

At the climbing walls, Jennifer proclaimed herself the photographer and wouldn't be coaxed up for anything. Troy surprised her by renting a pair of shoes and getting himself harnessed and roped. He listened to Aaron's instructions with a serious expression and slight nods. The respectful way he treated Aaron despite their huge age difference gave Jennifer a rush of affection for him. Her son's effort on Troy's behalf made her heart swell too. She wanted to kiss and hug them both. In a sport for the young and lithe, Troy did pretty well. More than that, he showed a fun side, a soaring spirit.

Chapter Eleven

Late October days brought warm sunshine as if fall refused to yield to winter. Troy's anticipated length of stay in Oklahoma City had long come and gone. He and Jennifer were on borrowed time.

A hat-buying expedition took them to Stockyards City. In a shop called Shorty's Hattery, Troy found a handsome brown Stetson made of brushed felt with a braided brim. Sturdy but soft, it would help him stay warm in winter. He sat in the passenger seat of the Jeep with his new purchase on his lap. He picked it up and turned it around in his hands, then cleared his throat.

"Russell's about finished with his other job. He'll be takin' over here in a week's time. Like I said, I've got unfinished business back in New Mexico, and I'm long overdue at the ranch."

His words were like a punch to the chest. It seemed unimaginable to return to her old life. Troy had changed it from dull gray to an aurora's brilliant color. She'd been in denial about his leaving and struggled to respond in a neutral tone.

"It's not like we haven't been expecting it." *I will not cry; I will not cry.*

Despite this mantra, tears filled her eyes. It became hard to see. *This is not happening.* She turned her blinker on, switched lanes and pulled into the first driveway that came along, an abandoned parking lot.

Cutting the engine, she threw off her seat belt and hid her face in her hands.

Troy reached an arm over to console her. "Hey, baby, it's all right."

"No, it isn't."

He hurried around to her side, opened her door, and pulled her into his arms.

She didn't meet his gaze. "I don't know what to say. I'm embarrassed."

"There's no need for words."

His brawny arms held her, and they rocked back and forth.

****

In the early dawn of Troy's departure, he stopped by Jennifer's house on his way out of town. She stood barefoot in the doorway in a flimsy nightgown and her curls wild. In her sleepy stupor, the unexpected visit and bewitching in-between hour emboldened her. She wrapped him in her arms and kissed him while she pressed her full length hard against him and felt his desire.

She urged him to come inside. "My warm bed is waiting."

His words were forced. "Can't. Gotta go, baby. Go back to sleep."

He kissed her and was gone.

By noon, he'd called twice.

Their phone calls grew more frequent than when he'd been nearby. Bedtime conversations became a ritual. When she missed a call from him, she played the message over and over to hear his voice. The envoys were simple, like, "Hey Jen, what'cha doin'? Sorry I missed you. Call me, bye," yet she found them sexy, and they drove her crazy with desire for him. No one else called her 'Jen.' She loved the way his voice deepened an octave at 'bye.'

Troy's leaving hurt but didn't break her the way she thought it would. In fact, it gave her pause to study their relationship. Five hours separated them. The distance would thwart a serious relationship. She'd lost sight of her plan to return to California, but it still existed. Troy was a fourth-generation Stanhope to run the ranch, with Okie roots dating back to the land run of 1889. The odds of him moving to San Diego with her were slim to none. Maybe her feelings for him were infatuation and would ease up. She'd see him on occasion and enjoy an easy companionability like mature adults. When Aaron graduated, and Stanhope Construction finished building the mall, she and Troy would part friends.

Each time Jennifer expressed to Troy her longing for the ocean and the San Diego hills, she found his answers condescending.

"You're restless. Give it time. You'll change your mind."

Was he right? She'd been settled here for twenty years. This longing to return to California sprung from discontentment over a situation now resolved. It was ill-timed. Her argument may have been valid, but to live in Oklahoma for the rest of her life still seemed unimaginable.

One Sunday while Jennifer and Troy relaxed on her patio, he said, "I like the way things are between us. No drama—just simple, honest, and easy."

Jennifer smiled. "Small town meets country."

"You're small town, and I'm country?"

"That's right."

"I like it. The hard part's the travel, and I've come up with a way to deal with it," Troy said.

"Oh?"

"I'll charter a Cessna. I can keep a car at Yeager Field."

"Take an airplane here?"

"Just a single prop two-seater."

"That would be a lot easier on you, but wouldn't it be expensive?"

"If I book ten tickets I can save a bundle. Publicly, it's a usual and customary business expense. Privately, you're worth it." He'd reached across their chairs and took her hand.

****

Physical intimacy continued to elude them, a topic always on Jennifer's mind. Men of Troy's age often had sexual dysfunction. He'd know about remedies—blue pills and such—though they weren't always effective. Maybe he couldn't perform at all. Was she too unapproachable for him to discuss so delicate a matter? She wished there were someone to talk to. Evelyn had sworn off men long ago. Jennifer's sister? Too ditzy. Her mother? Oh hell no. Her book club friends? Too private an issue for any of them. The other choices were a professional counselor or bear it alone.

A psychologist might help with another mystery. Her ex-husband traipsed through her dreams every night. Romantic, platonic, or a face in the crowd, it didn't matter. Kind or angry, there he was. Someone once said the number of years married equaled the weight of your soul. The comment had been part of a comedian's routine, but it had struck a chord with

Jennifer. Would her ex show up uninvited into her dreams for sixteen more years?

Jennifer pulled up to the apartments, got out, locked the Jeep, and put the remote into one back pocket and her phone in the other. Up and down the corridors of her apartment complex was a ragtag collection of tables and chairs the tenants had acquired who knew where. Ghetto Shabby, the year's new look. She'd like to provide patio sets, but at what cost? These men weren't vacationers at Alcove Resort. Perfectionism had caused her to overspend in the past, and she struggled to rein it in. Yet matching sets of outdoor furniture would look so nice. Her maintenance man had good sense about things like this; she'd ask his opinion.

She continued to meander with a notepad in hand to jot down chores for maintenance. Her thoughts shifted to Troy. Was he in the throes of a sexual relationship with another woman, bound to faithfulness? It seemed the likeliest scenario. Jennifer would not involve herself in some feminine competition to win him over. She wouldn't use overt gestures with Troy; they weren't her style. She'd carry on as usual and guard her emotions. Theirs was an intimate yet restrained friendship, an alliance between business associates. That's how she'd regard their odd liaison.

That evening, Jennifer lay on the couch and picked up a novel that had caught her eye in the library's new books section. She read the first page, tossed it aside, and did the same with a second book. She sighed. The day's resolute conclusions about her and Troy were useless. She drifted into a fantasy of making love with him until the phone's ring interrupted her. On the line was the very focus of her joy and frustration.

They spoke of the coming weekend they'd spend together, and Jennifer blurted, "You could stay with me rather than at the Wyndham."

"The company pays for my hotel."

"You are the company. You'd save yourself money."

"That's cute, but I get up real early to be at the job site. I'd hate to disturb you."

"I'm an early riser."

What was she, some pushy broad in combat boots stomping across the flowerbed of their delicate boundary?

She added in haste, "but I appreciate your thoughtfulness."

After the conversation, she chastised herself for cowering. As a healthy woman with normal needs, she had a right to expect sexual intimacy with Troy. The question had gone unanswered for too long. She needed to pipe up.

An opportunity arose by way of a suggestive phone message from Troy. "Hi Jen, sorry I missed you. You must be at the gym. It's the only place you don't take your phone. I swear you must take it into the shower with you. Not that I'd know. I'm just imagining."

She called him right back. "I got your message."

"Yeah?"

"The one where you imagine me in the shower."

"Uh-huh."

She summoned her nerve and gave a light laugh. "We could take a shower together. That way, you'd know if I have my phone. The mystery would be solved."

She'd never have made the cheeky suggestion in person, even in jest. Her voice came out too loud and bright, Susie Sunshine on crank.

"Showering together is over-rated. Someone's butt is always out in the cold."

Jennifer had come this far and would not back down. "A bath, then."

Troy laughed. At least there was that. "We wouldn't both fit in your little tub."

"Okay, the big one in your hotel room, Friday night."

"Whoa, what's this all about?"

There in her Jeep at the apartments, she drove her thumbnails into the steering wheel's spongy material and left crescent-shaped indentions. So what if they were permanent.

"It's about us moving forward, honey. I want to know what's up."

"I thought we were taking it slow, you know? Friendship first."

"I'm forty-five, and you're fifty. We've spent a lot of time together. You know I care for you. I'm ready for more."

There was a long silence.

"Can we talk about it later? I'm working right now."

"Of course."

"Great. See you soon, sweetheart." The phone went dead.

Fuck! What a plodding ox. Her scream was a release but not at all satisfying.

Chapter Twelve

Jennifer walked the perimeter of her apartment complex with Ramiro, the groundskeeper.

Crossing their language barrier for simple instructions like 'Please pick up the trash' wasn't a problem, but she struggled with more complex directives.

"*Por favor todas las semanas la basura, un poco major.*" The clumsy attempt to tell him to manage ongoing litter issues brought a premature nod from him. They'd be stumbling through this again in a week.

The roaring wind would've caused her to miss a phone call save for the phone's vibration in her back pocket. Instead of letting the call go to voice mail, she gave in to the chime's conditioned stimulus and picked up.

"Hello, Ms. Ellis? Sheriff Whiting here."

"Hello, Sheriff." She pointed Ramiro toward plastic grocery bags and other debris blown along the fence.

"I've got bad news."

His long pause unnerved her. To have stray cats and dogs rounded up from her mother's property was hardly bad news. "Is there a problem besides the animals?"

"Yes ma'am, I'm afraid so. Animal Welfare removed the cats from your mother's barn and discovered an active meth lab."

"What? Oh my god." Another blast of wind hit the phone, and Jennifer couldn't hear. "Hold on a sec while I find someplace quieter."

She waved a hurried goodbye to Ramiro and rushed behind a wall for shelter. With her back to the wind, she bent down and covered her other ear again.

"This meth lab, is it dangerous?"

"We believe it is. A Haz-Mat team is there now. The state narcotics bureau will assess the situation and arrest some, if not all, of the residents."

Jennifer didn't care that she now violated her own rule. She crouched and shouted directly behind someone's bedroom window. "Where's my mom?"

"She's staying with a neighbor, I believe."

That would be Lois. "Is she in trouble?"

"Your mother?"

"Of course my mother, who else?"

"Well, she hasn't been arrested yet. She's been issued an initial citation for possession of controlled substances, and a court date for several public health violations. If she fails to appear, a bench warrant will be issued the same day."

Still struggling to hear, Jennifer moved to a protected spot between two large air conditioners at rest. She squatted and leaned into the wall, missing some of his words.

"…more serious charges once it's turned over to the D.A. Here in California, operating a meth lab is a felony offense punishable by up to seven years in prison."

"They must know my mom isn't the one running it."

"A related offense is Conspiracy and Health Safety Code 11366.5. It addresses the law against allowing another person to operate a meth lab in your home or other structure."

His police-speak made her edgy.

"The law states any person residing or working where illegal controlled substances are being used, sold, or manufactured faces a mandatory ninety days in jail or a fifteen hundred dollar fine for a first offense. That would be the lightest sentence. It's a misdemeanor at this point, but it could be upgraded to a felony, and usually is from what I've seen."

Her mom would be overwrought, and Allison's hysteria would take over on that front. Jennifer had no choice. Her legs went numb, and she sat on the cement, wedged between the metal condensers.

"I'll try to catch a flight out tomorrow. May I come talk to you when I get there?"

"That'll be fine."

One of the air conditioners cycled on. *Why is someone running his a/c this late in the year?* She scrambled up and hurried toward her Jeep. "My sister lives in Del Mar. I haven't heard a word from either her or my mom about this."

"Yes, ma'am. Yours is the only contact number on file."

"Thank you for calling, Sheriff."

Jennifer headed toward the parking lot's exit. Her right tires ran over the curb and gave jarring thumps when she pulled into traffic. She clutched the wheel and sped toward home. The nerve of those lowlifes after her mom had thrown her door wide to them. How had her mother been so blind? An eighty-one-year-old jailbird, what a mug shot it would make. Allison had promised to keep watch on the place. Why hadn't she looked in the barn? Too busy with her own pursuits. Sheriff Whiting didn't escape Jennifer's ire either, though she didn't know why. She raged at herself more than anyone. The signs were all there. *Why didn't I figure it out? I should've followed up.*

She dreaded telling Troy about her whack-job mother and airhead sister. The thought of sharing this family sketch with an upstanding man from a distinguished family brought the familiar pounding sensation to the back of her head. She pressed it hard against the headrest. A few more miles and she'd be home. She knew the routine. Two aspirins, a glass of water, and a few bites of anything edible. She needed to see a neurologist.

Three different airlines quoted similar exorbitant rates for the next morning's first flight out. With no choice, she pushed the button on her computer's keyboard and booked a flight. She had to call Troy. It'd be so much easier to leave him a message about her urgent need to fly to San Diego. By the third ring, she thought maybe he wouldn't pick up, but he did.

She rushed through her explanation with her words tripping over each other. Troy missed most of what she said, and she had to repeat it.

"Why didn't you tell me about your mother before? Maybe I could've helped somehow."

"I thought that all I had to do was convince her to evict her tenants. She takes in stray young people and animals. I'm sorry to have to burden you with this."

"It's not a burden, but I wish you would've told me about it."

"Sorry." She'd apologized twice. It was too much. She moved between closet, bathroom, and bed, packing a bag.

"Sheriff Hamm came into the café yesterday talking 'bout this very thing. Meth manufacturing and use are epidemics out this way." Troy said.

"I'm surprised it goes on there."

"They're saying it's the main cause of the increase in cattle rustling."

"Cattle rustling? Sounds like something straight out of the Wild West."

"It's alive and well, and plaguing the livestock industry. Here in Oklahoma, a record number of cattle thefts were reported last year—eight hundred thirty according to the Cattleman's Association. Most of the rustlers are hopped up on meth and looking for quick money. Making off with the animals can be as simple as cutting a fence, backing up a truck, and shaking a bag of feed. Cattle come willingly. Law enforcement agents from the Ag Department track down most of the thieves. It's just a matter of time before they get 'em."

Despite the bleak topic, Troy's voice calmed her frayed nerves. She stopped rushing around to lie on the bed and let his steady tone deliver its unique brand of serenity.

By mid-morning the following day, Jennifer sat behind the wheel of a rental car and exited east off Highway 395 toward Las Casitas. The familiar beauty of soft, dusty hills rose around her. Other than the road itself and an occasional highway marker, the five-mile stretch of the valley floor carried few traces of human intervention. Continuing east through Manzanita Canyon, rolling hills grew into looming mountains, matching her rising angst while she drove into town.

There were two new gas stations, a strip mall, and a housing tract where fields had once been, but other than that, things had changed little. Las Casitas sat tucked too deeply into the mountains to fall victim to suburban sprawl like so many other towns.

Jennifer called her mother. No answer. She'd been trying since her plane touched down. Lois was almost deaf and slow moving, so Jennifer opened her screen door, knocked, waited, and knocked again. A bare wire stuck out of a crumbling hole in the stucco where a doorbell used to be. She called out, but no one answered.

On the short distance to her mother's, Jennifer's guilt welled up again, and she berated herself for her negligence. It had been eight years since her last visit. There were always things standing in her way, like her own family's vacation plans or being at odds with her mother. When Jennifer visited California, she stayed with Allison. Her mother didn't extend invitations, so their shallow visits took place in San Diego restaurants.

The house stood out in all its lime green glory, formerly Day Glo Pink. Jennifer pulled into the driveway and parked. The garage door was open. Part of it had been cleared and turned into a makeshift living room. Jennifer walked past a sagging couch and faded easy chair. A wooden spool sat on end with empty beer cans and ashtrays full of cigarette butts. She knocked on the door.

"Come in," her mother yelled.

Jennifer entered and inhaled the overpowering scent of her mom's signature fragrance, Jungle Gardenia. Jennifer remembered the scent on many a car trip, indistinguishable from rotting roses or funeral parlor wreaths.

Her mother stood at the kitchen counter removing the skin from a green apple with a paring knife. She didn't pause when Jennifer entered, nor did the two embrace. Growing up, the only time her mother touched her was in anger. Jennifer remembered her arm being grabbed by Blanche's cold, wet hand.

Her mom had aged. She'd grown thin and exuded a vulnerability that her hostility had prevented in the past. Jennifer hoped her mom's curly hair and short stature were their only similarities. Blanche's brassy orange dye job was an obvious do-it-yourself concoction and cause for endless complaints from Allison, Stylist Extraordinaire. Bright polyester warm-up suits and rubber flip flops were her year-round fashion choice. Today's color: Vivid Coral.

"Hello Jennifer, how are you?" She bit into her apple.

"Okay, I guess. The real question is how you are."

"I had the crap scared out of me when they found that damn meth lab. I almost had another nervous breakdown." She imitated craziness by pulling at her hair and mimicking a silent scream.

She'd been threatening breakdowns Jennifer's entire life. "You've never had a nervous breakdown."

"My doctor put me on Prozac and wants me to take Geodon."

"Are you taking it?" Jennifer knew she wouldn't.

"Why the hell should I? It's for certifiable nut cases."

Jennifer walked to the sliding glass door in the living room. Its lower third had always been muddy and scratched—no change there. Dilapidated chain link fencing, once a makeshift kennel, lay strewn about the backyard. A car without a driver's door sat in the weeds. Even from where she stood she could see a locked chain on the barn door.

She returned to the kitchen. "What's happening in the barn?"

"The county came by this morning. Other than some burnt spots on the walls, they said the damage is minimal. There're no plumbing or ventilation systems needing detox so it looks like I'll get a break in that regard. You want some coffee?"

She pointed to the carafe with enough in it to cover the bottom of the pot.

"No thanks, but I'll take an apple."

Blanche pointed her thumb over her shoulder. "In the fridge."

"Green apples are sour. I'll need something on it."

"Like what?"

Jennifer shrugged, "Yogurt, honey, cinnamon, anything."

"Just eat the damn apple."

Jennifer skipped it and slumped into a chair. "Why isn't the barn airing out?"

Blanche handed her a flier. "The county gave me this."

Jennifer read aloud with some ad-libbing: "To promote chemical dispersion into the air, the barn should be closed, and the temperature inside increased to ninety-five degrees for at least forty-eight hours."

"They set up a huge heater out there. I'm terrified of a fire starting. After that, it gets aired out for five more days. The SPCA took all the animals, Rex included. What a good dog." Blanche affected a sniff.

"Didn't you smell the lab chemicals?"

"You know I have sinus trouble. Besides, I'm not a chemist. I thought the cats caused it. So did that nice deputy."

"Then why didn't you do something about them?"

Blanche slammed her knife down on the cutting board. "Do not come here and lecture me. It wasn't that bad. I couldn't smell it in the house."

Jennifer had long ago stopped being intimidated by her mother's raised voice. She'd grown up with the screaming. In her teens, she'd delighted her friends with impersonations of her mother, whom she called 'Wild Banshee Woman.'

"I can't believe you didn't notice activity in the barn."

"The tenants said they were making jewelry."

"Jewelry? That's rich." She picked up a pamphlet and read aloud, "with pseudoephedrine, bleach, and hydrochloric acid? Weren't you curious about the process, or at least what the finished pieces looked like?"

"They told me the jewelry wasn't finished."

Jennifer closed her eyes. Oh, the sarcasm she could let fly with this if she had someone with whom to share her cruel mother jokes. Allison didn't comprehend their underpinnings, or else she'd get mad, perhaps even cry. No fun at all. She'd been too easy a target for Jennifer's swift verbal jabs when they were growing up. Early on, Blanche became protective of Allison and lashed out at Jennifer.

Jennifer didn't want to be like her mother. Nasty remarks would undermine her efforts to curtail her sarcasm. "Where do you stand legally?"

Her mom threw up her hands. "I don't know. They won't tell me anything. The citation states 'defendant's relationship to be determined at hearing.'"

She shuffled through a pile of papers and handed Jennifer a document the size of a traffic ticket. It had little information other than fragments: Premises-Hazard: Toxic Chemicals. Viol. California Criminal Code—Sec: J667. There was a long citation number, and a hearing date in two weeks.

"Are your tenants in jail?"

"I think so." Apple in hand, her mother sat down at the table and began to read a disheveled newspaper.

Jennifer filled a glass from the faucet and took a long drink. She couldn't resist one little jab. "Did the rodents leave for good, or will they scurry back when the coast is clear?"

"Those kids will never move back in."

"Do you plan to get new ones?"

Her mother rolled her eyes like a rebellious teenager. Their roles had reversed.

Jennifer glanced around. "Other than a little worse for wear, the place looks the same."

Cabinet doors had never closed for all the junk crammed inside. Rubber bands still hung on doorknobs, tarnishing the brass finish. At least the house appeared sound.

The two women poured over a packet of information from the county. In reading about chemical cleanup, it stated they would have to dispose of everything porous.

"Not to be flippant, but the barn needs cleaning out. It's full of junk. This isn't a huge problem so far. It says here all items have to be hauled to a chemical dump. Haz-mat will arrive with a mobile lab to analyze materials on site. They'll test dirt from the floor and seal the walls. Common household products can be used for the cleanup and shouldn't cost over three thousand dollars."

Blanche leaped up. "Shit. I don't have that kind of money."

"Don't worry about the cost."

"Who will clean it? I can't exactly call Merry Maids to come and scrub down a meth site."

"Calm down. Here's a list of contractors. We'll call some of them for estimates."

Jennifer had been with her mother an entire hour, meaning it was time for a break. She slung her purse over her shoulder.

"I think I'll go have a talk with the sheriff."

Chapter Thirteen

Jennifer drove through town toward the sheriff's department. She passed the cemetery where her father had been put to rest. He'd died before she could have him in her adult life, but he'd been very much a part of her childhood. Her father had loved her sass and spunk even more than her button nose, face full of freckles, and white-blonde hair. He'd been her tall, handsome hero who made her heart go pitter-pat. As a career Navy man, he'd taught her sea ditties and laughed at her recitations. *I'm gonna shave and shower and shine my shoes/when I get through I'm gonna put on my blues/I'm gonna go, go, go.* She remembered how nice it'd been to hug him and hold his hand. She missed him dearly.

The sheriff's station hadn't changed from its location behind city hall. In the waiting area, she tried not to stare at a teenager dabbing his bloody nose with a tissue. After ten minutes, a man with a crew cut and trim gray mustache opened the door.

"Ms. Ellis?"

Jennifer stood. "Yes?"

"I'm Sheriff Whiting, this way please."

He ushered her down a hall.

"What happened to that guy in the waiting room?"

"There was a scuffle."

Jennifer knew a dismissive tone when she heard it.

Sheriff Whiting opened the door to a small conference room like those in police shows.

"I can imagine the dramas that have unfolded here," she said.

"Have a seat. The state narcotics bureau has jurisdiction in your mother's case. They don't believe the meth lab had been operating long. It'll make the cleanup easier. Does your mother have a lawyer?"

"Do you think she needs one? I can't imagine my mom being thrown in jail. The charges would have to be negligent cluelessness."

Sheriff Congeniality didn't smile. "You'd be surprised by the number of people who've tried to use ignorance of the law as an excuse. She should get a good drug crimes attorney."

"Can you suggest someone?"

"I can't do that, ma'am. Call the State Bar Association or the Legal Aid Society." He withdrew a pen from his jacket, clicked it, and jotted the numbers of those organizations on the large envelope in front of him.

"What about the other people involved?"

"They're being held and facing three felonies: possession of hazardous chemicals, manufacture, and intent to sell controlled substances." He handed her the thick packet and stood.

The meeting had reached its end. Jennifer stepped outside the building and called Allison.

"In my opinion, Mom's problems go deeper than her legal issues. She's slipped since I last saw her. How can she not have known her tenants were cooking meth in the back yard? She can't handle the place anymore, or the people."

"The drug thing's terrible but other than that Mom's okay. She got a new roof and found someone to do the mowing. She doesn't want to move or live alone and thinks taking in boarders is the answer."

Allison's response had fallen back into her norm, defense of their mother regardless of facts. While still on the phone, Jennifer arrived at her car and stood leaning against the door.

"I wish she'd find decent ones. You need to keep a closer eye on things."

"I'll try, but it's a lot of driving, and I don't have time."

Jennifer's words shot out like bullets. "I can't believe I'm hearing this. I should not have had to fly all the way out here. Like it or not, you've got to make time. You will go to court with her, period. I'm not coming back for that."

"You wanna stay at my house tonight?"

Vintage Alli, focused on social plans rather than the seriousness of the situation. "Did you hear what I said?"

"I heard you, Jenny. I'll try to keep closer tabs on Mom, and I'll go to court with her, okay? But you need to do your part, too. You never even call her."

"That's not entirely true. I'll call her more often, but we both know she'd rather talk to you than me."

"So my house tonight?"

Jennifer loved Allison's pristine beach cottage with its bleached floors and ultra-modern glass and chrome furniture, but she felt like staying in Las Casitas.

"I don't think so. Why don't you come up?"

"I'm supposed to go out with friends after work, how about joining us? We're meeting at The Chart

House; it's right on the water."

"It'd be nice to see you, even if I am mad at you."

"Then come. Meet me here at the salon at six. We'll go together."

"Okay."

"Sure you don't want to spend the night afterward?"

"Nah, I think I'll drive back up here, but thanks for inviting me."

Allison's voice grew faint while she spoke to someone, and then returned to the line. "I've got a client; gotta go."

"Okay, see you at six. Bye."

Jennifer arrived at the salon on time.

Allison held a scissor over a client's short dark hair. "Jenny, this is my friend Ben. Ben, this is my sister Jenny visiting from Oklahoma."

Jennifer and Ben said hello.

Allison nodded to the row of chairs. "Have a seat, I'm almost done."

Jennifer sat. The place looked good, impeccably clean, very hip and swanky. Her glance flitted here and there. Her gaze met Ben's in the mirror. She looked away but was compelled to look back. His eyes remained fixed on her reflection. He had deep brown eyes below dark lashes and brows. There was a broodiness about him. He was tall. His shoulders rose well above the chair, and his knees jutted to the sides, a nice-looking man with a haunted look telling of some unmet need, a searching but not finding.

Music played through unseen speakers, people moved around and conversed, and hair dryers whirred. Through it all, she and Ben exchanged curious looks across the thousand miles separating their lives.

Dinner with Allison included a dozen people—beautiful Hollywood-types who talked nonstop about matters of no interest to her. Allison had invited Ben, and he'd said he might come. Jennifer kept looking toward the entryway. She imagined scooting over to make room for him and satisfying her curiosity about him through one-on-one conversation. Mystery Man never showed up. The evening served to remind Jennifer of why she didn't enjoy socializing with her sister.

The next day, she and her mom sat in the conference room of a San Diego sky rise and listened to an attorney.

"If you knowingly allowed these people to operate an illegal meth lab in your barn, you could face up to four years in state prison. Depending on the circumstances, prosecutors could also charge you with aiding and abetting or conspiracy. If convicted of one or more of these offenses as a misdemeanor, you face up to one year in the city jail and a maximum one thousand dollar fine. 'Knowingly allowed' are the key words here. I can provide a compelling argument for your defense. Based on your age, years in the community, and lack of a criminal record, you may be charged with nothing beyond a citation and the responsibility for adequate cleanup."

The attorney impressed Jennifer with his capability and positive outlook. Blanche liked his patience. They returned to Las Casitas and went on a tour of Highland Ridge, a new condo community specializing in independent living for seniors.

Blanche shook her head at the proffered sales

information. "The apartments are nice but too expensive. It's a waste of time because I'm not moving."

Jennifer took the packet. "Mom, there's a long waiting list. Let's have them add your name for the heck of it. There's no obligation."

Blanche mumbled her consent.

Two days later with her mother's problems handled, more or less, Jennifer rolled her suitcase outside and took a last look at the surrounding hills, her old stalwart friends. She filled her lungs with warm, dry air. Life had tricked her into leaving here, robbed her of the choice and promised a return, an unkept promise. She and her husband rented out their California house with full intention of returning when his work obligation ended. They arrived in Oklahoma with their three-year-old son, ready for the adventure of a different culture. They made friends, preschool began, and they settled in. Their California house went on the market and sold. California stopped waiting for them.

Jennifer left Las Casitas well before her flight time. She lowered her window and endured freeway noise to catch the first whiffs of ocean air. She parked and stepped into salty mist along Pacific Coast Highway. Waves crashed, and high rugged cliffs defined the beach's perimeter. She vowed to stay in better contact with her mom and sister. Despite the distance, she knew she'd be the one hiring a contractor to clean the barn. There'd be consults with the lawyer, calls to government agencies, and dates to remember. She resigned herself to the endless details to come.

Her thoughts drifted to Troy, and weariness pressed in on her. He still made her fluttery inside, but what would come of their relationship? She thought she could remain on the tightrope between friendship and romance, but she couldn't. The time for change had come.

She rolled up her pant legs and strolled toward the wet sand where once-powerful swells diminished and bowed in final flourishes, ending with quiet grace, gliding arches encircling the feet of their native daughter. Over and over the foamy tide whispered her name.

Chapter Fourteen

November's overnight frost lingered all day. It clung to crevices, gutters and gradients, along fields and fences—natural compasses showing north like the counterpart to moss on southern slopes.

Troy asked Jennifer to a holiday party hosted by the Oklahoma Cattle Breeder's Association. She'd berated herself for not speaking to him about their lack of intimacy. With that invite, her mind whirred with a plan like a precision machine warming up.

"I'd love to. Will there be music and dancing?"

"I believe so. These events always have an orchestra. It'll be held at the Oklahoma City Golf and Tennis Club."

"Oh, it's stunning there."

The thought of swaying in Troy's arms filled her with visions of a romantic interlude. With two weeks until the event she arranged for ballroom dance lessons, enough time to learn a basic waltz, two-step, and foxtrot. She didn't mention these lessons to Troy. More than ever she wanted to be in his embrace, to feel the heat of his body against hers. She'd never made advances toward a man but that would soon change. Upon their return to her house after the party, she'd invite him in for wine, a warm fire, sultry music, and hopefully much more.

On the evening of the event, Jennifer laid out her

new purchases—a lacy black push-up bra with matching panties and silk thigh-high stockings. She sat on the bed and put them on and then smoothed the bedspread. The bedsheets were fresh, and she'd added a few spritzes of Troy's favorite fragrance. She reached for her Asian-style evening dress of maroon silk. It buttoned at the neck in front and opened in a low-cut triangle. A side slit revealed a fair amount of leg. It would happen tonight. The future of their relationship was at stake. She arranged herself in the new bra, attached a dangling pearl earring to each lobe, slipped into heels and gazed at her image. Perfect. Hair shining with fresh highlights; curls uniform and behaving themselves for once. An hour ago she'd run by the salon to have her hairdresser apply her smoky-gray liquid eyeliner. She didn't have the knack. Perfumed and painted, Jennifer was ready for action.

More important than her appearance was the resolve she called forth like a spell. Troy might reject her advances; she had to be prepared and find the strength to tell him goodbye.

At his knock, she smiled and opened the front door. There he stood, fabulous in a tuxedo. The deep burgundy of his bow tie and cummerbund matched her dress, giving them a pre-planned appearance. Oh well.

"Hi, handsome."

He looked her over and whistled. "Hello, gorgeous."

He stepped inside and gave her a warm kiss. His broad shoulders in the fitted jacket appeared more expansive than usual in her small entryway. He picked up her fox coat from the couch and helped her into it. How seamlessly he transitioned from cowboy in jeans to elegant gentleman.

Winter's first snowflakes whisked up and over the windshield of Troy's truck, soft like the dusting of powdered sugar through a finely meshed sieve. Jennifer met the smiles of fellow travelers through car windows. Everyone was charmed by the small miracle of snowfall.

Troy took her hand.

They left the truck with the club's valet and stepped into the foyer. Jennifer admired fur coats in all lengths and colors, noting with satisfaction none matched the winter white of her own. She did a double take at tuxedos paired with western hats and boots. It took a few clandestine stares on her part to get used to the odd match.

A Christmas tree rising two stories dominated the reception area. It stood regally dressed in shades of white and silver, the party's grand dame in full holiday regalia. Glitzy ornaments were the size of beach balls, ribbons flowed like waterfalls, and pine scent filled the air. At its base, bejeweled ladies floated and swirled in their gowns of sparkling colors, some wearing long white gloves.

"Would you like a drink?" Troy asked.

"I'd love a glass of merlot." The color would go well with her gown.

They started toward the bar, but a zealous photographer in a Santa Claus hat corralled them to a spot in front of the tree.

They posed and smiled, then Troy steered her away by the elbow. "We're now memorialized in the Cattleman's Association annals."

"It'd be a great photo to have; I'd like a copy."

Jennifer glanced back, but a surge of partygoers had thronged the area.

She sipped a glass of wine, grateful for its relaxing effects. Troy introduced her as his lady. Her face warmed with discomfort at the title, but with pleasure, too. There were curious looks from the Belles, and Jennifer assumed her presence beside Troy brought his available status into question. She smiled and held fast to his arm, alerting female predators to back off.

A lull in activity at the photography station sent her hurrying back. She envisioned Troy and herself beaming from a glossy eight by ten, framed and displayed on her dining room sideboard. After she made arrangements to get a copy, she started back toward Troy. Their eyes met across the room. She knew that look. He wanted her. Head high and eyes on her target, she glided toward him with her own sultry expression. Being his romantic partner seemed so natural. Tonight would be the night; she was sure of it.

Before long, heads turned toward a bank of French doors being opened wide to a dining room beyond. Genteel migration began, encouraged by a soft gong. Round tables with floor-length white tablecloths displayed oversized red and white floral arrangements bursting with greenery. Place settings waited with iced tea, water, salads, rolls and swirls of butter. At Jennifer's inquiry, a waiter recited the menu: strawberry and arugula salad with vinaigrette dressing, filet mignon sear grilled and topped with chanterelle mushrooms in a Cabernet reduction on a bed of Durham risotto, creamy butter beans with crispy bacon bits and Dutch-oven corn bread dotted with fig jam.

She followed the stream of polite conversation at

their table until Troy's hand squeezed her thigh, slid a bit higher and rested there. After that, she lost all ability to follow what was being said, instead smiling and nodding when it seemed appropriate. It appeared she wouldn't have to play seductress after all; that is unless Troy wanted her to. Tonight she and Troy were of like minds. Why now, after so long? She hoped the answer would come to light.

During dessert of cherry upside down cake, Jennifer returned Troy's gesture by placing her hand high up on his leg. He smiled at their secret and put his arm around her. Someone approached the microphone and spoke, followed by applause. Jennifer didn't care who he was or what he said. Her head and heart filled only with thoughts of the handsome man beside her, calling her his lady.

The orchestra started with a waltz, and the room came alive with couples threading their way toward the dance floor.

Troy turned to her. "Would you like to dance?"

"I'd love to."

He held her close, his lead bringing to life her limited steps.

She inhaled the scent of his skin. Unable to resist, she brushed her lips along his neck. She wanted to claim him for every number but respected his adherence to the courtesy of at least one dance with each lady at the table. She swayed in the arms of another man and noticed Troy dancing nearby. Each time she peeked over her dance partner's shoulder at him, he was watching her.

Back at their table he leaned toward her. "You appear to be enjoying yourself."

She smiled. "I'm having a wonderful time."

"Save the last dance for me."

Champagne flowed, and so did glitzy women to their table. They used any remote connection to Troy to draw him into conversation. Each time a new one approached, he stood and introduced Jennifer. The women ignored her and flirted with him. Jennifer soon had enough and remained in her chair, thinking she'd pass the time with her polite table companions and leave Troy to it. He urged her up to stand by his side. Despite his arm around her waist, the vixens were undeterred. They pressed their augmented breasts against him in the guise of friendly hugs. A brassy redhead sashayed over.

Troy spoke under his breath and tightened his hold around Jennifer's waist. "Here comes trouble."

"Troy, I haven't seen you in ages. You look wonderful. Are you still lifting?"

"Hello, Cassie. This is Jennifer."

The woman gave Jennifer a deliberate once over, then turned back to Troy. "Isn't this our song? It's time for us to dance."

"It's great to see you, but I need to sit this one out."

"All right, darlin'." Her garish red lips turned upward. She slipped a card into Troy's breast pocket and sealed the gesture with a kiss on his lips. "The last dance is mine."

That's it. Jennifer wrapped her arms around Troy. "I've checked his dance card. That one's already taken."

Brassy gave her a hard smile and departed with swinging hips and clicking heels.

"You're popular," Jennifer said.

Troy let out a guttural laugh. "Have you ever seen so many grasping ninnies?"

"Never. Too much bubbly, I'd say."

"You're too generous. They're always like this, desperate and aggressive."

The last number was announced, and Troy led Jennifer toward the dance floor.

She slipped her hand into his. "Was I supposed to be your shield? I did a poor job of it."

"No, I brought you to be my arm candy, and you did a marvelous job."

"Glad I could oblige."

Troy's strong arms spun her one way then the other and brought her back into his embrace. "You're here as my lady, my partner, my other half. That's how I think of you."

She held him tighter. They carved out a corner on the dance floor and swayed in harmony.

Jennifer smiled up at him. "I could have danced all evening with you alone."

The music drew to a close, underscored by their tantalizing kiss.

"That's a taste of what's to come. Let's go."

Chapter Fifteen

Driving home from the party, pent up anxiety electrified the atmosphere. Troy removed Cassie's card from his pocket and handed it to Jennifer. She tore it in half, inched the window down and let it flutter away. She shifted sideways, ran her fingers through his hair, brushed the side of his face, and let her hand come to rest in his lap. He lifted it and rubbed it against his cheek with its hint of stubble more subtle than fine-grained sandpaper. She laid her head against the backrest and closed her eyes. He settled her hand back on his thigh and entwined his fingers through hers, giving a small squeeze now and then. Jennifer smiled. There was no need to speak. The thick silence said it all.

They stepped inside Jennifer's house, closed the door, and fell into a deep kiss. Restraint lay behind them. Troy clicked the deadbolt into place, swept Jennifer up, and carried her down the hall.

Her head rested against his shoulder. "It's been awhile for me, years actually."

"I'll be gentle. We'll take it slowly."

Troy lowered her onto the bed. Hallway light filtered in through the half-opened door. He removed his jacket and laid it on the easy chair, followed by his bow tie, cummerbund, suspenders, and cuff links, all in measured time.

Jennifer slipped out of her shoes and let them drop. There were so many parts to a tuxedo. Troy's promise to take things slowly sounded good a few moments ago, but she'd grown impatient. Her desire for him raged. She wanted to forego the tantalizing strip tease; tear both their clothes off, and get down to it, yet inhibitions would not let her carry out such a plan. Troy was in charge. That was fine with her. He appeared to savor each moment, now removing his dress shirt to reveal a tuft of blond hair above the V-neck of his tee. With fluid movements, he pulled the undershirt over his head and tossed it aside.

Jennifer stepped up to him and caressed his chest, "A lion's mantle."

She'd seen his body when they swam, but the unspoken dictate had been 'look but don't touch.' Her eager hands continued to his abdomen. She inched her finger from the fine line of hair at his navel to where it disappeared below the waistband of his slacks. They shared a wicked smile.

He moved behind her, buried his face in her hair, and kissed her neck. "There's something magical about your scent. One whiff tells me you're created for me alone. It drives me wild."

He eased her zipper down the small of her back, and the fabric's tautness gave way. He faced her and coaxed the sleeves from her shoulders.

Jennifer wanted this, but her nerves didn't agree. "I'm a present being unwrapped. We're holiday gifts to one another."

He lowered the dress to her waist, bent and kissed her neck and cleavage. "You're so soft. I couldn't ask for a finer gift than you."

He pushed the dress over her hips. It swished and landed on the floor. She stepped out of it, and he picked it up and laid it on the chair. She stood in her bra, panties, and stockings while Troy's gaze aroused her even more.

"I hope you like what you see."

His response was a low growl. He ran his hands down her back, cupped her bottom and pressed her hips against his. With her arms around his neck, they moved in a slow, swaying dance to imagined music. Troy's eyes were intense though veiled in softness. Jennifer knew he was savoring the moment, imbedding it in his memory. A wave of love for his effort swept through her.

He reached behind her, unclasped her bra and lowered the straps. "I want to see all of you."

Her breasts were no longer perky but nice enough that she wasn't embarrassed. Troy adored them. She moved to the edge of the bed and removed her stockings, inch by inch, and then slipped her panties off. He removed the rest of his clothes, and they stood at arm's length and gazed in full at each other.

"You're beyond beautiful," Troy said.

"So are you." She stepped into his arms.

The room was chilly, and the sheets were cool. They buried themselves under the heavy comforter. She wrapped herself around him, tasted his lips, his neck, everywhere she could reach without breaking from his snug embrace.

Before long she pushed the covers aside. "I'm warming up fast. It's like I have a space heater in bed with me."

"You're comparing me to a metal gadget?"

"Yes, one with an irresistible chest and arms and legs and…oh, my."

Troy moved farther down. He raised one of her legs and kissed it from her foot up along her inner thigh. He reached her center and lingered there. Her fantasies of this moment hadn't included such ecstasy. She arched her back and moaned, then relaxed into the moment. He gave her the same excruciating pleasure with her other leg.

Fiery with desire, she could stand no more of this tormenting foreplay. She urged him upwards. "I'm ready, honey, right now."

With one arm around his back and the other on his bottom, she pressed him hard toward herself, poised and ready when he eased into her.

"Am I hurting you?" he asked.

She wasn't willing to hold back. Her body met his thrusts and urged him for more. "No, I want all of you."

His intensity increased. "You're so damned tight."

"I want this so much."

"I know, baby, so do I."

Jennifer sought every bit of pleasure that was hers to take with no inhibitions.

"Switch places?" Troy asked.

Full sentences were impossible. "Uh huh, my favorite."

With dexterity, he turned them as one. She shimmied and swayed in bliss while he held her breasts, squeezed them and toyed with her nipples.

Her release began. She threw her head back, "oh oh oh."

"That's right, baby, take it."

Each thrust's shuddering force fulfilled an urge

she'd held in check since her first glimpse of this sizzling-hot man. After the ecstasy, she wanted to collapse but held herself strong for him. He gathered her up and turned her onto her back again, intent now on his pleasure.

"Jen…get ready."

She tensed, and his release came in final thrusts of raw power.

****

Dawn barely tinged the walls with soft gray light when Jennifer woke to a rush of chilly air. Troy had risen from bed, his backside pale and firm as he stepped to the chair for his pants.

She propped herself on her elbow and tucked her hair behind her ear. "Morning."

He looked back and smiled. "Hello, beautiful."

"Are you leaving?"

"Sorry, but I've gotta run by my hotel room and then get to the site."

"Can't you skip it this once?"

"They're expecting me. I'll make it up to you tonight."

She grinned. "How so?"

He answered with a kiss.

She started to get out of bed. "I'll make you some coffee."

"No, don't get up."

Back into the covers she went, where his body warmth and the heady scent lingered. Her womanly soreness was a mixed blessing; she liked its reminder.

Troy dressed in haste. His shirt remained loose and unbuttoned. "Why do you keep this room so cold?"

"I sleep better that way." Her smile widened. "Last

night was fantastic. Well worth the long wait."

He sat beside her, put an arm around her waist, and brushed her tangle of curls. "I know the wait was hard on you. It was for me, too. I figure I owe you an explanation."

"Yes, you do."

He looked down and back up. "There was someone else. I had to wrap things up with her."

Jennifer drew back. She pulled the sheet higher around herself, fisted her hand and laid it over her heart.

"Oh?"

"She lives in Albuquerque. Real connected there, comes from a family with a lot of sway. Fact is they think they own the town. She had our life together all planned out and wasn't a bit happy about my wanting to break it off. She had the power to make things difficult."

"Were you engaged?"

"Just dating."

"What harm could she do? Were you worried about your reputation?"

"I don't give a damn about my reputation, but it wasn't me who stood to lose. The woman was hell-bent on making someone pay, and Stanhope Construction's headquartered in Albuquerque. Russell and his family live there. I had to back away real slow-like."

Jennifer crossed her arms. "I wish you'd have told me. It would've been easier than trying to figure out our relationship."

He hung his head. "I'm sorry. I didn't want to make you the other woman, or lose you."

Her arms remained folded. "Is it over?"

"Completely."

She looked into his eyes and knew his words to be true. "I'm glad."

"So am I. You have no idea how much."

The barest tickle of a thought came to her. She narrowed her eyes. "Was she at the party last night?"

Troy sighed. "You don't miss a beat, do you?"

Their eyes locked and Jennifer had her answer. "Which one was she?"

"She's not like the women you met. Once she accepted we were through, she had class enough to keep her distance."

"How long's it been since you had sex with her?"

"Long enough. Every trace of her is purged from my life."

Jennifer had a hundred more questions. "What does her…

Troy placed a finger over her lips. "How 'bout we concentrate on us."

Her arms relaxed. "Okay, but there's still the California matter to figure out."

"You're not gonna give up what we have for some elusive dream of moving back there, are you?"

"My plan looks more distant at the moment."

"Maybe it's time to make a new one."

A lot had happened since yesterday. She needed time to process it. "We'll see."

He slipped his hand under the sheet and caressed her breasts. "How 'bout we get together around five tonight? I'll come over."

She nodded.

He kissed her temple, her lips, and left her smiling.

Another woman. How obvious it now seemed. Jennifer had thought of the possibility but more than that, she'd imagined Troy dating many women, a sought-after playboy. She thought perhaps Stanhope Construction had financial troubles and she'd worried about how it would affect her bottom line. There'd been no inside source to tap. The obvious had eluded her.

Apartment business claimed most of Jennifer's day. The ongoing 'punch list' needed prioritizing. No sooner was a host of small issues resolved than a new bunch arose. It had nothing to do with good maintenance. Faucets dripped, converter valves leaked, drains clogged, and dishwashers died. Window screens had to be put up, taken down, repaired, or replaced. Some residents wanted to be present for repairs; others didn't. There were tenants who wouldn't change a lightbulb themselves. Worse still were the ones who 'fixed' things on their own, doubling the repair job. Maintenance contractors had quirks too, a whole slew of them. Managing it all required an astute hand.

Jennifer floated through the day's issues with a bright outlook. She spent an hour at the gym, ran by the grocery store, tidied the house, and had time left over for a nap. She dressed in a chambray sweater dress and knee-high leather boots and waited for Troy's arrival.

They decided on takeout from Lemongrass Thai with a plan to eat at home and re-watch *Bourne Identity*. Jennifer set the cardboard containers of food on the coffee table, and Fuego meandered over to investigate. Troy grabbed the dinner and carried it into the dining room.

"It's a party of two. No cats invited."

Jennifer scooped up her ginger ball of joy and put him out. He jumped onto the window ledge in full view of the dining room and expressed his indignation with loud meows.

"The poor thing's cold. I'll put him in the garage with a heater by his bed. That should quiet him down."

She washed her hands and rejoined Troy at the table. "You don't like cats, do you?"

"Nothing personal, but I'm not a cat person. They make me itch."

"I've had Fuego since he was a kitten. He won't be in the house when you're here."

"I appreciate that."

Jennifer dimmed the lights, chose a blues CD and lit a candle. She went to the kitchen for her latest purchase—rosewood chopsticks carved into cranes—while Troy laid out the meal. They shared an order of sea-salted edamame and pad Thai with spicy green fried rice.

The previous evening's lovemaking continued atop the rug in front of the fire with a nest of pillows. Inquisitive eyes, fingers, and lips caressed soft, sensual places before giving way to desire.

Chapter Sixteen

A brief season of unimpeded happiness followed Troy and Jennifer's first night together. He called her from the ranch or from whatever city he was working. On Fridays, she stepped through her day with lightness, knowing by evening a silver bird would deliver Troy into her open arms.

She expected him any minute and had cooked up a special dinner. For lack of space, she kept her good china in a storage bin. Memories rushed forth as she removed the bubble wrap from each piece, a luxury tax for enjoying the dishes.

All those years ago, Jennifer's new mother-in-law had insisted she select a pattern. Out of her element, Jennifer stood in front of a lighted wall of china on glass shelves in a fancy department store. Until now, selecting mess kits for camping had been it for her. An elaborate design caught her eye of hand-painted red and pink cabbage roses with tiny green leaves on an ivory background, and she chose it. Her mother-in-law stood back and offered no help except a credit card at the end.

To Jennifer's mature eyes, the dishes looked like a seven-year-old's tea set, the approximate age Jennifer had been when she'd lost interest in such things. Still, the china had served her and her family well. She and her husband had spent holidays dressed in wool socks, flannel, and fleece, immersed in cooking. Jennifer would create a beautiful table with the china, and the small family would sit down to a delicious feast.

When the marriage ended, Jennifer wanted the china but left it behind thinking it wasn't hers to take. Her ex requested she come and get it, and she did so in haste. There was no place to display it in her small house, so it remained packed in bins and pushed into a corner of the spare bedroom where it went unused and took up space.

Jennifer's tastes evolved, and she found the china's style too fussy and countrified. It carried the cobwebs of a failed marriage. She offered it on eBay but didn't get a single nibble. An antique dealer wanted the set on consignment. Through conversation, Jennifer learned the dealer's intent was to use the pieces to decorate her tables and hutches, enhancement for their sales. It caused her to hold off relinquishing the china.

One year, Valentine's Day fell on an evening Jennifer hosted a book club dinner. The china lent itself to the romantic holiday. She had fallen back in love with it. Of its bittersweet memories, she focused on the sweet.

Jennifer carried two place settings into the dining room and set the table with care. She lit a large cranberry candle, replaced its glass cover, and then stood back and admired it all. In the kitchen, she slipped into a red ticking apron with 'Betty' stitched across the front to protect her new tunic and leggings. A knock at the door sent her running to answer it. Troy held a cheerful bouquet of jonquils and a bottle of Chablis.

"Nice apron, Betty." He leaned down and gave her a kiss.

She threw her arms around him. "I've missed you."

"Me too, baby. I always do."

They shared a long embrace in the front hall. Afterward, Troy perused her music collection. He chose Van Morrison rather than his usual country western. The upbeat tempo of "I Wanna Woo You" resonated through the house. He walked into the kitchen and wrapped his arms around her from behind while she worked at the cutting board.

"Smells great, what're you making?"

"I bought rainbow trout at the new fish market on May Avenue. We're having it with capers in garlic-lemon sauté, wild rice, and let's see, tossed salad and baked tomatoes topped with crumbled rosemary." Her words were sporadic because of his soft kisses on her neck.

She arranged the meal on plates, added parsley sprigs and seared lemon wedges, and set them on the table.

Troy looked on. "You went to a lot of effort."

"It's fun. I thought it'd be a nice change from restaurants."

He held her chair. "I haven't had a home-cooked meal in a long time."

"How long's it been?"

"Since before my divorce, and even then she didn't do all this."

Jennifer laid her napkin in her lap. "You mean the women you've dated didn't cook for you?"

"Reservations were the only thing they made for dinner."

"'Made' as in past tense?"

He stopped and looked at her; eyebrows raised, and

then reached across the table and brushed her cheek with his fingers. "It's just you and me now. I thought you knew that. I care about you."

"I feel the same way. I'm...I could be falling for you."

He rose, stepped over, and kissed her. "Same here, I spend all week waiting to see you. I can imagine you and me building a life together."

He sat back down, and they reached for each other's hands while the CD player glided from Van to Emmy Lou.

She smiled. "Let's eat before the food gets cold."

Troy took a couple of bites. "This fish is delicious."

"Wait 'til you taste some of the things I plan to cook for you."

"That right?"

"Uh huh."

"Well, I intend to try it all."

Jennifer's new intimacy with Troy made her realize she knew very little about him beyond their Oklahoma City existence. She thirsted for more.

"Do you cook?"

"Not much, but I'm wicked with a barbecue. I grill steaks, burgers, and vegetables, all with my special seasoning."

"What's in it?"

"Secret ingredients. You'll have to try it."

"I'd love to. When might that be?"

"Soon as I can take you with me to Cimarron for a visit."

"Matter of fact, Aaron and I have a ski trip planned for the twenty-second of this month. Maybe we could visit you on the way."

"That'd work. Let's plan on it."

"Great. I need to run the idea by Aaron, but I'm sure he'll go along with it. What's your place like?"

Troy shrugged. "It's a cattle ranch. Nice enough I guess, but not all gussied up."

"Is the house good-sized?"

"By some accounts. My great-grandparents had a large family, so it has five bedrooms. I made changes to the place when I took over. Here lately I've taken to calling it my 'warming hut' because I'm hardly ever there."

"Five bedrooms? That sounds huge."

"It's a good sturdy house. Could use a woman's touch but comfortable enough."

They finished eating and carried their plates to the kitchen.

"There's not much for dessert, but try this."

She held up a melon ball dipped in whipped cream, and he took her fingers into his mouth along with it. They embraced in the middle of the kitchen and had more bites of sweet melon, then refilled their wine glasses and stepped onto the patio.

Troy looked out beyond the yard. "I like the woods back here."

"The trees are the reason I bought this place— elms, pecans, and oaks. They're bare now, but in summer they form a wall of green leaves and in autumn their color matches the flames in the fireplace."

She pressed her back against him with her head on his chest. He wrapped her in his arms.

She turned, put her arms around his neck, and looked up at him. "I realize you don't plan to move from your ranch but would you consider living in California part-time? My mom's house sits on a small acreage with mountains all around. We could have horses."

"Listen, I want to be with you, but me living in California? That's as likely as herding cats."

Fuego appeared, rubbed himself against Troy's leg, and was eased away.

"And when you retire?"

"I'll stay where I am. There's plenty of room for you, too."

"I'd consider it, but I want ties to California too."

They held each other at arm's length, and the chill beyond his embrace enveloped her. Why wouldn't he consider her desires? A second home seemed an easy solution.

"Why are you clinging to your San Diego plan? I thought you and I had something special," he said.

"We do. We're in a committed relationship, but I'm from San Diego. I have roots there."

"You have roots here too. This is where you raised your son. You've lived here a long time. Oklahoma's your home."

They unclasped hands, and she crossed her arms. "I'm a Californian at heart. Aaron became serious about leaving Oklahoma, and it struck me—I want to go back. You and I could be snowbirds, spend the cold months in a warm climate and…"

Troy jammed his hands into his pockets. "I know what snowbirds are. I'm not interested in moving to the coast or anywhere else. These ol' Okie roots of mine go way back. You knew it before takin' up with me."

She'd expected that line of protest. "Living in

California part-time is a fair and reasonable solution."

"It may seem that way to you, but it's not a solution for me." He picked up his glass, downed his wine, and headed inside.

She followed on his heels. "You haven't seen the town or the property. It's better than you imagine."

"How do you know what I imagine? I'm sure it's nice as you say, but I have no desire to live in California. Never have, never will."

The pitch of her voice became higher. "So I do all the sacrificing?"

His voice grew loud. "Sacrifice? That's an odd concept in connection to our relationship."

"That's not what I meant."

They moved around the room like wary opponents circling each other at a distance. A log in the fireplace shifted. The fire crackled and emitted a loud pop.

"You know damn well I'm tied to the ranch and its right where I wanna be. I have no desire to be uprooted."

She lost the battle to stay calm. "Oh, but it's fine for you to uproot me, right?"

"You want to be uprooted. How many times have you said so?"

"This argument's going nowhere." Jennifer collected the wine glasses and started for the kitchen.

"Leave those; we're in the middle of a discussion."

She hesitated then set them down with a clatter. With folded arms, she glared at him. A new CD slid into place. Rod Stewart began his sultry rendition of "It Had to Be You," a perfect choice earlier but awkward now. Jennifer jabbed the player's button, and it shut down.

Troy spoke in a controlled voice from across the room. "I'm offering you my love and my home. You've got a decision to make so I hope you think long and hard about what you want."

She gaped at him. "Is this an ultimatum?"

"I'm tired of listening to you whine about California. It's time you got your pretty ass off the fence."

Her forehead and palms grew clammy. She took a step in his direction. "We're getting ahead of ourselves. I mean, are we ready for that kind of commitment?"

Troy frowned. "I'm not suggesting we change our living arrangements right now. I'm asking you to commit or decide once and for all to move away. I'm not hanging around until you're good and ready to leave."

She couldn't stand her pleading but continued it. "A winter home in Las Casitas is reasonable. Why can't you see that? Don't you care how much it means?"

"I care, and I hate to see you sad, but I'm sticking to my plan. I'm sorry but what I said stands."

"Your way or the highway, is that it? How can we have a loving relationship if you won't compromise even one bit?"

"I've said what I have to say. I'm leaving now so you can start on all that pondering. It's okay to vacillate for a while, but it's time to decide which side has the greener pasture."

"Troy…"

He shook his head. "Let me know." His goodbye wave felt more like being waved off. Frigid air from the open door blew into her face. The truck started with a roar and then grew dim as it carried him away.

Wide awake in bed, Jennifer checked the time. Quarter to two. Damn. Did she think the answer to her dilemma would tiptoe in on the slippered feet of a dream? She went to the living room, settled on the couch, and drew up a blanket. Electric light would interrupt the room's hush. The soft chalk of moonlight angled in and illuminated unexpected surfaces.

To live in Southern California meant surrounding herself by mountains, ocean, and mild temperatures. Her mother wasn't ready to move, but the time drew near, and she'd made her wishes clear; the home was to pass to her daughters. Allison didn't want it. Jennifer loved the house and property, or at least its potential. Through the years she'd held a vision in her mind of how nice the place could be. What a shame to miss the opportunity of purchasing her sister's share and allow the family home to slip away.

Jennifer got up and made a cup of chamomile tea. She carried it to the couch and tried to get comfortable. Even with the blanket drawn up to her chin she was cold, so she turned up the heat and spread another cover over the first. The hours to come would be long and sleepless.

She wanted her relationship with Troy to continue as it had been, at least a little longer. Would he follow through on his threat to end the relationship? She knew the answer was a decisive yes, and she couldn't let it happen. Asking him to withdraw his ultimatum was pointless; he'd thrown down the gantlet. Earlier in the evening she'd opened the discussion convinced he'd come around to her way of thinking. Her plan had backfired.

She and Troy had a solid relationship now, but it

might change. What if she gave up the Las Casitas house and then they broke up? California was a sure thing.

Chapter Seventeen

Daybreak arrived with a thin pink cast to the freezing December air. It reminded Jennifer of the old proverb, 'Red sky at night, shepherd's delight; red sky in the morning, shepherd's warning.'

She stood beside the Jeep while Aaron loaded the last of their gear. They were bound for Colorado's ski slopes over the holiday. Light snowfall and dry road conditions were forecasted by last night's weather report. Jennifer took the wheel first. Snowflakes brushed the car's windows and melted before they reached the ground.

The city disappeared from the rear view mirror while the travelers settled into the comfortable rhythm of the open road. Rather than their usual northerly direction, they chose a southern route with plans to visit Troy and stay the night at his ranch.

"I'm looking forward to this time with you. Plus, it'll be nice for you and Troy to get acquainted," Jennifer said.

Aaron turned the heat down. "What's his place like?"

"He's got a lot of land, with cattle and horses. This will be my first time there. He's been vague about it, so I guess we'll find out."

A five-hour drive lay ahead. Aaron caught up on the sleep he'd lost in getting up so early.

Jennifer had decided between Troy and California two weeks ago. Life in Las Casitas would be no Shangri-La without him. She wanted Troy more, even if it meant spending the rest of her life in some woebegone corner of Oklahoma. The night had paled before she'd made up her mind and then fallen into peaceful slumber. A few hours later, she woke and called Troy.

"I'm in this relationship all the way, even if it means giving California up."

"Gimme twenty minutes, and I'll be over."

"Can you make it sooner? I've got an oatmeal pecan pancake recipe I'd love to try out on you."

"All I wanna taste is you."

They'd made sweet love all morning and then roused themselves to go out. Jennifer had apartment business to tend. For once Troy had no work of his own. He'd tagged along with her, making the errands fun.

Jennifer exited I-40 northbound in El Reno. Aaron woke up, yawned and stretched. He took stock of their progress and had some coffee from the thermos.

"I meant to tell you. I'm not moving to San Diego," she said.

"How come?"

"Because of Troy, there's something special between us."

"I'm happy for you. He seems nice based on the one time I met him. Will you move to his ranch?"

"We're not ready for that. California's out is all."

Aaron tilted his head and studied her. "You sure you're okay with that?"

"Uh huh." She smiled and looked away. How odd

it felt to verbalize her decision to someone other than Troy.

"Speaking of not moving, I've changed my mind about going to Seoul," he said.

Great news for sure, but Jennifer kept her cool. "Why's that?"

"I don't know. The State Department's taking too long to complete my background check. I've had time to think it over and I've decided not to go. Instead I'm researching grad schools."

"Great. For once I'm thrilled with federal bureaucracy."

In the town of Kingfisher, they turned west. The weather shifted. A north wind swung telephone wires and bent the tall winter wheat. Occasional sharp bursts rocked the Jeep. After Watonga, the two-lane highway eased northwest toward Woodward, the last town with more than a grain silo and a gas station for the rest of the journey.

Once there, Jennifer stopped to fill the tank. She unlatched her door, and it flew open. An icy wind blew hard across the plain. She gripped the door's handle with both hands and pulled it closed. Aaron crouched beside the pump and struggled to button his coat and pull up the hood.

Jennifer checked the weather report from her phone, lowered the window and read in a loud voice, "winter storm warning, low-pressure front with seventy percent chance of precipitation. Sleet and freezing drizzle likely. Road Advisory: Travelers should avoid interstates in the panhandle counties of Harper, Beaver, Texas, and Cimarron until eleven P.M. due to blowing snow and poor visibility."

Aaron got back in.

"We're headed that way. Not good. I wonder if we should turn back," she said.

"No way, Mom, we're already this far. They make Jeeps for rough weather. Let's see what this thing can do. Besides, they always exaggerate the weather forecast."

"That's true of TV, but this is a public service broadcast and it's not hyped up. I hate driving in sleet."

"I'll drive."

"This isn't about who'll drive. I wonder if we should chance it at all."

Jennifer called Troy to let him know where they were.

Aaron mumbled beside her, "Sensationalistic journalism, that's all it is."

Jennifer tuned him out and focused on Troy's words. "Y'all need a hotel room there in Woodward. Storm front's coming, and it won't be pretty."

"I agree, but we're not very far from Cimarron. A few hours and we'd be there."

"Too risky, you'd be out in the middle of nowhere. You wouldn't even have phone reception."

"Okay, we'll look for a hotel and drive out tomorrow."

Aaron huffed his displeasure.

The town's hotels were full. Up and down the two main streets neon *No Vacancy* signs were lit. Jennifer pulled into two motels just the same. The clerks called other lodgings but with no luck. Even out-of-the-way places were full or no longer in business. It seemed Woodward's development of half a dozen new oil operation sites had brought drilling crews numbering in the hundreds.

Jennifer studied the sky. The wind blew furiously but carried only wisps of snow. They were closer to Troy's here in Woodward then they were to Oklahoma City. Turning back made no sense. Plenty of daylight remained. Aaron persisted with his urgings for them to continue on their way. She saw no choice and decided to press on without notifying Troy. He'd tell her to turn back, citing too great a danger. She disagreed and knew him to be over-cautious.

"How about I drive?" Aaron asked.

Jennifer glanced from him to the horizon. "Promise to switch back when I say?"

He looked at her with his dad's sincere blue eyes. "I promise."

She paused and then got out and moved around to the passenger side.

An hour west, they hit the blizzard head on. Bursts of wind roared down on them and screamed through the window's edges. The high-pitched wail drove her crazy. I'm a complete dumb-ass, she thought, putting my son and myself in danger this way.

Aaron fiddled with the radio. She shooed his hand away. "You concentrate on the road. I'll search for a weather station."

Scratchy reception from televangelism and Spanish-language channels was the only offerings.

"Try AM," he said.

"I did, there's nothing." She switched the radio off.

Troy's house wasn't far, another hour or so under normal conditions, but it could have been a full day's travel at their current pace. The Jeep crawled at twenty miles per hour through hard snow and wind coming at them sideways. The low-pressure light came on; an indication the right front tire needed air. Aaron didn't seem to notice, and Jennifer internalized her alarm.

He squinted and leaned forward in a struggle to see. She fished out her mask with an amber lens designed to ski in snowfall, loosened the straps, and handed it to him. He put it on to block the white-out's harsh glare but soon tore it off.

"It's just a distraction."

He tried sunglasses, found them too dark, and took them off. With each switch from sunglasses to no eye protection, his eyes looked more bloodshot. He wore a frown, unable to let up on his close vigil. It had been miles since they'd seen another vehicle.

She handed him an open bottle of water.

He shook his head. "It'll make me have to go."

"Take a few sips."

He ignored her. "We're barely moving, but I still have to focus on staying in the tire tracks made by semis."

There was no distinction between land and sky; no visible perimeters to the road, nothing but a white abyss lay before them.

An eighteen-wheeler came into view from the opposite direction. Aaron white-knuckled the steering wheel. The driver barreled toward them, heedless of the danger. Within seconds, the rig spewed a wake of slush on their windshield. Visibility dropped to zero.

"Stop!" Jennifer yelled.

Aaron slowed to a roll. The wipers were useless against the concrete-like load dumped on top of them. Panic rose inside her at the thought of being trapped in a small space.

Above the racket of sleet hitting metal and glass, Aaron called to her in a voice of careful control although Jennifer made out its undercurrent of terror. "Take it easy, Mom."

She peered behind. "At least no one's behind us that I can see."

He looked ghostly white, and she felt the same way.

"The car wash from hell," he said.

The dumping of slush onto their windshield continued, more like a freight train going by than the twenty seconds it took for the rig to pass. The etched lines in her son's brow deepened.

"Aaron, I'm gonna drive now."

"There's nowhere to pull over."

"Our agreement was you'd switch places with me when I said so. Climb over the back. I'll scoot across and take the wheel."

"You're distracting me. Let me drive."

Mile after mile they scanned the roadsides for even the dimmest beacon of light from any structure, be it a rest stop, gas station, or at this point even a private residence. Bladder issues arose. They had no phone signal, no radio, nothing out there but hard-blowing snow and the north wind's wail.

An unexpected curve in the road caused Aaron to crank the wheel. The Jeep hit a slick patch, shimmied, and slid sideways.

"Shit!" Aaron yelled.

Jennifer dug her fingernails into the cushioned armrests and held her breath. They plowed into a snowbank, and she kept silent, afraid of the terror in her voice if she opened her mouth. Neither of them moved for a moment. Aaron put the Jeep into reverse and pressed the gas pedal. The tires spun out a plaintive whine, but the Jeep didn't move.

"How do you put it into four wheel drive?" he asked.

"It's automatic. Push the anti-skid button and try again."

The wheels continued to spin.

"Jesus, Mom, now what?"

"Try again. Press on the gas, put it in reverse, then forward, and repeat."

He tried it, but nothing happened. "We're screwed. I hope we don't get hit."

"Turn on the hazard flasher."

She'd thought about buying sand bags a week ago. Why hadn't she done it? Aaron turned the wheel and tried again. Still nothing. They were alone and stranded.

Jennifer unbuckled her seat belt and bundled up. "I'm gonna take a look. If I'm not back in five minutes, send out a search party."

She brushed snow off the tire with a gloved hand, examined it from various angles, and hurried back into the Jeep.

"We have a problem. The right front wheel hit a rock, and the impact knocked the tire off the rim. We'll have to move either the car or the rock, and it doesn't help that we're on an incline."

"Oh, crap."

"We can do this. I've got your dad's old army shovel, a spare tire, and the tools to change it. We'll be okay."

"I don't know how to change a spare, Mom." The agony in his voice made her grow hot. How had her ex overlooked teaching his only child this essential skill?

She took the Jeep's manual from the glove box and flipped through the pages. "I've never changed one either, but there are instructions in here."

The first two lines read 'Park the vehicle on a firm, level surface. Avoid ice or slippery surfaces.' She didn't read the words aloud.

"I pushed on the rock, and it gave a little. If we shove it out of the way, we can dig enough space around it to change the wheel. We should put on all the clothes we've got."

Aaron zipped his coat. "I want to see it."

A minute later he got back inside. "Yep, you're right. The rock will be easier to move than the Jeep."

Jennifer climbed over the seat and dug through their bags for warm clothes. While back there she opened her emergency box. A quick inventory showed water, a first-aid kit, rain ponchos, a flashlight, and batteries. She and Aaron were vulnerable. Her pepper spray wouldn't do much to someone with ill intent. A gun would've been more reassurance.

When they were ready to get out, she said, "We look like astronauts or homeless people in a frigid climate."

Her transparent enthusiasm met his scowl. "Don't. You'll make it worse. Our situation is not funny. We could die out here."

"We'll be okay. First we should set our gear outside to reach the tools."

They opened their doors and plunged into the whiteness. Aaron shoveled a clearing around the rock. Together they heaved it out of the way and then clamored back into the Jeep.

Jennifer picked up the manual. "Good. Now we need to set the jack on the ground and ratchet it up high enough to get the wheel and tire off without letting the car tip. It'll be tricky at this angle. We can't get inside while it's jacked up."

"Okay, you ready?" he asked.

She nodded. He worked the wheel with a wrench, and she yelled above the wind. "What are you doing? The instructions read 'jack the Jeep up.'"

"I've seen my friends do this. If you don't loosen the lug nuts first, then get it jacked up and torque 'em hard the wheel will keep spinning."

Her nod was more like a small bow due to her snowman-like layers of clothing.

It took some fumbling and false starts, but they got the jack set up and then ratcheted. When the tire cleared the ground, and the lug nuts were off, he tried to remove the wheel.

"It's too slick with ice. I can't grab it."

She gave it a go, with no luck. "I'm freezing. I've got to get back inside."

"Then we're screwed. You can't."

"Un-jack this fucking thing, I'm going in."

Aaron did so, and they climbed inside. The coffee remained warm in the thermos. There had to be a way out of this predicament.

"What if we chip away hand holds on the tire?" Aaron said.

"Let's try it."

They geared up once again. Aaron pounded at the tire with a screwdriver, and Jennifer used a hammer. He took it from her. "It's easier if I do it myself. Go back inside, Mom."

She remained beside him and watched him make little progress before she walked to the back of the Jeep and stared inside. Her eyes lit on the bag of rock salt she used at the apartments. She carried it to where Aaron still toiled in vain.

"I wonder if this will work."

She took handfuls of the mineral and massaged it over the tire. Aaron used the hammer's claw to roughen the ice and the back of the shovel to press the course granules into it. Task completed, they folded themselves back into the Jeep amid the rustling nylon shells of their bulky ski suits.

"I hope this works. If it doesn't we're up shit creek," Aaron said.

She offered a bored expression. "Can't you come up with more imaginative vulgarity?"

"Look who's talking. You're the one who said 'un-jack this fucking thing.'"

"Touché."

Fifteen minutes passed.

"I gotta take a leak," Aaron said.

She watched him bend over and check the tire, straighten, adjust his clothing, and pee on it. Oh geez. She turned her head away. Not a bad idea, but he might have warned her. When she looked again, he was pressing more rock salt into the tire. Once inside, he reported that it was still frozen.

"It needs more time." Jennifer didn't know if there was any truth to what she said, but she couldn't bear her son's grave expression. More chiseling with the claw of the hammer would be the next step.

Their wait continued.

"That must've been quite an experience," she said.

"What's that?"

"Urinating in a blizzard."

"I wouldn't recommend it."

She smiled. "When your dad and I were expecting you, 'I wouldn't recommend it' was the obstetrician's pat answer to every question we asked him."

Aaron looked somewhat interested. She interpreted his silence as an okay to continue.

"…like whether I should continue jazzercise, or ride on the back of your dad's motorcycle, or something else of a personal nature."

He cringed and held up a hand. "Don't."

"So, it became a standing joke between your dad and me. We worked the phrase into our everyday conversation."

Talk and movement lessened until the only sounds were the wind's maniacal howl and frozen rain hitting the Jeep with the fury of machine-gun spray.

Chapter Eighteen

Stranded in the Jeep, Aaron tilted his head back and closed his eyes. Jennifer saw her ex in his profile. For so many years, they'd been a family on these winter treks to Colorado's ski slopes. The Three Musketeers were no more. Family hugs were a thing of the past. Her son was robbed of an intact family. The thought made her heart ache.

Aaron's intuition had always been keen regarding her. His eyes remained closed, but he reached over and took her hand, bear-like in its thick glove. She adjusted the wool blanket spread across their laps.

"Have I ever told you what a good son you are?"

"About a thousand times."

"Because you are. You're the best. I'm proud of your accomplishments and the compassionate person you've become."

"Thanks, Mom."

"You don't deserve divorced parents."

He shrugged. "Aw, it's okay. Everybody's parents are divorced."

"That's so sad. I carry a lot of guilt about the way you had to live with your dad and me fighting all the time. You didn't even have a sibling to commiserate with you. I'm so sorry."

"It got pretty bad. I used to wish you guys would split up. The summers I spent in California helped me get away from it."

"You're close with your grandparents because of it, so we did one thing right."

"Don't beat yourself up, Mom. You did a lot of good stuff while I grew up."

"Thanks buddy. I love you."

"Love you, too."

They squeezed hands.

Sending Aaron off to stay with her mother may have been the highest level of self-sacrifice. It was an odd contradiction. Blanche had foisted oppressive hatred on Jennifer her entire life. Jennifer wanted her child to know gentleness, so she didn't speak ill of her mother to Aaron. He and Blanche enjoyed a close relationship. Blanche also loved Allison, had lots of friends, and was well regarded in general. Jennifer alone was the recipient of the black side of her heart.

Another check of the tire showed the rock salt had worked, at least enough for them to grab hold of it. Despite agonizing slowness, they jacked the Jeep back up, removed the tire and fitted the spare into place. Aaron pulled a glove off to hand-tighten the lug nuts, lowered the Jeep, and wrenched them tight. Jennifer even had an air pump for the spare. They cleared snow from around all four tires and made a pass at roughing up the ground behind each one. Jennifer repacked everything and then took the driver's seat before Aaron could reclaim it. The four-wheel drive kicked in, and the Jeep lurched backward toward the road. With whoops, hollers, and high fives, their journey continued.

She paid strict attention to the road so she wouldn't veer into another snowbank or a ditch. Good fortune came by way of an eighteen-wheeler with a well-lit back end. The rig defined the road's edges and created fresh tracks.

"I'm gonna stay right here behind it," Jennifer said.

"Like we have a choice?"

After five miles the semi's hazard lights came on, and it slowed to a crawl. If it had to stop, there'd be no way around it. They couldn't turn the engine off because of the cold, and with a quarter tank of gas left, they'd run out. She inched up closer, and the semi's red, yellow and white lights threw confetti-like bits of bright color into the Jeep.

"Look over there," Aaron said.

A square of light shone in the near distance, and they struggled to figure out its source. "It's not a house. It looks more like a business."

They drew closer.

"It's a diner!" Aaron started to gather his things.

"Thank Goodness. The truck driver's been signaling to us that it's here."

Jennifer put some distance between the two vehicles and flashed her headlights in thanks. The trucker responded in kind and then sped up and disappeared into the white night.

"Our angel trucker. He's been driving slowly for us all along," Jennifer said.

Aaron stared in the direction the truck had disappeared. "That's so awesome."

Jennifer navigated the mounds of accumulated snow at the parking lot's entrance and pulled in beside four cars and half a dozen big rigs. She stepped into the diner and inhaled the welcome aroma of hamburgers, fries and onions. Fresh coffee brewed, dishes clanked, and TV voices filled the air. The weary travelers shook off the snowflakes that had gathered during their sprint to the door. They nodded to the people in the room.

Aaron tossed his coat into a booth and headed to the men's room, then returned and sat sideways with his feet sticking out the end. Below his disheveled hair, the worry lines across his brow had already started to soften.

Still without phone reception, Jennifer asked about telephone service and the cashier nodded toward a pay phone. *Those things still exist?* She dreaded the call. Troy wouldn't be happy. She dropped quarters into the slot and listened to the plop and slide of the ancient mechanical ingestion.

Troy picked up right away. "Thank God you're safe. Where the hell have you been? I've been trying to reach you all day."

"Would you believe I'm on a payphone?" She explained their situation.

"Any number of plans would've been better than yours. What were you thinking heading straight into a blizzard?"

"It wasn't a blizzard when we left Woodward. I thought we'd dodge it and make it to your place."

He let out a deep sigh. "At least you're all right. Where are you now?"

"We're at Mona's Café on Highway 3, between Fort Supply and Hardesty."

"More 'n eighty miles between those towns. Can you narrow it down?"

"Hold on." She leaned around the corner, asked for an address, and returned to the line. "Mona's is at the junction of Highways 23 and 3, northeast corner."

"Gus and I'll head your way in a six-wheeler with snow tires. We'll drive you and Aaron here and go back for your Jeep when the weather clears. Sit tight, we'll be there when we can."

Irma stood at their booth and chatted with Aaron while he spooned the mound of whipped cream from his mug of hot chocolate. Her husky voice and sinewy form were all wrong for the ruffled pink and white uniform. Jennifer slipped in across from Aaron.

"I guess y'all got caught in the storm."

"Big time, we're glad we found this place," Aaron said.

"We're glad too, hon. Where y'all comin' from?"

"Oklahoma City. The weather report last night didn't mention this."

"We got us a handful a folks cussin' the weather center."

Irma brought another hot chocolate, and Jennifer told her and Aaron of the plan.

"I've got an idea. Hang on a sec." Irma bustled away and came back again. "Manager says y'all can leave your car parked 'round in the side lot where it'll be more protected from the nor'westerly squall if you'd like."

"We would. Thank you," Jennifer said.

"I'll move it, Mom."

"Okay, but rest first. There's no rush. We've got a long wait ahead."

"I'd rather do it now before the Jeep gets buried in snow."

"Good point." She handed him the keys.

Through the window, she saw him struggle in the blizzard—coatless. The forgotten parka lay in a heap on his seat, a great wad of down-filled polyester. She couldn't protect him from youth's impulses. He'd have to learn.

The diner's atmosphere held an alliance among the stranded motorists. A local weather broadcast came on, and someone turned up the volume. The report stated the storm would lessen by evening.

"Like hell it will," said a burly man at the counter. He glanced around for allies and found them in a collective grumble.

Two seats down another man said, "The so-called experts didn't know about the storm this afternoon."

People tsked and shook their heads.

Jennifer didn't agree. The experts had predicted the storm would be farther north and were wrong, but Oklahoma's weather center was state of the art and forecasts were usually spot on.

She and Aaron did little more than play games on their phones during the long wait. They peered through the window for the umpteenth time when a huge white six-wheeler with a cattle guard and steer images on the doors pulled up to the café's entrance. The truck remained at an idle, and its engine caused vibration to the window beside Jennifer. It pulsed through to her core.

"That's gotta be them," Aaron said.

She caught Troy's silhouette in the passenger seat. Two long weeks had passed since they'd been together. Her stomach fluttered. With haste she scrunched her hair, applied lipstick, and dabbed perfume on her wrists.

Aaron watched her and laughed. "You ladies are funny. You look great, Mom, no worries."

She noticed him glimpse his own reflection and handed him her comb.

The diner's door opened to Troy and Gus. In hats and heavy coats they appeared larger than life in the small café. Their presence stirred the settled atmosphere. Jennifer and Aaron scooted out of the booth and stood to greet them.

Troy strode over to Jennifer with a smile. "Hey, darlin'." He swept her up and gave her a warm kiss.

She threw her arms around him. "I'm so glad to see you."

She liked the chill of his face. He smelled of coffee and a certain Eau de Troy, a familiar aroma that did things to her.

He nuzzled her ear and whispered, "I've been worried. What a relief to find you safe and sound."

"It was rough out there. Aaron drove through the worst of it."

Troy turned to him, nodded and extended a hand. "Good job, Aaron. You got your mother and yourself to safety."

"Thanks. I've driven in snowstorms before but none like this. I don't know what we would've done if this place hadn't come along."

"Let's be glad it did. This is Gus, my ranch foreman, and this is Jennifer and Aaron."

Gus nodded and touched the brim of his hat. "Ma'am."

"Nice to meet you, Gus."

He and Aaron shook hands.

Gus stood six feet tall with a stocky build. Not quite fat, but beefy, and close to Troy in age—mid-fifties. His size and round, wire-rimmed glasses weren't much of a distinction but his walrus mustache covering the bottom half of his face made an impression.

No one made a move to sit. They'd all done a lot of that already.

"Weather's not getting better, and we need to make use of the daylight. Ready to go?" Troy said.

Jennifer and Aaron nodded.

Gus addressed Aaron. "What say you and I go out 'n take care a gittin' the bags and such outta yer vehicle?" He had a much thicker accent than Troy.

"Sure." Her son grabbed his coat this time.

Troy motioned Jennifer toward the side of the booth that faced away from the room. He tossed his hat and coat on the opposite seat and slipped in beside her. "I've missed you."

His hazel eyes changed color based on the light or the shirt he wore. At the moment, they were their deepest green.

"I've missed you, too." She pressed herself against him and kissed his warm lips. So what if they were in public.

"I can't figure out why you didn't turn back when the storm worsened."

"Turned back to where? The hotels in Woodward were full, every single one of them."

"There must've been something."

"There wasn't. Clerks in two different motels called around for us. We would've stayed anywhere. Maybe we should've gone to the police or found a homeless shelter, but I thought we were close enough to Cimarron to make it. Aaron did the hard driving. He was amazing."

She looked down and willed her eyes to stay dry,

but a couple of alligator tears landed on her hands where they rested in her lap.

"Hey, everything's fine now. At least Gus and I didn't have to pull you out of a snowbank. Let's be grateful you're safe, and we're together." He touched his forehead to hers.

The truck pulled up, and its doors slammed, one and then the other. A blast of frigid wind swirled around her ankles when Gus and Aaron entered.

Jennifer gathered her things, nodded goodbye to Irma, and stepped into the blizzard. Troy opened a rear door for her and helped her up. He took the driver's seat, and Gus climbed in front. She wanted Troy with her, but Aaron got in beside her. He arranged a pillow between his head and the window and fell asleep. She didn't expect to so much as catnap, but warmth, the road's hum, and the deep muted voices in the front seat soon lulled her into an easy rest.

A shift in the truck's rhythm caused her to stir. It had turned dark outside. Streetlights gave meager luminosity through the storm. She cupped her hands on the window's frigid glass to block the dashboard light. When her eyes adjusted to the night, solid blocks of darkness became structures defined by roof lines.

She leaned forward. "Are we in Cimarron?"

"Yep, not much farther now," Troy said.

Would this become her home? Through blowing snow, she strained to see what she could of the town. It looked well-ordered, a Mayberry kind of place with a small downtown of two story buildings dressed up with awnings and old time western facades. The buildings became farther apart until darkness and open highway once again claimed their small party.

Troy rolled to a stop and turned onto a rutted road. It rocked her side to side and woke Aaron. The truck lurched and downshifted in response to an incline. Up ahead, a pinpoint of light beckoned from Troy's beloved home, the Lazy J Ranch.

Chapter Nineteen

Troy pulled the truck close to the front door. He and Gus got out and unloaded luggage from a compartment below the truck bed. They piled it in the entryway. By the time Jennifer and Aaron had shrugged into their coats and emerged from the back seat's warm cocoon, the two men had finished and stood stomping their feet on the frozen ground.

Troy gave Gus a hardy slap on the shoulder. His voice carried through the storm, "Thanks for everything, man."

Through puffs of white breath Jennifer and Aaron also bid Gus heartfelt thanks and a safe drive to his home nearby.

Troy motioned to Jennifer and Aaron, "Come in, come in, welcome to the Lazy J Ranch."

She stepped through huge wooden double doors, like those of a castle. From the wide foyer, a great room stretched out before her with rough-hewn ceiling beams and a stone fireplace big enough to roast an ox. The place was a massive man-house, far grander than the image she'd gathered from Troy's sketchy description.

For months, she'd entertained him with pride, ignorant of how small and simple her house was in comparison. Had she imagined a basic ranch house or had he misled her? Did he see a true description as bragging, or did he hold back so she wouldn't feel inadequate? Maybe he wanted to be liked for himself and not for his family's wealth.

Aaron gazed around. "Wow, this is nice."

"Thanks." Troy ushered them into the living room. "Please, make yourselves comfortable."

Mom and son exchanged a glance.

"We've done a lot of sitting. We'd rather stretch our legs if you don't mind." Jennifer said.

"I know what you mean. Let's go to the kitchen for a hot drink. Delia, my housekeeper, has been looking forward to meeting y'all. She's around here somewhere. Aaron, how 'bout a whiskey?"

"Um...sure." He looked at Jennifer and blushed.

She knew her son. He preferred orange juice or a tall glass of milk to liquor but was manning up in Troy's presence. She wanted to intervene on his behalf, but he'd put an end to that in fifth grade. He'd shown his mettle during the storm, managed himself like an adult, and Troy treated him as one.

They entered the kitchen, a spacious area in need of an update from its Seventies style. Jennifer often remodeled people's homes in her mind's eye. Within a few seconds, she'd done a complete renovation. Delia stood at the counter, and introductions were made. She filled a tea kettle and set it on the stove to boil. Troy left and came back with two glasses half-filled with golden brown liquid. Aaron took his, thanked Troy, sniffed it and frowned. The kettle whistled, and Delia removed it from the heat. Troy said something to her in Spanish, and she stepped aside to let him prepare Jennifer's tea. He handed it to her with a smile, and she took it in both hands.

"Having you host will be fun. You've been on my

turf for the past, what, five months?"

"Has it been that long?"

"Nearly."

"It's about time you visited. How 'bout a tour?"

"Sure." Aaron made for the kitchen's exit with his drink left tucked among various objects on the counter, untouched. After the shock of seeing this opulent home, Jennifer wanted to grab it and guzzle. She'd minimized the signs of Troy's wealth. Ownership of a ranch was no indication of money. Ranchers struggled with a plethora of problems from weather to the price of feed. The construction company belonged to his son, with Troy as a fill-in until they found a replacement. She'd attributed his plane trips to the city as an extravagance, his desire to be with her at any cost.

He led them to a library with handsome walnut bookcases lining three walls. The room had a pleasant lemon oil scent.

"These books have been collected over four generations," he said.

Most were on animal husbandry and agriculture, but there were also shelves devoted to popular fiction and classics. The room doubled as a family history center, with leather-bound albums and framed photos.

Troy pointed to one. "These are my maternal great-grandparents, George and Florence."

Like most photos of that era, a stoic couple in stuffy clothes stared at her from the past. Jennifer moved on to a picture of Troy at about ten years old with a blond crew cut. He posed with his arm around a sheep and holding up a blue ribbon with pride evident in his gap-toothed grin.

"I like this one," she said.

He chuckled. "I used to slide nickels between those teeth."

From there, they paused in the doorway of Troy's office. It had the same built-in bookcases. A huge desk dominated the room, covered with all the electronic trappings of an active workspace. Jennifer tried to suppress her anxiety over this home so she wouldn't ruin the atmosphere for Aaron.

"This is where you made those initial calls to me."

Troy smiled and nodded.

Aaron leaned in close to her. "We're in his bubble." He'd carried that phrase home from second grade, and he and Jennifer adopted it.

They moved on. Down a flight of stairs, they came to a gym with a sweeping view of snow-covered fields below the plateau where the house stood. A pool beckoned to her the way they always did. Starlight reflected through a sunroof into the water, making it sparkle. She strode farther into the room.

"You even have a Jacuzzi. You didn't mention that."

"I wanted it to be a surprise."

"That it is."

They headed back upstairs, and Troy spoke over his shoulder. "That's not the whole thing, but we've hit the highlights."

Aaron grabbed his duffel, and Troy showed him his room. He pulled his computer out and flopped onto the bed. "I'm gonna hang out here."

Troy's bedroom was at the end of its own hallway. Jennifer walked into its center and turned in a slow circle. The opulent lair wore heavy drapes in deep jewel tones that prevented daylight from penetrating, like a chamber of hidden riches. Dense furniture the color of dark chocolate included a huge four poster bed. Above it in a gilded frame, lion and lioness laid side by side.

She turned to Troy, who leaned against the door frame with his arms crossed. "Who's your decorator?"

"Was, as in past tense, and I'm smarter than to answer that one."

Jennifer strolled across a zebra rug to a river rock fireplace. An unusual object d'art rested on the mantel. She picked it up, realized it was an ivory carving of a couple in the act of intercourse, and hastily set it down.

The amateurish decorating wasn't for want of effort. She pressed him. "Was it your ex?"

The edges of his mouth turned up, but he remained silent.

"An old girlfriend?"

"It wasn't a professional. That's all I'm saying."

"Was it you?"

He snorted. "Hell no."

"My taste runs to simplicity and modernism. I'm glad your eccentric designer limited herself to this room."

She smiled, took hold of a bedpost and whirled around it. Alighting on the edge of the bed, she ran her hand over the silky maroon spread. "I have to admit, there's sexiness to this room. We can make good use of it."

Troy hurled himself onto the bed, grabbed her and pulled her into the middle. "I'm sure we can."

****

Troy left to check on the animals. Jennifer looked for Delia and found her in the kitchen.

Over tea, Delia said, "I am working *con la familia*

para trenta, pues, thirty year. *Muy simpatica.*"

"Wow, thirty years. That's a long time."

"Troy, he is a good man."

Jennifer nodded. "Yes, he is."

On cue, yours truly appeared. He and Delia conversed in Spanish. Jennifer followed along enough to get the gist of what they said. Delia had delayed her departure so she could meet Jennifer. Troy wanted her to stay the night because of the storm. Delia picked up the phone to call her husband while Jennifer and Troy went into the living room. He poured a drink and sat beside her on a couch facing large windows that looked out on the snow.

"So this is your warming hut?" she asked.

Troy gave a snicker. "Did I call it that?"

"Yes."

"Sounds like something I'd say. Do you like the place?"

"It's stunning. Why didn't you tell me you live in a lodge nice enough for the nation's top brass?"

He leaned forward and set his glass on the coffee table, then took her tea mug and set it down too. He stood and urged her up. "C'mere." He wrapped her in his arms. While holding her, he stepped a few feet away and leaned against the back of a chair with his legs straddling hers.

She allowed Troy to hug her but didn't hug back. Instead, she crossed her arms and looked him in the eye. "I want my cowboy back."

"What do you mean?"

"You never told me you lived in such luxury. It's not what I pictured. My whole image of you has changed, and I don't know this new person."

"I'm the same ol' me."

"Anything else you haven't mentioned?"

He looked up and to the side, holding the expression. How would a body language expert interpret that? The question wasn't a hard one.

"I have a condo in Paladora where I'm taking you this summer."

She'd driven through Paladora once and remembered the charming mountain town near the Rio Grande National Forest in Southern Colorado.

"Another warming hut?"

"It's a condo, Jen, much smaller than this place."

She resisted his gentle urging toward an embrace. "Now I know why you won't consider the California house. You already have a second home."

"No. That's not it at all."

"You haven't even seen it."

He continued to hold her. "Let's not stir up that old argument."

She looked down where their bodies pressed together and said nothing while her mind raced. Troy's house and vacation home were grand discoveries, yet the one request she'd made that together they make plans to keep the California house and live there part-time had been refused. It didn't seem fair.

"You were asking about other surprises? There's JaRay," Troy said.

Jennifer waited, unwilling to ask the obvious question.

"She started out as my personal trainer, but her job's evolved into a general assistant. She helps Russell and me in the construction business; runs errands for us, that kind of thing. She lives in Albuquerque, not far from headquarters."

"What kind of errands does she run?"

"All sorts, whatever we need her for."

Jennifer looked out the window. Troy and Russell had dozens of employees, why mention this one? Personal trainer turned business assistant? Something didn't sit right. Jennifer got a bad sense of this JaRay person and ugliness filled her heart.

"What kind of name is JaRay? Sounds like a hillbilly made it up."

Troy shrugged.

Jennifer persisted. "Why bring her up?"

He dropped his hands from around her waist and let them hang. "You're trying to be difficult. I'm thinking of things, or people, in this case, who are a luxury rather than a necessity."

"Please say she wasn't the one who decorated your bedroom."

"I won't grace that with an answer."

She hoped that meant no. "Have you been romantically involved with her?"

"Absolutely not."

Jennifer studied his face. He wouldn't lie to her, not counting minor omissions like his mansion.

He smiled, dimples and all, and then returned his arms to around her waist and pulled her closer. "Have I appeased the inquisitor?"

She nodded. His embrace helped ebb her confusion. She never wanted to be released.

Chapter Twenty

Colorado's Transportation Department posted the closing of Independence Pass on its website. Jennifer and Aaron spread a map out and studied it. She ran a finger along the section of their route in question. "As I thought, it's the pass we need to take to reach Aspen."

"So let's get tire chains and take Highway 24 instead."

"It means an extra three hours, removing the chains twice, and the chance of those passes closing. We'd end up stuck in Denver."

"Then let's find a closer lift."

"We don't have reservations."

"There's always someplace to crash for the night."

Jennifer smiled at youth's impetuousness. "Maybe if I were eighteen I'd be up for a ski-or-bust adventure, but I'm not sleeping in the Jeep or who knows where."

Their attempt to find lodgings at other resorts failed. Aaron's frustration grew. He stormed away and made himself scarce for the rest of the evening.

Snow fell all night. By the afternoon of their second day at the ranch, it had yet to let up. Troy rested his elbows on the kitchen counter with a bottle of water in his hand. His slender hips swiveled to one side, and his brawny shoulders leaned in toward her. She enjoyed the alluring pose from her perch on a bar stool.

Swishes and clomps announced Aaron's approach.

He appeared in full snowboarding regalia. "We should've been heading up to the slopes by now."

"I know, honey. I wish something could be done about it."

"I need to get outta the house. Troy, is it okay if I check out the horses?"

"Sure. Hang on a sec. I'll go with you." He finished the last of his water and disappeared down the hall for warm clothes.

Jennifer wanted to go too but hung back so they could get to know each other one-on-one. She sat in the living room with an afghan over her lap and stared out at the snowfall's hypnotic beauty. An hour later, noisy shuffling at the front door broke her reverie.

"We're back!" Aaron's bellow reverberated through the open space. He strode up to her. "Quite a spread Troy has here. We might take four-wheelers out tomorrow."

His sour mood had vanished. Troy's time with him had done it. Aaron picked up his book, yawned, and stretched. "Time for *mi siesta.*"

He seemed to be making up for the rest he'd sacrificed during the school year. At the front door, Troy stripped off a one-piece cold weather suit that reminded her of a thick mechanic's coverall. He joined her on the couch in his flannel shirt, jeans, and woolen socks. She wrapped herself around him and pressed her face into the crook of his warm neck. He put his arms around her.

"You're real friendly all of a sudden. Does this mean I'm forgiven for my lack of disclosure about my house?"

"Yes, but no more surprises."

"You could've asked me what it was like."

"I did. You were vague. Still, you have a point. I formed a picture in my mind and left it at that. It's one of my few faults, assuming certain things and not asking enough questions."

"Few faults? Don't break your arm patting yourself on the back."

She nudged him with her shoulder. They watched the silent flurries.

"What'd you guys do outside?"

"Went to the barn, fed the horses some apples."

"You were gone awhile."

"Yeah, well, Aaron was going stir crazy cooped up in here, so we chopped some wood and carried it to the front door."

She looked up at him. "Should we make a fire?"

"How 'bout we go for a swim first, get our exercise in for the day?"

"Okay."

"I'll meet you at the pool; towels are out there."

Jennifer padded through the house in her bathing suit and bare feet. She slid into the water and clenched her teeth. Goosebumps rose on her arms, and her nipples stiffened.

"Not exactly warm."

Troy pulled on his goggles. "Cool temperatures encourage vigorous swimming. The trick is to start right away. Should we try for half a mile?"

She nodded, pulled her cap and goggles on, and pushed off. All repetition becomes monotonous. Her solution was to alternate between the crawl, back, side, and breast strokes. She paused and watched Troy do the butterfly from the other end. He drew up beside her.

She ducked into his lane, entwined her legs in his and gave him a wet kiss.

"Umm, salty."

"You taste the bromine I use to treat the water."

"Aren't you romantic?"

"I prefer it to chlorine. Ready for a soak in the Jacuzzi?"

"Sure."

Troy's quick turn of the timer started a riot of bubbles. She eased into the steamy bath, a luxurious reward for her energetic workout. A bottle of wine and two glasses sat on the edge of the tub. Troy reached for them. "Wine?"

"So you are romantic. I'd love some."

Soaking this way reminded her of another hot tub waiting in Aspen. The relentless snow would make her and Aaron's trip impossible.

"This was going to be my last time to ski with Aaron. I've gone with him since he was three. It's fun, but I'm tired of chapped lips, thick sunblock, wet gloves, and lugging gear between room and slope in blistering ski boots. On our last few trips, I spent more time in the sauna than on the slopes."

"It's hard to let go of things. I've had to do it, too, with three kids."

His feet found hers below the gurgling water. "Why are you sitting way over there, darlin'?"

She didn't move toward him. "I can't shake the sensation of being one of a long line of women who've been here."

"I may live out in the sticks, but no one's ever accused me of being a hermit. I've brought women here before, and we've sat in this tub like you and I are

166

doing. But I'll tell you, none of 'em could keep pace with me in the pool the way you do. They were afraid to get their hair wet."

She leveled him with a look. "So I'm your first tomboy. At least I'm your first something."

"You've been on edge since you got here. Where's it coming from? I want you more than I've wanted any woman. You know that."

He set his wine glass on the tub's rim and reached for her. "I'm all yours, Jen."

She floated into his lap, set her glass down, and held him. He traced the outline of her bathing suit. It was of simple design; a no-nonsense one-piece made for swimming laps. His fingers slipped under the elastic and then cupped her breasts through the taut fabric. She felt him stir beneath her. Their kisses grew deep and lingering.

"We need to find a way of getting together more often. If you like it here, you can visit all you want. I'll fly you out."

"I want to be wherever you are."

He toyed with her bathing suit strap. "This thing's as impenetrable as a chastity belt."

She arched an eyebrow. "Shall I remove it?"

"Definitely."

She looked toward the entry to the pool area.

"Delia never comes in here," Troy said.

Jennifer considered his words. "Arron's not likely to break away from his computer, but I'd hate to get caught in the act, especially by my child."

His caresses urged her on. She squirmed to release her arms from the straps, and then peeled the suit down her torso and cast it aside. The jets stopped. The silence was interrupted only by the echoing plink of water dripping from Troy's arms when he raised them to caress her breasts. He pulled her onto his lap, ran his hands down her back and squeezed her bottom. They fondled and pinched each other's nipples, teasing them to perkiness. He cupped her mound and pushed his fingers inside of her.

She closed her eyes. "Mmm, I like that."

He lifted her off his lap, slid out of his swim trunks, and pulled her into a straddle on top of him. She pressed her mouth hard on his. Their tongues mingled. With foreplay forgotten, she mounted him and rode with abandon, lost in the exertion of deep penetration. With his hands on her hips, he raised and lowered her, meeting each of her thrusts with his own. His face expressed self-pleasure and something more. He was happy for the bliss he gave her. She held him tighter for the knowing. Her moment arrived. She arched, threw back her head, and cried out in ecstasy.

Chapter Twenty-One

In the morning, Jennifer stopped by Aaron's bedroom on her way to the kitchen. He'd already risen and made his bed. A dazzling sun reflected off the snowy landscape and threw white light across the pale walls.

She continued to the kitchen where Troy stood at the stove with a spatula and a ready smile. "Morning, there are bagels, orange juice, and Biff's Coffee, ordered for you. I'm making eggs and sausage."

"Smells great. Morning, Aaron."

He waved hello from a counter stool with a knife and fork in hand and plate of food in front him.

Jennifer put her arm around Troy's waist and kissed his cheek. "What a beautiful day."

"Sure is. Aaron and I are taking four-wheelers out later this afternoon, along with whoever else wants to go." His three children and their families would arrive throughout the day.

"How fun."

"You wanna come along?"

She reached for a coffee cup. "No, thanks."

Aaron looked up from his plate. "See? I told you she wouldn't want to."

"I prefer quiet activities like swimming." She almost said skiing but caught herself. Time constraints meant a canceled trip.

She leaned against the counter. "I thought downtown Cimarron looked kind of interesting when we drove through the other night."

Troy nodded. "It sits at the crossroads of two major highways and is the closest town to Black Mesa Mountain."

Aaron piped up, "At five thousand feet; Black Mesa is the highest point in Oklahoma."

Troy and Jennifer looked at him.

"Just a little factoid I picked up."

She smiled. "Sounds like you're Oklahoma Proud."

"Nothin' wrong with that," Troy said.

Jennifer sipped her coffee, still looking at Aaron. "No matter where you go, you'll always be an Okie at heart."

He flushed with pleasure.

Mug in hand, she walked around the counter and kissed him on the head. As a pre-teen, it had been the one place he'd allowed her to do so, and it became the norm. She sat on the stool beside him. "I'd like to go downtown. Anyone want to come along?"

"Can't Mom, we're going four-wheeling."

Troy set a platter of scrambled eggs and sausages in front of them. "Downtown Cimarron isn't that big. There's enough time for both. I can't go myself, I have catching up to do, and I'd like to be here when my kids arrive."

Aaron speared a sausage. "I'm not thrilled with boutique shopping, but I'll go with you for something to do."

Troy arranged for a ranch hand to give Jennifer and Aaron a lift downtown just before ten. They meandered along Cimarron's main street and passed a young woman who looked out of place in this prosaic little town on the southern plains. Aaron and Jennifer's eyes met. The girl had long, disheveled blonde dreadlocks. Her thick sweater's scruffy sleeves dangled below her hands, and she wore no coat. On her feet were thin canvas shoes. As their paths crossed, she stared at the ground.

Aaron looked back. "I wonder what her story is."

"I don't know. She has to be cold."

They reached the raggedy end of downtown. Beside them, an antique shop's windows were opaque with dirt. The name 'Painted Pony Antiques' arched across the front in chipped and peeling gold letters. It seemed Cimarron's beautification efforts had overlooked this shop.

"The land time forgot," Aaron said.

Jennifer smiled. "Real treasures are in places like this. Let's check it out."

No surprise, they were the only customers.

"Mom, look at that." Aaron pointed to a statue on a high shelf behind the counter. "It's a duplicate of one I saw in the background of a snapshot in one of Troy's albums."

They asked to have a look at it and watched the ancient proprietor balance a ladder against the cluttered wall.

"Can I help you with that?" Aaron asked.

"Oh, no thank you, honey. I can manage. It's been on display so long I forgot it was up there."

Jennifer cringed when the woman started her slow ascent. She reached the second to the top rung, leaned sideways and pushed things aside. Jennifer held her breath and watched the trembling hand near its quarry.

Aaron moved around the counter and held the ladder steady. He reached up, took the object, and helped the woman down. When both her feet were on the ground, Jennifer exhaled.

Aaron held the item up. It was a metal sculpture of a cowboy on horseback lassoing a steer. Its wooden base doubled as a wind-up music box and spun out the tune "Red River Valley." Though coated with grime, the statue appeared intact. The steer's eyeballs were wide and turned back in fear. The horse's swiveled neck, swinging tail, and galloping hooves conveyed power. Its frothing mouth and sculpted muscles seemed taxed to the limit. Flared nostrils of both horse and steer evoked heavy breathing. The edges of the cowboy's hat curled as if from wear. His twists and turns were evident in the folds of his shirt and jeans. Minute details included chaps, spurs, snaps, pockets, and rope.

Jennifer took the statue from Aaron and examined its underside. "There's no artisan's mark, but the craftsmanship's good."

"We should get it for Troy," Aaron said.

Jennifer turned to the shopkeeper. "If we can get this cleaned today we'd like to buy it. May we take it to the watch shop down the street to see about that?"

"You mean Chester's place? Sure, if you don't mind leaving a twenty dollar deposit."

"No problem." Jennifer handed her the money.

The shopkeeper, with bejeweled arthritic fingers, took pains to write a receipt in shaky cursive. They left the overheated shop and were hit full force by the icy north wind.

In the timeworn repair shop, another elderly person, a man with a drooping white mustache and bushy eyebrows, shuffled forward in response to the tinkling doorbell. On his heels was a rheumy beagle.

"Einstein," Aaron whispered.

She nudged him. "Hush."

"How can I help y'all?"

Jennifer slid the scarf from her head, causing a crackle of static. "We'd like to give this as a gift. Can it be cleaned today?" She smoothed her flyaway hair.

He took the music box in both hands and examined it through thick reading glasses worn low on his nose. "This is delightful. Sure, I can shine it up for you folks. I'll need about an hour."

Once outside, Aaron said, "Is everyone in this town geriatric?" Encouraged by his mom's snicker, he added, "Should we get them together?"

A delicious scent of baked goods filled the air. Aaron sniffed. "Where's that coming from?"

"Let's find out."

They approached a bakery just as the young woman they'd passed earlier slid down the wall of a building and sat on the sidewalk with her arms and legs tucked in close.

Jennifer didn't hesitate. "Will you join us inside for a hot drink?"

The girl paused and glanced toward the bakery door. Her soft voice contrasted with her rough appearance. "Ah, okay."

"Hello, Misty," came the greeting from the bakery clerk.

Her long expression didn't change, "Hi, John."

Aaron pointed to a huge cinnamon roll. "I'll have one of those and a hot chocolate."

Jennifer turned to the girl. "What would you like?"

"Hot chocolate, please."

"Three cinnamon rolls, two hot chocolates, and one spiced cider," Jennifer told the clerk.

Chairs scraped as they settled at a table. The two young people were silent.

"I'm Jennifer Ellis. This is my son Aaron."

"Hi," Aaron said.

"I'm Misty Meadows."

Jennifer draped her coat on the back of her chair. "That's an interesting name." Had the girl made it up?

Misty frowned. "It's my mom's idea of poetry."

As they warmed up, Misty's body odor and tobacco smell grew more pronounced. She had a pretty face despite gaunt cheeks and a pale complexion. Jennifer tried not to stare while Misty wrapped her shaky hands around the steaming mug.

"I don't mean to be nosy but do you mind if I ask why you're coatless in this frigid weather?"

Misty's eyes remained downcast. "I left the house without it. I guess I wasn't thinking."

"So you live nearby?"

"My mom does."

Getting information from Misty would be tough. Jennifer didn't want to bombard her with questions but if she knew the girl's situation maybe she could help. She tried the conversational approach.

"Cimarron seems like a nice town. Aaron and I are visiting here for a few days."

Misty's response was a slight nod while she picked at her roll.

Jennifer persevered. "On our way to Colorado, we got caught in the storm."

Still nothing. Aaron didn't help. He chose to be

engrossed in his roll. Jennifer remembered her tried-and-true method of coaxing information from him when he was little, asking questions requiring open-ended answers.

"We're from Mustang, near Oklahoma City, where are you from?"

"I grew up here, but I got out when I was seventeen."

It didn't appear to be the case, but at least it was a crumb. "Where'd you go?"

"San Francisco. I'm going back when my boyfriend sends me a bus ticket."

"San Francisco's a beautiful city. What does your boyfriend do for a living?"

"Construction, he got work up north. When he gets back, he'll send for me."

Her plan sounded sketchy, perhaps even delusional. "That's nice. Anyone ready for more hot chocolate?"

At this, Aaron found his voice. "Sure, I'll take some."

"Misty?"

"Yes, please."

Jennifer rose and then returned with two hot chocolates and another cider. She blew on hers. "Misty, I'm a mom, so indulge me."

Aaron groaned. Jennifer ignored him and focused on the waif. "I'm concerned about you in this weather without a coat or warm shoes. Can we give you a lift to your mother's house?"

Misty gave a wistful smile. "That's nice of you, but I don't like being there when her boyfriend comes over. He stinks up the house with cigarette smoke."

Were cigarettes the only problem with the mom's boyfriend? Misty appeared to have left in a hurry, not even wearing socks.

"That's understandable. I hope I'm not too forward, but will you let us take you to a store for a coat and shoes? We'd like to."

"Oh, thank you so much, but I don't need those things. I have them at my mom's."

Jennifer reached into her purse and removed a one hundred dollar bill. She handed it to Misty.

Misty looked at the money and shook her head. "Oh, no, I couldn't."

"It's too cold for you to be outside. You can have a meal and then save the rest in case this happens again. Please?"

"No, I can't. It's too much."

Jennifer put the hundred away and brought out two twenties. She laid them on the table. "I'm afraid we have to go. If you change your mind and want a ride home or anything, meet us at the café up the street in half an hour. I forget the name, it has a red awning. Aaron, what's it called?"

"Something western like Wrangler's or Round Up."

"Rustler's," Misty recited in a flat voice.

"Yeah that's it," Jennifer said.

Misty managed another almost-smile. "Okay. Thank you for the hot chocolate and everything."

Jennifer smiled back. "You're welcome."

They stood and put their coats on. "It was nice to meet you, Misty."

She hated to leave the girl there with the arms of her dirty sweater stretched half way down her hands and her fingers still wrapped around the mug of hot chocolate. Jennifer tucked her bare hands into her coat pockets and turned up her collar as she and Aaron hurried back to the watch repair shop. She'd left her gloves and scarf resting on the back of the chair in the bakery.

The statue sat on the counter in a cone of light from a pendulum lamp. Chester had conjured magic. Jennifer examined it from different angles.

"It's like new but with the patina still intact."

"I cleaned and oiled the little motor, so the horse and rider go 'round and 'round." He wound it to demonstrate, proud of his handiwork. The melody's simple chords continued to plink after the statue disappeared into a brown bag with handles. Jennifer paid him more than the meager fee he asked for his labor. Inside the display case, a large violet cocktail ring caught her eye.

"What kind of stone is that?"

Chester removed the ring and took a look and then handed it to her. "This here's an amethyst."

She slipped it on and turned to Aaron, "Your birthstone. It's too big, can it be sized?"

Chester took it back and checked the band. "Yep, it surely can."

Aaron picked up the bag with the statue and cradled it in his arms. He walked to the door and stared back at her. He'd always hated to shop. She turned away from the jewel and joined him.

"Come back and visit again soon. Likely as not, the ring'll still be here." Chester gave her a wink.

"We will. Thank you for the wonderful job."

"Yeah, thanks, Chester."

They returned to Painted Pony Antiques and paid the balance, then ran-walked through the icy air to Rustler's Café. Their driver nursed a cup of coffee at the counter, no doubt happy to be assigned this cushy task rather than one involving ice and cows. The no-frills eatery catered to locals; men in western hats, jeans, and boots, and a few in overalls. They sat four per booth or hunched over coffee cups at the counter. Few women were present other than waitresses. Like Painted Pony Antiques, Rustler's hadn't been touched by downtown's prairie-themed makeover; the difference being this place dodged the town's exuberant renovations rather than having been overlooked. There was no sign of Misty.

Chapter Twenty-Two

Jennifer and Aaron returned from their downtown jaunt to a full house. Troy's daughter, his two sons, and their wives had all arrived. His six young grandchildren ran in an excited pack, and the adults beseeched them to use their inside voices and not run. Troy had gone out to the barn, so Jennifer introduced herself and Aaron amid the polite smiles and veiled curiosity.

Troy came back in, and Jennifer asked for a private word with him. She told him about meeting Misty Meadows. At the mention of the girl's name he sat forward, hand on chin, and heard her out.

"Leave it alone, Jen."

"I can't. How can this town ignore her?"

"There're folks working on the problem. She's a troubled young woman who resists help. You saw it yourself."

"So they leave her to freeze on the street?"

"You know nothing about her background or what's being done."

"Where does she live? I'll to go out right now and buy her some things and bring them to her house."

"It's Christmas Eve."

"All the more reason."

Troy laced his fingers together on the desk. "I appreciate your compassion, but we've got a houseful of company. Like I said, people are looking after her."

"No, they aren't. You didn't see her today."

He stared at her a moment. "Tell you what; I'll call my buddy Calvin Hamm. He's the sheriff. I'll see what he can do."

"Will you call him now?"

Troy pulled his phone from its holster, scrolled, pushed a button, and held the device to his ear. "Calvin? Troy Stanhope here. Sorry to bother you on the holiday but Misty Meadows is out wandering 'round town again. She's got no coat or warm shoes. What's being done to help the girl?"

Jennifer pointed to his phone and mouthed the word 'speaker.' He shook his head, so she leaned in and grew still. She heard the sheriff's voice but couldn't make out his words. All Troy said was 'uh-huh' or 'yeah' until the conversation ended. He had yet to slide his phone back into place before she pounced.

"What did he say?"

"They're sending someone to check on her."

"Who?"

"The deputy on call."

"What else did he say? I mean, he did a lot of talking."

"Calvin said he'd take care of it, and I know he will. You can relax. Let it go."

She wasn't about to, but for now Troy's words and the set of his jaw ended the conversation. She'd look into the girl's welfare later.

Troy's daughter Susan reached out to Jennifer. The two forged a genuine connection. Susan came up with gifts for them of fleece sweatshirts, thick and soft. Aaron's featured a pack of howling wolves, and hers read 'Cimarron, Oklahoma' in machine embroidery.

Troy gave her silk pajamas lined in wispy-thin flannel.

She held them against herself. "They're beautiful. I love the color." They were pastel peach, her most flattering shade.

After an appreciative kiss, she gave him his present, a multicolored wool sweater in a roomy size XL.

"Is it too impersonal?"

"No, it's great, especially since it's from you."

Aaron brought out the musical statue and presented it to Troy, who sat forward on the couch and inspected it, handling it like a precious relic. He spoke more to himself than anyone else.

"I'll be damned. This might be the one that went missing when I was a boy."

He wound it, set it on the table, and watched it rotate while releasing its simple tune. He didn't bother to hide his tears.

Aaron sat nearby. "You want to see the picture?"

"Nah, I remember it. We had a temporary housekeeper when I was about nine who disappeared with it and a few other things. After today, I'm gonna set it back in its old place."

He addressed Aaron. "You spotted this in a snapshot and again in an antique shop? Good eye for detail. Thank you."

There was pleasure in her son's smiling eyes. "You're welcome."

The musical statue became too great an attraction for Troy's boisterous grandchildren, and he moved it to a high shelf. They begged him to wind it. The familiar tune became the theme song of the holiday, sung or hummed by family members when it rested from producing its tinny music.

Come and sit by my side if you love me/do not hasten to bid me adieu/But remember the Red River Valley/and the cowboy who loved you so true.

****

The holiday drew to a close. Troy's family departed, and quiet fell over the house like a sigh. Jennifer stood in the doorway of Troy's office. "Aaron and I have to go. We need to get back to our jobs."

Troy looked up. "Come in. I have to ask you something."

She bypassed the empty chair in front of his desk. Sitting there made her uncomfortable in its formality, like being on a job interview or in the hot seat of the boss's office. Instead, she perched on the edge of the desk.

He pushed his chair out and patted his lap, "Right here, darlin'."

She needed no further encouragement.

"I like having you here; it feels right. Can you stay another week?"

"I'd love to, but I can't."

"Dean's been home with his family in Albuquerque. He's due here on his way back to Oklahoma City. How 'bout if Aaron catches a lift with him? I can send a third man with them to Mona's Café to drive your Jeep back here."

She crinkled her nose. "I don't think so. I don't want to leave Alcove without management any longer."

"I figured you'd say that. How 'bout if Dean keeps an eye on things for you?"

Jennifer wanted time alone with Troy. His proposition was tempting. "My HVAC guy has a set of keys, and I can handle most issues by phone. It could work. I'll talk to Aaron, and make sure Dean's willing."

"I already passed it by Dean. He's fine with it."

"Presumptuous, aren't you?"

"I took the initiative; there's a difference."

She toyed with his shirt collar. "Honey, you're used to being in charge, but not everyone's your employee. I wish you would've asked me before you spoke to him. I would've preferred to do it myself."

She found Dean hard to read. He might be fine with Troy's directive, or he might resent the increased workload. On the other hand, her ignorance of Dean's mindset was minor compared to the ease of Troy's adroit handling of the situation.

"Point taken. I'll keep that in mind," Troy said.

"Thank you."

She went in search of her son with the old familiar mom-guilt roiling through her. The point of this trip had been to spend time with him. He'd been a good sport about their misfortune—the blizzard, the closed mountain passes, and a canceled ski trip. In return, she schemed away at pawning him off on strangers so she could be with her boyfriend. Aaron was an adult, but he was still her son. The word *skank* came to mind. Self-deprecation did not stop her from approaching him with the plan.

Aaron didn't hesitate, "Sure Mom. No problem."

His nonchalance took her aback. To distance one's self from a parent is natural, but he might have expressed regret at their separation. Then the shame would be too great, and she'd change her plans. She threw a coat on and went out for air. Her footsteps in the untrodden snow made pleasant squeaks and left fresh waffle weave boot prints. Aaron would graduate college soon and embark on a new life. Her existence was transitioning, too. To build a life was good for herself and her son. She took a deep breath of winter air. A vigorous walk did wonders to clear one's head.

****

During the following week, the vastness of the prairie impressed Jennifer. She and Troy drove through open rangeland to check its condition. Miles from nowhere they encountered Gus on horseback and with two stock dogs.

Troy eased the truck beside him. "Gus does things the old way."

The three of them spent an easy hour on the tailgate of the truck discussing rest and recovery of the land, animal impact, and wildlife maintenance. Jennifer took in every word. Land maintenance involved far more than she'd realized. A new world had opened to her.

Troy took her to a cattle auction. She sat in dusty stands immersed in a sea of blue jeans. Folks around here weren't aware of the rule against double-denim. Men and women alike committed the fashion faux pas. The western hat rule was clear, though, straw in summer, wool felt in winter. Today Troy's innate sense of style set him apart. He'd opted for a T-shirt in the warm arena rather than his usual long-sleeves. She wrapped her arm around his muscled arm and remembered him on her doorstep in a tuxedo. His versatility impressed her.

Delia left dinners for them, spicy enchiladas one day, tortilla casserole another, yet her discretion made her invisible. Each evening Jennifer and Troy swam laps and made sweet love. They woke in each other's arms. The end of her stay arrived quickly. The week seemed a mere tease, a taste of what could be.

Chapter Twenty-Three

Ice storms were inherent to Oklahoma winters, and February arrived in the grip of one that raged until dawn. As a transplant from a semi-arid climate, Jennifer gazed through the window of her Mustang house in child-like wonder. Sunshine displayed a landscape of sparkling diamonds. Winter's thin rays were fickle so she dressed in haste and then stepped outside into the courtyard of a fairytale ice castle. Evergreens, heavy with permafrost and glittering, were nature's models for tinsel-laden holiday trees. Beyond an uneven row of icicles on the house's eve, each blade of grass and red holly berry wore a casing of ice. How enchanting this otherworldly brilliance was, like nature's sincerest expression of regret for its bad behavior the previous night.

She longed to share the moment with Troy. He visited when he could, but the freezing rain made flying impossible. Driving the distance wearied him, and she discouraged it.

Mid-February came with an interval of mild weather, so Jennifer and Troy were quick to make plans. Before there'd been time to reconsider, Jennifer peered with unease out the window of a two-seater plane destined for Cimarron. She thanked the heavens to have arrived in one piece and took a brisk walk across the small landing field into Troy's arms.

As soon as they arrived at his house he received a call, disappeared into his office, and came out a half hour later.

"I'm sorry, Jen. I have to go to Albuquerque and meet with a guy we're looking to hire as general manager. There's a push to get him on board."

She sat cross-legged on the bed, sipping tea. Her shoulders sagged, "I just got here. Can't it be done by phone?"

He set an overnight bag beside her and unzipped it. "Some things have to be face-to-face. Hiring a key employee's one of 'em."

She never noticed how loud a zipper could be. "Let me guess. Russell's too busy to do it."

"He already has. I'm giving my opinion."

"Why all of a sudden?"

"The guy's available right now. We need him on a job. That'll free me up to spend more time with you." He leaned over and kissed her, then started to pack.

After an overt exhale, she scooted off the bed. "I'll check on a flight home."

He caught her around the waist. "Hang on. I'll be back tomorrow evening. Why not stay here and relax, work out, read, do whatever you'd like?"

"Yeah, I guess I can." This won her another kiss.

"Good. I'll try to hurry things along."

She watched TV until she thought he'd be in his hotel room for the night, and then dialed his number.

He answered, and she said, "I'm lying between your dark satin sheets right now, where are you?"

The husky voice that had mesmerized her from the start came through the line. "I just got in. I'm undressing at the moment, about to shower."

"I'm getting a nice visual."

"So am I. What are you wearing?"

"What makes you think I'm wearing anything? I love these sheets on my skin. They carry your scent." She hugged his pillow and buried her face in it.

"What else do you love?"

"Your rough face when you kiss my stomach, and I love your body."

"Yeah? Which parts?"

The bedside lamp cast too much light for this conversation, even being alone. She reached over and switched it off.

"I love your broad shoulders, your arms of steel when they hold me, your butt in snug-fitting jeans."

"That all?"

She flipped over and propped herself on her elbows. "No."

"What else?"

She snickered. "Your majestic staff."

"My what? I didn't quite get that."

"Your instrument of passion. What's your favorite part of me?"

He didn't hesitate in his gravelly whisper. "Your pot of honey."

On her back again, she held the phone in one hand while the other one started to roam. "What would you do once possessing it?"

"Depends on my appetite."

She listened to him grow mute and breathe harder.

****

The long winter warmed, and early spring blew hard against Jennifer's front door. On a Sunday afternoon in late March, she and Troy snuggled on her couch. His weekend bag sat in the front hall, packed and ready for his flight home in an hour.

Jennifer rested her head against his chest. "Saying good-bye is never a happy time for us, is it?"

He stroked her hair. "I'm weary of all this back and forth. I never see you enough."

"Winter's over so I can come out more often."

"It still won't do. I want you with me every night." He drew away to see her face. "I love you, Jen. Move in with me."

"The apartments…"

"You've gotta loosen your vice-grip on them. They won't fall apart without you. Someone else can run them."

She did tend to micro-manage Alcove, but Troy didn't realize how much hard work, costly upgrades, and sheer grit had gone into its success. Besides, what about his tight control of the Lazy J? Moving there meant a huge adjustment in her life, yet his would change little except to improve with her presence.

She looked down and picked a piece of lint from her jeans. Her throat tightened. At nineteen or twenty, she'd have thought nothing of jumping from one life-altering situation to another. Had she developed an aversion to change, or did the advance of years mean less inclination toward risk?

"What would I do with myself on the ranch, honey?"

"Plenty to do 'round the place. There's no scarcity of jobs if you want one. You could help manage the office or look after animals. For sport, there's riding horses and hunting. It all depends on what appeals to you."

Hunting held none; the rest sounded okay. What does anyone do on a ranch far away from a city? She'd figure it out. More than anything, she wanted him. If he couldn't leave the ranch, she'd make it her home.

"Troy, I…" She cleared her throat. "I love you, too. Yes, I'll move in with you."

He took her face in his hands and gave her a long kiss. "It's gonna be great."

By the time he left, they had a plan. She'd move to the ranch in three weeks. A whirlwind of arrangements followed. She and Dean agreed on a management fee for his services. Her HVAC guy would be the on-call maintenance person; he'd fallen into the job anyway. Ramiro would see to her yard. She'd work from her computer, open a post office box, and travel back to Oklahoma City on occasion. The move was experimental; she'd see how it went.

On the day of her departure, Evelyn came over, and they stepped onto the patio.

Jennifer picked up a dried leaf and tossed it into the grass. "You'll be visiting, right?"

"Soon as I get some vacation time." Quiet settled around them. Did Jennifer's moving away signify the end of their friendship? Evelyn had been there for her when she'd moved in next door four and a half years ago. It had been the darkest time in Jennifer's life. For that, she'd forever hold Evelyn dear. Over time, each of them held fast to her privacy. A measure of emotional distance was needed to compensate for the physical closeness of living side by side.

"I'm gonna miss you, Ev."

"I'll miss you too, Jenny."

They weren't demonstrative, so their heartfelt

embrace bespoke the camaraderie shared over time.

There wouldn't be a moving van for furniture, no boxes taped and labeled, no winter things. Any number of return trips would come. Jennifer loaded the Jeep with her computer, her summer clothes, and a final crate containing precious cargo. She arrived at Troy's and unloaded her things in the driveway for him to help carry into a bedroom slated to be her office.

She walked into the room with two cold bottles of mineral water and handed one to him. "I guess this means I'm abandoning my plan to move to California once and for all."

"I thought the notion had been put to rest a long time ago."

She smiled. "It's hard to let go of it altogether. I'm exchanging one dream for another."

"I'm glad to hear you say so."

"Considering everything that's gone on with my mom, though, I'm due for a visit out there."

"Sure, let's get you settled and talk about when you want to go."

She pushed a few boxes aside and sat in the bay window's covey. "There's something else. We never finished our discussion about Fuego. I can't keep leaving him with Aaron; he's too busy."

"Who's too busy, Aaron or the cat?" Troy chuckled.

At her glare, he dropped his smile. "There's a policy of no fur balls here. Can't it live with Evelyn?"

"Her dogs would eat him for dinner. Besides, Fuego belongs with me. He's an outdoor cat in all but the coldest months. He catches gophers and moles, and since I've had him, I've never seen a live mouse. He'd be a companion for Jango."

She knew the last point was a stretch the second it left her lips. Jango was Troy's old yellow lab who spent most of his time lying on his bed in the kitchen, inert as a plaster of Paris statue. Only when a vehicle pulled up were the jingle of his tags and click of his toenails heard as he managed a stiff lope outside, wagging his tail. Jennifer doubted Jango had ever felt the tug of a leash around his neck.

Troy guffawed. "The last thing that ol' dog wants is some feline usurper."

"So you're Jango's spokesperson?"

"Hell yeah, we've been together his whole life. We know each other's thinkin'."

"The same can be said for Fuego and me."

This battle of wills ended before it'd begun and Jennifer knew herself the victor. Troy wouldn't change his mind about her moving in because of a cat. Still, she wanted it stated out loud that the ranch would be Fuego's home.

She sat up straight. "Love me, love my cat."

"That's going too far." He took a long pull from the water bottle then let his arm dangle. "I don't see as I have a choice, looks like this is the little pest's new home."

She gave him her biggest smile. "I'll make it worth your while."

He brightened. "Yeah, when?"

"Whenever you'd like."

"I like the sound of that."

He moved toward her, but she dodged him and ran outside to free her beloved cat from his carrier and into the limitless plains.

Chapter Twenty-Four

Two weeks passed with Jennifer living on the ranch, and all was well. Jennifer wheeled her big red shopping cart through the aisles of Wal-Mart, the only supermarket in Cimarron.

That morning, she noticed herself taking quick breaths like those while in full swim mode. It made her smile. Her laps in the pool had become so frequent she was breathing like an amphibian. Troy kept the water at a cool seventy-five degrees. Before getting in she'd wet her hair and rub conditioner through it, warm up in the Jacuzzi, and then splash cold water on her arms and legs. After that she'd tuck her hair into her cap, lower her goggles, and ease in.

Yesterday, Troy had paused in his laps. "I'm halfway through my set when you're just dipping your big toe in. If you'd quit pussyfooting around, get in and go, you'd finish sooner."

Jennifer rounded a corner in Wal-Mart and almost collided with Delia on her day off. An infant in a carrier slept in her cart. The baby's wispy white hair and cottony pink blankets gave her the look of a cherub shrouded in clouds.

"What a beautiful baby. Is she your grandchild?" Jennifer doubted it because they looked nothing alike.

"*No es mi familia...*" Her glance flitted like a fugitive's.

Jennifer wasn't an intrusive person, but Delia's odd behavior encouraged her. "Are you babysitting?"

"*Sí.*" She took a few steps to leave.

"Whose baby is it?"

"*No es mi nieta, Señora.*" Delia looked miserable. Jennifer couldn't bear the woman's agonized expression and released her psychological grip. "Okay, well, see you at the house tomorrow."

"*Sí, mañana.*"

Jennifer watched Delia make a hasty retreat toward the checkout line. *I'd make a lousy interrogator.*

The next day, Delia didn't pause for a cup of tea with Jennifer the way she'd been doing. Jennifer approached her in the kitchen.

"I'm sorry, but I've got to know. Whose baby did you have with you yesterday?"

Again Delia's eyes jumped around. "*No puedo hablar sobre el bebé.*" She gripped the counter and looked everywhere except at her inquisitor. It made Jennifer glance around too.

Something suspect was afoot, Jennifer's intuition screamed out the knowing. "Troy's not here. Did he tell you not to talk about it?"

Delia frowned. Jennifer hated to pry, but she'd stumbled onto an important matter, a secret. She'd meant to tell Troy about how she'd run into Delia with a baby yesterday, and about Delia's odd behavior, but the incident had slipped her mind. Blatant curiosity overwhelmed Jennifer's gentler senses.

"Who's the mother?"

"Señora, I can't say."

Jennifer bore into Delia with a hard stare. "Yes you can; it's okay."

"Troy—he knows."

"He won't be home for hours. I'm asking you now."

"You know Misty…?"

"Misty Meadows?"

"Sí."

"Is Misty the mother?"

"Sí."

An alarm rang in Jennifer's head. Dare she ask? "Who's the father?"

Delia shook her head over and over. Either she didn't know, or she refused to answer, but her pleading eyes told Jennifer to ease off that question.

"Why is the baby with you?"

Delia's explanation came in a rush of Spanish.

Jennifer pushed her hands in a downward motion. "Wait, you're saying Misty didn't want it, and then she did; now she doesn't know?"

"*Sí.*"

"And Troy said 'make up your mind?'"

Delia nodded.

Jennifer's mind spun. Did Misty become pregnant by her mother's boyfriend? That didn't explain Troy's possible involvement by way of his housekeeper. She couldn't ask Delia if he was the father. The question refused to form in her larynx.

Jennifer lay down in the bedroom and stared at the ceiling. Did Troy father Misty's child? Did he imagine he could keep the secret from her? She remained there until her sense of dread eased.

When he came home, she kissed him hello with a calm façade. He might be guilty of a serious misdeed but to hold her presumption from him was joyless.

He lifted the lid on a pan of pork chops simmering in wild rice. "Smells good."

She gave a tight smile. "What's up with Gus?"

Troy slumped onto a stool and stared at the counter top. "There was a calf born this morning. Real hard birth—needed a lot of help. We lost the heifer."

"Oh, what a shame, I'm sorry."

His eyes remained downcast. "Yeah, so the new babe'll have to be bottle fed."

She set a colander in the sink and rinsed some lettuce. The salad spinner's whir filled the room. Normally she'd be eager to hear about the calf, and to get a look at it. The care and feeding of a motherless newborn would consume a lot of somebody's time. It presented a chance for Jennifer to be of help. However, the other issue took precedence. They sat down to eat.

"What's the matter, Jen?"

"Nothing."

"Are you sure?"

She didn't want to ruin dinner. "I have to talk to you, but it can wait."

"Seems the cat's out of the bag. Might as well talk now."

How to start? All afternoon she'd churned through answers he might give to the baby's birthright and hushed existence. "I ran into Delia at the grocery store yesterday."

Troy sliced his meat, set the knife down, and took a bite. "Uh-huh, and?"

"She had a baby with her." There, out in one fast exhaust of breath.

Troy continued to eat, a little more slowly.

"I bullied the poor woman into telling me the

mother of the baby is Misty Meadows."

He didn't look up. "Go on."

"Naturally, I have questions."

He sipped his wine.

Her mouth became dry, and she did the same. "What's your involvement with Misty and her baby?"

Troy aligned his fork and knife on the edge of his plate and looked at her. "What do you think it is, Jennifer?"

He never used her full name. It sounded sarcastic. One of her hands played with the stem of her glass, and the other one squeezed the napkin in her lap. "I don't know. That's why I'm asking. You didn't tell me Misty had a baby."

"I didn't think it was your business, frankly."

"I think it is. You asked me to share your life with you."

"You don't want to get mixed up in Cimarron's affairs."

"Your housekeeper is caring for the baby. Why the secrecy?"

He finished his wine and set the glass down with pointed gentleness. "Not that it matters, but Delia's daughter Alicia keeps the baby. It's not a secret so much as a private family matter. Delia knows that and respects it."

Troy hadn't answered her question about his role. The house grew silent and waited for an answer along with Jennifer.

His icy tone reached all the way to her bones. "Do you think I'm the father?"

She rubbed the chill from her upper arms. Tears formed in her eyes.

His stern voice implied it was she who had explaining to do, rather than him. His neck grew crimson, and the color crept into his face, a bad sign.

Her small fib avoided an ugly confrontation. "Of course I don't think you're the father, but what is your connection to the baby?"

He didn't answer her question. Instead, he threw his napkin on his plate and got up. "You think I'd have sex with Misty Meadows? I believe you underestimate who I am."

Jennifer dabbed her eyes with her napkin.

Troy walked to the bar, poured a drink, and stood at the dining room window with his back to her.

Nervousness made it hard to sit still, so she gathered dishes.

"Leave those for now."

She sat down, refilled her wine glass, and emptied half of it in two gulps.

He squared his shoulders and took a sip of whiskey. "Russell's the father. He couldn't keep his fuckin' zipper up and got her pregnant on a one-night stand."

Jennifer exhaled in relief.

Troy turned in profile and frowned into his drink. "He's gotten himself into a real mess. His wife's wound real tight. Now she's pregnant and likely to go off the deep end over this. One way or another she'll find out."

"What'll Russell do?"

"Everything's up in the air. The girl can't decide whether to keep the baby or not. Leaves town saying she doesn't want her and comes back saying she does. With Russ living in Albuquerque, I guess she figured I was his closest kin. One night she showed up here and left the child. Delia's daughter has young children and volunteered to take the baby in."

Jennifer hated the thought of Troy being tangled up in this, despite his automatic involvement as the grandfather. She walked over and rubbed his shoulders.

He continued, "Misty Meadows has nothing going for her. Lives with a mother who brings different boyfriends home all the time if you know what I mean."

"She's a prostitute?"

"She's no book club regular. Hangs out in bars and truck stops without visible means of support."

"Is Russell sure he's the father?"

"After Misty confronted him he took a paternity test. He's compensating Alicia for the baby's care. There are plenty of folks who'd want to adopt her. We're looking into it. When that girl takes off again for places unknown, we'll get the courts involved."

Jennifer had nothing to offer. She had no experience with these sorts of things. Tomorrow morning she'd research legal rights of various parties, abandonment issues, and the state's adoption process. Also, there must be someone, or some agency to help Misty. If not she'd step in.

"Let's go have a nice soak," she said.

"Good idea."

They carried their plates into the kitchen, scraped the half-eaten dinner into the trash, and loaded the dishwasher.

The Jacuzzi's soothing heat relaxed Jennifer's body, but her mind fluttered at the revolutions per minute of a hummingbird's wing. Family secrets had a way of wrangling their way into the open. Russell's wife would have to deal with it. Jennifer's arm came to rest against Troy's, and he took her hand. Misty must be in a state of agonized confusion. Jennifer's heart went out to the girl. She was sorry for the pain Russell's trouble caused Troy, yet she'd been unburdened. Her man wasn't the father.

Chapter Twenty-Five

A shrill ring cut into nighttime's curtain of peace like the jagged tearing of black velvet. Jennifer lifted the dead weight of Troy's arm from around her waist. She patted the top of the bedside table in search of the intrusion's source. A glimpse at the clock showed twelve fifteen. She croaked into the phone. "Hello."

"Jenny, guess what? Mom's ready to move into Highland Ridge."

"It's after midnight here."

"Oops, I forgot."

"That's what you said last time."

Troy's pillow muffled his growl as he turned away. Jennifer didn't want to further disturb her slumbering bear, so she tiptoed into the bathroom and eased the door closed.

"We've wanted this for her."

"I know. Isn't it great? Someone needs to sort through everything and get Mom moved. I can't do it; I don't have time. Can you come out?"

There it was—Allison's angle revealed. Create a wave of excitement hoping to lock in a quick promise from Jennifer.

"I flew out for Mom's meth lab debacle last October. I'm not the on-call janitor. This one's up to you."

"With my schedule and Matt's kids staying with

us? It doesn't look good for me to do it."

How did Allison manage her over-booked clientele and still be a social butterfly? "Work on it, Sis. You can do this. I'll call you tomorrow."

"But, but…Jenny!"

Jennifer hung up and got back into bed, then lay there wide awake. The likelihood of Allison stepping up? Slim to none. A backup plan took shape in her mind.

In the morning, she stood guard over the coffee machine so Troy wouldn't pull the pot out and fill his cup before the brewing finished. He wore his robe in a disheveled fashion.

She ran her fingers through her lopsided bed hair and grinned. "Aren't we a pair. I guess the honeymoon's over."

He returned her smile and adjusted his robe. "What'd your sister want last night?"

"My mom's ready to move into that senior place I told you about. It seems enough of her friends are there now."

"Good. I'm glad she's going ahead with it."

"We all are. Looks like I'll have to help her settle in and get the house ready to sell."

"What about Allison?"

Jennifer crossed her fingers. "I'm hopeful she'll handle most of the sorting so I won't have to stay for more than a week. I'll call her this afternoon."

Allison's stance during their next conversation hadn't changed. "I'm buried in work. Plus, you're the organizer of the family. Your patience for this kind of thing goes way beyond mine or Mom's."

"Your attempt at manipulation won't work. If I

couldn't do it, you and Mom would manage."

The pitch of Allison's voice went up. "I'd throw everything away, and Mom would freak out. We'd both be miserable. I know you, Jenny. This is right up your alley."

Jennifer loved nothing more than to roll up her sleeves and delve into projects like this. She'd long imagined her mom's house freed of its burgeoning contents. She paused, sighed, and paused again.

"I'll think about it."

"There isn't much time. Mom has to give the people at Highland Ridge an answer before the next person on the waiting list gets it. She can leave a deposit to hold it, but the house will have to be sold soon."

"I need to talk to Troy."

She found him at his desk behind two large computer monitors. His office looked out on a red barn and outbuildings, with fences and green fields beyond. Jennifer appreciated the pastoral view considering the long hours Troy spent in that spot. She stepped up to the open doorway and tapped. He pivoted in his chair to face her.

"About my going to California, I'll have to do most of the work. I thought I'd give myself plenty of time, say, the rest of May."

He gaped at her and dropped his hands from the keyboard to his lap. "Today's the second. Are you talking a month? What about Allison? She's right there."

Jennifer leaned against the door frame. "I love my sister, but her head's in the clouds. All she can manage is her own frantic life. She's always been that way."

Troy's frown displayed every line on his face. He leaned back in his chair and crossed his arms. "Maybe it's because y'all have enabled that kind of behavior."

Jennifer shrugged. "She isn't in Las Casitas. It's a forty-minute drive for her, and longer in traffic."

"Whereas for you, it's a mere fifteen hundred miles. Why don't the two of you hire a professional organizer or some such person? Then you can fly out and finalize everything."

"My mom's always been oppositional. She's difficult about almost everything now days and might change her mind out of sheer orneriness. The move has to be handled with care. It wouldn't work to bring in a stranger. Besides, I can do a better job than someone like that."

Troy turned his head toward the window and clenched his jaw. "You just moved in here. You're barely unpacked. I can see you going for a week, but the entire month of May? Don't you think it's too much time for us to be apart?"

"Yes, and I'm sad about it. I'll miss you, but I have to do this. Also, I thought I'd drive." *Might as well heap it all on at once.*

"Drive? What the hell for? It's a long trip, especially alone. Why not fly and rent a car?"

"I'll need to haul my mom's stuff to her new place. The Jeep will be handy for that. Plus, I might want to bring some things back."

"So rent an SUV and ship the stuff."

Her stance in the doorway slumped. "It's too expensive."

"I'll cover it."

"It's a waste of money."

"There must be long-term discounts on car rentals. Have you checked?"

On and on went the discussion, a badminton game with a leaded shuttlecock. She wearied of it. Committed relationships include differences of opinion and compromise; Jennifer realized that, but she wouldn't be swayed.

The night before leaving, she emerged from a bath and surveyed her pretty bottles of perfume Troy had provided a steady supply. Old favorite, new, or go natural? He loved Organza, so she spritzed a little behind her ears and in other key places. With an ear tuned toward his approach, she stared into her lingerie drawer. The saucy red and black negligee was for a different occasion. Tonight was about romance. Her silk nightgown would be buttery-soft in his hands. She lit candles and slipped into his side of the bed to warm it for him.

Sweet and tender lovemaking was their parting gift to one another. Warm lips, scents, and softness, the curve and bend of each other's form, all were savored as memories for the lonely nights and untold miles that would separate them. Afterward, they lay side by side.

"When you get back we'll drive to Paladora for a vacation if you'd like."

"That'd be nice. I've wanted to see it."

He raised himself on his elbow and gazed into her eyes and then sat up and urged her to do the same. He took her hands in his.

"Will you marry me, Jen? I know this is sudden, but we've talked about it before. We could go to the Justice of the Peace in Paladora. I don't have a ring for you yet but…"

She let loose a joyful scream and threw her arms around him. "I love you so much. Yes, I will marry you."

In the morning, she shared her smile with the sunrise while waiting beside the Jeep for Troy to finish his shower and join her. They were engaged. When talk of marriage had come up in the past, his eyes sparkled, and her pulse raced. No biological clock or financial need influenced her decision. Neither of them was pressured by a person or dogma. Jennifer was in love with Troy and wanted to commit to him, to be his wife and spend the rest of her life with him, pure and simple.

He approached, and she reached up to embrace him. The smell of vanilla soap, shaving lotion, and deodorant exuded from his skin. These artificial fragrances were pleasant, but she preferred his natural musk.

"Do you remember what you asked me last night?" she said.

"Of course."

"And you still mean it?"

"With all my heart. Do you?"

"More than ever."

Their kiss lingered, and they held one another until she eased away, slipped behind the wheel, and buckled up.

"Thank you for being so good about this."

He shoved his hands into his pockets and kicked a rock. "Yeah, well, I agree under protest. Don't pick anyone up."

Of course not, she knew the dangers and wouldn't do such a thing.

"Don't drive at night."

She had night blindness; he knew that.

"Don't stop for stranded motorists, be careful, call me every day, do you have your phone charger?"

"Yes dear, I'll be fine."

Chapter Twenty-Six

Jennifer spent her next two days in monotony behind the wheel. The endless empty miles allowed her to contemplate her mother's situation. Blanche balanced on the edge of a life-altering change. It couldn't be easy. Jennifer resolved to get along with her no matter what, beginning with a hug when she arrived.

She pulled up the drive, and Blanche stepped from the doorway. Jennifer got out of the Jeep and reached toward her but let her large purse tip forward from her shoulder as a safety barrier. The two managed an almost-hug. Her mother felt frail. Time may have worn away her acidity along with her bulk.

Blanche's preparation for Jennifer's arrival amounted to a stack of fresh sheets. Jennifer cleared clutter and dusted. With ghastly images of the room's past occupants, she sanitized and opened windows. Blanche stood in the doorway and chattered like a magpie. A realization hit Jennifer. Her mom couldn't enter because of the intimacy such movement implied. Jennifer freed some wire hangers from a tangled pile and hung her clothes as she pitied Blanche her constricted heart.

"I'd like to get started first thing tomorrow morning. How do you want to approach it?"

Blanche shrugged. "How do I know? You're the organizer."

Her words taunted. It grated on Jennifer's nerves to hear them straight from the horse's mouth. "Don't label me. We'll start at eight a.m."

"That's early, isn't it? I can't get my breakfast and shower by then."

"Eight o'clock sharp, Mom."

Blanche gave another shrug.

In the morning, Jennifer called the trash company and ordered a dumpster. She worked out a three-pile system—keep, donate, or toss—and began in the garage. From the start of the monumental job, Blanche carried things from one pile to another. She flitted like a desultory butterfly. They talked about having a yard sale, but it meant a lot of added work for Jennifer, and she didn't want to. There were her father's things to consider, two table saws, a vise, and a multitude of hand tools that were miraculous survivors of the procession of tenants. Jennifer researched their value and placed ads to sell them through the local newspaper and online.

Lunchtime highlighted each day. Blanche made sandwiches of sharp cheddar cheese, mayonnaise, lettuce, and alfalfa sprouts on sunflower bread. They drank iced coffee with cream. Despite their adversarial history, the two got along with little abrasion provided Blanche wasn't pressed into any real work. Jennifer sifted through forty years accumulation of household trash and treasure in a week's time.

On the last day, they stood outside and watched the full dumpster being hauled off.

"After spending all this time together I know the complete history of each of your friends, their children, and their children's children," Jennifer said.

"Smart ass."

Am Vets pulled in for their lot. Jennifer surveyed the garage, empty for the first time since 1968. She swept it out and sashayed across the vast concrete floor with the broom as her partner.

On the morning of Blanche's move, Allison arrived her customary one hour late, greeted by their mom's gushing attention. She presented Blanche with a kaleidoscopic bouquet the size of a funeral display, and Blanche almost went apoplectic. Jennifer surveyed her sister. As manager of a full-service salon and spa, Allison had access to all the latest beauty treatments. She adopted every one, a walking billboard for the business. It saddened Jennifer. Fake eyelashes, hair extensions, lip filler, a boob job, and all the rest of that crap hid her sister's natural prettiness. Five foot six wasn't tall, but Allison's svelte figure and signature stilettos gave her the look of a car lot model.

"Mom, do you want to walk through the house one last time?" Allison asked.

"Yeah, sure."

Jennifer waited until her mom was out of earshot before she addressed Allison. "I don't want to part with this place."

"Why not, it's a freaking albatross. I can't wait for it to sell."

"This is where we grew up. We're about to let go of something my heart tells me not to." Jennifer waved her arms toward the hills. "Look around, it's beautiful here."

"Maybe to you, you're used to nothing but flatland."

"That's not true, Allison."

"You'd have to drag me kicking and screaming up here to live."

Jennifer shrugged and smiled. "I like it."

Blanche returned with her head hung and her feet dragging. "It's lost its soul."

They lingered in the driveway until Jennifer locked up and pushed the remote to lower the garage door. Allison got into the back seat of the Jeep to leave the front for their mother, but Blanche insisted on sitting in the back next to her. Allison and Jennifer had to rearrange boxes, bags, and odds-and-ends. Satisfied, Blanche planted herself in her dictated spot like Her Royal Highness awaiting her conveyance.

Jennifer pulled into Highland Ridge and parked. She retrieved one of the large bins and insisted Allison carry the other. They walked single file up the narrow sidewalk. Blanche refused to part with the massive bouquet while she struggled to unlock the door.

Allison set her bin down and reached for the key. "Here, Mom, let me help you."

Blanche gripped it tighter. "No, I have to learn. We never locked our door on Gallatin Road."

Jennifer hoped this wasn't the start of some habitual comparison on her mom's part, her apartment to the house. An intense energy drain made her flop down on top of her plastic tub to wait out her mother's door-unlocking session. Every pore in her body sighed with the release of tension, like a deflating balloon. The heavy lifting and carrying weighed nothing compared to the comments she'd held in check while her mother did the opposite all week.

Jennifer hired an old acquaintance for a turnkey renovation. He began the next day. His crew hauled off yard debris and prepped the outside of the house for paint. She needed a real estate agent; someone she knew from high school expressed interest, but Jennifer wasn't ready. She wanted Troy to see the place.

"Won't you come out and visit?" she pleaded to him over the phone.

"I can't. I'm busy, Jen. I miss you. C'mon back soon."

"I miss you, too."

She knew his next words. Sure enough, they arrived on cue.

"Have you listed the house?"

She made herself comfortable on the bed in case he belabored the subject. "It's almost ready."

"You've said that before."

"I know, but the real estate person says it'll sell quickly, so the work has to be done before it goes on the market."

"Make sure the agent you hire can handle things without you there."

This new topic had grown old. "Yes, I will."

After they had hung up, Jennifer went outside. A scrubby gray-green blanket of chaparral covered the hills. It adapted well to yearly fires and droughts. To the east, a footpath once meandered up the hill. As a girl, Jennifer had gone there to pick poppies and goldenrod and nibble wild anise. The hills were full of rattlers, but she'd never crossed paths with one or heard its chilling sound.

Around the side yard, a slackened metal clothesline wore random wooden clothespins, some merely broken halves swinging on their springs. Jennifer always liked the crunch of weedy gravel underfoot when she hung laundry. Once dry, the stiffness of her Levi 501's reminded her of the snug fit to come. She recalled breezes brushing soft cloth against her cheeks and the fragrance of cotton dried by the sun.

She strolled down the driveway to the split-rail fence that defined the yard. It wasn't strong enough to perch on like she'd done years ago. She gazed down the road and remembered her and Allison's barefoot walks to the store for ice cream during the scorched brown days of summer. It had to be at least two miles one way. She inhaled the sagebrush-scented air, the elemental smell of her youth.

So many things she loved had disappeared from her grasp. Aaron grew out of childhood and slipped from her reluctant arms. Her marriage had failed and it, too, had to be set free. She couldn't manage the family home in Mustang and had to give it up. She later came to realize the property wasn't meant to be hers for more than a prescribed measure of time. Her reward for being its good steward had been the pleasure of the yard's dappled beauty. She had a new life, a good one, but it didn't keep her from a backward look at all she'd once held dear.

Now the Las Casitas house would join the many-pocketed garment of her past. She closed her eyes, spread her arms wide, and took a deep breath.

"I release my hold on you."

She made a vow. This would be the last time she'd remain a passive player in Fate's hand. Empowerment meant she'd decide for herself what parts of her life needed archiving. Her resolve solidified an idea she'd mulled over for a week. The press of her phone in her back pocket propelled her to take the first steps on her course. Straight to the house she went, and into her boxy bedroom with its small window. She pulled out her phone, sat on the bed, and pushed Troy's number. He answered on the second ring. Her words tumbled out.

"I've made up my mind. I'm spending the summer here, at the beach."

She sealed herself for his response whether hurt or angry.

"You want to stay the entire summer? You've been out there most of May, and that's too long. What the hell's next, a year?"

"No, just this one summer. I'll miss you, honey. I have since I've arrived, but I need this."

"Did you plan it all along? Is that why you drove?"

"Of course not. I would've told you. I'm listening to my heart."

"Yeah? You said I was your heart."

Tenderness wrapped itself around her guilt. "I love you, Troy, and I'm grateful to you for allowing me to hire Dean as manager of my apartments and free me to do this, but I'm asking for your support."

His sigh blew through the line. "Moving your mom into retirement and selling the family home is a mental and physical strain. I get that. Why not take a week or two at the beach and then come on back?"

"I need more time than that. Can you at least think about it, let it sink in for a few days? Then it won't seem so far-fetched."

"I don't see my thinking changing any."

He'll come around. She researched lodgings for rent in the beach towns along San Diego's north county coast. Four days passed while she and Troy skirted the subject of her extended stay, but a silent strain had emerged between them.

The construction crew finished the outside of the house. Its stucco walls were a color called 'Soothing Sand' with sage green trim, colors harmonious with their surroundings. A good mow, edge, and trim of the yard gave the property curb appeal. The workers waited to begin the inside of the house with their other jobs on hold. She could put it off no longer and again spoke to Troy about her plan.

"I've e-mailed you the websites of available rentals, included an estimate of costs, and how I intend to pay for it. I'll use furniture and household items from my mom's, and then donate, sell, or take them with me when I go back to Oklahoma. I'll live simply and cheaply." An accounting wasn't necessary, but she wanted him to know she'd been through in her planning.

His voice sounded small. She almost preferred anger to its bare pain. "Perhaps you'll recall us discussing a wedding in Paladora this summer."

She had a ready comeback for him. "Can we delay it a little and get married in the fall? I imagine Paladora to be beautiful then. The trees will be full of autumn color. It's a romantic time to wed, symbolic of our having met later in life. Ours is an autumnal romance."

"You've got a solution to everything, don't you?"

Jennifer let the remark pass. Silence went on so long she looked at the phone to make sure he hadn't hung up and then forced herself not to fill the void with words.

A weakened version of his husky voice came through. "I can tell you're determined to do this.

You've been talking 'bout living in California since we met. I guess you think this is a reasonable compromise."

"Yes, I do."

"I'm dead set against so long a stay but go ahead and get it out of your system."

"Oh Troy, thank you for going along with this."

With the phone at her ear, she jumped up from the bed and bounced around the room's small space.

Chapter Twenty-Seven

Jennifer settled into an apartment atop a hill near the ocean in Encinitas where she'd usher in the summer. May gray was in the past. June gloom meant foggy mornings or even whole days, but in this beautiful climate she didn't care. A town whose largest industry was flower growing would be her home through August.

Her excitement bubbled through the phone to Troy. "You should see it here. There's a small space outside my front door bursting with bird of paradise. The patio's covered with bougainvillea. I'll send pictures."

"It's okay, you enjoy it, Jen."

He sounded blue, but she was excited and wanted to share her new surroundings with him.

"My apartment's tiny, but the walls have fresh texture and white paint. There's distressed plank flooring that may be faux but looks good. I have a pine table and four chairs from my mom's. Her old couch will do. I bought an off-white linen cover to hide its ugly print."

"Sounds like you have everything you need."

"Everything but you. My furnishings are spare, but I like it that way. And the weather, there's no need for air conditioning. I open the windows to salt air and eucalyptus."

"I'm glad for you."

"Thank you, but I miss you. Please come out, even for a week. We'd have so much fun. When's the last time you took a vacation?"

"Maybe."

It didn't sound promising. "I listed the house. The agent says there's a lot of interest."

She hoped it would brighten his mood, but his next words were monotonous, like the others.

"That's great. Glad to hear it."

Jennifer spent her time introspectively. Each day began with a walk on the overcast beach. Weekdays included people watching from her favorite perch in a coffee house on Pacific Avenue. She explored the streets of the town on foot or rode her apartment manager, Robin's, beach cruiser with its wide nubby tires and wicker basket.

"Borrow it whenever you'd like. I keep it on the back patio," Robin said.

In the afternoons, Jennifer read second-hand paperbacks. Like the turn of a dimmer switch, the room shifted in smooth silence from sunshine to shadow when clouds moved across the sun. Late afternoon rays wove their way through patio slats and horizontal blinds to perform a shadow play like a disco ball.

Aaron liked her once a week calls, but Jennifer knew her son; more often would've smothered him. He'd been busy with plans of his own.

"I'm moving to the San Diego area, too. I've been accepted into the MAS program at Scripps. Grandma and Grandpa Ellis want me to stay with them until I find an apartment."

"What does MAS stand for?"

"Master of Advanced Studies, it's a hybrid degree

to develop a career at the interface of ocean science and public policy."

"Is that what you want to do?"

"Yeah, I mean, it gets me in the door."

"When are you coming?"

"I'm staying in Oklahoma through the summer to work with Dad. He ordered a hundred fifty trees for his place and needs me to help plant them and build an irrigation system."

"Sounds like an epic undertaking."

"Not really, he has two tractors. He's paying me a full wage. I'll save my money and move out there in the fall."

"Congratulations, honey. You're a free bird, soon to soar."

A sharp longing to be with him pressed on her heart. "Our timing's out of sync. Fall is when I'm going back to Oklahoma. I guess we'll wave to each other from our cars as we pass on some empty stretch of I-40."

"No, we won't, Mom. We'll pull over and visit for a while."

"Ha ha."

"It'll be all right. I bet we'll see more of each other once I move out there than we did when we both lived in the Oklahoma City area."

She doubted it but appreciated his attempt to cheer her. "Let's try to overlap our time so we can be here together. We'll go trippin' down the boardwalk and hike in the mountains."

"You sound so sixties."

She knew he'd say that.

****

Downtown Encinitas offered vintage clothing shops worth exploring. At an open-air farmer's market, Jennifer bought a bromeliad for the kitchen table and a small African violet that soon lost its blooms. She'd never had luck with indoor flowering plants but like cut flower bouquets, they were so pretty at first.

Just north of Encinitas was the small town of Leucadia. On Saturdays, its flea market came alive. Her first time there, the festive atmosphere drew her in. She bought a pair of sandals with thick soles made from recycled tires, but failed to bargain and paid too much. She'd never wear the chunky things.

In an antique store, she admired an ancient trunk with a distressed black patina, leather lashings, and iron trim. Another piece of furniture that caught her eye was a handcrafted birch dresser with simple wooden dowel pulls in a natural finish. She returned three times, filled with dread that the pieces would be gone. At last, the owner delicately suggested she purchase them and threw in free delivery. This gentle nudge did it. She bought them with a plan to have them shipped to Oklahoma when the time came.

Jennifer continued her once a week treks to check on her mother. Each time she visited her mother a little more had been done to personalize her new condo, neon pink silk roses here, dingy odds and ends there. She made sure Allison kept her promise and did the same. Jennifer's visits were met with indifference. She'd expected no more and knew she'd done right by her mom. That's what mattered.

Dean was performing well as manager of the apartments. Jennifer's texts, emails, and phone conversations with him were ongoing. She paid bills online, monitored cash flow, and addressed the day's apartment issues, a chore started, carried out, and finished while a life beyond her window waited for the close of her laptop's lid.

Troy announced he'd fly out. "I can get away for a week, no more."

"We'll make every minute count. I can't wait to see you."

She picked him up at the airport and drove straight to the beach. She wore a dress, and he rolled his pant legs up. They strode hand in hand and kissed along empty stretches of wet sand. One night they used a fire ring at the beach for a campfire and cuddled on a blanket with a bottle of wine. Phosphorescent waves broke below a crescent moon that hung so low its sharp horn seemed to prod the waves forward.

Despite the coastline's beauty, shells and other gifts from the sea were scarce. On an early morning stroll, they passed a chunk of driftwood entwined in a large heap of smelly seaweed.

Jennifer stepped closer. "Look at that, it could be a prized find."

Troy grimaced. "You'd need a Hazmat suit to rescue it, let's keep walking."

Jennifer stood her ground. "I want it."

She pushed her sleeves up, took a big breath, and plunged in to free the gnarled branches. Sand fleas swarmed while she dragged the mass clear of the decaying kelp.

"It's heavier than I thought."

Troy shook his head. "What now?"

"I'll set it on the patio to dry out and see what kind of shape it's in afterward."

"Lemmie guess, you want me to haul it up to your apartment."

"Would you mind? I'll take one side."

He sighed. "I got it."

He picked it up with both hands and headed toward the hill. "This thing's waterlogged. I can't believe I'm going along with this kooky idea."

Jennifer flitted around him. "Should I get the Jeep?"

"You wouldn't want this in there. God knows what's living in it."

"Careful not to break a branch."

He shot her a look that said she was pushing her luck.

They stopped so he could rest. He set the driftwood on the sidewalk and sniffed his hands. "It's rotten."

"Saturated with sea water is all. I can see through to its beauty. With the intricate twists in the wood, it'll be gorgeous when it dries."

Only once did Jennifer and Troy venture beyond the coastline's mile-wide stretch. The farther east they drove, the hotter it became. Behind the wheel, Jennifer stewed about the obligatory visit to Blanche. Never had her mom gone out of her way for Jennifer's friends. She hadn't welcomed her new son-in-law into the family. When Blanche was in the presence of Jennifer's then-husband she acknowledged his existence by way of flirtation.

Troy and Jennifer sat on Blanche's sofa, sipped tea, made small talk, and then got the hell out. Forty-five minutes max, as planned, sooner if Blanche started in with her Betty Boop routine.

Jennifer drove Troy to the property and showed

him around.

"It's a nice place to grow up. I see why you're so fond of it."

"I spent countless hours roaming these hills."

"I understand what it's like to have strong ties to a place. You can always come back and visit."

"It's the past. My mom needs the money from its sale for her living expenses. I've said goodbye." The problem with goodbye is that it's so final.

She hadn't called the real estate agent to unlock the house. The grounds were the draw. They peered into the barn. All traces of the meth lab had vanished.

"What was the legal outcome for your mom?"

"I told you, honey, remember?"

"No, I don't."

Jennifer didn't like to talk about it. Maybe she'd glossed over the subject. "Two of her tenants were convicted of manufacture and possession of meth with intent to deliver. As for my mom, we worried about the aiding and abetting law, but all she got was a heavy fine. The meth lab incident will have to be disclosed to potential buyers, but the real estate agent said it shouldn't hurt the sale."

Allison had told Jennifer that Blanche's 'Woe Is Me' act in court could've earned her an Academy Award. "Either the judge bought her story or rewarded her for the entertaining performance. He lowered her fine by more than half."

They left the property and drove toward one more place in town Jennifer wanted to take Troy. Las Casitas Cemetery was where her father had been laid to rest. On the way, she noticed a Brittlebush in full bloom and pulled over.

"I'm gonna pick some of those flowers for a bouquet."

"You can't wander into somebody's yard and help yourself to their flowers. Don't they have florists in California?"

"The bush is growing wild in the field."

"Jen, it's in a tended garden."

"It's in between. Those bushes cover the hills."

Troy glanced around. "First the driftwood, now this. You're becoming a scavenger. If you get caught, flower girl, I don't know you."

"If I get caught, I'll die of embarrassment. Besides, I'm not doing anything wrong."

Troy chuckled and then rubbed his temples. "Those are opposing statements. You're not making sense."

"There's no logic in matters of the heart."

She approached the bush from the field side, gave a last furtive glance around, and plucked a handful of the bright yellow daisies on their long golden stalks. How amused her father would've been by her shady method of procurement. She could see his pale blue eyes smiling at her. At the cemetery, she tidied the area around his grave and laid the flowers there. Troy stood beside her and put his arm around her shoulders.

"He loved me so much. I wish you could've met him. Fifty-seven is too young to die. He could've prevented his heart attack if he'd taken better care of himself."

Jennifer's thoughts were on her father during the drive home.

****

Other than dinner with Allison and Matt twice, Troy and Jennifer spent their days alone together in the throes of love. They spoke of their marriage vows and the wonderful life they'd share as husband and wife.

The morning of Troy's departure, an offshore storm caused dense fog and chill that kept them inside. From the living room, Jennifer heard the soft thud of Troy's suitcase hit the bed. Plastic clothes hangers clicked together as he pulled his shirts from them. A dark mood gathered in the air and Jennifer turned lights on to brighten it.

She called into the bedroom, "Can I help you with anything?"

"No."

She heard Troy tap his toothbrush against the sink with excess vigor and let a drinking glass clank onto the porcelain. He dropped the suitcase to the floor rather than setting it there. She couldn't ignore his noises.

"Are you okay?"

Troy didn't answer. She had to go in. "What's wrong?"

He turned from packing his carry-on bag to face her. "I think you should come back sooner than the end of August."

She let her body slouch. "Honey, we've been through this."

"I don't care. It's all wrong. We're not in a long-distance relationship anymore. Stay 'til the end of the month and then come home."

She shook her head. "I've always given in to you, content to follow your lead because we've wanted the same things. I gave up my dream of living in California and moved in with you while you sacrificed nothing. Oh wait, I take it back. You cleared out a few of your dresser drawers and allowed my cat to live outside."

Troy scowled, pulled out his phone and glanced at it. "It's time to go."

"There's two and a half hours until your flight."

He picked up his bags and started for the front door. "I'll wait at the airport."

Jennifer interrupted the silent drive one time. "Please understand. I need to do this before I'm forever land-locked."

"You make it sound like the ranch is a prison sentence."

"I don't mean to. I look forward to it, but you always get your way. We have to give and take."

"We've decided to spend our lives together, not apart. This isn't what I had in mind. Why am I the only one who feels this way?"

"You act like it's ongoing. It's a onetime thing. I don't think it's too much to ask."

"Something about it doesn't sit right, a gut instinct."

"My instinct says I need this."

They said goodbye at the curb and gave a peck on the lips, icy and passionless, while other drivers inched their cars ever closer and glared with impatience for the spot. Jennifer pulled away, and her muscles relaxed for the first time that day. Troy had left. What a relief.

Chapter Twenty-Eight

Like Alice in Wonderland's white rabbit, Allison was always on the go, phoning Jennifer while in a rush from one engagement to another. *"I'm late I'm late for a very important date/no time to say hello goodbye/I'm late I'm late I'm late."* In place of the white rabbit's pocket watch, Allison forever consulted her latest electronic gizmo.

One day Allison called while Jennifer was on her patio examining her handiwork. She'd used distilled water and a brush to remove the decayed parts from the chunk of salvaged driftwood and then left it to cure in the sun. She'd bought sandpaper and beeswax for the next part of the project. She examined the wood from different angles.

"I want to see you, Jenny. It's why you're here for the summer, right?"

Not quite. Jennifer kept silent on the subject. A solid reason for her stay had yet to reveal itself. She'd just moved in with Troy, so her timing couldn't have been worse. To tell people she had this vague need made them blink and stare with blank expressions.

"Come out with Matt and me. Meet our friends."

"I don't fit in with your party crowd."

"You make them sound like a bunch of debauchers. They're nice people; you'd like them."

"I didn't mean to insult your friends. I want to see

227

you too. Let's meet for lunch and a walk on the beach."

"I can't take a whole afternoon off. You have all the time in the world; I don't."

"I worked my ass off for it." *And my relationship with Troy might suffer, so this indulgent summer of mine comes at a price.* "Can we meet on the weekend?"

Allison's pause told Jennifer the idea was a no-go.

"Jenny, listen. I've been helping plan a dinner party for a good friend of mine who's turning fifty. We're holding it at the Pacifica Hotel, near your apartment. Come with us this one time. Please? You can leave whenever you'd like."

"Geez, what I have to go through to see you. I guess so, but I want to sit with you and Matt. Visiting you guys is my one reason to go."

"Great. I'll make sure of it."

Jennifer had nothing to wear to this stupid event. All she brought from Oklahoma were casual clothes. She'd bought some sundresses from sidewalk vendors, but they wouldn't do. In a shop called Petite Boutique, she stood in front of a three-way mirror in a festive green and white print dress cut in a classic sheath.

The sales clerk looked on. "It's lovely on you. It matches your eyes and shows off your figure."

A pair of nude high-heeled sandals and a straw clutch finished the ensemble. She didn't want to go to the party, but at least she had the perfect dress to not enjoy it in.

The Pacifica Hotel's banquet room didn't stop with a view of crashing waves. Its architecture seemed to go for visual immersion, like standing before a huge aquarium minus the serenity. A glass wall, low causeway, and narrow strip of sand were all that separated Jennifer from the violent surf.

Allison and Matt were across the room. Matt spotted Jennifer and waved; she waved back and walked toward them. Allison was in director mode. She pointed waiters toward tabletop bouquets and place settings, moving her hands as if using sign language but with her mouth in motion too. She stopped when Jennifer drew up. They hugged and held each other at arm's length.

"You look great, Alli, a vision in beige silk."

"Thanks, you too. Can I borrow that outfit?"

The comment poked fun at a difficult time in their past when they wore each other's clothes. If one of them borrowed a favorite garment on the other's forbidden-to-wear list, it resulted in cruel words and screaming. Physical fights were rare but spiraled into kicking and hair pulling. Allison kept a twirling baton under her bed that made an unruly weapon. At forty-five years old, Jennifer still carried guilt from the hateful words she'd spewed back then. Older than Allison by two years, she should've set an example.

Jennifer gave Matt a hug. "You're looking well."

"Thanks, so are you. Would you like to sit down? We saved a seat for you right here." He drew out the chair beside Allison's.

The long table sat ready for at least thirty people, and Jennifer's seat faced the waves, no doubt considered a prime one. She accepted the chair and didn't mention she'd rather sit with her back to the window. That way, when a powerful wave shattered the glass wall, she didn't have to see it coming.

Allison started in with the intros. "Jenny, this is Michael and Anna."

"Hi."

"And this is…"

On and on went the introductions. With each one, Jennifer performed the perfunctory smile and "nice to meet you."

At last she whispered to Allison, "Can we bypass some of the intros?"

"I want everyone to know you're my sister. Besides, it's rude not to."

Allison's teaching me manners? That's rich. She motioned her head toward the other end of the table. "Right, but I don't need to meet people way down there."

At the first opportunity, she ordered a glass of wine to help her through the ordeal. Everyone settled down to the meal. Jennifer relaxed and enjoyed herself with another glass. After dinner, the group moved to a night club on the premises. Music started up with no way to converse over its blare. Jennifer had to bellow her dry martini order into the server's ear.

"I can't remember the last time I had a mixed drink. It's delicious," she shouted to Allison. She danced with a few of Matt and Allison's friends but didn't enjoy it and passed on further invitations. Boredom set in, and she threw back her third or fourth martini. When she decided to go home, neither Allison nor Matt was around. She wobbled toward the valet, stopping once to remove her high heels, and again to empty the contents of her clutch onto the floor in search of her ticket. She then waved it above her head.

"Here it is!"

A valet ushered her to the side. She stood and waited while a procession of guests collected their cars and drove away. When she stepped up to ask the reason for the delay, the concierge led her to a private corner of the lobby.

"Excuse me, ma'am, I've consulted with the manager who believes you're not in a state to drive at this time. We're happy to keep your car in our secure lot until you're able to pick it up at your convenience."

"What?"

"I'm sorry, ma'am."

"'At my convenience' is right now. I'm not...I only live a few minutes away."

"Again, I'm sorry about this."

She rolled her eyes. "I'm sorry, I'm sorry. What are you, a parrot? Squawk, Polly want a cracker? I need a van or shuttle to take me home."

"There are none tonight. I'm..."

She turned away. High heels weren't fit for the walk home. She considered going barefoot. On second thought, a five-minute drive might be a long walk, at night, alone, in an unfamiliar place. No. She should've left after dinner or when the loud music started.

Back in the nightclub, she found Allison and explained her predicament. "Can you or Matt drive me home?"

"You mean right now? The party's going strong. Stay and have fun. We'll take you home later."

"You said yourself I live nearby. Can't one of you duck out for a few minutes?"

"I don't know where Matt is, and I've had a lot to drink too. C'mon, let's dance together." She took Jennifer's arm.

Jennifer pulled it back and looked around for Matt but didn't see him in the dark club. When had the place become so crowded? There were no cabs this far from San Diego. She was stranded.

"I'll wait for you in the bar. Don't forget to collect me before you leave."

At the opposite end of the lobby, she entered a cocktail lounge with a whispered atmosphere. Her ears still pulsed to heavy bass. She ordered a sparkling water and watched the bartender pour it and set it in front of her. She carried her glass and the rest of the bottle to a small table and had a seat. A man got up from the bar and walked toward her. She recognized him; he'd been a member of her dinner party. She watched him approach, tall and slender, dark, close to her age, with salt and pepper hair at the temples. His rimless glasses gave him an intellectual appearance, not unattractive. She was unavailable, but she could still look.

He smiled. "You're Jenny, right?"

"Yes, we were introduced at dinner but I forgot your name."

"It's Ben. I noticed your trouble in the lobby."

She grew wary of his having been in the same two places as she. "Were you leaving and then changed your mind?"

"No. I left my phone in the restaurant and went to find it."

"And did you?"

"Yes. The server left it with the concierge."

"Oh him, the Parrot."

Ben's non-aggressive style impressed Jennifer, towering there above her. "Would you like to sit down? I'd be happy for the company. I have to wait until Allison and Matt are ready to leave, and it won't be anytime soon."

His words came with a warm smile. "Sure. I'd offer you a drink, but it might not be a good idea."

She smiled too. "That's what got me into this fix. I'm not used to the hard stuff. A glass of wine with dinner is it for me."

"So it would seem."

"Still, I like those spiky vermouths. I dread tomorrow morning."

She studied his face. "I remember now, you're a doctor, right?"

"That's right."

"Forgive me, but I don't want to focus on your specialty right now."

"It's complicated, not one of those one-word answers like 'dermatologist' or 'cardiologist.' I tell people I'm in research and leave it at that unless they ask for details, and that's rare. Listen, I'd be happy to give you a ride home."

"Oh, did you think my comment about having to wait for Allison was a hint that I wanted a ride?"

"No, you need a ride, and I'm offering is all."

"I don't know...you're almost a stranger, a tall, mysterious one."

Ben laughed.

"Excuse me, I have to go find my sister. I won't be long." Jennifer scooted her chair out and rose, but lost her footing and stumbled. Her hand slammed onto the corner of the table, and the table toppled and crashed to the floor. Down she went, flat on her butt along with their drinks.

Ben leaped up and pushed the table aside. "You okay?"

She rubbed her upper arm.

Ben crouched down and examined it. "Does it hurt?"

"A little. I feel like a total ass. The worst bruise of all will be to my ego."

Everyone stared, and a few people offered help. The bartender and a server rushed over with towels. Jennifer shifted sideways and tossed the sandal she'd been sitting on aside. The wetness beneath her soaked through to her skin.

"Can you move your arms and legs without pain?" Ben asked.

She rotated her ankles and tested her limbs. "I'm okay."

"There's no broken glass. Other than this scrape you seem okay. Let's get you up."

She grabbed her handbag and let Ben help her to another table. Once there, she straightened her dress and patted her hair in an attempt at decorum while people stared and staff cleaned up the mess.

"Is your offer of a ride still on the table?"

They laughed at her unintended pun and glanced over at the two employees who lifted the fallen table back into place.

"The offer stands."

Ben declined a replacement drink. She caught the bartender's eye. She'd made a scene and then laughed out loud. Her behavior didn't fit with this first-rate establishment.

She rose with care. "I still need to talk to my sister a minute. I'll be right back."

"Do you want me to come along?"

"No, I'll be fine."

In the nightclub, Allison reassured her. "It's fine to

get a ride home with Ben. I've known him for years. He dated my girlfriend Cheryl, and she still talks about what a decent guy he is."

"Why'd they break up?"

"Cheryl said he's commitment phobic."

Jennifer forgot she'd been mad at Allison thirty minutes ago. She bear-hugged them both. "I'll see you guys later. Thanks for inviting me. Matt, take good care of my little sissa. I love you guys. When are you gonna get married?"

Allison extracted herself from Jennifer's octopus-like grip. "Jenny, where are your shoes?"

"In the bar."

"This isn't the place to go barefoot."

Even in Jennifer's present condition she wouldn't give Allison the upper hand. "It is for me."

"The bottom of your feet will be filthy."

"I don't care."

Allison took her by the shoulder. "C'mon, I'll walk you back."

"No, you can't leave your precious party."

Allison went with her. Ben stood as they approached.

"I'd appreciate that ride, especially from a handsome gentleman like you."

"Jenny!" Allison looked at Ben. "She's never like this."

"I understand. So, Jenny, sis here says I'm safe, right? Are you ready to go? Don't forget these." He picked up her wet sandals and handed them to her.

She waved them at Allison in goodbye.

Once in Ben's car, she directed him toward her apartment. "I shouldn't have come tonight. This isn't my style."

"What do you mean?"

"You know, clubbing and loud music. I gave it up in my twenties."

"What's your style?"

She thought about it. "Quietude."

"Quietude's nice."

Soon they were at her apartment. His car's headlights cut through the darkness and lit up the door like a grand opening. She unbuckled her seat belt and felt around for her sandals.

"Thank you for the ride."

"My pleasure."

She stepped into the glare and extended her arm toward the doorknob, then realized she didn't have her key. "Oh shit."

She padded back to Ben's car. "The keys are at the hotel."

"Sorry, I didn't think about that. Climb in, we'll get them."

Her maneuver back into his car held no grace. "Why are you sorry? It's my dingbat fault."

"You have an excuse, too many martinis. I should have thought of it."

"No way is it your fault."

They picked up her key and headed back to the apartment. Her stomach lurched. Waves of nausea pulsed into her throat. She covered her mouth and tugged at Ben's sleeve. His eyes widened, and he frowned. With a sharp turn of the wheel, he swerved to the curb. In one swift movement, she flung off her seat belt and opened the door. They weren't at a full stop when she leaned out and hurled the remains of her drinks onto the edge of someone's perfect lawn, then sat back in her seat and groaned.

Ben opened the glove box and handed her some napkins. He reached behind his seat, produced two bottles of water, and handed one to her.

"Take small sips. It'll reduce dehydration and help you feel better in the morning."

He sprinkled water from the other bottle on the curb to clean up. Flood lights from the house came on, illuminating an expanse of lawn that stopped a foot short of where Jennifer waited for the next wave of nausea to hit. She and Ben stared wild-eyed at the house. He jogged around the car and got in.

"Let's get outta here."

He sped away like a criminal, his eyes darting between road and rear view mirror. "Can you hold on a few minutes?"

"I think so."

"Take some slow deep breaths."

She rode with the window down and her head on the sill, oblivious to the night's chill. At the apartment, Ben came around to help her inside.

"I'm okay. I can get myself to bed."

"Sure?"

"Yes, thank you."

She closed the door and turned the deadbolt into place, certain Ben waited on the other side to reassure himself of its click. He seemed nice like that. Then she went straight to the bedroom and crashed.

Chapter Twenty-Nine

Jennifer opened her eyes and braced for the blows of a hangover. Instead, a dull throb suggested a low-level headache that would hang on for days. She knew the routine—aspirin, water, and food—sometimes twice. She washed off the previous night's smudgy makeup, slipped into a sundress and cable sweater, and headed to the beach for a jumbo-sized dose of fresh air.

Her sandaled feet slapped the asphalt on the steep descent as if she wore rubber fins. Troy liked her in dresses, and she'd worn the sun-bleached styles of the locals here without him. His angry words during their last conversation played in her mind. "It hacked me off when you said you were stayin' in California for the summer, and I still don't like it. Now you barely call. When we do talk, it's like you're not there. Seems I've been the only one reachin' out. From now on, it's up to you."

At the time of the call she told herself she'd reconnect with him and show him how much she cared. Soon after, though, calls to him fell back into being a chore. Their conversations were hollow. She no longer bubbled over with details of her experiences. Troy read meanings into her words and searched between them for clues. She knew he sought answers to why she'd pulled back from him, and she didn't blame him, but there were none. A week had passed since they'd last spoken.

At the bottom of the hill, Jennifer stepped out of her sandals, picked them up, and walked across the cool sand. A ribbon of foam at the water's edge covered her feet. Her California state of mind put her in the here and now. She wanted a mental break from Oklahoma. Troy refused to grasp her desire to step out of her old life, to be free and unencumbered for a brief period.

Early morning's calm wind and glassy water made for the best surfing. Surfers in slick wetsuits faced the western horizon and bobbed atop their boards. Like black rooks in a chess game, they waited for the right move, the perfect swell.

One of them turned his board toward shore, lay prone, and paddled. He stood up with arms spread wide and steered below a wave's crest for a long ride. The shore break signaled his ride's end, and he let out a joyful hoot.

Surfers were easy to spot around town by their sun-bleached hair and shoulders broadened by paddling. In high school, surf racks on cars were status symbols. Ron Sands was a surfer who'd resembled a young Robert Redford. He and Jennifer had a longstanding crush that never amounted to much. She'd been too shy and immature back then for a relationship. Years had passed since she'd thought of Ron.

She walked along the water's edge. Dry sand gave her legs a good workout and provided her feet with natural pumice. When she reached the place where pale sandstone walls jutted into the water, she turned back.

She'd been denied her Jeep last night because of inebriation. How humiliating. Did she tell that nice guy Ben he was hot or something like that and throw up in his car?

She started up the hill, crested it, and there stood Ben in the parking lot beside his car. After last night's calamity, she had no particular desire to see him again, but neither was she opposed. She studied him. Yep, still good-looking, long and slender in corduroy shorts, a T-shirt, and flip-flops, very Southern California. His elbows rested on the roof of his silver BMW with one leg crossed over the other, every inch of him a glossy magazine model who oozed sexy nonchalance.

He smiled when she approached. "Good morning, Jenny. I see you're up early. How do you feel?"

He had the same offhanded manner she'd noticed last night.

"Hi Ben, oddly enough I'm in pretty good shape."

"I noticed you coming up the rise just now and thought you could use a ride to your car."

"I planned to walk over but sure, I'll take a ride."

Something in his stance, the turn of his head, unlocked a buried memory. She scrutinized him. "You and I have met before; I mean before last night."

He nodded. "At your sister's salon, last October."

His expression revealed the same unfulfilled searching she'd read into it that time months ago. The hair on her arms stood on end like thousands of tiny radar antennas tuned to him.

"Did you recognize me last night?" she asked.

"Right away, at dinner. I wanted to talk to you but didn't get a chance. When you walked into the bar and sat down, there was my opportunity."

"And I didn't recognize you. I'm sorry."

"Our introduction was brief back then."

Right, but they both remembered their eyes

meeting in the mirror, their flitting away and back again, a flirtatious dance of eyes while Allison finished his haircut.

"Are you in a hurry, or can you come in for a cup of coffee?"

"Coffee sounds good."

"C'mon in."

Jennifer measured beans and water, started the grinder and then the coffee machine all by rote with her mind on Ben in the other room. She looked around the corner at him bent over the chest of drawers in a close examination of the driftwood on display. She walked up beside him while the coffee machine bubbled and churned behind her.

"Where'd you get this?" he asked.

"I found it on the beach."

He gave it a partial turn. "It's interesting, polished and all, very nice."

"Thanks. I like the way it turned out."

Soft brown eyes under dark brows and lashes moved from scrutiny of the driftwood to Jennifer's face.

"Do you live nearby?" she asked.

"In Del Mar."

"So you drove up this morning just to give me a lift?"

"Sure, it's not far."

She remembered the loss of dignity she'd suffered the night before and wanted to justify it. "Was I really that drunk?"

He chuckled. "I've seen worse."

"I didn't stumble around or make a fool of myself, did I, except for when I fell?"

"Don't worry about it, you were fine. How's your arm?"

She removed her sweater from where she'd tied it around her shoulders and raised her arm. "It's bruised, but it doesn't hurt."

He gazed at her and smiled.

She tilted her hip and rested her hand on it. "Why are you giving me that look?"

"What look?"

"The proverbial Cheshire cat grin."

"You were cute last night."

Her face soured. "I hate that word."

"What word, 'cute'?"

"Yes. Short women detest it. I've heard it all my life, including at the most inappropriate times, as in 'what a cute wedding dress.' Never use it again in reference to me."

"How about 'cutie'?"

She turned and stormed away. From the kitchen she called, "How do you take your coffee? Be warned, it's as robust as espresso."

"In that case with cream and sugar."

She struggled for the sugar bowl on a high shelf. He stepped in and reached it with ease. *He's a giraffe, too tall for me, not that I think of him in that way.* They carried their coffee into the living room. The couch was the only place to sit.

"Have a seat but be warned, it's hard to get up from this shlunky old thing."

She sat at one end and relaxed with her feet on the trunk. Ben took the other end and lifted a corner of the cover.

"A study in mauve floral."

"At least it's hidden under this nice linen throw."

He nudged a stack of paperbacks out of the way and rested his feet beside hers.

"Um, about last night, I may have said some embarrassing things," Jennifer said.

"Oh? Like what?"

She read his tilted head and widened eyes as feigned innocence. "You know what, my drunken references to your looks. Are you trying to coax a repeat of last night's inebriated flattery out of me?"

His grin turned up on one side, adorable.

She grimaced. "Sorry about throwing up."

"You couldn't help it."

"I'll clean your car."

He rested his cup on his thigh. "No need. You had spot-on trajectory and cleared it. So Jenny, what's your line of work in Oklahoma?"

"I own a corporate housing business. It's not real big. I managed it myself for a long time, but I've hired someone to take over, and I'll see how it goes. I'm a beach bum until the end of August."

"You're only here for the summer?"

To lay her plans bare held no appeal. "I'm in a transitional phase."

"A woman of mystery, I'm intrigued."

"Are you?"

"Very."

They looked at one another, and then Ben touched toes with her. She didn't move her foot away but stared at them.

"What kind of doctor are you?"

"I'm a bio-med researcher, also called a research neurologist. I work in a lab."

"What do you do besides work?"

He looked at her with those deep eyes. "Attend functions like the one last night and wish I wasn't there. The social scene has burned me out. I've been at it too long, but I didn't feel that way last night."

She dropped her gaze, this time to hide the delight that bloomed inside her like a flower, or was it a cancer? She rose and carried their empty mugs to the sink.

"Ready to go?"

"What if I said no?"

"The question's rhetorical. We should go."

On the drive he said, "Seems we've been here before."

"This makes the third time."

He gave her a brilliant smile with white teeth. "Third time's a charm. I have no idea what I mean by that."

How nice it was to share laughter with him. She reached into her purse for her sunglasses. "Things are brighter today."

"Meaning?"

"No idea."

She relaxed into Ben's easy company. To spend the day alone became unappealing. "Do you like to swim in the ocean?"

"I haven't done it much, but yeah, sure."

Encouraged by his lighthearted manner, she asked, "Would you like to go to the beach today?"

He peered at her over his sunglasses. "Okay. I have errands this morning, but I can be back by, say, one? The fog will have burned off by then."

"Great. I'll see you at one."

They pulled up to the Pacifica Hotel. After a final wave, she turned toward the lobby and adjusted her demeanor to one of seriousness. She had to apologize to the concierge.

On the drive home, she thought of Ben. Something existed between them, and she'd steered straight into it. What woman wouldn't? An innocent flirt here and there never hurt anyone. She was on vacation, why not cut loose and enjoy herself? What harm could there be?

Chapter Thirty

Jennifer lay almost naked on a blanket in the hot sand with a dashing man beside her. This made two events she couldn't mention to Troy, her martini adventure being first.

She wore her only swim suit. It used to be bright tangerine but had long since faded because of pool chemicals and wear. Salt water and sun would ruin it once and for all. The afternoon heat pulsed around her. Jennifer liked to body surf rather than lie out and fry. She'd stay in the water until forced out by the chill.

She turned to Ben, "Ready for a swim?"

His sinewy stomach muscles flexed as he sat up. "Sure. Let's go."

Entering the cold water was like a polar bear plunge but worth the initial shock. When Jennifer was waist high and dodging waves, she dove in. Ben disappeared underwater and resurfaced into a wave's frothy aftermath.

"Listen to the sizzle," she yelled.

He looked toward another set of waves approaching. "Incoming!"

She ducked under and fought gravity to stay on the calm ocean floor while a wave agitated above her like a washing machine. After it had passed, she popped back up.

"I love how buoyant I am in the salt water. I'm like

a cork. Let's go farther out and try to catch a ride."

Ben shouted over the roar. "Have you ever seen dolphins?"

"Sure, but if you spot one tell me, and I'm outta here. I don't want to get nosed by them or end up in the middle of their pod."

After a while, they returned to their blanket. Jennifer patted her face, "how refreshing." She arranged her towel as a pillow, lay back, and closed her eyes. Ben lay in a similar position beside her.

"So where are you from, Ben?"

"I'm a transplant from Albany. I came to San Diego to attend UCSD and stayed. I work for Scripps Institute."

Jennifer turned over and rested her head on her arm. This smart, attractive single man piqued her curiosity. "Can I ask you a personal question?"

"Sure."

"Have you ever been married?"

He joined her in lying prone. "Can you believe a forty-nine-year-old has never found the right one?"

"You've been in love before, haven't you?"

"I've had long-term relationships. I fell real hard for one woman, even bought her a ring."

"What happened?"

"I think we waited too long. We dated for three years. When we broke up, she got depressed. She wanted to get back together, but I'd moved on."

"A breakup is always hard. A lot of people have emotional scars visible on their faces, but not you."

"It was a long time ago; I've dated since then."

How like pillow talk this was, face to face with their heads cradled in their arms while the sun reclaimed drops of seawater from their skin. She wanted to ask him why his relationships hadn't worked out, but it seemed too personal. She sat up and applied sunblock.

"How'd you meet Allison?"

"The Del Mar singles crowd is a small group. I'd seen her at parties before we met. I go to her for my haircuts. She's a sweet lady, but she tries to set me up with her friends. I don't need help in that area. Besides, I'm on a hiatus from dating."

What a good thing to hear. Jennifer liked Ben and wanted to get to know him. Another woman in the picture would put the kibosh on it. She held the tube of sunblock out to him, and he shook his head.

"Dating can be brutal," she said.

"It sure can. Most of the women I meet want more than I can give."

"What do you mean?"

"It gets to a point where they start in with demands, a life commitment, a diamond ring—they smother me."

"So do you want to get married?"

"I barely know you," Ben said.

Jennifer shoved his shoulder. "I'm not quite that fast."

"I wouldn't mind a live-in girlfriend, but I've never had a desire for marriage, and I won't be coerced. How about you; is there someone in Oklahoma?"

There'd be no getting around a discussion about her other life. "I have a fiancé."

Ben turned away and looked into the distance without a word.

Jennifer continued. "It's funny; here in California I feel like I've stepped into a different life. I'm two people, and my Oklahoma self is obscure like it doesn't exist."

More than the physical distance was how far she'd traveled on an emotional level. In Ben, she'd found a fellow soul at odds with life's prescribed order.

He didn't probe but instead rolled onto his back. "I imagine it was great to have grown up here. You must miss it."

"I do. Until age seven or eight my family's visits to the shore meant unruffled bays. Any hints of waves were made by speed boats. I'd rush out and play in their wakes, surrounded by engine exhaust. Then I got older and discovered the ocean."

"Big difference between the two."

"There sure is. My mom preferred the bay and had final say. She refused to be swayed."

They lay in the heat's saturation before Jennifer spoke again. "When I was little I used to pretend I was a mermaid."

Ben turned on his side to face her. She did the same, and their bodies formed an intimate corridor. His smile invited her to continue.

"There were no rocks for me to sit on and sun myself or comb my hair like a proper mermaid. Instead, I made up a Southern California version. I'd sit sideways in the wet sand with my legs together as if conjoined and my feet splayed sideways like fins."

She sat up and demonstrated the position. "The water would come up and wash over my iridescent green gills, essential in keeping them damp and supple."

Ben grinned, then reached over and held a string of her wet hair. "That's a nice fairytale."

"I've never told anyone."

She brushed a strand of hair from his forehead. He lay back and closed his eyes with a lingering smile.

All the attention Ben showered on Jennifer put her into conversational overdrive. "Have you ever had a phobia?"

"I have a thing about heights. I stay away from windows when I'm in high buildings."

"My phobia story's longer than yours."

"I'm listening."

She lay back with her knees up and her hands at rest on her stomach. "The summer I turned fourteen, the ocean was inundated with jellyfish. They weren't the frail creatures you see in aquariums that look like delicate parasols floating with the current or like a troupe of ballerinas in pink tutus with ribbons flowing behind. The jellyfish that year looked like plastic bags with translucent purple veins. Their long tendrils were like barbed wire. They stung me, and the pain was intense."

Despite Jennifer's riveting narrative, Ben had fallen asleep before she'd even reached the part about how she developed a fear of the ocean and her two-year struggle to overcome it. She looked at the specks of sand that glistened from his wiry muscles. His skin radiated a heady mix of sweat and sea salt. A stir of desire for him came from a place deep inside. Time for a cold ocean plunge. She stood, brushed the sand off her seat, and walked toward the water.

When afternoon passed, they packed up and began the steep ascent to the apartment. They stopped to rest halfway up.

"I'm glad you came today, Ben."

"I'm glad too. I live near the ocean, and I've taken it for granted. Let's do it again soon."

"Okay. If you can get away on weekdays, it's less crowded."

They continued up the hill. "My schedule's flexible, late afternoons, in particular," Ben said.

He unlocked his car and tossed his gear inside. "Let me give you my number." He rifled through his wallet and pulled out an insurance agent's card, turned it over and wrote his number on the back.

"I have no use for business cards, a perk of my job. Can I get yours?"

She gave it to him without hesitation. He turned from a sideways position in his driver's seat to facing forward. "I'll see you soon."

"Okay, bye."

Jennifer watched him give a last wave through his open window. In a rush to wave back before he disappeared, she dropped her blanket and beach bag. She scooped them up and stared at the driveway's exit.

She was drawn to Ben. He lifted her spirits. To meet another person who evoked such emotion was a rare gift, a thing to cherish. Her apartments were a responsibility, Troy had expectations of her, and Oklahoma represented both. At present, life held the ability to make her heart sing a much different melody.

Chapter Thirty-One

On Ben and Jennifer's next beach outing, the hot sand below and the sun above conspired with Ben's nearness to make Jennifer fiery with desire. Unlike the last time, she didn't use cold ocean water to extinguish her arousal. Instead, she lay still while her breasts heaved, her nipples hardened, and warmth surged between her legs. Ben napped beside her. Her thighs trembled when she looked at the bulge in his swim trunks, so she pressed her knees together. At that moment, a future intimate encounter with Ben seemed inevitable.

After the beach, Jennifer invited him in for a glass of iced tea. She motioned toward the couch.

"Make yourself comfortable. Don't worry about getting it dirty. I can shake the cover off or toss it into the wash."

The living room filled with the scents of sea salt and Ben's coconut oil. They sat in the same places as last time, Ben at his end, Jennifer at hers, with their feet close together on top of the trunk.

Apropos of nothing, Jennifer began. "Allison and I used to explore tide pools. We'd stick our toes into small anemones while their tendrils contracted. Barnacles covered the rocks and hurt our feet, but we kept going back. I used to go barefoot so much that the bottoms of my feet were shiny-hard like worn moccasins."

Ben rubbed them with his own feet. "They're soft now."

She laughed and returned his touch. "They've had thirty years to turn that way. Yours are hairy."

He cocked his head to the side and looked at them. "They are not."

Jennifer flexed her toes. "My dad used to say the gap between my big toe and the second one could fit a sixth toe."

Ben lifted her feet, set them on his lap, and massaged them with skillful hands.

She smiled. "Feels nice."

He finished and rested his hands on her ankles with his legs crossed in that easy way of his. "Why'd you ever leave California?"

"Because of my husband's work; he's an engineer. His temporary assignment in Oklahoma turned permanent, our son Aaron started preschool, and we settled in. With all Aaron's talk of leaving Oklahoma after this term, the idea struck me—I could move back."

Ben reached to the floor where he'd set his tea and took a long sip. His off-handed manner didn't disguise the heft of his words. "Is that what you want to do?"

Jennifer looked at her feet still resting on his lap, and then into his face. "Until I met my fiancé, yes, but he's Okie born and bred; his roots run deep there."

"But what about you, how deep are you rooted to Oklahoma?"

Jennifer looked away with a one-sided lift of her shoulder. "That's a good point to ponder."

"Can you stay a while longer?"

"I have responsibilities there."

"What if you had a reason?"

Frankness seemed her one choice. Would it be the death toll of their new friendship? "I'll be here for the summer is all."

Ben leaned forward and picked up his keys from the chest. The movement jostled her feet, and she withdrew them.

He stood. "I should go."

"So suddenly?"

He looked away and didn't answer.

She rose. "Do you want to get together tomorrow?"

"Maybe."

Such a tepid response. He got into his car and backed out. From the doorway, she hand-signaled the 'call me' motion. Either he didn't see her or pretended not to. His car hadn't yet disappeared from view when she began to miss him. She carried the tea glasses into the kitchen, set them in the sink, and then stared at them. He'd left for good; she knew it, and it was best. To play with his emotions wasn't right.

She'd neglected Troy for over a week, so she picked up the phone and pushed his number.

"Why haven't you returned my calls?" His gruffness came as no surprise.

"I'm calling now, honey, and it's nice to hear your voice. What's been going on?"

"What do you care?"

It took effort to soothe without mollycoddling. "I care very much. I hope you're glad I called."

"It is nice."

"So, how are things?"

"My sons and I are drivin' out to Gila National

Forest next weekend. This year I drew out for an archery elk hunt there." Talk of hunting caused his voice to take on an excited lilt.

"What do you mean 'drew out'?"

"In New Mexico, hunters apply for a specific animal and firearm. Big game drawings are carried out by a quota system."

"I didn't know you were a bow hunter."

"I started at fifteen or sixteen, soon as I could drive myself."

"What do you do with the, ah…bodies?"

He laughed. "My favorite game meat is Oryx steaks. I marinate and grill them.

"I didn't know such an animal existed in New Mexico."

"Oh sure, there are others as well—black bear, pronghorn antelope, elk, ibex, and Barbary sheep. The exotics are from other places like Nairobi and Iran. I used to feed my family with the meat I harvested. Nowadays I have it processed and donate it to Albuquerque's food pantry. In fact, I've agreed to volunteer there once a month."

"That's generous of you."

"It's for a good cause."

Talk of hunting wound down and so did his spark. "We've got a severe drought around here. My ponds are dry, and I'm thinkin' hard about selling off some of the cattle to help keep the ranch going."

"I'm sorry about that." Her sympathy was sincere, but she hoped he'd continue to do most of the talking so she wouldn't have to. Her world held nothing to share with him.

"The panhandle's in its driest year for the past

twenty-five. High winds kick up and cause dust storms."

"That's too bad; it sounds like the conditions of the 1930's. What will you do?"

"Not much I can do. Cull the herd 'n wait."

"It's tough to have your livelihood dependent on weather."

This woeful topic wore itself out like the soil of a mismanaged crop field. They drifted into silence until Troy came up with something to break it.

"The neighbors and I are talking 'bout putting down road salt."

"Isn't salt for icy conditions?"

"In the warm months it keeps the dust down."

"I've never heard of that."

Her words were mechanical while her mind wandered to whether Ben had walked out of her life. Being only half invested in the conversation wasn't fair to Troy, and she struggled to focus. "I read in the paper Sunday's full moon will be the largest one of the year."

"Is that right?"

"Yes. If we look at it, we'll see the same one."

This attempt to conjure emotion fell flat, and the knowledge pained her. She and Troy had exhausted all general talk. The subject of their relationship would soon come up. Jennifer didn't want to discuss it.

"I should go. Enjoy your hunting trip."

"What's your hurry?"

Jennifer grew weary of being Miss Sparkly Voice. "I'm not in one. We've had a nice conversation, and it's winding down, that's all. I'd like to end it on a positive note. We'll talk again soon, okay?"

"Yeah."

Clearly it wasn't. She wanted to cry. "Love you."
"Love you too."

****

Jennifer met the quandary head-on rather than sit by the phone and wonder if Ben would call. She phoned him on his lunch hour the next day. He sounded receptive, and her shoulders relaxed in relief. Either she'd misjudged his hurried departure, or he'd reconsidered his rash action.

"Apartment life's getting old; I'm looking at some houses next weekend," Ben said.

"Is this a sudden decision?"

"Nah, I've put it off for a long time. Do you want to come along? I could use a second opinion. Dinner's on me afterward."

"Sure. I love house hunting."

Five long days strung out before their Saturday get-together. Jennifer carried on with her old routine although time spent with Ben dulled all else. She met Allison one afternoon for lunch; on another she began reading a novel. A bike ride turned into a bike walk because of the steep residential streets of pastel bungalows landscaped with drought-tolerant plants.

Ben picked her up on Saturday looking suave in a knit polo shirt, jeans, and loafers without socks. The look was a tad bit campy for her taste but a nice change from swim trunks and flip-flops. They knocked on the door of the first house and waited for the real estate agent to answer. Like all close spaces, the boxy front porch brought her and Ben's vast height difference into focus. He claimed to be six-foot-one, but he was taller than that. Jennifer remembered the joy of being on Troy's arm, a will o' the wisp beside his stocky five-foot-eleven frame. People had smiled at them in passing.

She and Ben surveyed the house and found it outdated beyond repair. On to the next one. The agent drove them in her Coupe de Ville and jabbered non-stop to Ben about issues unrelated to real estate. Jennifer sat alone in the back seat. Ben had introduced her to the agent simply as Jenny and left the woman to draw conclusions as to their relationship.

Inside the second house, the agent asked them, "Do you have children living at home?"

Ben put his arm around Jennifer's shoulders. "They're grown and gone, at least for now. Right, honey?"

Jennifer didn't like the agent. Her overdone makeup and platform shoes were forgivable, but the way she ignored Jennifer wasn't.

"Sure baby. We want a layout with a mother-in-law plan. That way the kids will be further away from us when they get stoned and have weekend orgies."

This caused the expected double take from Ben and the agent. Jennifer gave him an innocent smile. *You wanna play? I'm good for it.*

It was too much fun, so she continued. "We never imagined our doing so when the children were growing up would rub off on them. Did we, sweetheart?"

One-upped, Ben became fascinated with another room. Jennifer behaved herself after that. She continued the game but limited her comments to practical ones peppered with terms of endearment. One house had a patio with a high wall around it. She couldn't resist one more zinger.

"Look, honey, we can enjoy our lifestyle out-of-doors." She turned to the agent. "Did I mention we were nudists? Perhaps you'll be our guest sometime."

The woman's discomfort gave Jennifer wicked satisfaction.

Over dinner, Ben shook his head. "You went way too far."

"Having a little fun is all. We'll have to 'fess up to the agent."

He shrugged. "'Fess what?"

"Our true identities."

"Which are?"

"We didn't raise our children to behave that way." She laughed and waited for Ben to chime in with some clever comeback, but he didn't. He sipped his drink and then set his glass down and rested his hand on the table between them.

"I like people thinking we're a couple. It has a nice sense about it."

Jennifer withdrew her hand and rearranged the napkin on her lap. "You're my good friend, Ben."

He gave a deep frown and his brow furrowed. She saw his unhappy face for the first time. "Fine, this 'good friend' will straighten the agent out."

Chapter Thirty-Two

A routine evolved for Jennifer and Ben. On weekends, they house hunted and then had dinner and drinks in nice restaurants. Weekdays included late afternoon swims followed by meals in Jennifer's apartment where they chopped and sautéed together in the tiny kitchen.

During one of her touch-and-go conversations with her sister, Allison said, "I saw Ben at a party last night. He wasn't with anyone and looked bored."

An internal alarm sounded. Jennifer assumed Ben spent all his free time with her, other than work, rest, and personal chores. His attending parties didn't fit that image.

"I don't care. It's none of my business what he does."

"Uh-huh. I talk to both of you. You guys are together, what, every day? It's obvious you have feelings for each other."

"I'm involved with Troy, remember? We're getting married."

Allison harrumphed.

Hours later, Jennifer remained unsettled by the conversation. She sat at the kitchen table, checked her posture, and rolled her head side to side. The phone's presence before her urged her on with silent insistence. It wouldn't dial itself. Jennifer inhaled, exhaled, and picked it up with a heavy hand. She pushed Troy's number. The ring tones were out of sync with her rapid heartbeat. They dragged on as if he were deciding whether to answer the summons.

"Hello?"

"Hello, Troy."

"Why, Jennifer, what a surprise. How nice of you to call."

This wouldn't be easy, and he'd be no help. "I tried to pick a good time. Can you talk?"

"Yes."

"It's been awhile. I should've called sooner."

"Oh? Why's that?"

Her voice was flat. "Please don't."

"Don't what? We used to talk several times a day. I miss you and wonder why the hell I'm sleeping in a cold bed."

For Jennifer to say 'I miss you too' would've been untrue. "You agreed to my summer here."

"Something's going on. Am I losing you, Jen?"

She didn't answer.

"It's time to come home."

She closed her eyes and took an even breath. "I think I shouldn't accept your financial help out here anymore. I'll take over the rent." She pushed her laptop away as if it were his unwanted funds.

"Why? What's changed?"

"It's better that way."

His voice grew loud. "You know that's bullshit. You're cutting yourself loose, that it?"

She paused. "Maybe."

"I see."

Her next words came in quick succession. "It's not

that I want to be free. I always have been. I need space."

Her phone beeped with another call. She didn't answer but knew it was Ben. What uncanny timing. The mechanical click of Troy's easy chair told her he'd gotten up and started to pace.

"What the hell do you mean by 'need space'? You're half way across the country, and that's not enough space? This California trip's been a death knell for us from the start. Is there someone else?"

She knew Troy. He used anger to cover pain. She'd wounded him. "I'm not having an affair. I need time to sort things out."

Ice clinked at the other end of the phone. Troy's schedule operated like clockwork, including one whiskey after dinner. It was nine-thirty Oklahoma time, so this would be his second.

"Fine, Jennifer, take some time. Take all the fuckin' time you need. Then call me. Or don't. I can't say I'll be around."

The table lay bare except for the computer with its dark screen. Her compulsive tidiness left nothing to grasp in her shaking hands, no pen and paper for scribbling, no napkin to shred.

"What do you mean by that?"

"We both know what's going on. I wish you'd tell me what you want that you don't get from me."

Troy's wounded voice bruised her heart. "It's not you; it's me. I'm going through something I can't explain. I'm torn between there and here."

"Don't expect me to understand. I never will. Look, if you get in a jam with money or anything, call me. Otherwise, don't. Not until you figure out what the hell you want."

"I'll try harder to explain."

His voice caught. "I reckon not."

The line went dead. With it, a place at her core reserved for him alone emptied of joy and filled with sadness.

The conversation left her immobile there at the kitchen table. Twilight turned to darkness. It seeped around her until her halted state became an urge to get out of the apartment. The phone showed the earlier call had been Ben. She pressed his number, and he picked up right away.

"Hi, Jenny."

"Hi. I saw you called. What's up?"

"Remember the house with the Spanish tiled roof?"

"Of course."

"I'm seriously considering it."

Jennifer's heart was an anchor because of Troy. The walls of her apartment were too close, yet Ben sounded happy. "I love that house, very Mediterranean. Not that I'm an expert on Mediterranean."

He didn't pick up on her lackluster tone. Evelyn or Ally would have noticed right away and coaxed the angst from her.

"It needs updates but not an entire renovation," Ben said.

Jennifer struggled to keep her voice from breaking. "I hope you'll keep the cobalt tiles in the kitchen."

"Of course, aside from the view they're my favorite feature."

"My favorites are the archways and terra cotta floors. Ben, this is great news, but would you mind if we talk more about it later? Something happened just now. Not dire, but can we meet somewhere so I can tell you about it?"

She pictured him raising his sleeve to glimpse the time, one of his simple, elegant gestures. "Okay, how about the Pacifica Bar?"

"That'll work. When can you be there?"

"In half an hour."

"See you then."

Jennifer combed and fluffed her hair, applied lipstick, tied her sweater around her shoulders, and left. She'd arrive twenty minutes early but couldn't stay in the apartment a second longer. Did she break up with Troy? Her pulse raced, and her chest thumped. She remembered the same sensations minutes before her first dive from a high board as a girl. Philosophically, it's what she'd done. At the Pacifica, she turned the Jeep's motor off and began a deep breathing technique she'd learned during her brief yoga phase.

Ben appeared outside her car door. They walked into the bar and found it jam-packed.

"I forgot about happy hour." He looked anything but happy. At least he was well turned out. In a button-down shirt and slacks, he fit in with the business crowd. Jennifer's shorts and sweater were out of place amid the suits. A couple at the bar started to leave, and Jennifer sidled through the crowd to stand behind them. She and Ben sat down. They hadn't been here since they'd met.

"The usual?" Ben asked her.

"Sure."

He signaled the bartender with a two-fingered wave, "Two frozen margaritas with salt."

Their drinks arrived in heavy stemware glasses the size of fish bowls.

Jennifer gaped at the monstrosities. "We forgot to ask for small ones. It'll take both hands to lift them."

Ben shook his head. "They're going back."

He got the bartender's attention. "These are too big."

The harried barman said he'd charge them for small drinks, and then he was pulled away by the needs of the crowd.

"Fine, but we're stuck drinking from mixing bowls on pedestals," Ben mumbled.

Jennifer brushed at the salt on the rim of her glass and swiped its condensation. The vibe between her and Ben wasn't right for her news.

"I feel under-dressed."

He saw her as if for the first time. "You're fine."

"We were lucky to get these seats."

Ben nodded and remained silent. Though patient by nature, he seemed to want her to get on with the purpose of this meeting. She rubbed the goose bumps on her legs.

"You cold?"

She nodded.

"Here, take this."

He lifted a jacket from his arm and spread it across her lap. It had an inviting wool smell and carried his body warmth.

"Thanks. I bet you haven't eaten. Should we order something?"

"I'll eat at home."

She wanted to mention how different the bar's atmosphere was now than the night they'd met, but his mood stopped her. Perhaps he'd had a bad day. A few gulps of her drink caused a painful brain freeze in her head. She'd have to slow down. When the tequila took effect, she leaned in close to him because of the room's din and the private nature of her news.

"I broke up with my fiancé."

She expected him to react with surprise. One of pleasure would've been nice. Instead, he maintained an even expression.

"I thought you might be at a crossroads regarding him."

"Not until recently. Things have changed."

"Because of us, you mean?"

She ran her fingers over her glass. "Mm-hm."

"You told me I was a friend. I took it to mean just a friend. In fact, I felt rebuffed."

So validation of his feelings for her wouldn't be forthcoming. Their stances in the relationship had done a sudden flip-flop.

She nodded at him like a bobble-head doll. "You're right. We are just friends."

Ben watched her. "You're wading through some heavy issues right now. It can't be easy."

More nods. She wanted to crawl under her bar stool. Ben's sophistication and the complexity of their relationship should've told her he wouldn't react with child-like simplicity to her news. How could she have imagined it differently?

"I can't help you with your decision. You'll have to make it on your own," Ben said.

"I realize that."

He took a sip of his drink, set it down with a soft thud, and slid it away. "It's a work night. I should go."

"Yeah, me too."

They walked to her car, and she handed him his

jacket. "Thanks for meeting me. I needed to get out for a little while."

Her gaze may have stayed on his face too long, her smile too wanting. He leaned over and kissed her. Not a brush of the lips, but firmer. His hands cradled her head, and the kiss held urgency. Then it was over.

"Good-night, Jenny." With his jacket flung over his shoulder, he walked away.

She drove to a convenience store and bought a pack of Marlboro Reds. At her apartment, she drew one out and threw the rest into the dumpster. She settled into her patio chair, flicked on a tapered lighter, lit up and pulled a deep and deliberate inhale. The deliciously dry flavor bit her tongue. Smoke swirled into her lungs and filled them, a satisfying sensation. She tilted her head upward and exhaled. The smoke mingled with the night and disappeared.

The last time she'd pulled this stunt was the day her divorce became final. Before that, it had been on her wedding day when Allison showed up with a single cig. They'd giggled and shared it in the bathroom before the ceremony.

Jennifer didn't care for the dizziness it caused. The nicotine rush failed to halt her whirring mind, even for a moment. Foreboding seized her. Ben's kiss was a quandary, but it paled in comparison to what she'd done to Troy.

Chapter Thirty-Three

Jennifer applied a thick layer of sunblock to her face and hands. She dressed in roomy shorts and a long-sleeved blouse. Behind the wheel of her Jeep, she flipped the visor down to shield her eyes from the new day's glare. In a valley due west of Las Casitas, she stopped for a bottle of chilled water en route to Mount Kincaid.

Hilltops loomed above the dense fog. She continued east, and the straight swath of road became one of steep curves. Rock walls stood to the left and right like fortresses. They hefted the burden of her anxiety, carried it upward to their boulder-strewn peaks, and released it.

She had a particular trail in mind though it'd been years since she'd been there. After two wrong turns, she found its base. The early hour hadn't kept others away. Two cars were parked in the gravel lot.

Jennifer had no daypack, so she made do with a slouchy cloth bag worn cross-body. The number one rule of hiking is 'Never Hike Alone.' Jennifer found it an impossible one to follow. Instead, she left a note under her wiper blade with her name, cell number, destination, the date, and time. Also listed were Allison's name and number as an emergency contact. In a broad-brimmed hat, she began her hike. Her wide stride and brisk pace brought her joy. The simple movement was one she'd taken for granted. She breathed in the scent of chaparral. How fortunate she was to have good health, this day, and the mountain.

Up ahead, three men with ropes and harnesses rappelled on boulders. She called out a hearty hello and exchanged a few words with them. Beyond basic friendliness, her greeting served to note her presence, another safety precaution. So far she'd seen no other hikers. Good. None but the stalwart made it to the peak. Once there, they lingered, and Jennifer wanted the summit to herself.

When she reached the top most of the fog had lifted. She stood on an outcrop while a dizzying expanse of valley opened below her. She stepped back. The twenty-foot monoliths behind her more than connected her with something solid. She took in the view with her back pressed against the warm granite. Downtown San Diego's skyline appeared to the southwest. If the horizon straight in front of her had been clearer she would've glimpsed the sea, a chip of sapphire inset between hills. She'd seen it before from this spot.

Jennifer sipped her water on a flat surface shaded by a boulder. The endless space invited her to open her mind. Troy must be so hurt though he was no angel either. For months after they'd met he'd strung her along, filling her with self-doubt. All along there'd been another woman. They'd moved on to a nice relationship, and she held no resentment. He'd brought her out of a four-year withdrawal from society but had awakened a tigress, it seemed, because she now hungered for a different man. This trek revealed no change of heart in that regard.

Like a sure-footed mountain gazelle, Jennifer stepped across small boulders toward the trail head. She'd rather hike up a path than down one. Ascents challenged her leg muscles and lung capacity, but descents came after hours on the trail when fatigue had set in. Gravity's constant nudge added danger to loose rock underfoot. Jennifer took her time and stepped with care.

With Las Casitas nearby, she stopped at her mom's apartment for the week's obligatory visit. Blanche and another woman sat at the kitchen table.

"Bev, this is my daughter Jenny. Jenny, Bev, who lives next door."

The woman's face lit up, and she gushed in a loud voice, "Oh, is she the one who runs the salon? I've heard so much about you!"

Jennifer's mood soured. "No, I'm the other one."

"Blanche, you never mention this daughter. What does she do?"

Jennifer strode past them toward the bathroom.

Blanche mumbled, "Oh, something with rentals."

****

One must forgive to heal. Jennifer drove back to Encinitas with those words on her mind. They'd been recited over and over, carted out by a horse grown old from boredom. For her, they'd never rung true. Psychological sages be damned, certain acts were unforgivable. Blanche's jealous cruelty had abraded Jennifer since infancy, a lifetime of hateful words hissed so no one else could hear and screamed when the two were alone. It wasn't Jennifer's fault her father favored her over Blanche or Allison.

Her mother's words used to linger inside Jennifer

for weeks, like toxic smog from L.A.'s gridlocked freeways. Yet something occurred to her at that moment while she navigated the mountain road. Other than for a moment, she realized she no longer harbored the negativity. She'd left it back at her mom's condo. In fact, it had been a long time since she'd suffered the torment. When had it stopped? The cursed condition had slinked away, a feral cat having fed on rancid offerings for the last time. Jennifer became wide-eyed and smiling at the richness of her discovery. Let the bells toll and the trumpets herald. She was free at last. Duty decreed she care for Blanche, who'd grown old and powerless. Jennifer would carry out the duty with neither unkindness nor affection.

The thought of newfound freedom made her mind shift to Ben. She'd become too dependent on his company and needed to foster other friendships. A plan took shape.

Once parked at her complex, she went straight to her manager's door and knocked. Robin opened it while drying her hands on a dishtowel.

Jennifer smiled. "Hi. This is sudden, but would you like to go with me to the Farmer's Market tomorrow? We can sample the new melons."

Robin gaped and then collected herself, "Sure."

From where Jennifer stood outside, a TV commercial's blare accosted her. She didn't own a set and had grown unaccustomed to its racket. From the kitchen, the aroma of spaghetti sauce wafted through the doorway. Her stomach growled. She'd eaten little, a granola bar in the morning and half a tuna sandwich at her mom's. She longed for her dear neighbor Evelyn, who would've invited her in and insisted she have a big plateful of the delicious-smelling dinner.

"Let's go for lattes first, about nine?" Jennifer asked.

Robin squinted and shifted her gaze sideways. Jennifer had seen her use that gesture before and counted silently, one thousand one, one thousand two, one thousand three…

Robin looked back at her. "We should make it earlier so we can get the best produce. Let's go at eight, and skip the lattes."

What was this, debate team? Robin didn't get it. The point was to build friendship, not perform a chore. *Let's sleep 'til ten, skip the market altogether, and shimmy up to Joe's coffee bar.*

Still, Jennifer wanted to accommodate. "Okay, see you at eight."

She walked toward her apartment. Her muscles quivered, and each step made her wince. All those treks up and down the hill to the beach hadn't been enough preparation for today's strenuous hike. How would she walk tomorrow? Oh, what she'd have given for the powerful jets of Troy's Jacuzzi.

The next morning Jennifer limped beside Robin through the open-air market. Skinny vegans carried babies in slings. Earthy locals with gray ponytails wore Birkenstocks and carried environmentally responsible hemp bags. Beneath an expansive patio cover, tables held an abundance of fresh produce. Jennifer liked being part of it all despite her painful muscles. By the time she and Robin left, she was weighed down with bags of vegetables dangling on each arm. She'd make a big pot of soup, give some to Robin, and enjoy the rest with Ben.

Jennifer had a pleasant enough time but went home empty inside. She and Robin didn't click. The woman made a poor replacement for Ben, with his off-handed intelligence and breeziness. At present, the seams of her and Ben's friendship were tested by strain. Jennifer had given him the come hither she thought he wanted. He'd rebuffed her and then kissed her. Everything was jumbled. She longed to talk to him but wanted him to call first. Two days passed. Maybe he preferred the thrill of the chase to its conquest. Had his kiss been one of goodbye?

The call finally came. "Hey Jenny, how've you been?"

"Confused, but relieved you called."

"So we're okay?"

I haven't lost him. "Far as I'm concerned, we're fine."

"The last grains of sand have cleared out of my ears. I'm having withdrawals and need a beach fix. Are you free this afternoon?"

She laughed. "Gimme thirty minutes."

After their ocean plunge, they settled on the blanket and wiggled to make comfortable indentions in the sand. Lying prone with her chin in her fist, Jennifer watched Ben write her name in the sand with a stick.

"Any news about Oklahoma?" he asked.

"What do you mean?"

Neither one looked at the other. Instead, they stared at Ben's handiwork.

"Have you figured out where you'll live?"

How typical of Ben to toss out a loaded question as if commenting on the weather. "I'm going back to Oklahoma at the end of summer. My plan hasn't changed."

The long lashes of Ben's dark eyes held golden specks of sand. He turned his head away. Crashing waves and nearby voices filled the silence until he turned back.

"You all but said you broke up with your fiancé because of me."

"You're right, I did. I've been confused about him, but I have obligations in Oklahoma. My livelihood's there."

"I see."

The sun's heat spread across Jennifer's skin like butter. She scooped some sand and let it sift through her fingers. The granules formed a small pile and rolled down the sides, an hourglass's measure of time.

Ben sat up and brushed sand off his shoulders and arms. "We should get going."

They labored up the hill in silence. Jennifer stood beside his car while he put his beach gear into the trunk.

"You're coming in, aren't you?"

"I'm covered in sand, and my swim trunk's still damp."

She rearranged the gear in her arms, shrugged, and smiled. "What's new about that?"

"Today's different."

She looked straight into his face. "You could take a shower in my bathroom."

Any hesitation she had toward Ben self-destructed at that moment. Its ashes rose with the breeze and floated back to the hot sand where she'd laid enveloped in his essence.

Ben gave her a direct look. "I could do that."

While he showered, Jennifer brewed tea,

transferred it to a pitcher, and put it in the refrigerator to cool. Ben emerged, and it was her turn to shower. She closed the bathroom door, and the unexpected musk of a man assaulted her senses. It smelled like sex. She leaned back against the door. Closing her eyes, she imagined Ben's skin on her lips and tongue, his body urgent against hers as her legs wrapped around his hips in response. In her mind, he whispered his urgency into her ear. She hesitated no further but shed her clothes and stepped into the shower.

Before she left the bathroom, there was the coo of Grover Washington singing the bluesy track "Mr. Magic." Ben loved jazz and thought the sound quality on hand-held devices didn't do it justice. He'd brought in a CD player from his car. Jennifer walked over to where he lay on the couch, his sinewy length at ease there. He wore no shirt or shoes, just plaid Bermuda shorts. She inhaled the scrubbed version of his beguiling scent. If warmth had but one scent, it would be that of Ben's skin.

"You look comfy."

He looked at her with half-closed eyes, and brushed her thigh with his finger, just above her dress's hemline. She gave a small smile before going for the tea, and then returned to the living room. Ben furled his limbs to make room for her. She sat sideways in the center of the couch with her legs tucked up.

After a long swallow he looked at the glass. "Is this a new flavor?"

"Honey Vanilla. Like it?"

"It's good." His Adam's apple moved while he finished the glass.

"You must've been thirsty."

"I'm always thirsty after the beach."

"Want more?"

"Sure."

She carried his glass to the kitchen and called out, "I made chicken salad."

Why offer that? The atmosphere promised lovemaking. To suggest wine or offer chocolate, cherries or oysters made sense, but chicken salad? In the past, when Jennifer received unwanted attention from a man she'd chatter about her husband and son. Words were her firewall. Was the mention of chicken salad a last ditch effort to halt an encounter she both craved and feared?

"Later, Jenny. I've got a place on the couch for you."

Chapter Thirty-Four

Jennifer shrugged off all extraneous thoughts and returned to the living room. The music changed to George Benson's "Living Inside Your Love." Ben's profile showed his high forehead and strong Roman nose. He leaned forward and set the half-full glass of tea down. How fluid his movements were, like the natural grace of a large exotic bird.

She set her glass beside his and relaxed back into the couch. "I don't know how to resist you." Her soft laughter didn't disguise the intent of her words, nor did she mean it to.

Ben leaned toward her. "Jenny."

Their kiss tasted warm and salty-sweet. More kisses followed, deep and intense. He cupped her breasts, and she ran her hands over his chest. He reached under her dress, but she took his hand and stood. She led him to the bedroom. She lifted her dress over her head and removed her bra. Then she remembered the sharp contrast between her tanned and pale skin and covered her breasts with her forearms.

"It looks like I'm wearing a white swimsuit."

With softness, Ben swept her arms aside and brushed her nipples with the backs of his fingers. "No. You're beautiful."

He removed his shorts, and she slipped out of her panties. They lay on the bed, and Ben explored her body with long fingers and a touch so feather-light she pressed her hands on top of his to show him her need for a firmer touch.

She kissed his lips, his neck, and on down to his firm manliness.

He stroked her hair. "That's good, Jenny. I like that."

She paused, and he eased her head back down. "Nice, keep going."

She continued until he urged her up. "Are you ready?"

"Uh huh."

She opened herself to him, and he took her eagerly. They tossed and tumbled until both were satisfied. Afterward, he drew her close, arranged the sheet around her, and kissed her hair. She laid her head on his chest and drew herself into his snug embrace.

****

June eased into July while Ben and Jennifer lay in each other's arms. Afternoon siestas followed love-making on her double bed's sagging mattress. It rolled them together into its center. They'd rise with ravenous appetites and walk a block down Highway 101 to Jose's Taqueria for sizzling fajitas or fish tacos.

On the weekends, they let the sun chase away any remnants of fog before emerging from the apartment with beach gear in tow. Ben's skin became burnished. After a swim, it dried with a layer of salt and a dusting of silky sand. At such times, Jennifer found him more irresistible than ever, and they'd hurry back to the apartment for a hasty interlude. Even she became tawny-hued despite strict adherence to sunscreen.

They fed each other papaya from a street vendor

and laughed at the juice that ran down their chins. Jennifer modeled skirts for Ben at a tourist stand, and they tried on straw hats in a dollar store. When he wasn't with her, she ached for his touch.

For the first time in Jennifer's adult life, she turned away from society's conventions. To give one's self to another was the ultimate expression of love, with no room for possession. One should embrace the present to its fullest; tomorrow would take care of itself. This rationale lessened her guilt toward Troy and the woman he loved, the one who resembled her but was a stranger. Troy belonged in a distant life. He existed in abstract. Jennifer began to journal about her new perspective. Thus, the first two weeks of July sped by like the thumbing of a book's pages.

Jennifer intended to stay in California through August, but life had a calendar of its own. A hint of unrest stirred within her. To live in the moment had a wearisome element. Life was more than an endless summer. She and Ben didn't gaze into their collective future the way most couples do. The closest they'd come to addressing it had been on a drive to the mountains. She'd taken his hand from where it rested on the console and threaded her fingers through his.

"I care so much for you, Ben. I love being part of your life."

"I care for you too. I always will."

They'd remained hand in hand but looking straight ahead. Maybe their shared time had run its half-life and began to wind down. Though Jennifer's youth had been left far behind, she was still vibrant at forty-five. She felt sexy and beautiful with Ben. Natural aging would diminish certain aspects of her life. A last hurrah, is that the full measure of her romance with him? Their relationship had plenty of chemistry, but it lacked some other key ingredient. Ben was like the coastal mist. If she tried to hold tight to him, he'd evaporate in a way steadfast Troy never would.

Ah, Troy. She may have traveled too far down her current road to salvage her relationship with him. Would he even want her? Stanhope Construction remained her primary tenant. If she formally ended her relationship with Troy, she stood to lose the majority of her renters, all of them at premium rates. Yet she'd sever ties with him if it were her true heart's dictate. She thought of the small mound of sand on the beach, and how the granules slid in haste through their narrow passages between her fingers. She had to decide.

Afternoon light dipped low across the living room wall. Jennifer roused herself from her contemplations. Four o'clock, time to get ready for Ben's arrival and the swim they'd planned.

Jennifer carried a towel and a small tote. Ben's ever-present backpack hung over his shoulder. The concrete and tarmac under their feet radiated with all the heat of the day, so Jennifer and Ben hurried toward the beach's temperate relief. They walked along the water's edge to where the crowd thinned out, tossed their things in the sand, and made straight for the water.

Out beyond the breakers, the ocean belonged to them. They dove and frolicked like otters.

Jennifer called out, "We're Muskrat Suzie and Muskrat Sam."

Ben didn't respond.

She called again, "Did you know sea otters hold hands so they won't drift apart? Should we move closer to shore and catch the next big one in?"

He still didn't speak, and she glided closer to him.

His words held whispered alarm. "I...I...I've been stung. Something..."

Bluish masses floated nearby. "Jellyfish, we have to get outta here; c'mon, Ben!"

"Can't...paralyzed...help."

Jennifer waved her arms toward shore. It was useless. No one was nearby. They'd entered the water too far down the beach. Her lifeguard training from ages ago kicked in. She reached crosswise for Ben, grabbed his arm and gave it a quick pull so he faced away from her. Without letting go, she cupped his chin with her other hand to keep his head above water. Alternating arms, she slung one across his chest, clasped her hands together, and held tight. For someone her size to rescue a grown man would've been impossible if he'd panicked. He was lethargic but too large for her to handle. She swam on her side with Ben above her and scissor-kicked with all her might. Though submerged, a good hard thrust brought her to the surface for a breath when necessary. The same ocean that gave sustenance to the creatures that hurt Ben then helped him by way of lifts and forward thrusts.

"We're almost there," Jennifer said.

Ben's eyes rolled up in his head. His body was limp.

"Ben, say something."

No response. He didn't seem to be breathing. She'd never struggled so hard in her life, not even in childbirth. This rescue was well beyond her ability, but she couldn't give up. Her toes brushed the ocean floor—encouragement to keep going. She and Ben were still too far away for anyone to hear her shouts, and besides, exhaustion prevented them. She reached a depth shallow enough to push off the bottom and lunge forward. The second she could brace herself and Ben against the waves she started mouth-to-mouth resuscitation. Between breaths, she checked to see if he would start up on his own. Nothing happened.

She gripped him hard with one arm, waved the other, and screamed for help. People noticed. Someone ran for a lifeguard. She continued the resuscitation.

Two lifeguards rushed in, high-jumping through the water.

Jennifer fought to catch her breath. "Jellyfish," she told them.

They took Ben from her arms and started CPR. Though exhausted, she remained upright through terror-induced adrenalin.

One lifeguard shook Ben and yelled, "Hello sir, can you hear me?"

He pressed his fingers on both sides of Ben's neck. "No pulse."

They carried Ben to shore with Jennifer right behind.

"I'll start compressions. Travis, check his airway."

They pumped, and the lifeguard named Travis used a radio to call 911. He looked at the huge welts on Ben's legs.

"Looks like part of the tentacles of a jelly are still wrapped around his calf. He's been stung by a big one."

A crowd gathered, and someone approached. "Need help? I was an Army medic in Afghanistan."

"We might. Stick around."

Jennifer strained to hear the rescuer's words. She frowned toward the ocean's taunting roars and then turned her back to it. *Blink, Ben, move a finger, give some sign of life.*

On a count of three the lifeguards moved him twenty feet onto dry sand. Jennifer knelt beside him. Shouldn't he have come around by now? *Oh Ben, please don't die.* She tasted salty wetness on her lips. Her tears mingled with those from the sea. Poseidon flexes his muscles and then weeps. She loved the ocean too much to blame it for the deep misfortune.

Two EMT's zoomed up in a beach vehicle. They examined Ben while the lifeguards continued rescue breathing. Every few seconds someone glanced toward the parking lot for the ambulance.

"This man's had a severe sting with paralysis." an EMT said. He slid his hands into rubber gloves, removed tentacle fragments, rinsed Ben's leg with sea water, and poured vinegar on the stings.

Jennifer kneeled as close to Ben as she could without being in the way. She remained vigilant to the rescuers' every move. In her mind, a mere glance away invited disaster. The lifeguards sweated and strained with effort. They attached EKG pads to Ben's chest.

Where was the ambulance?

The compressions stopped, and paddles were applied. Everyone watched the monitor. It remained blank.

A lifeguard yelled, "I'm getting airway resistance."

"Stop for a second." An EMT felt each side of Ben's neck. "Nothing. Resume CPR. John, get two amps of epi. And oxygen, hurry."

One of them addressed Jennifer. "Does he have any

known allergies?"

"I don't know. He hasn't said. I haven't known him long."

She sped through her and Ben's conversations. *Idyllwild, hiking, his day pack...* "Bee stings, severe allergy!" It came out so loud everyone looked at her.

The senior EMT shouted over his shoulder, "Get the syringe and an ampule. Let's give him epi."

The younger EMT opened the glass ampule to draw the fluid into the syringe. His wet hands shook when he tried to insert the needle. He stuck himself. Pain made him drop the vial. It landed open end down in the sand. The life-saving fluid ran out.

"Get the other one, rookie, STAT."

"Sorry, sir. We used it this morning."

He looked at Jennifer. "Did you say severe allergy?"

The obvious struck her. "His pack, he must have something in it."

"Get it, quick."

Jennifer sprinted to where she remembered they'd left their things, but they weren't there. She ran across blankets and zigzagged around chairs while seconds passed like drum beats. She spied their stuff where they'd left it with carefree abandon a short time ago. In a real-life relay race, she grabbed the backpack and sped back to where Ben lay motionless.

The senior EMT searched the bag and found a zippered pouch with five vials of epinephrine and a syringe. He readied one and injected it into Ben's jugular. Nothing happened.

C'mon Ben, breathe. Jennifer wanted to release a primordial scream, like the woman in the Munch painting.

Assisted breathing and chest compressions continued. "How's the resistance?"

"Getting worse."

Jennifer threw her hands over her mouth to stifle a sob.

"He's having an anaphylactic reaction."

Someone covered her shoulders with a blanket. She wrapped it around herself and clung to it.

"Second vial, NOW."

It was injected. They pumped his chest. "Check for pulse."

Everyone was quiet.

"No pulse. Check the machine. He's in V-fib. I'll charge the paddles, keep going."

The barked orders, pauses, shuffling, the rescuers' heavy breath—all became white noise to Jennifer as she willed Ben to breathe.

"Everybody clear. Ma'am, you must not touch him now."

Jennifer let go of Ben's hand and scooted back. They rubbed gel-coated paddles together and placed them on Ben's chest.

"Set to one hundred. Clear?"

Ben's body jerked. They checked again. "No pulse, second shock."

Jennifer looked away. Ben's unnatural spasms were unbearable. She wanted to collapse beside him. For the world to lose this bright man was unbearable.

Injections, chest pumps, compressions, pulse checks, on and on it went. Preparations for a third shock began. Jennifer didn't look away fast enough. When Ben's body convulsed, she gasped and sobbed.

"We've got a pulse."

Another vial was injected, they waited and then checked.

Ben stirred and muttered, "What the hell…"

Jennifer's body stilled, and her heart raced.

He coughed, was turned on his side, vomited sea water, and passed out.

Chapter Thirty-Five

The ambulance's wail reached a crescendo and stopped. Its bright lights continued to flash as the driver pulled into the parking lot. Two female EMT's rushed over. They moved Ben onto a gurney, and then a crew of four hustled him away. Jennifer gathered her and Ben's things and climbed into the ambulance with him.

The medics inserted an IV. They carried out their tasks with a swiftness of economy. It helped quiet Jennifer's nerves. After the initial flurry of activity, the medics settled in to wait. In front, the driver's radio emitted scratchy directives. Sideways remarks often garner revealing information. Jennifer strained to hear the medic's muted conversation at the other end of the ambulance.

"It's July. ER's full of new interns," one of them said.

"Yep, start of a new training year, busy month for the coroner."

A grunt of agreement, "If you're gonna get sick, do it in June when the trainees have put in their year."

Jennifer couldn't resist piping up. "What are you talking about?"

The glances of the medics were synchronized, to her and then one another.

"Nothing," one of them said. They didn't speak again.

The siren wound down, and the ambulance stopped at the emergency entrance of Scripps Hospital. Inside, a doctor stopped to talk to Jennifer.

"Did you see the jellyfish?"

"Yes, they were large and boxy-like."

"Sounds like the Australian species. He's suffering from paralysis caused by jellyfish neurotoxin. He's lucky the paramedics recognized and treated both reactions."

He looked at his clipboard, and then to Ben. "This man's familiar. Ben Gillespie. He's been researching post-vaccine neuropathy."

Jennifer nodded.

"He presented his data at last year's meeting. Innovative man, let's get him cured. Nurse, call the pharmacy for two vials of anti-venom, STAT."

Judging by his age, the physician wasn't a student. "Are there doctors-in-training here?"

"There are, and I supervise them. Don't worry; we won't turn green interns loose on a case like this."

Ben became somewhat responsive, and Jennifer took his hand. An administrator asked him about next of kin. Unable to speak, Ben wrote his sister's name and number. She lived in New York. There was no one else.

"I'll call her right away," the administrator said.

Jennifer was still in her wet swimsuit. She shook from the cold. "Would you have something for me to change into?"

A nurse gave her a set of pink scrubs, baggy, soft, and warm. Perfect. She stayed at Ben's side and tried to keep up with all that went on in order to give his sister an accurate report. In ICU, they hooked Ben to tubes and a ventilator. An x-ray of his chest had the doctors worried about aspiration pneumonia. They gave him Cipro for it.

Jennifer called Allison. She wouldn't be able to help with medical issues, but she'd be a comfort.

"I'll be right over," she said.

Ben began to breathe without the aid of the ventilator. He coughed and removed the tube himself. "Jenny, a whole lot of thanks while I got through."

His words didn't quite make sense, but his ordeal wasn't over, and a lot of drugs were in his system.

Jennifer stepped out of the room. From the far end of the hallway, Allison approached in her long, determined stride with her heels tap-tapping on the polished linoleum. The two hugged, and Allison listened while Jennifer recounted the disaster and Ben's condition.

After the pertinent questions, Allison said, "You look like something the cat dragged in." From her, the comment held only concern.

"More like a primeval amphibian that crawled out of the ocean. I don't even have a comb."

"Go home. Shower, change, and eat. I'll stay with Ben."

"Thanks, but I can't."

"Go, Jenny. I'll be right here."

"I'll have to borrow your car."

Allison searched through her purse and handed a remote to Jennifer. "It's Matt's new Mercedes. If you wreck it, I'm dead."

"I won't wreck it. Thank you."

"You're welcome. Hurry up."

"Let me check on Ben first."

He'd thrown the covers aside, and a nurse stood beside him. "I only have partial feeling in my legs. Look at the blisters. They've enlarged, and they're spreading."

The nurse took a look. "I'll call your doctor." She left and reappeared soon afterward. "They've ordered neurology and dermatology consults."

Jennifer hurried home then returned to Ben's side. Allison left, with a promise to return soon. Jennifer settled into the bedside chair for the night. His sister Liz would arrive sometime tomorrow.

The next day, doctors came and went without a word.

"Why aren't they talking to you?" Jennifer asked Ben.

"This is a teaching hospital. They're specialists. Their findings are funneled through my primary doctor."

Another group of white-coats examined Ben. Jennifer had to press her lips together until the doctors left to resist asking them about Ben's condition. The nurse came in.

"What was their impression?" Ben asked her.

"Dr. Gillespie, you know it's against hospital protocol for me to read your chart to you."

"Please read it."

The nurse studied him and then picked up the chart, "says it's a drug-induced bullous dermatosis. I know what caused the blisters, jellyfish. I'll call your doctor about this note and then see if the nerve lab can get you in."

Within the hour, Ben's primary physician showed up. "Your blistering could become serious if it progresses. I'm stopping the Cipro, and I concur with the recommended immune-globulin."

The nurse stood beside him. "I've already called the pharmacy. They can't get any until tomorrow."

Ben was coherent enough to handle these issues, and Liz would arrive soon, yet he could suffer setbacks, or Liz's flight could be delayed. Jennifer insisted the doctor explain everything to her in simple language while she took notes.

"Ben has paralysis brought on by neurotoxin exposure from jellyfish tentacles. He also has Stevens-Johnson syndrome, which is blistering from a drug reaction."

Tests were run and a neurologist reviewed the results with Ben. "I recommend a second dose of antitoxin."

"Would you mind getting me copies of the findings and your notes?" Ben asked.

"Sorry, hospital policy. They can't be released while you're a patient."

When Ben and Jennifer were alone, he grumbled, "These people think they're holier than thou. My status as a physician and neuroscientist should entitle me to my records if not more respect. Who the hell do these bastards they think they are. Can you get your laptop so I can do some research? These blisters itch like sons-of-bitches."

She'd never seen Ben like this and didn't want to leave him in such a state. An internal medicine resident arrived, read the chart, shared the findings with Ben, and attempted to calm him. Ben persuaded the resident to read the note verbatim.

Afterward, Ben asked, "What do you plan to do?"

"I'll call my supervisor and read it to her."

The intern came back ten minutes later. "She wants me to give the second dose of antitoxin."

"Tell your supervisor no dice. I refuse. I'm improving, and I have enough trouble with these blisters that still haven't been nailed down. I will not be burdened with reactions from additional anti-toxin. Tell her thanks for nothing."

Who was this person in Ben's body? He was bullying this poor resident, someone barely more than a medical student. His voice had become loud and his hostility more obvious. Jennifer feared the need for different intervention, a shot of Valium or something more powerful. If they gave him sedatives and he reacted adversely to them, things could go wrong in a hurry. Without them she feared he might tear out his IV's and bolt.

"Ben, honey, they're trying their best. Why don't I put off going for the computer and read to you instead? I have Grisham's latest right here."

An hour later, Ben's primary physician popped in. He smiled and straightened his polka-dot bow-tie. "I hear you're doing fine, Ben. How'd your lab visit go? I see they recommend more anti-toxin, I would have done the same."

What was he, fresh from the golf course? The man was clueless.

Ben shot back his response. "Not so fast, Doc. Read my chart and then read my lips. No more anti-toxins. I don't need the complications. No more nerve testing, either. They can find someone else to torture. I'm going home tomorrow with or without a discharge order. Nice tie, by the way."

Jennifer hated seeing Ben like this. She escaped to the cafeteria for hot tea. When she returned, he'd calmed down.

"My sister called. Her plane just landed. She's coming straight here. She'll be able to help filter some of this crap."

Thank God.

Ben moved the covers aside. "Join me."

Jennifer didn't want to. The antiseptic smell and compendium of clinical sounds were hardly mood-enhancing.

"Your legs, I might hurt them."

He patted the mattress. "We'll be careful."

"I might break your blisters. Besides, what if someone comes in?"

"So what?" He smiled for the first time since before the disaster and then struggled to lower the bed rail.

"Ben, don't. You're about to get your hand caught."

She took over for him. Having no choice, she eased herself onto his bed with her legs draped over the side. Ben wrapped his arms around her and pressed his upper body against hers. She waited the shortest time possible within reason and then escaped from his needy clutches with a restroom excuse. When she returned, he was asleep.

She studied his beautiful, injured form. Emptiness swallowed her up. She had affection for him, but her desire had disappeared. No, worse than that. When he'd encouraged her to join him in bed, she'd felt aversion. Her mind screamed out the unfairness of her emotion. *He's bedridden for god sake, vulnerable and in pain. Of course he's not exuding sexiness. What the hell's wrong with me?* Her internal protests changed nothing. Heavy-hearted, she tucked the sheet around him, straightened and smoothed the blanket, and wished she could do more.

There was a soft knock, and a woman appeared in the doorway. "Hello?"

Jennifer gave a small smile. Liz and Ben were almost duplicates, tall and distinguished-looking, but instead of Ben's casual manner, Liz appeared starched, even after her long flight. She nodded to Jennifer and then gazed at her brother's sleeping form. Her expression warmed. She bent over and looked at Ben, read the clipboard, frowned, and gestured to Jennifer toward the door. They walked out and eased it closed.

"I'm Liz. You must be Jenny."

"Yes, I am. I'm so glad you're here."

Liz motioned toward the hall. "Shall we talk in the visitor's room?"

Jennifer recounted to Liz the accident and Ben's care. She made a point of sharing her concern over his temper. They exchanged phone numbers.

"Why don't you go home and rest? I'll stay here," Liz said.

"You must be tired, too. I'll come back this evening or sooner if you'd like."

"I'll be fine. Sleep in your bed tonight."

They stood. "Please let me know if there's anything you need," Jennifer said.

"I have a rental car with my suitcase and personal things."

"Will you call me with updates?"

"I will."

"Okay. I'll be back in the morning."

Liz leaned in and gave Jennifer a hug. "Thank you for everything you've done for Ben."

Liz had no idea. Everything she'd done to him, more like. "You're welcome. I'll just get my things."

They entered Ben's room where he struggled for a coherent conversation with his doctor, saying he'd been followed by government agents since his admittance to the hospital.

Jennifer stared. She turned to Liz and shook her head. Liz nodded and held up a hand. She stepped forward, all confidence.

"Ben's suffering from drug-induced psychosis, a reaction to the cortisone. My brother has never had delusions. He shouldn't stay on it. I'd appreciate you using an alternative therapy now."

She had the doctor's attention. "And you are?"

"I'm Doctor Elizabeth Gillespie, Chief of Medical Pharmacology at Sloan-Kettering. We see a dozen drug-related cases every week. We use IVIG and have better results both with safety and efficacy."

Jennifer smiled to herself. *Kudos to you Liz, give 'em hell.* With a plan to call her in an hour, Jennifer gathered her purse and sweater, slipped out, and went home.

Chapter Thirty-Six

The hospital's double doors opened with a mechanical whoosh. An attendant wheeled Ben out with Jennifer and Liz on either side. Once at his apartment, the women fluttered and fussed to make him comfortable. Jennifer did her best to meet his needs. He wanted certain books, so she picked them up from a bookstore and brought them by. When he felt up to it, the three of them went out for lunch. She kept in touch by phone. Days passed, and she waited for her passion toward Ben to return, but it had fled.

Jennifer once considered her little beach apartment sleek, but it no longer appeared so. She came to see the clutter-free white walls as stark. She had personal items in three locations; her Mustang house, Troy's ranch, and here. The nomadic life wasn't for her. It contrasted with her tidy nature and left her disconnected. She could pull her mom's house off the market and settle in there on her own. It'd been her original plan before either Troy or Ben had come along. She dismissed the plan as quickly as it formed. Her mom needed the money from the sale of the property. Jennifer could try to buy it, but since she'd met Troy her image of life in Las Casitas had always included him. She'd visualized him about the place, walking the unused acre while planning the layout of horse fencing, and bringing new life to the old barn. Living there without him no longer held appeal.

Jennifer refused to let Ben's ordeal revive her old jellyfish phobia. She changed into her swimsuit and grabbed a towel. She'd be most visible in front of the lifeguard tower, so it's where she entered the surf and forded the mild current until she reached the choppy calm beyond the breakers.

Alone save for a curious seagull, she let the sea rock her in their guarded reunion. Fellow creatures shared the water with her, but she ignored them and let them do the same. Children's squeals and deeper adult voices carried over the waves and reached her submerged ears in wavering echoes. She was at peace there. From time to time she drifted off course, and a dozen lazy back strokes realigned her with the lifeguard tower.

Her astrological element was water, emotional and intuitive. She'd grown up with her mother's belief in such notions, and she could never quite shake them. Troy was earth, strong and steady, grounded, of the land. Water and earth were compatible. She should have nurtured him, supplied him with life-giving sustenance rather than running off to let him face the summer's drought without her.

Ben was air. She'd never asked him his sign, but she knew. He was a rare winged creature too elusive for her with his almost indiscernible touch and the hint of scintillating breath on her bare breasts. She held herself partially to blame for his accident. Before she'd come along, he didn't go into the ocean, instead content to stroll its shoreline. He'd wanted to be with her and followed her into her watery realm. She'd led him to danger like a siren. He'd mentioned bee stings in an off-handed way, making little of it. She should've honed in on the subject, asked what he carried in his faded blue backpack. The signs were there, and she'd paid no attention.

Jennifer checked her position in the water, found all to be well, and returned to her thoughts. If she went back to the Lazy J Ranch, would she and Troy reunite or would she end up in Oklahoma City where she'd started? Trading California for a cowboy? She'd have to be crazy, or crazy in love with a man whose only connection to an ocean were waves of flaxen wheat and a prairie's endless sea of tall grass.

Something brushed her leg, and she bolted upright. A piece of kelp bobbed beside her, and she flung it away. She'd become chilly anyway and made her way to shore. At her apartment, she checked her phone messages and returned a call from Ben.

"I thought I'd come over," he said.

He deserved to know her mindset, but she'd been stalling. Who ends a relationship with another while they're in recovery from a near-fatality? Her mother's taunts of 'monster' rang in her mind.

"You're still healing. It's better to wait."

"I'm much better. My doctor gave me the green light to drive, no pun intended."

"Now isn't a good time."

"You've said that twice."

He was a smart man who'd chosen to ignore her clues.

The time had come. "Come on over."

Jennifer answered the door with red-rimmed eyes. Ben's hopeful smile dropped into a frown. "What's wrong?"

She shook her head.

"Jenny, what is it?"

He reached to hug her, but she stepped back and opened the door wider for him to come in.

"I've been doing a lot of thinking."

"This can't be good."

They sat on the couch in their old default positions—he at his end, she at hers.

Her words came softly, "I'm going back to Oklahoma. We both knew our time together would end."

Ben hung his head and let his shoulders sag. He wouldn't fight for her; it wasn't his way. "I can't change your mind, can I?"

"You're a wonderful man, but no."

"I'll miss you, Jenny."

"I'll miss you, too."

They dropped into silence. The sun, wind and clouds set shafts of light to dance across the walls in mockery of the moment's gravity.

Jennifer scooted closer to Ben. "There were obstacles to my staying here, yet a magnet-like power drew me."

Ben gave a sad smile.

"That must sound ridiculous to you, a scientist."

"No, it doesn't. I'm glad you came."

He rose with deliberation and looked around, went into the bathroom and came out with his swim trunks. "All I have to show for our time together is wear and tear on these."

She laid her hand above her heart. "What I have is in here. You made my spirit soar. I've never felt as free as I have with you, and I never will again."

The corners of his mouth turned up, and his eyes warmed. "When will you leave?"

A plan materialized at that moment. "I'll pack tomorrow. If there's anything you want, a memento…?"

She scanned the room. There must be something to give him. She went into the kitchen and came back with the bamboo-handled corkscrew her father brought back from Singapore years ago on a tour of duty.

She held it out to him. "You and I used this more over the summer than in the past forty years put together."

He reached over and touched the sharp end, then frowned. "So I'm screwed?"

She let her arm drop. "It's emblematic of the wine we've shared and, you know, everything that followed."

"It's a family heirloom. You should keep it."

Finding a suitable keepsake for Ben seemed of dire importance. Time casts fleeting romances like theirs into the surreal. It reduces them to trinkets in the back of desk drawers. A hand might graze one or an eye glimpse another during a rifle for something more pertinent like a letter opener or reading glasses. Those tidbits of past lives are laden with memory denser than a flash drive at capacity. At the end of the day, they have a purpose. Still, Jennifer wanted something more substantial to give Ben.

"How about the little sauce pan we used so much? I bought it new, and we're the only ones who've used it. Will you take it?"

Ben shrugged. She went to get it, came back and handed it to him; handle extended. At the precise moment he took it, Jennifer's mind formed a picture of a little girl with dark eyes and hair like his. The pensive child sat at a kitchen table while Ben prepared something in the pan. He was almost out of time, but Jennifer hoped his future held a loving wife and child.

"Goodbye, Jenny. I never thanked you for saving my life."

They embraced and shared a lingering kiss, the last petal to fall from a faded summer rose.

"Goodbye, Ben."

He stepped out the door and walked through the parking lot. His arms hung at his sides with a cooking pan in one hand and swim trunks in the other. The picture was all wrong. She wanted to hold fast to her images of him, but not that one. He turned and looked back to where she stood in the doorway. A harsh sun beat down on the empty asphalt. It cast an over-exposed glare on him as if he'd been abandoned in a black-sand desert. He ducked into his car, backed out, and disappeared.

Swallows flocked to Mission San Juan Capistrano each March and took wing in October. Ben and Jennifer's sultry, salty affair ended, though, unlike the swallows, there would be no return.

Chapter Thirty-Seven

Loud knocks startled Jennifer from a nap. She jumped up, hurried around the bed, and slammed her shin on the metal frame. In searing pain and sheepish from being caught in a midday nap, she bent down and rubbed her leg while opening the front door.

There stood Troy with his feet planted and his beefy arms crossed like a commando ready for a siege. Weeks, months, a lifetime had passed since they'd been in touch. She'd grown unaccustomed to all that solid muscle mass.

"Troy! What are you doing here? What's wrong?" Her thoughts reeled. The apartments had caught fire; someone had been injured because of an oversight on her part.

He wore no smile. "We need to talk."

Reality is a sobering wake-up call. He knew about Ben. She stepped aside. "Come in."

His eyes darted around and paused on the gnarled wood, a remnant of a happy time they'd shared.

She motioned him toward the living room. "Have a seat. Would you like something to drink?"

"No thanks." He crouched on the edge of the couch as if ready to spring.

Jennifer lowered herself onto the other end. Small talk was pointless. "I need to tell you; I've been seeing someone."

"No shit. Even a dumb Okie like me figured it out, but I wanted you to look me in the eye when you said it."

He glanced toward the kitchen and then to the bedroom's open door. "Is he here?"

Jennifer was still in shock over his presence. "No. It's over. I told him I was going back to Oklahoma."

"How could you do that to me? We were engaged, for god's sake."

He rose, turned away, and pressed both of his hands on the door frame as if to restrain them from harming her. Taut muscles quivered along his strong back. Pulsating veins stood out on his neck, the skin red with rage.

She'd seen him furious once before when a ranch hand saddled the horses at night and let a bunch of drunks ride. "Fire him," Troy had bellowed at his foreman, despite the man having been with them for ten years. Would he fire her now, too?

The room was too small for defensive anger, so Jennifer forced her voice into one of calm. "You and I broke up. You were the one who ended it."

"I may have left things vague, but I never thought you'd turn around and screw someone else."

Jennifer got up and stood at the kitchen table. "It wasn't like that. He was a friend, and things got out of hand."

Troy remained with his back to the room, arms extended and hands pressed on the sides of the door. Jennifer hoped the frame wasn't of flimsy construction.

"How long's it been goin' on?"

"Sometime after that conversation you and I had."

Troy's head dropped even lower. He sniffed and

wiped his eyes.

Jennifer wondered if she should offer him a tissue but instead she didn't speak or move.

He turned to her. "Do you love him?"

"I ended it. I want to be with you."

"That's not what I asked."

"I cared for him, but I knew it wouldn't last."

"And you never thought about us?"

Jennifer pushed at her cuticles and tucked her hair behind her ear. "I did, but it's like I stepped outside myself. Everything became compartmentalized. It was impulsive. I'm really…"

"Who the hell is he?"

"His name is Ben. He's a biomedical researcher. I met him at a dinner party with Allison."

"I didn't know you were making the social scene."

"Alli's so busy it was the only way I could see her. It was just that once. Besides, what's wrong with going to a dinner party?"

"Seems seeing your sister wasn't your only reason to go."

Hurt was the basis of his insinuation, and she ignored it. "I hope you won't hold anything against Alli. It was all my doing. To say I'm sorry doesn't come close to being enough, but I am, with all my heart."

Troy opened the patio door and stood there a moment. He ran his hands through his hair and then sat on the couch, elbows on his knees and hands slack. The ocean breeze from the open door would reach him there. Jennifer hoped it would soothe his injured pride with a caress to his cheek, an action she wished she could perform. Maybe the sea air's salty breath would convey the spell it had held over her.

Troy sat up. "We need to figure this thing out, and the ranch is the place to do it. I make no promises about the way things'll go between us, but I'm asking you this one time to return with me. I'm staying in a hotel near the airport 'til tomorrow morning. Decide if you want to come back and let me know."

He'd had the luxury of time and the advantage of surprise while she'd been caught unprepared. Her thoughts raced to catch up. Did hopefulness hover there in his eyes?

She shook her head. "I don't need time to decide. I want to go with you."

He spoke in a softer voice. "Take the time. You need to be sure."

He pulled an airline ticket from his back pocket and set on the trunk. "You and I are booked on a ten o'clock flight. Do you remember JaRay, who works for the company?"

Oh her. "Yes."

"My plan is to have her drive your Jeep back and haul a trailer with your things."

Information overload. Like a built-in safety mechanism, her mind filled with insignificant thoughts. *Library books, I have to remember to return them.* Jennifer hadn't yet formed a coherent response when Troy rose.

"I'll call you later."

In the early evening, she called him. "I'm going back with you."

"Nice to hear."

She wanted more from him, some small hint of his feelings. "I hope we can get through this."

"You're coming back's a good start, but remember, I promise nothing."

"I'll do whatever it takes. There is one small issue. I don't want JaRay handling my things."

"She's trustworthy and can manage the move."

"Is she in town?"

"No, she's waiting on my call."

"I'd rather drive back and pull a trailer myself. You could go with me, and we'll use the time to talk."

"I'm not interested in driving, and I don't want you to either. A lot can go wrong with a trailer hitched up. JaRay's been hauling heavy farm equipment and what not since her teens. She's more than capable."

"I'm capable, too."

Troy released an obvious sigh. "Look, can you do it my way for once?"

"Okay, I'll see you at the airport tomorrow."

"You need a ride?"

"No, I'll get one."

Their conversation ended. Though still stunned, Jennifer got busy. She knocked on the apartment manager's door and found her home.

"I'm leaving tomorrow."

"You mean ending your stay? You've paid through August. Is there a problem?"

"No, the apartment's been great. In the next few days someone named JaRay will clear out my stuff and take my Jeep. Mail my deposit to the address you have on file. Do you mind if I leave my car keys with you until JaRay picks them up?"

Robin panned the parking lot over Jennifer's shoulder as if the answer to this turn of events waited there. "That'll be fine."

"Thanks, I'll drop them off tomorrow morning."

"You're welcome. Will you be back next summer?"

"No, I don't think so."

Jennifer arranged for a cab ride to the airport and phoned her mom to say goodbye. The next call was to Allison. It wouldn't be as easy.

"What's going on?" Alli whined in response to the news.

"It's time to go home; that's all."

"You aren't due to leave yet."

"My plans have changed. I hope you don't mind, but I don't want to talk about it right now."

"So when are you leaving?"

"Tomorrow morning."

Allison's voice held concern. For all her faults, she had a big heart. "I'll come up tonight."

Jennifer needed serious alone time, so she told an almost-truth. "I'd love to see you, but I have so much to pack and everything. There wouldn't be time to visit."

Allison's pitch reached the squeaky level. "Are you sure?"

"Yes, but thanks."

"Okay, I'll be there tomorrow to see you off."

"I called a cab for a ride to the airport." Damn. Jennifer wanted to bite back her words. They would stimulate a new barrage of questions.

"The airport? You're driving, aren't you?"

"No. An employee of Troy's will drive my Jeep, and I'll fly."

With the phone at her ear, Jennifer ruffled through kitchen cabinets for items she might need. She set an unopened box of her favorite tea on the counter. Stress lay in her near future; it was a given. She'd need the tea's calming properties, and Cimarron's grocery stores didn't carry her brand.

"This is so sudden. Are you sure everything's okay?" Allison asked.

Jennifer's eyes filled with tears. There'd been dozens of times her emotions could've spilled over and didn't. Why now? "I'm fine, sweet little sister."

"Can I at least drive you to the airport?"

"That'd be great. I'll cancel my cab and fill you in on what's going on then. Do you want my bromeliad and an African violet that refuses to bloom?"

"No thanks. You know me, minimalist to a fault."

Jennifer carried the plants to Robin's apartment and left them on the stoop. She composed a list for JaRay of the household items she wanted to keep, and a specific charity for the rest.

The next day, Allison arrived late as was her tendency. Jennifer had allowed for it by giving her an extra early time to be there. A last-minute arrival at the airport would give Troy the message she couldn't decide whether to come or not, and she'd never been more certain.

Jennifer hefted her suitcase into Allison's trunk, and they pulled out of the complex. From the hilltop, she gave the sparkling ocean a long look. Late July meant plenty of warm weather ahead. Over time, chill and damp would change the beach from summer's brilliant blues and whites to various shades of gray. The western horizon would become a pale thread between sea and sky. On shore, crashing waves and cawing gulls would be alone, the party's last revelers beckoning in vain to fair-weather friends. Jennifer said a silent goodbye to the continent's edge. She'd be back, but her stays on the coast would never hold that summer's magic.

Chapter Thirty-Eight

Jennifer neared the boarding gate and slowed her pace. Across the crowded corridor, Troy checked his phone and glanced up without seeing her. The intensity of her attraction for him reached the level it had been close to a year ago when she'd first laid eyes on him. His jacket and hat lay on the seat beside him, to save her a place no doubt. The western jeans and boots he wore with ease were out of place here. He was of the heartland, a rancher born and bred. The prairie's red dirt ran through his veins. He could no more live in Southern California than delicate coastal flora could weather harsh plains.

She drew near, and Troy gave a nod. She wanted to throw her arms around him and kiss him but settled for a restrained smile and hello. They exchanged few words while waiting for their flight, as if an invisible barrier stood between them, impenetrable like Plexiglas. Jennifer hadn't expected flowers or declarations of love, but neither did she envision so cold a reception. Tears rolled down her cheeks. She fumbled through her purse for her movie star sunglasses and disappeared behind them.

With the plane underway, she turned to Troy and spoke in a low voice so no one else could hear. "I don't know how to say this so you realize I mean it. I regret everything that's happened. I blew it, and I'm sorry, so very, very sorry. I hope you can move past this and find a way back to me."

Troy's jaw tightened and he remained looking straight ahead. Long after she expected him to respond, he said, "I'll give it a try, but I'm not sure I can forgive you."

So there's a chance. She slipped her hand into his, finding familiar comfort there. Maybe he felt it too.

Amarillo met them with the bliss of an uncrowded airport. The city soon lay behind them, and an open highway stretched ahead like a sketch artist's graphite rendition. Next to Troy in the pickup, Jennifer set aside her angst for a time. She noticed her emotional transition, one region to another. She'd traveled full circle or at least three-quarters of one. It was nice to be back. Would Fuego be happy to see her or would he keep his distance to punish her for abandoning him?

A question rose from Jennifer's deep thoughts without small talk's gentle prelude. "Is Delia's daughter still caring for the baby?"

"You haven't asked in all this time. Do you think we'll just go back to business as usual?"

"Of course not."

It wasn't regret consuming her at that moment, but anger. *You asshole.* She stared out her side window. The two-hour drive to the ranch would be tortuous. Her next words were icy.

"I thought you wanted me to return. Was I wrong?"

"Like I said, I want this settled. The place to do it is the ranch. I'm torn between forgiveness and sending you on your way."

"I understand." She resigned herself to a silent trip.

"Misty gave up her rights to the child. Russell and

Brandy will raise her."

Jennifer snapped her head in his direction. A response from him was unexpected, doubly so it's content. "You're kidding?"

"No."

She let the news sink in. Troy turned up the air conditioner, and she spread her denim jacket over herself like a blanket.

"Is it too cold?" he asked.

"With this on I'm fine. So Russell's wife accepted her husband's and another woman's child. I'd never have imagined it."

"Not at first. She went ballistic, like he thought. Took the boy and stayed with her parents. Lotta tears and fightin' the way Russ tells it. Things settled down after a bit. Russ said he'd put the baby up for adoption, but Brandy took one look at the little thing and fell in love with it. Brandy's parents helped steer her toward her decision."

"Where do they live?"

"Right there in Albuquerque, 'cross town."

"Brandy has more character than I've given her credit for. She's about to have her hands full with a toddler and two babies."

"We've got the general contractor on board, so Russ will have more time to spend with his family. That's the idea, anyway. Plus, I've wanted to step outta the business."

Jennifer smiled. "I've heard that before."

"It's a process, but we're getting there."

"Congratulations are in order. You have another grandchild, and she's beautiful. I mean, you have had all along, but it's more official now."

Troy nodded.

"What's become of Misty?"

"We're doing what we can to help her. Got her into an apartment in town. Russell's seeing to her rent and some other things for now. He set her up with a car. She's workin' at the bakery."

Jennifer slipped her sandals off and drew her legs up under her jacket. "That's great. Does she still have her dreadlocks?"

"Her what?"

"Her hairstyle, is it the same?"

Troy shrugged. "I haven't seen her and wouldn't have noticed besides."

"Any talk of her seeing the baby?"

"Some, but she still thinks she'll head west, so who knows."

Jennifer thought she'd drop by and visit Misty soon.

Once at the ranch, Troy carried her suitcase into the guest bedroom and set it squarely on the floor. He mumbled something about business to tend, and disappeared into his office. Delia welcomed her back, but with bad news.

"*Lo siento señora, pero ha sido un mes desde que su gato estaba aqui.*" Under stress, Delia reverted to her native tongue. I'm sorry, she'd said, it's been a month since your cat has been here.

Jennifer sank onto the couch. She should've known. Fuego had fallen prey to a wild animal, a coyote most likely. It happened to domestic animals back in Mustang all the time. She'd left her beloved pet in dangerous surroundings. Would there be no end to the repercussions of her reckless summer? She'd wreaked havoc with the emotions of two good men, and held herself to blame for a serious accident, at least in part. She probably deserved to be back in Oklahoma City, alone and desperate like she'd been when Troy's call had filled her with hope.

To lose Troy would be devastating. She knew every line in his face, his every expression. She thought about how he never hesitated to lend a hand, his fair treatment of hired help, and his kindness to animals. It's the little things that endear. Jennifer loved the way he drank his morning coffee in the big blue mug his daughter once made for him; how he tucked his shirt in haphazardly, and carried so much in his pockets, they became threadbare. He kept a pair of rubber boots upended between his truck's cab and bed. Though he rarely used them, the look said 'working man.' The thought made her smile.

Troy carried a heavy burden because of her. Would the imagery of her summer dalliance be too much for him? She pictured him approaching her with sadness in his voice saying 'I tried, Jen, but it's not gonna work.'

Hours became days while she pressed upon him her regret. One such conversation took place after dinner on her third evening back.

"I can't imagine how you must be hurting. Would it help to talk about it?"

Troy opened the refrigerator for a beer. "I know you're trying to make amends, but things are too raw right now."

"What'll happen when JaRay gets here?"

"I don't know. Do you want to go back to Oklahoma City?"

Had she not made her desire abundantly clear? I

mean, she'd bombarded him with it. She stopped loading the dishwasher. "No, I don't want to go back to Oklahoma City. I want to stay here with you and make things right."

Troy shook his head. "It'll never be the same."

"It won't be the same, but it can be wonderful again."

He unscrewed the bottle cap and threw it in the trash. "Let's wait until the U-Haul gets here."

Mid-afternoon the next day, the dreaded arrival announced itself by way of chains slapping against the U-Haul's metal sides and a chassis'groan with every rut and bump in the dirt road. Jennifer watched from her bedroom window as the Jeep rolled to a stop with 'California' emblazoned in bright orange across the trailer's side like a taunt.

There'd been no progress with Troy. Jennifer didn't know if she'd be ushered to the rig and sent on her way, so she packed her things and then sat on the bed to wait out her destiny. With the door left open a crack, she stayed alert to the nuances beyond her room. JaRay entered the house, used the powder room, and got a drink from the kitchen faucet. One needed no intuition. JaRay's vibe announced her thoughts as if by bull horn—curiosity and the anticipation of meeting Jennifer there in the house. Jennifer stayed put. She owed the girl no appearance.

JaRay and Troy drove the rig to a large metal barn nearby. Jennifer went to another room for a better view. JaRay got out and opened the wide doors, and Troy pulled inside. A white truck arrived, and a ranch hand joined them. Thirty minutes passed. What are they doing in there, standing around visiting? Finally, the ranch hand left. Troy and JaRay emerged and walked toward the house. Jennifer studied the woman—dark-complexioned, long brown hair, early thirties, and five-foot-five with an athletic build. She appeared tomboyish with her determined stride in jeans and boots despite the heat. In place of a purse, she carried a daypack.

From this distance Jennifer couldn't make out JaRay's facial features, but noticed her jaunty step and swinging ponytail with her head tilted up at Troy. Anyone could see it. The girl was in love with him. It's natural to be flattered by a crush, but Jennifer knew Troy didn't care for JaRay in that way. He was principled and wouldn't be tempted by a younger employee in search of a father figure. She had to admit the girl performed well in whatever she did. Troy would reward her with professional appreciation and no more.

They entered the house and moved around the kitchen while Jennifer remained in self-imposed captivity. The events surrounding her return were personal. She didn't know how much JaRay knew and had no desire to meet her under the circumstances. Instead, she found a hard copy of *Mansfield Park* in the nightstand drawer and lay down to read. The pages wouldn't open wide enough, so she forced them a bit and heard the brittle spine crack as the book went slack in her hands. *Oops.* It brought to mind a diminutive lit professor she'd had in college who used to tear his nine-pound texts in half to lighten his load. Jennifer couldn't mutilate her books like that despite their weight as she lugged them across campus.

The volume lulled her to sleep. She woke to the sound of a soft knock on her door.

"Yes?"

Troy spoke through the pencil-thin opening. "I'm taking JaRay to Cimarron airport and returning the trailer. I'll be back soon."

So she wouldn't be issued to her Jeep and sent on her way, at least not yet. "Okay."

She waited until the road dust settled and then entered the barn through its side door. Her things were in careful stacks against the wall. The dresser and chest were in good condition; everything was in order. Even the chunk of driftwood was here. Jennifer remembered the journals she'd written and dug one out of a box. A random page stated: To own romantic love is like trying to own the sky or the sea, it cannot be done honestly. Another page read: I reject the concept that I must share myself with only one other. I know this to be false. I've shed a heavy shell and am in a new body, one of lightness and simplicity.

At best, these words were fanciful whimsy. At worst, they were scratching's of embarrassing immaturity and complete self-indulgence. She collected all six volumes and tossed them into an empty trash can, gleaning pleasure from the thud and metallic reverberations.

Chapter Thirty-Nine

A week passed with relations between Jennifer and Troy far from settled. Yet an unspoken truce came to exist under the flutter of a white flag.

Her phone rang one evening as they watched TV. "It's Alli. I won't disturb your show." She went into her bedroom and closed the door.

Allison began in a rush. "I saw Ben today. He's so hurt."

The statement annoyed Jennifer. Ben wasn't the only one hurting. "Don't you think I know it? It's on my mind a lot. How's his recovery from the accident?"

"Fine, you can't even tell he'd had one."

"Good. Maybe he'll get over his heartache soon too."

"I told him you were going through a mid-life crisis."

Jennifer closed her eyes and took a slow deep breath. Allison's tidy summation didn't convey an episode significant to three lives.

"It's more complicated than that. Letting go of Mom's house was like cutting all ties with the past. It wasn't that way for you because your attachments are different than mine. After we listed the house I wanted a break from everything. My friendship with Ben went too far. If I'd loosened up earlier in life and not been so uptight, maybe it wouldn't have happened."

"What do you mean?"

"If I'd taken myself less seriously I wouldn't have swung so far the other way and bailed out on Troy, who means everything to me. It's just a theory I made up, or heard somewhere, but it makes sense."

"Aren't you being kind of hard on yourself? You're only human."

The usual three-beep sequence of Allison's car door began. She'd arrived somewhere, and the conversation would come to an abrupt end. Jennifer spoke in double-time. "Promise me you won't try to fix Ben up on dates. He can get them himself. He likes being in your circle of friends but hates when you guys pester him about his love life."

"I gotta go."

"Listen. Promise me you'll be his friend but not hound him about dates, and keep your girlfriends from doing it, too."

"Fine, I promise."

Either Allison had picked up on Jennifer's earnestness or she wanted to get off the phone. Either way, she was influential in her crowd and would keep her word. Ben could socialize without the badgering; a small thing Jennifer could do for him.

The call ended, and she remained cross-legged on top of the bed. Her time with Ben had been an affair of the heart, an unforgettable adventure. Years from now when she was very old, she hoped its residual pain wouldn't prevent her from pulling the memory out of a pocket of her house dress, along with a rumpled tissue, to elicit a sparkle in her eye and a secret grin.

She stared out the bedroom window at her reflection and the darkness beyond. The romance with

Ben happened. She didn't regret it. To say she did was denial, lying to herself and Troy. Did he disregard her entreaties because they rang false? Her thoughts continued to churn. Troy caused himself pain because of his unspoken expectations. They weren't hers.

She strode out to where he sat. "We need to talk."

He aimed the remote and turned off the television. Without its bright flicker, the room dimmed and stilled.

He crossed his legs and tapped the arm of the chair with his thumb. "I'm listening."

"I've been thinking. Until now I've shouldered full responsibility for the summer, but the problem is ours to share, not mine alone."

"How do you figure? I didn't leave you to go off and have a fling."

"We left things open-ended. I'll take fifty percent of the blame, maybe more, but we're both adults, and it's a shared mishap."

Troy didn't look happy. "I don't appreciate your standing over me. Sit down, will you?"

She walked around the coffee table and teetered on the edge of the couch.

He continued. "I hear what you're saying, but I don't agree. Even if we'd parted ways, I wouldn't have turned to another woman so soon. How you could've done what you did, and so easily, baffles me."

"You don't know if it was easy or not. In fact, it was hard, but it happened, and we have to move on."

Troy reached for the lever on his chair. She knew about its loud ratchet but jumped at the sound anyway.

His frown deepened. "We don't have to do anything. I'm not ready to move on. If you don't like it get in your Jeep and go back to Oklahoma City or wherever the hell you want."

Jennifer stood, and the Afghan slid to the floor. "There's something called taking responsibility and the rescue of a relationship that's worth saving."

Troy's scowl deepened. "Who said it's worth saving? A salvage operation is more like it. What'd your sister say to you to get you all riled up?"

"Nothing relevant to our issue, I see things more clearly is all."

"You get a call from her, disappear into the bedroom, and come out spitting nails 'bout this being my fault."

"I didn't say it was your fault. Try shared responsibility."

"Shared responsibility? That's one hell of a spin you're putting on it. You're dreaming if you think I'll admit to any wrong doing in this soap opera. Delusional, they call it. You broke things off between us and then turned around and slept with someone else."

She jabbed an angry finger at him where he sat in his chair. "You're so full of yourself. Your mind's made up, so why bother it with facts? I said I was confused and needed time off. You lost your temper, said 'take it', and hung up. You dumped me. What I did after that was none of your damn business."

He was on his feet now, shaking his head and wagging his finger side to side. "Not so fast. You called me intent on breaking up."

"You know it all, don't you? So now you're a mind reader?"

"It was obvious. Let's say for a minute I left it hanging. In that case, we'd have patched things up rather than you running to the arms of another man."

Jennifer's tone mocked. "I didn't run to the arms of anyone."

"Seems that's just what you did, planned it all out before you called me."

"You don't know how I felt. You can't read my thoughts. I was confused and did the honorable thing. I said I needed a break from the relationship."

"Honorable, huh? That's not what comes to mind when I think of you."

"Meaning what?"

He started to walk away. "Nothing, forget it."

Jennifer stopped him with her words. "No, now's not the time to turn retiring wallflower on me. I want to know what you meant."

"What if I hadn't figured out what you were up to out there? I'd sure be playing the fool, wouldn't I?"

"I was about to call and tell you when you showed up at my door. You may recall I told you what I'd done at that time. This is all about your wounded pride rather than our relationship, isn't it?"

"It's about your cheating and sneaking around, ya two-timing little hussy." He kicked the ottoman and sent it tumbling on his way to the window where he stared out.

The gloves were off. "How dare you! I did neither of those things, and I'm not a hussy. I suppose you've always wanted to control your women, or they're hussies, is that it?"

Troy moved his hands through the air in a gesture of waving her off. "We're getting nowhere. It's a waste of time to fight with you. My throat's parched."

He went to the kitchen and used the tap for a drink

of water. She picked up the afghan, sat down, and stared at the blank TV screen. Troy returned and did the same. They remained silent for a while.

Jennifer folded her hands on her lap. "If we could quit this he said she said crap the wounds would heal. There are better memories waiting."

"Look, I consider myself a man of action and resolve, but you've got me on the ropes with all this, bruised good and bleeding some too. I'm hunkered down with a wounded heart. I know you're waiting for word from me on our life together. I'm hopeful, but I'm not gonna rush something that'll determine our future."

"Do you still love me?" She hadn't planned on asking, but there the question hung, exposed.

He looked at her for a long time. "You think I'd hurt this much if I didn't? You might say I love the woman but hate the goings on."

"It sounds like your ox is gored and I'm to blame. It's a game I no longer play. Things happen. People live, laugh, love, and then die, so we have to move on."

Once again, silence engulfed them before Troy broke it. "You asked if I love you. When you're near, I feel a stirring. I love your tussled hair with the untamed curls you complain about, and how you look in that silly apron while you're stirring up something nice for me. I love your easy affection. I can't give all that up and not be the biggest dope of all."

She gave a small smile. "So can we start over?"

"The problem is, sometimes bitterness and anger well up inside me. You betrayed me, Jen. No matter how you spin your little tale, my bullshit alarms have gone off big time, and they're about to deafen me. You can't piss in my beer, and then come back expecting me to welcome you with open arms. What's worse, I was foolish enough to finance your affair."

She fidgeted. "You're not foolish. I…"

He held up his hand. "Let me finish. The other night my outrage was unbearable. I jumped into my truck and hauled ass down the road like I was trying to outrun it. Driving around for an hour didn't end my fury, and I was all set to come home and tell you it was over. Then I found you waiting in a deck chair, arms around your knees hugging yourself. You looked so miserable I didn't have the heart to do it."

Jennifer waited to make sure he'd finished. "I'm well aware of your moods. You've got a short fuse that gets lit pretty easily. When you're like that, I can't speak to you about forgiveness. Things will cool off, and then we can try again."

"Seems there's not much more to say or do. There's a lot to ponder. I left the phone conversation hanging; I'll give you that. It was hang up or say some things I'd regret. I never should've gone weeks without calling. That trip was ominous from the start. I tried to insist on a shorter stay, but you wouldn't have it."

He picked up the remote, aimed and pressed the on button. The racket and toxic glow from the idiot box again dominated the room.

****

Jennifer sensed she was home alone one night. It caused fitful sleep. Earlier that evening Troy headed out the door saying something about Gus. It was well after midnight when the sound of the truck's engine caused a deep rumble through the house. The front door opened and closed, and then Troy's keys clanged onto the entry table. In the kitchen, cabinet doors banged, and the refrigerator whooshed open. Wide awake, Jennifer tossed her covers aside and walked into the kitchen where Troy rooted through a deep drawer full of cookware.

She tried for a soft tone, "Late night?"

He looked up, startled despite her attempt. "I can't find the omelet pan."

He didn't tend to go drinking, yet she suspected he'd done so. "It's in the dishwasher. I'll make you some eggs if you'd like."

"Yeah, sure."

He removed his hat and hung it on the corner of a chair, and then sat at the table with a heavy thud, letting his arms and legs sprawl. Jennifer set to work. She stood at the stove barefoot and in a thin cotton nightgown. The night was warm, and she hadn't bothered with her cardigan. Later she'd realize there'd been a different motive for appearing that way in the kitchen.

While she stirred the eggs, Troy came up behind her, put his arms around her waist, and pressed himself against her. His boozy breath on her neck confirmed the drinking. Be it right or wrong, his touch felt good. She tried to concentrate on the eggs, but a snicker and a squirm got away from her. He reached for the burner's knob, shut it off, and then turned her at the waist to face him. He took the spatula from her, set it down, and positioned her arms around his neck. Their kiss was hard and hungry.

Things happened without pause after that. He ran his hands over her body. She raised one of her legs and wrapped it around his upper thigh. They inhaled each other's essential scents. He scooted her over to the kitchen table. She fumbled with his belt, got his zipper down, and discovered him ready for her despite the influence of liquor. The moment was an urge for sex, nothing more. She didn't care because she wanted it, too.

He turned her around and lifted her nightgown. "Bend over for me."

She did as he asked. He fumbled with his pants and spread her legs with his own while feeling for her wetness. There were a few awkward attempts and some help from Jennifer before he entered her. Her body jostled to his uneven thrusts. It was all she could do to keep herself in position, elbows locked on the table top and hands gripping its edges. She'd derive no satisfaction from this base ritual. This was for Troy, who in the past had done the same—sacrificed his pleasure for hers. He released a series of loud moans and the jarring of her body increased. She didn't know how long she could remain like this. A few more heaves and Troy finished.

He withdrew and zipped up. Jennifer lowered her gown, stepped into the powder room, and then returned to the stove. She finished cooking and set two eggs and some toast in front of him, along with a jar of the apple butter he liked.

He stared at his plate before reaching for the salt and pepper with a quick glimpse toward her. "Looks good, thanks."

She washed the pan and then sat across from him and grinned. "That was riveting."

He remained silent and intent on his food.

"I think I'll go back to bed." She waited, but he didn't respond. Her voice took on a lilt. "Care to join me when you're finished eating?"

"It's not a good idea."

She'd been dismissed. Her disappointment wasn't crushing because she hadn't expected him to go along with it. "Okay, goodnight."

"'Night."

****

The next morning Jennifer approached the kitchen with her mind made up. Last night happened, so be it, but for a repeat performance, this holding pattern they were in would have to change. She was an early riser, but Troy always made it to the kitchen before her. He sat at the table with his blue mug and the newspaper.

"Good morning," she said.

"Mornin'."

Jennifer poured herself some coffee, leaned against the counter, and surveyed him.

He rose and stood beside her to refill his cup. "Did I hurt you last night?"

"I'm sore."

He dropped his head and shook it.

"I'll be okay. How about you, how do you feel?"

"Been better."

"Want some aspirin?"

"Already took some. I'm sorry about what happened between you and me. Lori's off visiting family this week, so Gus is a bachelor. He and I sat out on his porch with a bottle of Jack Daniels that got the best of us. I took the dirt roads home."

"It wasn't just you. I could've refused."

"Maybe so, but it won't happen again. Not like that, and not until things are resolved between us."

Jennifer shrugged, "So let's resolve them."

"It's not that simple. I don't like the cavalier way I treated you. I'm not that guy. You deserve better."

"There were two consulting adults present."

"Still, I'll have to give some serious thought to my motives."

Damn the man's self-righteous sensibilities. "Or to the motives of Jack Daniels. There's room in this life for spontaneity, you know."

"Not in important matters."

Jennifer walked out of the room. Time to dress and start another day.

Chapter Forty

The final week of August approached as if on the cautious pads of a cougar. Jennifer and Troy had met one year ago that month. She wanted to acknowledge the anniversary before it slipped away.

A rummage through kitchen drawers didn't produce what she sought. Most households had blank all-occasion cards tucked away somewhere. Sure enough, she found an unopened package of small ones in the dining room credenza. Though yellowed with age, one of them would do. As a leftie, Jennifer wrote upside-down with her wrist curled like a hook. It took effort not to smudge 'Happy Anniversary' written in an arch above the card's faded bouquet. Inside, she spoke her heart in the timeless ink and paper method.

Dear Troy,

How well I remember first hearing your voice on the phone, so deep and gentle. With it I anticipated our meeting. When the moment arrived, I fell in love with you, or at least in lust that turned into love.

Knowing you over the past year has been one of the most exciting experiences ever. I want to spend every day of our life together showing you how much I love you.

Yours,
Jennifer

It would've been fun to leave the card for Troy to

find on the kitchen counter beside homemade cupcakes with frosting and sprinkles. Yet the gesture would've been more for her pleasure than Troy's since he didn't like sweets. Her plan of a homespun gift didn't pan out, so she took the drive into town. She peered through the scratched and clouded glass of the watch repair shop's ancient display case. A money clip would do. Chester adjusted his loupes and turned on the engraving tool's tiny motor. Its low hum, like a dentist's drill, heightened her misgivings about the whole scheme. If her attempt at reconciliation didn't reach through Troy's tough façade, maybe nothing would. To block the incessant buzzing, Jennifer concentrated on the items in the case. There sat the amethyst ring she'd long admired. It appeared not to have been touched in its velvet box with the open lid.

Back at the house, Jennifer wrapped the money clip in brown butcher paper. She rooted through the tool shed and came up with two kinds of twine to use as ribbon. Dinner wound down, and Jennifer hid her uncertainty behind a brave smile. She reached over to the seat of the chair beside her, drew up the card and gift, and set them in front of Troy.

He wiped his hands on his napkin. "What's this all about?"

"This month is our anniversary. I didn't want it to pass unnoticed."

He opened the card and read it. To her relief, he smiled and stood it upright on the table. The package appeared tiny cradled in his large hands.

"Nice wrapping."

"Homespun," she said.

He pulled the twine's bows loose, opened the lid,

and lifted the money clip from the box. Lowering it to his lap, he read and re-read the inscriptions. One side had his name in bold script. On the other, fancy lettering spelled out 'Jennifer's Love.'

"Thank you, I can use this." He reached for his wallet, secured the bills to the clip, and then leaned back and slid it into the front pocket of his jeans.

"I'm glad you like it." She should've stopped there, but she was pumped up with happiness. "I'm thrilled you'll be carrying it around with you. We were supposed to have had our wedding by now."

She threw her hands over her mouth. "Oh, crap. I didn't mean to say that. It makes things worse. I meant I regret our plans falling through." That came out wrong too. She didn't go for a third try.

"Yeah, same here." Troy left with a tight close of the door behind him.

****

Jennifer had time on her hands and liked to cook. She took over for Delia, who'd grown elderly and was gracious about stepping down. She weaned Troy off red meat and replaced it with healthier fare. One small grocery store in Cimarron catered to its Hispanic population. The store carried everything needed for the Mexican food Troy loved. Jennifer resisted preparing meals with too much flourish. She may have wanted to win back Troy's heart, but she had her pride. Fancy cuisine would make her appear desperate, 'the way to a man's heart' and all that. To serve it would force a festive air unbefitting the household's pensive mood. She reasoned if she kept to the basics, south of the border dishes were commonplace and, therefore, acceptable. With that rationale, Jennifer indulged Troy with chili and cheese rellenos for weekend breakfasts and pulled pork enchiladas or string beef jalapeno tacos with shredded cabbage and maize for dinner.

Evenings found Troy in his easy chair reading ranching articles on a laptop. He watched the news or some other program on TV. Jennifer didn't care what was on; she just wanted to be near him. She'd lie on the couch with a book and a multicolored afghan thrown over her legs. The blanket's granny-square design had been crocheted by Troy's grandmother. Similar ones lay folded across the foot of each bed.

At the end of an evening, she'd rise from the couch, wish Troy a goodnight, and receive his clipped 'goodnight' in return. It was all very polite. Jennifer hated it. She'd fall asleep saddened that another twenty-four hours had passed without their unifying, yet grateful for the next day's opportunity to show him how much she cared.

Their existence was a slush of dichotomies; familiar but estranged, isolated together. The days pushed on. It took a single walk with Jango for him to expect them daily. At Jennifer's morning footfall, he'd be up and waiting at the back door. Not only did his tail wag, but his whole hind end swiveled in anticipation.

Unlike Jennifer's desperation last summer, she was unemotional about the fate of her apartments. When Stanhope Construction finished its work and moved on, she'd find new tenants, try to sell Alcove as a business, or auction the contents and list the building with a commercial real estate agent. Whatever Alcove's fate, it had ceased to be her orbit. Troy occupied that sphere.

Alcove Apartment's front doors needed fresh paint, and she wanted to choose a new color. The soffit's plywood bowed in places, and her eye for detail would come in handy for the repairs. The time had come to visit Evelyn, and to check on her Mustang house. There were her yearly vision and dental checkups, and her woman's exam as well. She decided to put it all off a little longer. Her relationship with Troy took precedence over everything else at the moment.

Even a homebody like Jennifer grew restless. She had to remind herself of her tenuous situation. A seed on the head of a dandelion or a single strand of a spider's web could hold up to blowing wind. Not so the bind between her and Troy. Surely a fresh start would soon come to be.

Jennifer imagined visits from friends and family. Troy would host a reunion for his children like the one last December. Evelyn might take time off work and drive out. Aaron would fly in; he sounded homesick when he called from San Diego despite relatives nearby on both sides of his family. An e-mail from Allison stated, 'I want to visit a real dude ranch. I'm an experienced rider, you know.'

Jennifer responded, 'I'll talk to Troy, but you realize in light of last summer it might be a delicate matter.'

Alli's response came fast and furious. 'I HAD NOTHING TO DO WITH YOU AND BEN.'

'I told Troy as much, but emotions are still raw around here. It's best to hold off for now.'

Jennifer kept in touch with her book club friends back in Mustang. An e-mail came from one of its members. 'We've settled on a name. We're now the Lit Chicks.' Jennifer laughed. The name was perfect. They loved their wine as much as their novels. The e-mail continued, 'four of us thought we'd take you up on your offer last spring and make the trek out there for a few days' restorative retreat.' A visit from the Lit Chicks meant the house would resonate with gossipy whispers and riotous feminine laughter. They'd flirt and fuss over Troy unless he eluded them. It pained Jennifer to have to hedge around the request.

She and Troy met in the kitchen each morning. They'd been lovers in the past, of course, but weren't now, and she was self-conscious appearing braless in the thin cotton camis she liked to sleep in. One day, in particular, was no different. She rose and grabbed her lightweight cardigan, secured it by a few well-placed buttons, and followed the scent of brewing coffee. The first few sips were best.

"Has anyone in your family mentioned visiting?" Jennifer asked.

"There's been talk of it."

"I've had several people say they'd like to come out. I don't know what to tell them."

"Tell 'em now isn't a good time and leave it at that."

Would there ever be a good time? Still in her pj's, Jennifer took her coffee and walked out to the barn. Her furniture stood under a large tarp, waiting to be allowed into the house. So many times she'd come out here and thought how pretty the dresser would look in the guest bedroom with an arrangement of dried flowers on top. She'd worked it all out in her mind. The steamer trunk could go at the foot of the bed, and her mother's pine table and chairs might fit below the window without too much crowding. A braided rug would finish the room's country look. She couldn't do much with the other two bedrooms. Their old-fashioned wagon wheel bunk beds with the western-themed spreads served well in accommodating small groups.

She sat on a box and watched dust motes float across the slant of sunlight from the barn's open doorway. I've had enough, she thought. No more mooning around like a lamb with separation anxiety. There'd been plenty of time for Troy to come around. To live this way didn't benefit either of them. She had to leave, and right away so she wouldn't talk herself out of it.

She raised her mug for the last sip of coffee but found it empty. Into the house and straight to her room she went, and then dressed without pause. Her movements were familiar—she pulled her suitcase from the closet and packed.

Troy stepped through the open doorway. "What're you doing?"

She zipped her suitcase and set it on the floor with a thud more vigorous than intended. "I can't stay here like this anymore. I'm going back to Mustang. At least I have a life there."

In and out of the adjacent bathroom she went with handfuls of toiletries to load into the large carry bag propped open on the bed.

"You're a bit impulsive, aren't you? I didn't ask you to leave."

Jennifer continued to pack. "If it takes impulsiveness for me to motivate myself, so be it."

He watched her. "What brought all this on?"

She slung her purse and bag over her shoulder, took hold of the suitcase's handle, and strode past him. "Call me if you thaw out."

An hour later she was well underway. Views from the western Oklahoma highways all looked alike, flat and with enough space to accommodate the whole world's homeless population. She headed east at a determined speed, pushing beyond her desire to whip a U-turn and head back. She would not be a spineless wimp.

Road weary at day's end, she pulled into the driveway of her Mustang house. It looked as though debris from the entire neighborhood had blown against her garage door. Shin-high grass stood in scraggly clumps. Ramiro should've addressed it. She'd have a talk with him tomorrow. The remote for the garage door lay in a kitchen drawer, so Jennifer parked and entered the house through the front. She stepped inside and felt like an intruder in her own home. She didn't belong there but rather in Cimarron building a life with Troy. How wrong it all seemed.

Dean and Jennifer worked well together when separated by vast distances. With her sudden appearance at the apartments the next day, he neither made eye contact nor smiled. He persisted in calling her ma'am despite requests to use her given name. His wariness suggested she'd shown up unannounced to catch him in the act of something, but, in fact, it pleased her to find everything in order. The tenants had grown used to Dean's low-key management style. They liked him and were eager to know whether Jennifer would take over.

"We'll see" was her best answer.

For the next week, Jennifer made appointments for medical checkups and had her Jeep serviced. She renewed her friendship with Evelyn. Good ol' Ev, who may have suspected Jennifer's trouble with Troy but accepted her presence without so much as a raised eyebrow.

Jennifer even braved a book club meeting. She kept her fingers crossed behind her back, so to speak, and talked about her need to be in the city for business. The Lit Chicks started in with a barrage of questions.

"How long will you be here?"

"What does Troy think of your leaving?"

"How are you two getting along?"

"So, have y'all set a date yet?"

Jennifer's finesse equaled that of a seasoned politician. She said plenty and revealed nothing. The Chicks' consensus was that Jennifer's return must be a welcome change from the boonies. Nothing was further from the truth.

She'd given Troy a courtesy call upon her arrival. Conversations followed that were sporadic and brief.

Hey, how ya doin', Jen?"

"Fine."

"What're you up to today?"

"Interviewing a painter for the apartments, and I'm running late."

"Okay, how 'bout if I call you tonight?"

"I'd rather you didn't. It's better that way. I need some distance to look at things logically and figure out what's best for me."

"You had a whole summer of that. It got us nowhere, and that's an understatement."

"Living with you outside of a relationship got us nowhere either. I'm late. Gotta go."

A flurry of busyness was her stance to everyone including Troy. One by one, she checked off the items on her To Do list. The time came when daily workouts and trips to the apartment complex to oversee minor construction didn't fill her days. She ached for Troy, doubly so for not being able to tell him so.

Evelyn had vacation time saved up from her job in media resources at Oklahoma City University. The two made plans to travel the Talimena Scenic Byway. They began the fifty miles of breathtaking views at Winding Stair Mountain in Eastern Oklahoma, and continued the drive into Arkansas. Historic towns dotted the curving road. There were two nights in quaint bed and breakfasts and side trips to study landmarks amid mild fall weather.

The adventure improved Jennifer's state of mind. She returned to Mustang with a fresh outlook. An opening arose with a personal trainer at the gym, and Jennifer took it. Her strength improved, and she found renewed confidence. Organic grocery stores sold luscious leafy green vegetables. She shopped there and made meals of salads with pumpkin seeds, cranberries, and blue cheese crumbles. A floral shop called 'Bloom Where You're Planted' in downtown Mustang posted a notice in the window that read 'Temporary Help Needed.' Years ago, Jennifer had worked briefly as a floral designer. She considered the shop's name to be a good omen and adopted it as her personal motto. Quirky, yes, but the concept motivated her to inquire about the position. The regular employee was on maternity leave. The owner, Mrs. Chang, agreed to give Jennifer a try. Jennifer rose each morning and looked forward to the new day.

Chapter Forty-One

Jennifer told Troy about her new job. "I guess this means you won't be returning anytime soon."

"Not unless things change between us."

"Might take time, that's how I reckon these things work."

"You've had more than enough time. I care about you, but I'm not going back to the way things were. It's crazy to live that way. I won't do it."

Troy couldn't have missed her sniffles. She tried to stifle them, but they carried through the phone. "Your calls upset me. For now, I want no more controversy in our conversations than the chance of rain in the forecast. Either that or none."

"Fine then."

"Okay, goodbye."

Jennifer hung up and kept her hand pressed on the phone as if to reinforce her words and keep another call from Troy at bay.

Her new regimen with the personal trainer gave her an energy boost. She liked her job. Not only did she design floral arrangements, but she took phone orders, made deliveries, picked up supplies, washed and gassed up the van, swept and cleaned the shop—whatever she saw that needed doing. Mrs. Chang appreciated Jennifer's efforts and rewarded her with leftover flowers at the end of each day. Jennifer's earnings became her spending loot, leaving more of the apartment income for her retirement account.

One particular call from Troy caught Jennifer in a talkative mood. "I'm trying to find a painter who won't have his teenager do the work. Either that or they want to bring in laborers and then barely show up again except to collect the pay. I shouldn't have to manage those guys."

"I understand, Jen. Finding good help is a common problem in every profession. By the way, do you imagine you'll return here when the apartment work's done?"

"I can't say. It's nice to be self-contained. I see why some people, like Evelyn, remain single. It avoids complications."

Her words had a mean edge and were insincere. It wasn't at all a lifestyle she'd choose. More than anything, she wanted to wrap her arms around Troy's firm torso, kiss the smile lines on his handsome face, have and hold him as her life partner. Was he seeing someone else? She didn't think so since he wanted her to move back. She'd stay put and take the chance of losing him. She thought of the saying by Kahlil Gibran:

"If you love somebody, let them go, for if they return, they were always yours. If they don't, they never were."

****

The girl on maternity leave from the flower shop had her baby and wanted to return to work. It seemed too soon so she must need the money, Jennifer thought. A new employee, sixteen years old and hired for deliveries, had so far shown up when expected and did his job without causing anxiety for Mrs. Chang. Three employees were too much overhead. Jennifer's time there drew to an end.

Her personal trainer got the position he'd interviewed for in one of Oklahoma City's large call centers. He gave notice to Jennifer and the rest of his clients. She'd absorbed the bulk of his knowledge regarding the best use of the gym's machines, and had been keen to bow out. Six weeks had passed since she'd left the ranch.

"Sounds like things are wrapping up there. Do you expect you'll be comin' back soon?" Troy asked.

"Coming back to what?"

"Well, you've got a lot of clothes and such here. I imagined you'd be returning at some point."

"Do you miss me?"

"Well, yeah. You're there, I'm here—it's a record we've played too many times."

"I miss you too, but I want things to be different between us. I need a reason to return."

"Nothing's gonna get resolved with you there. I'm askin' you to please c'mon back, baby."

That's all it took. His voice with its crack of emotion moved her. She mentally tallied the space inside each cooler stacked in the garage for its capacity to hold the perishables she wanted to bring back. Maybe she should've waited, held out for a more solid commitment from him, but she didn't. The year's theme seemed to be 'no impulse control whatsoever,' or maybe 'matters of the heart trump logic.' Either way, the next morning's first light saw her skedaddle out of Mustang. Her place lay with Troy in whatever scope his ability to love her allowed.

Jennifer's return to the ranch held little fanfare. She

had no illusions it would. Troy wasn't home when she arrived. Back into the guest bedroom went her things. She unpacked the groceries and had a dinner of Chicken Kiev and a bottle of chardonnay ready when he arrived.

Her presence elicited a rare smile from him. "Glad you're back."

"Yeah, me too."

****

North of the living and dining room windows lay rolling prairie and native trees; Ponderosa Pine, Redbud, Bur and Sawtooth Oak, and Pecan. The views were beautiful, but Jennifer spent her time on the redwood deck facing south off the kitchen—a large, unpretentious space. A balustrade ran its length, and a forsaken barbecue grill stood covered at one end. An abundance of patio furniture sat in disarray, a good place for a barefoot morning's measure of joe in a glazed ceramic mug.

At the entrance to Lazy J Road, three mailboxes shared a single post, and an obscure sign read 'Lazy J Road.' It's where Troy had waited in his truck as Jennifer drew near on her initial solo trip to see him. The turnoff would've been hard to find otherwise.

In speaking of the road, Troy explained, "The three of us neighbors went in on a tractor. The Whetsels use it to farm in exchange for grading and maintenance."

Jennifer asked about the three-sided shelter beside the mailboxes.

"My kids and I built it a long time ago to protect them from the elements when they waited for the school bus. I oughta tear it down."

He didn't tend to let such tasks go. The shelter's

planks had turned a weathered gray. It remained there out of nostalgia.

Troy's house had been built on a rise. From the deck, visitors in cars and trucks were mere puffs of dust as they started up the road. Sounds carried with ease. Vehicles reached the wide arc of the road's mid-way point with their engines droning like horse flies. As they drew near Jennifer could distinguish the blue of Delia's sedan and the red truck of Dan the Pool Man. Her heart quickened each time Troy's brown pickup came into view. The crunch of gravel replaced flying dust when the vehicles pulled into the driveway.

Sometimes Jennifer spotted roadrunners, so similar to their cartoon counterparts. Scissor-tailed flycatchers had a set of long graceful tail feathers. She heard the pleasant coo of wild turkeys, so unlike the raucous honks of geese that flew low toward nearby ponds. Small bats took wing and sliced through the dusk in pursuit of insects before the start of an owl's deep nighttime hoots. A bobcat's yellow eyes reflected in Jennifer's headlights one night as it ran in front of her car. She heard the howl of coyotes and watched one cross a field with a rabbit in its mouth, the likeliest fate of poor Fuego.

The prairie met the edge of the deck with no yard to serve as a buffer. Jennifer liked it that way. On the west side of the house, a thick row of junipers had been planted ages ago as a shelter belt to block strong spring winds and dust that churned up at planting time. Other than a grove of mature oaks off to the east, this side of the property remained the windswept expanse it had always been.

With the aid of a wheelbarrow and thick leather

gloves, Jennifer retrieved her gnarled driftwood from its storage place in the barn. She set it on the edge of the wide deck steps. In an instant, the weathered wood ceased to belong to the coast and transformed itself into a sun-bleached piece of the prairie. Her former beach combing expeditions became a search of the fields for interesting rocks to arrange on the steps, just so.

Troy joined her outside one day. He handed her half a geode the size of an abalone shell. "For your collection."

She cupped it in her hands. "It's lovely. The color reminds me of a ring I've had my eye on in Chester's shop."

She tucked the geode in among the other rocks as he watched. Its presence suggested their flinty outsides also beheld these lavender gems. It caught the sun's rays. Jennifer turned and looked up at Troy. Was that a trick of the light or a spark of love in his eyes?

Chapter Forty-Two

Early one morning after autumn's first heavy rain, Jennifer started down a footpath with Jango beside her. She retrieved her tent-like poncho from the Jeep because of the drizzle. She wanted to see the field flowers washed of dust, and spider webs with silver droplets more voluminous than a summer morning's dew.

A loamy scent permeated the warm mist. She passed a gully with its iron-rich soil washed away by the night's deluge. Stepping with care around a crevasse, she spied a rose rock camouflaged in the red earth. She bent over and examined it. What a great find! Rose rocks weren't valuable, but they were rare and uniquely Oklahoman. They weren't known to have formed in the panhandle, but rather in the central part of the state between Pauls Valley and Guthrie. Rock hounds and weekend adventurers went in search of them with buckets and shovels in tow.

Jennifer built a cairn of flat rocks and then hurried back to the shed for a trowel. She returned to the site and cleared the wet clay-like soil from around the rose rock. This was the first time she'd seen one in its natural state. Her eyes were first to befall something millions of years old. With the trowel, and bare fingers for the intricate parts, she persisted with the dig until she'd unearthed a cluster of several perfect specimens.

Her poncho was rain-slicked and splattered with mud. It clung like a second skin. She held the front of it bucket-style to carry the rocks. In her haste to dress that morning, she'd slipped into yesterday's shorts. Her legs were now bare to the elements. The poncho's loose-fitting hood had blown back. She didn't need a mirror to know humidity had turned her hair wild. She'd ruined her sneakers for anything but her daily tramps. No matter how many times Jango shook himself off, he couldn't keep the moisture from his coat.

Jennifer neared the house and saw Troy step onto the deck with his blue coffee mug in hand. He must've been watching for their tiny party. One look at the spectacle before him and his hearty laughter rang clear over the quiet prairie.

She yelled a greeting and crossed the sodden ground between them. "I found a rose rock colony down the trail."

Troy left the shelter of the house's eve to admire her treasure. "You've got some real nice ones there."

"I'm gonna display them on that big turquoise platter."

With some maneuvering of her makeshift bucket, she lined the rocks along the balustrade. Jango shook himself off again with clanking tags.

"You two need to come inside and dry off," Troy said.

"Would you mind getting that stack of old towels from the laundry?"

Troy left and came back with the towels. "I'll see to Jango. Why don't you get yourself out of this dampness?"

"I like it out here."

With her poncho draped over a patio chair, she stood on a towel in the kitchen, wiped herself off, and watched Jango enjoy his rub down.

Troy squatted and checked the dog's ears. "Looks like you've picked up a few ticks, old boy. Jen, you'll want to check yourself for them. I'll give you a hand in a minute."

Ticks were nothing new to Jennifer. She started to search, on the lookout for chiggers as well. They liked tight places, so she looked under her waistband and around her ankles beneath her socks.

With a pair of tweezers, Troy grasped the unwelcome hitchhikers burrowed in Jango's skin and examined each one afterward.

"Gotta make sure I pulled the whole thing out. Lemmie wash my hands, and I'll look you over."

Being second to a dog? No problem.

Troy examined her. He checked the back of her legs with gentle hands. Even this innocuous touch aroused her. It had been a long time since he'd done so. She didn't want him to stop.

"I believe you're tick free."

"That's good."

He stepped away, busy with towels and wiping the floor.

She threw open the back door. "Isn't the air fresh? It's like there's a communal sigh of relief from the parched earth and thirsty plants."

"Right, and it seems to be makin' a poet of you."

Jennifer was unfazed. "Finding rose rocks on a path I've walked dozens of times is exciting. I think I'll keep the location a secret from everyone but you."

Troy picked up a clean towel and began to dry her

hair. He smelled like wet dog and vanilla soap.

She panted with lolling tongue. "Woof. This feels good. Now I know why Jango smiled when you dried him off."

Troy laughed again, more softly than before, a sound pleasant to the ear, like the first notes of a tenor sax. He drew her face up toward his and kissed her. Her eyes widened. When he finished, she smiled and waited for more, but the magic had passed in a heartbeat. He headed off with an armful of dirty towels, leaving her in a pleasant daze.

A few days later, two booklets appeared on the table beside her favorite patio chair. They were titled *Gems and Rocks of the Southern Plains* and *Oklahoma Prairie Country*. Returning to her was the sweet man with whom she'd fallen in love.

The prairie booklet described native grasses. Her success in identifying them was limited, but she liked their names; Indian, switch, tall prairie, cord, and blue stem. The flowers said to bloom in August were easier. She spotted broom weed, goldenrod, tickseed, ashy sunflower, and mare's tail.

In return for his gift, she left a heart-shaped rock balanced on the arm of his chair. Smooth as glass and sun-warmed, it would feel nice cradled in his palm. With each small kindness that passed between them, hope bloomed like one of the field flowers.

Jennifer didn't leave the ranch, save for weekly errands to the grocery store and a roadside stand for eggs of pastel blue, green, and beige-pink. The seller told her they were from a breed of Chilean chickens called Araucana. The idea of raising a clutch herself took hold, and she researched it on the Internet. Troy agreed to fix up an old coop, and together they added wire fencing for an enclosed yard. Jennifer Ellis, Chicken Farmer. It had a nice ring.

There'd been a trip to the beauty salon in town for a hair trim and pedicure. Mostly, though, she was content to let the remnants of summer settle around her. The ranch was a restorative retreat where she and Troy could heal their wounded hearts. Winds blew clean and clear with no impediments like buildings, mountains, or complicated souls to get in its way. Sometimes Troy joined her on the deck, and they passed a pleasant hour.

"The land is showing me its secrets. I'm becoming a part of it," Jennifer said.

"It'll do that to a person when they're open to it. We've seen plenty of mule deer and whitetail bucks around here. Every so often there's an elk sighting or the sound of their bugling. The panhandle's one of the few places they still live in Oklahoma."

"I'd love to see one."

"Maybe you will, one of these days. There's a prairie dog town the other side of Beaver Creek. Gus thinks they're pests, but people travel a long way to take a look."

"There's one in the Wichita Mountains, too. You should see all the tourists pulled over snapping pictures."

They sat side by side in patio chairs with their shoulders touching. "You know to watch out for rattlers when you're out walking, don't you?" Troy said.

"I'm careful about that. I used to borrow my mom's Irish setter, Amber, to take into the hills with me so I wouldn't be alone."

"If you're gonna go very far you should have

another person with you."

"Would you like to join Jango and me some time?"

"Why would I do that? I have a truck. If it breaks down, there's a horse."

Jennifer rolled her eyes and clicked her tongue. "Years ago when I did a lot of hiking, I tried to bring girlfriends along. One friend wore bright clothes and floral perfume in hopes of attracting a rugged mountain man. The only attention she got was from a swarm of bees that terrified her."

Troy chuckled, and his eyes softened when he looked at her. "Have you hiked in Oklahoma?"

"Quite a bit. I was in the Ouachita Mountains once in the fall. It rained the whole weekend, but it was worth it. All along the trail were weird mushrooms, pink and purple lacy ones, red and white polka dot pin cushions, shiny yellow banana peppers, and rows of formal-looking black and white ones. Have you been to the Wichitas?"

"Down by Lawton. Sure, my kids and I used to ride there. We stayed in Medicine Park a time or two."

"That range became our regular stomping grounds when Aaron was growing up. Sometimes we'd come across bison standing their ground on the trail, and we'd have to turn back."

The Wichita Mountains were similar to those around Las Casitas. They'd been Jennifer's sanctuary when she longed for home. She shrugged off the sharp pang of nostalgia. Life was full of long backward glances. So be it. She'd raised a good son and felt a rebounding closeness to the man she loved. She was almost exactly where she wanted to be.

Chapter Forty-Three

'Love is patient' begins a romantic poem from Corinthians. With those three simple words in mind, Jennifer spoke to Troy.

"I'll wait as long as it takes for things to heal between us. All I need is to be near you."

His comeback was better than a direct response. "I'm headed to the Country Store. Wanna come along?"

"Sure."

It was the only invitation he'd extended to her since her return to the ranch. Maybe they were getting somewhere. She wanted to spin in circles, pirouette out the front door, and leap into the truck's cab like an excited ballerina. Instead, she glanced down at her faded cut-offs.

"I'll go change."

"No, don't. I like you in those."

"Okay. I'll grab my purse."

In her bedroom, she applied lipstick and then wiped most of it off. This wasn't a date, and she had her dignity to consider. She scrunched mousse into her hair, just a dab mixed with water in the palm of her hand. Her earrings were cinnamon-colored beads that matched her T-shirt. She stepped into her sandals and turned side-to-side before the mirror. *This'll do.*

Troy waited behind the wheel of his truck. In his Stetson, he looked every bit the handsome gentleman

351

rancher.

The Country Store was a massive no-frills warehouse with agriculture and ranch supplies, sporting goods, and hardware. She followed him around the place. He looked up and grinned occasionally. In pet supplies, he picked up a bag of dog chow and then went to gardening for an organic insecticide to use on the junipers infested with bagworms.

"Anything you need?" he asked.

She glanced around. They were in dry goods. Metal shelves held western hats; folded blue jeans sat in stacks on tables fashioned from plywood and sawhorses.

"No, I don't think so. They even carry Levi's; I'll remember that for later."

Troy stood in the checkout line, and Jennifer wandered over to a low animal pen. Thick straw covered the cement floor, and a partition ran down the middle. One side held yellow chicks. On the other, pudgy Lab puppies played. A group of kids had gathered around them. She scooped a puppy up and nuzzled it against her cheek.

"Oh, you're adorable." From across the wide aisle, she called to Troy. "Look at this little fellow. We need to adopt him."

Troy looked away. She'd embarrassed him, and she checked her enthusiasm. Outside, the Smokin' Okies Bar-B-Cue truck enjoyed a red banner day. The aroma of pork and sweet sauce permeated the air.

"I believe I'll try some of those ribs, how 'bout you?" Troy asked.

"I'd love some."

He put the purchases away then they walked over.

The ribs were the best she'd ever tasted. Meat slid off the bone, and the sauce was perfect.

"You think we oughta get a puppy?" he asked.

Jennifer's heart leaped. She wanted one, but more than that he'd used the plural 'we.'

She nodded. "Yes, I do. Fuego's gone, and Jango's getting on in years."

Troy frowned at the ground, and his shoulders slumped so she added, "It's not so much Jango's age but he could use a friend. This is spur of the moment but feels right."

They finished eating. Troy wiped his face and hands and threw the napkins away. Jennifer spotted a jumbo-sized container of sanitizer on the ledge of the food truck and brought it to their picnic table.

"I've been thinkin' 'bout a new dog," Troy said.

"Let's take another look at the puppies."

He glanced at the building's front door. "Wouldn't hurt."

Jennifer reached the pen first. She lifted a puppy by its round tummy and handed it to Troy. "Here's the biggest one."

"Hey, Boss." He examined it. "Boss here's a girl. We'd have to call her Bossie."

"Do you want a male or a female?"

He gave her a sharp look and then set the pup back in the pen. "Males are less trouble."

"Oh? How so?"

"They're more loyal."

Hands on hips, Jennifer harrumphed. "Say's you and who?"

He picked another one up and tried to cradle it. "This is a lively one."

The puppy Jennifer held had nestled into her arms. "I like Snuggly here."

"Let's have a look at him."

They passed the pup between themselves and laughed at his grunts. Jennifer inhaled Troy's alluring scent.

"He's good sized, and he's got a shiny coat that'll go from white to blond when he gets older," Troy said.

She reached over and held one of the puppy's paws. "He's gonna get big. He's a Jango Junior."

"Let's take him home," Troy said.

"Seriously?"

"Yeah, I'm serious."

They beamed at each other. A sales clerk stood nearby. "Do y'all need supplies for him, puppy food and what not?"

Troy glanced up from stroking the pup's round head. "We'll need a few things, I guess."

"You can take him with you inside if you'd like."

Jennifer got a shopping cart while Troy cradled the pup in his strong arms. What a picture it made. She pulled out her phone. "I've gotta get a shot of you two."

"Wait 'til we get to pet supplies."

Once there, Troy posed with the pup, and Jennifer took several shots. She'd frame one and mount it on the kitchen wall.

"So what do we need? Let's see—puppy food, bowls, a dog bed, and chew toys. What about a gate to keep him out of certain rooms?" she asked.

"Probably a good idea."

They selected a soft bed and set the puppy in it. He sniffed around and then lifted a leg and marked his territory.

"We just bought ourselves a dog bed," Troy said.

Jennifer lifted the edge. "The liner's removable. It's washable." Jennifer turned away. "Here we go, a rubber steak that squeaks." She squeezed it and tossed it into the shopping cart.

Troy picked out a length of rope with knots on each end and a red ball. They headed to the checkout line.

Back at the truck, the puppy wiggled around on her lap. It was like bringing a newborn home for the first time—their newborn.

"Should we name him Snuggly?" Jennifer asked.

"He'll resent me for it when he weighs in at eighty pounds."

Jennifer laughed. "I think a huge dog named Snuggly is cute."

"Nothin' doin.' How 'bout 'Critter'?"

"I like it." She lifted the puppy to eye level. "Hey Critter, do you like your name?"

Troy changed the radio station from livestock commodities to classic country. Jennifer sang softly along to familiar refrains. What a great day they were having. Her plan to be patient and wait for his affection needed a revision. Neither she nor Troy opposed a casual romp between consenting adults, but their relationship sprung from the notion that romantic and carnal love is synonymous. The unspoken knowledge encouraged her. The time had come to make her move.

Chapter Forty-Four

A mild sun shone into the truck's cab as they headed home with their new puppy. Troy steered with his left hand and rested his right arm on the center console. He had strong hands, capable of rough work yet tools of exquisite pleasure. They'd become suntanned over the summer, and the thick hair had turned golden. Jennifer longed to brush her fingers over his hand, mere inches from her own. If only she were bolder in the ways of love. She willed Troy to take hold of hers, but he didn't.

The drive took them into downtown. Troy eased the truck to the curb in front of Chester's shop with no offer of explanation.

"Do you need a watch battery?" Jennifer asked.

"Be right back."

He left and returned soon after, handing her a tiny drawstring bag. "I got you a little something."

She raised her eyebrows, smiled, and let Critter slip to his bed at her feet. When she took hold of the bag, she knew what it contained, and drew it out.

"It's the amethyst ring I've wanted. How beautiful. Thank you." She slipped it on and held it up.

Troy grinned. "Glad you like it."

He sat facing forward with his fingers hooked over the steering wheel. Mr. Stoic. More than ever she wanted to lean in and kiss him, but even in so tender a moment she wasn't sure how he'd react. She stilled her urge and kept to her side of the cab.

Once at home, they busied themselves with the puppy and dinner. Afterward, Troy sat in his chair in front of the TV with Critter on his lap. Jennifer took her usual place on the couch and thought about Plan B, the one that involved a seduction. Pup or not, it had to be now. Easy enough to manage—change into a negligee with a bathrobe over it, sit on the couch, and discreetly untie and open the robe. Yet it wouldn't happen because she lacked the seduction gene.

She sighed and scooted down the couch. "Would you turn that off? I'd like to talk."

Troy frowned and moved in sluggish motion to pick up the remote, push the off button, and toss the device back onto the table. It landed on top of the newspaper with a soft thud. Should she even try? Critter bounded toward her. She slipped to the floor and played with him while addressing Troy.

"Things are going well between us, don't you think?"

He waited a few beats before answering. "They are."

Jennifer engaged Troy in Critter's game of chase by tossing the red ball his way. "I've tried every way I know to show you how badly I feel about the past summer. I miss your arms around me and long to hold you in mine. Is there hope?"

"You expect me to forgive just like that?" He snapped his fingers.

"Yes, I do."

"'Round here we had one of the worst droughts in history. I had to sell half my livestock for next to nothin.' The grass was dead, and I struggled to maintain the rest of the herd with the sky-high cost of feed."

Maybe the negligee would've been a better choice.

Despite Troy's disheartening words, he and Jennifer continued rolling the ball back and forth between themselves like the strengthening of an invisible bond. She coaxed the ball from Critter's mouth.

"You've told me about the drought, but isn't it that way every summer?"

"Like I said, this year was worse, bone dry by June and hot as hell. I'd come in, eat dinner alone, and go to sleep in an empty bed. I didn't even have you to talk to by phone. I needed you, and you were off on some fantasy, not even bothering to call."

"You didn't call either."

"You stopped calling me, Jennifer."

She rolled the ball to him. "I'm sorry. You must know that by now."

He scooped it up and held onto it. "You want to reunite; I get it. And you know how torn I am. That's why I haven't asked you to leave."

She toyed with her new ring. "I'm getting mixed signals from you. How can we resolve this?"

The puppy sought Troy's attention but didn't get it. Troy's full focus was on Jennifer. "I don't want you to go. When you're near, I want you like crazy. I love your ways. I can't give you up."

Her arms were slack. She gave a tentative smile. "Then let's make up."

His expression remained stoic. "Before you headed out to California I asked you to be my wife. When I think about what you did afterward, I see red. I wanna trust you, but I'm struggling big time."

He stood, picked up the puppy, and strode out of the room. The ball dropped to the floor and rolled under the couch.

That morning, Jennifer had been sure she could wait forever. She'd been wrong. If they were through, so be it. What a shame their steady progress would be for naught, the wonderful day a tease—a glimpse of how things might have been, and the ring a goodbye gift. Heaviness pressed on her chest, and her heart cried out for release. Driven to act, she approached the doorway of Troy's office where he sat in his chair and stared out the window.

She tapped on the doorframe and he turned toward her. "I've made a decision. I'm putting an end to this now. You need to trust me. It's time to either move forward or not, but I won't go on like this anymore. If I leave again, I'm gone for good. I'll be in our bedroom, yours and mine. Please join me there."

He took in her presence and words with quiet eyes. She read no inner thoughts behind them. She entered the bedroom for the first time since her return from California. She hadn't been the only one vanquished. Delia's dust cloth hadn't come near the place. The air was stale, a lion's lair. Jennifer didn't flip on the light. Instead, she pulled the heavy drapes aside and threw open the windows. Evening air surrounded her.

Come morning she'd wake to the sweet sunshine of Troy's embrace. Either that or she'd rush around in a gray gloom to collect her things and make arrangements for the transport of her furniture. She'd have to reach the border of Oklahoma City before dark because of her night blindness. Strung out by a man and moving into her Mustang house echoed her painful post-divorce days.

The mild temperature didn't stop beads of sweat from forming at the back of her neck. She turned and lifted her hair to the breeze. The bed lay in her line of sight, an unmade twist of sheets. She approached it and sat on Troy's side. His usual things lay on the nightstand; a heavy silver watch, black-rimmed glasses, and ranch supply catalogs. She'd teased him about his choice of light reading material. His pillow had an indent from where he'd laid his head. She picked it up and hugged it. Eyes closed, she inhaled his warm scent.

When she looked up, Troy stood in the doorway with his thumbs tucked into the front pockets of his jeans. His broad shoulders filled the space, and his slender hips tilted at the same rakish angle she'd first glimpsed a year ago. His look smoldered. He wanted her. Her body tingled, and her heart raced. She set the pillow aside and met his gaze. She didn't suffer long silences under stress.

"Where's Critter?"

Troy tossed his head back toward the kitchen. He spoke in a voice thicker than usual. "In the box with a blanket and his toys. He'll be fine."

They looked at one another. Jennifer heard herself swallow and then a new sound carried through the house, the squeak of Critter's rubber steak being gnawed.

Troy grinned.

Jennifer giggled and covered her mouth with her fingers. The window sheers expanded and collapsed in whispered encouragement. Lightheartedness in so serious a moment opened a passageway.

"I guess I've been a real horse's ass. That sound about right?" Troy asked.

Jennifer gave a small smile. "Uh huh, but a kissable one."

He neared the bed with his arms at his sides. "You're right about somethin.' It's high time I got past the hurt. I don't want to lose you again. Havin' you here feels like home. I love you, Jen. Will you forgive this ol' cowboy?"

Jenifer stood. "I already have."

One long stride on each of their part brought them together. Their kiss held the first sweet taste of a new and enduring love.

A word about the author...

Karen Ginther Graham is a long-time Okie but hails from Southern California. Her writing often reflects these two places. Her livelihood includes management and renovation of apartments in a reemerging part of Oklahoma's inner city. She studied literature at the University of Oklahoma. She and her husband live in Edmond, Oklahoma.